BOOK OF HORTUS

LEVITY BROWN

This novel is entirely a work of fiction.

The names, characters and incidents portrayed are the work of the author's imagination. Any resemblance to actual persons, living or dead, is purely coincidental.

Book of Hortus

ISBN: 978-1-9192577-3-0

Editorial support and publication assistance from Creative Words Ltd
www.creativewords.cc

www.levitybrown.co.uk

A secret only remains a secret if kept from general knowledge or view.

With the rich getting richer, the poor getting poorer, and the ice caps melting, it suggests this secret is no secret at all.

So why do humans ignore it?

The story unfolds in four seasons…

TREES HAVE THEIR CHARACTERS…

Legendary hero, Quercus Coccinea, Lord of the Oaks, guided by his spiritual advisor, Sage.

COUNCIL MEMBERS

Ilex (Holly)

Acer (Maple)

Tilia (Limes)

Alnus (Alder)

Jubaea (palm)

Betula (Birch)

Fraxinus (Ash)

Syringa (Lilac)

Juglans (Walnut)

Sambucus (Elder)

Salix Caprea (Pussy Willow)

Fagus Sylvatica (Copper Beech)

ASTRONOMER, HOPELESS FORECASTER OF WEATHER

Zelkova (Elm)

JUNIPERUS PIRATES

Captain Twist and the Handsome Thief

RULER OVER A WORLD OF TWO NATIONS

The immortal Cedrus, giver of life, taker of death.

…AND CAUGHT IN THE SEARCH FOR THE BOOK OF HORTUS,

A doctor and his sister, unaware that their Cornish coastline hides the gates to another earth and sea.

SPRING CHAPTERS

With the arrival of spring, the land is soon awash with colour, some is provided by flowering trees and shrubs, and by myriad rock plants, but most come from an abundance of flowering bulbs.

THE AWAKENING

He was no ordinary man. Destined to crush his enemy, this hero was rooted to earth where the dead were no longer dead, the living not necessarily alive. His predicament was such that a century ago, he risked everything in search of the missing half to the Book of Hortus. And it was his nemesis that turned him into a scarlet oak.

As the rain abated, leaving shafts of sunlight squeezing through a canopy of new foliage, he was sat in a puddle of mud with a sense of bewilderment. Running his mud-caked fingers along a mud-caked chain hung round his neck, tracing the outline of a metal Q, he wondered if this was the only tangible evidence of his existence. For all that he knew of himself was his name, Quercus Coccinea. Sucking his muscled frame out of the quagmire, he strode naked through a copse until his limited horizons opened up to a new and more generous vista. There, standing in its own wilderness of blooms, was a pink-washed cottage that felt strangely familiar, yet unfamiliar.

At the back door, he ducked into smooth, cold surfaces, glowing dials, patterned china and shiny cupboards hanging on shiny walls, bounty never known before, step by cautious step, treading over someone else's life-story waltzing across the floor. In the washroom, which appeared like crystal fields of glass, he looked at his reflection and let out an angry sob of despair. Who was this man covered in mud and encrusted by twigs? Where were his memories of better years, a time when he could touch and smell the fragrances of life? Once those strong legs had carried him over tracks of fells and paths on rocks towards the sea, and once those arms had held other warm bodies, that mouth had kissed as well as eaten, spoken as well as drunk. Soon his rage would be fed because one hundred years does not make a man forgive or forget.

Now he measured the utilities of this cottage, worked the taps and ransacked the rooms. His life was becoming a series of guesses, which brought grief or the rewards of accomplishments. He studied himself again in a tall mirror fixed to the stonewash wall by the front door to consider the man of this household was certainly shorter than him. Grey flannel trousers finished above his ankles, leather shoes worn tight and a blue jumper sat short and strained. But his eyes were burning gold, and his hair was a lengthy mutinous mop of scarlet waves, somehow mapping his tormented mind in gratitude.

And just at the moment when he was about to leave, the front door flew open and what he had mistaken for shock was instead a shine of surprise. He never moved nor did she speak, observing her as she observed him, her smile becoming stretched, his mind becoming unsettled. *Err* was all that came out of his mouth, and he left.

Whatever small indulgences that cottage held or did not hold, misbegotten Quercus went in search of answers. He discovered the substantial evidence of a seaside port locked down by an historic walled town. Its glistening glass fronts and labyrinths, the strangeness of people, and his inability to distinguish between sexes made it all the more frustrating. The sights, the sounds, the smells, the likes of which he could scarcely imagine were all new to him. Someone hurried past talking into their hand and he wondered if this person was madder than him. Paying less attention to where he was going, a shrieking hazard zoomed by on a piece of rattling wood, followed by another. Springing back, he tripped into a cluttered passageway, accompanied by cheers and catcalls, by the anger of youths looking for a fight. It was their mistake and his misfortune.

Leaving the last to groan in the gutter, Quercus spat his contempt, nurturing a profound importance to seek shelter as the moon coursed its way to the sky. His choice was good, a wooden shed where the pink-washed cottage windows shone spectacularly bright. There he kept vigil with his pain and empty memories, crouched like a cur dog expecting to be driven away.

Then suddenly the shed door flew open to a militant figure. 'What makes you think you can use our home like a damn hotel!' She folded her arms, her face a mask of stern resolve. 'You left a trail of muck on the carpets, used the bathroom like a potting shed and took my brother's clothes. What is it with you people? Have we got a sign saying come this way or what?'

Wincing he struggled upright. 'I shall follow another sign.'

'Yes, exactly. Follow another sign.' Then her words fought the logic of her argument. 'You'd better come in and let me take a look at that before you bleed all over the mower.'

He summoned what he hoped was a winning smile and followed without an upward glance, thinking his way round every awkward situation he might possibly encounter.

'What is your name?'

'Quercus Coccinea.'

'And I'm Doctor Dolittle.'

'Then indeed I am fortunate.'

'Whatever,' she said with a fastidious sigh, indicating to a stool. She lifted the jumper, prodded and pried beneath his rib cage, then gave her verdict. 'You're lucky. It's not that serious.'

He said nothing but agreed and watched her shrug out of a worn tweed jacket to make preparations. It was minutes for him to observe the tilt of her neck, the flick of her dark eyelashes and the way her hair fell in coils of midnight as she cleaned and bound his injury.

'How did this happen?'

'Doctor Dolittle does not wish to hear of such things.'

She looked up. Her features bunched together and sparkled. 'Actually, my brother is the doctor. He specialises in taking out tonsils. Earlier, I thought you were his colleague.'

'Am I of similar appearance?'

'Apparently not,' she muffled, tearing off a strip of sticky plaster with her teeth. 'Do you make a habit of breaking into people's homes?'

'The door was unlocked.'

'So that excuses you walking in and taking what you want?' Their talk hung in the kitchen like a distant cloud. She was the inquisitor, the intrusive wave that tried to sweep his empty mind. 'Well,' she said, 'at least you look suitably guilty. I suppose you're hungry.'

Ah, the recollection of food. A leg of lamb, roast beef or a succulent pheasant might be on the menu. So he remained sat, hunched over the worktop with his clenched fist supporting his chin to concentrate on her skilled movements against all that shiny material, so wonderfully stylish and so odd. She opened a door and a light came on to show a stacked arrangement of packages that threw out a breath of cold air. Next, a frosty slice of something disappeared in a slot, a round tin groaned under grippers and a white china bowl revolved behind glass that hummed louder than a bee. Moments later, the bread popped up crispy brown, washed over with some kind of pallid substance and the humming bee went ping. His face went impassive, his body still when his eyes flicked to beans on toast. Hunger had no limitations.

'Your doctor brother, where is he?'

'Michael? Oh, he often works late at the hospital. Otherwise, he sees his dopey girlfriend and stays with her. Mind you what she lacks in the head, she certainly makes up for it in looks.'

'Looks can be deceiving.'

'You can say that again.'

'Looks can be deceiving,' he repeated and she chuckled, which made him wonder if he had possibly delivered a joke. 'The beans taste a little unusual.'

'Michael always buys the cheaper brands.' She switched on the kettle. 'You can certainly taste the difference.'

'Your garden is expansive. Why not make use of it?'

'Quite honestly, I hardly have time nowadays, so I just let it do its own thing.'

'Perhaps I can be of some assistance; a way to repay your kindness.'

'Are you a gardener?'

'I have knowledge of plants.'

'Mmm...I wonder what Sonja would say if she knew I had my own gardener. I think she would be very envious or perhaps irritated, yes, preferably irritated.'

'This Sonja,' he said, placing the utensils aside, 'why do you find her offensive?'

'She only goes out with my brother because he's a surgeon, soon to climb another rung on the social ladder.' She poured hot water into two mugs, squeezed the tea bags with a spoon and then dumped them in the sink with another desire to quell her curiosity. 'So, mystery man, who raids wardrobes, says very little and has a compelling head of red hair; what's your story?'

A question he was hard put to answer. 'Perhaps my story is the same as yours except one chapter behind.' Now the unease had returned and he stared moodily into his mug.

'It's hard,' she consoled. 'Work is difficult to come by at the best of times. I have a spare bed. It has to be better than the shed.'

Anything would be better than the shed. 'Will your brother be agreeable?'

'Now that is a debatable point. Unfortunately, he has a short fuse, so keep your presence circumspect. He won medals at university for boxing.'

'If you are not Doctor Dolittle, what may I call you?'

'You can call me Nina of the Atlantic,' she teased, gathering her laptop and milky tea, indicating to him to follow. 'Mum called my brother Michaelmas. It's actually on his birth certificate so I can understand why he's reluctant to get married. I mean, imagine having that name read out in front of a church-full.' At the top tread she motioned with her head. 'That's my room. That's my brother's and that's where you go. Once inside, you stay inside until I give you the all-clear. Are we on the same page?'

'I do believe we read the same words.' He dipped his head. 'Goodnight, Nina of the Atlantic. Sleep well.'

Fundamentally, Quercus was misplaced, floundering on a clash of negative inertia and her active temperament, speaking in metaphors and similes. He placed his mug to one side, sat on the bed to reason things out and covered his face with his hands. This was a nightmare he wanted to wake up from. He had seen people wearing similar attire, had heard clicking heels with shrilling laughter, and others hung in doorways with smoke billowing above their brooding heads. Sometimes their expressions were serious, almost earnest and sometimes they shrank away. Nobody apart from Nina had offered him a cordial smile or a hand of friendship. Did he really belong in this world?

It was a little while later he flayed back on the duvet with a sense of hopelessness and slept until he woke to plodding footsteps clambering up the stairs. It went quiet for a while and he drifted back to sleep, chasing empty dreams through jungles, swamps and steppes of wheat, while hares made love in the silver grass. Woken once more when he heard the same footsteps, this time going down instead of up, he went to the bathroom and prized off the itching plaster to view a miraculously healed wound. Next, he studied his reflection telling himself he was not out of the ordinary. But he was out of the ordinary.

Paying no heed to last night's warning, Quercus made his way downstairs where he regarded a chalked striped suit with a slick centre parting, dragging his heels, making a cup of coffee above a pair of rimless spectacles. It was a mistake for him to think the encounter would be cordial. A balled fist propelled him against the dresser. China went chinking and clinking to the floor. Twice he had encountered incivility, twice his recovery was quick, and gripped Nina's brother in a headlock. A small win of sorts.

'You're so dead!' Michael gasped.

'Since I have the advantage, when do you propose my demise?'

Michael was merely the initiator of events at whose conclusion he would still appear the innocent party when Nina walked in dumping her laptop on the table, her black patent shoes crunching china. 'What did I tell you last night?' She scolded Quercus. 'Look at this mess!'

The marvellous gritted-teeth smile had not endeared him. A back-handed slap round the head and he growled his contempt at Michael. 'Do you wish to be taught a further lesson?'

'Just try it again, carrot top.'

Nina swiftly wriggled between them, her attention swung at Michael. 'Don't you have to be at the hospital?'

'What? And leave you with this prick?'

'It was just a misunderstanding. I should have sent you a text but I forgot. Okay?'

'Not okay. He's wearing my trousers!'

'Oh, for heaven's sake, you are such a baby.'

Michael's manner suggested he found it hard to walk away and leave the matter unresolved. For seconds he stood motionless and upright, his black eyes narrowed to Quercus who returned the look. Then he adjusted his necktie and took his leave, a begrudging acceptance that he had no choice.

'What am I going to do with you?' Nina admonished Quercus further. 'Just look at this. It was my Mother's dinner set.'

'I am truly sorry, Nina of the Atlantic. I did not goad or bait.'

'I warned you last night to stay in your room. You never paid an ounce of attention. I mean, just look at you. Is it any wonder Michael went berserk? You better let me take a look at your injury.'

'My injury is not the problem.'

'Then what is your problem?'

Shaking his sorrowful head, Quercus wondered if he could possibly speak of his pitiful tale. Could he place the fragments of his broken thoughts into her lap like he placed the fragments of broken crockery into the bin. He cleared his throat and held a finger toward her. 'Do not say a word. Follow me and I shall explain.'

Sandwiched between the late sleepers and early risers, they picked their way through the garden, a place Nina could never control or clear - merely cherish whatever was there. Taking a worn path into the woods, he located the spot and stared at a flat piece of ground. Surrounded by trees that bore no genetic similarities, which, by a kind of alchemy, made his own achievement appear the greater, he wondered if he had lived where the dead were no longer dead, the living not necessarily alive.

'I had not the mind to diagnose my condition in the symmetry of change,' he said. 'But this is where I rooted.' She was surprised; he could see that. 'Consider where the scarlet oak has gone. Was there not a tree here? Where are the roots? Did the rain wash them away? Did they dissolve like ice cubes in a warm tub?'

Her glance was long, salacious and disapproving. 'I suggest you go back to your little world of make-believe and do what you seem to do best.' She turned on her disgruntled heels. 'Some people have to work around here.'

'Yes,' he voiced aloud, 'it is a moment of madness.' Now her attention was drawn, he continued. 'I do not know how it was achieved or why. All I have are too few memories, memories of rising from wet earth, memories of my name.'

'So, what is your name?'

'You may know my name as Quercus Coccinea. In botany, as in other scientific disciplines, the use of Latin has been found to be a convenient and precise basis of a universal language.'

'That is the most ludicrous thing I've ever heard.'

'Yes, ludicrous. I would not disagree.'

'Who tried to harm you?'

'I do not know,' he replied looking down at his tight borrowed shoes. 'I ventured beyond your home to establish my identity, set upon for no apparent reason.' His rheumy and baleful gaze returned to her. 'By instinct I was drawn to your home.'

'Maybe you were a threat to someone. Believing they may have killed you, they buried you alive. We had a terrible rainfall yesterday. Then you saw trees; somehow you reached out for a name.'

'No,' he disagreed and showed her his pendant. 'Q is for Quercus.'

'Q for Quirky more like. Has it not occurred you might be from another country? Maybe English is not your spoken language. You certainly speak a little odd.'

He was ready to accept that. 'What countries speak Latin as their first language?'

'Well, none really. Latin is mainly spoken by Catholic priests or scholars of history. Perhaps we should get in contact with the police…no, on second thoughts that might be a bad idea. They might lock you up in a lunatic asylum. What we need is to jog your memory banks to give us more clues, then we can establish your status.'

'Perhaps I am a botanist.'

'Do botanists claim to be trees?' She tilted her head and smiled. 'I once knew a chap who thought he was Prince Albert in another life.'

'If my status can be proven, would I be accepted in your society?'

'Quirky, this country is like Liquorice Allsorts. We have bombers, drug addicts, murderers and rapists mingling among extraverts and introverts, any colour, any creed, so I cannot see why someone who claims to be a tree cannot be accepted,' and she walked on, laughing. 'Let's see what we can muster.'

Quercus glowed. He did not want to think of failure, only success. 'How shall we muster, Nina of the Atlantic?'

'We shall muster on this.' In the kitchen she unzipped her laptop. 'But first a cup of tea.'

'And breakfast; preferably one without beans.'

'They make Michael fart too.'

Her deranged sense of fun and her metaphors intrigued and perplexed Quercus as the world around him came alive with a flurry of happenings and smells. Bacon sizzled, fried eggs curled, smoke whirled and mushrooms shrunk to half their size. In between all this, Nina grabbed her mobile and held her nose, sent nasal excuses for her absence at work while frantically pointing her foot at the smoke billowing from the toaster. Quercus flustered, put his finger in the slot and let out a yell. She rolled about laughing. Nothing was taken seriously until they were physically soothed by food.

'Where do you labour, Nina of the Atlantic?'

'I work at the library under the direction of Paul Death. Death by name and death by looks, but I cannot complain, not really. I love to work among literature, even more amazing to read how literature can be so conflicting. Take Henry VIII. We all know he was a villain, chopped off several heads and changed his religious status to suit his whims, yet do we admonish him? No. Instead we immortalise him.'

'Immortalised for his head chopping or status?'

'Well, both certainly had an impact. Pity we cannot chop the heads off government. I would certainly sit in the front row with my knitting. And you, Quirky, do you have a feeling you might have been in the priesthood?'

He shook his head. 'For certain I feel these hands have held a woman.'

'Maybe the Q might stand for a secret society called Quixotic.'

'Quixotic?'

'Yes, after Don Quixote, the knight in Cervantes's 16th century Spanish romance. After all, you felt sure you held a woman in your arms. Who knows, perhaps the woman had a husband and he tried to bury you six feet under.'

'Indeed, you have a vivid imagination.'

'Look who's calling the kettle black. Not so long ago you claimed to be a tree.' They laughed and she waved her hand in front of her face. 'Oh dear,' she said exhaustively, 'this will never do. If you were drawn to this house, it might be you were tracing its history. It has quite a reputation you know. It used to be part of an old mill used by smugglers. There is a legal letter dated 1897 in our library archives which refers to the mill having been unproductive and suggests that the tower be converted to provide additional accommodation. Now James Farrow, tenant of the mill and suspect of certain illegal trades, fought against this. What he suggested was to convert the mill into an alehouse. The row continued for a number of years, until Farrow suddenly disappeared without a trace. His wife claimed he ran off with another woman. His men claimed he was murdered by the authorities so they could get back the property. It caused headline news. In the end, the mill was demolished with just this part left. And in so doing, a number of stolen items were discovered, plus illegal contraband. To this day, no-one has ever found proof of what really happened to James Farrow.'

'And you think I may know?'

'Don't be silly. Michael used the story for his dissertation. Lots of people have been interested in the old mill. I just thought you may have been an historian since you claim to have had a feeling about this place. Other than that, you might be a horticulturist.'

'What does this tell you?'

Pushing her plate aside, she explored his proffered hand, her concentration powers shown in her face, her mouth partly open with her tongue pressed between her teeth. 'You have no calluses,' she said looking up. 'Rather a contradiction wouldn't you say considering how much you know about plants. Perhaps we're barking up the wrong tree.' She giggled, prodding him in the rib. 'That was an involuntary joke. Do I see a smile?'

'I have a constant smile in your company, Nina of the Atlantic. You too are a contradiction. For one so rare, you too wear a mask of secrets.'

'What? Are we a psychoanalyst now.'

'I hear discord in your voice.'

'Quirky,' she said rummaging in her bag, 'I'm like the Hindenburg of love. Every relationship I've had ends in disaster. Not to put too fine a point on it, most men are only interested in one thing. Gregg was Michael's choice, a blind date, so I agreed to keep him happy and just look what happened. I bumped into you.'

'My appearance must have been daunting.'

'Surprising, yes. Daunting, no.'

'Yet you said nothing when you thought me Gregg.' He paused to her blushing response. 'Even the blandest of flowers attract the honeybees. It is the way of things, more so when the flower is rare. Rather than adopt a disguise, learn to close your petals to the weakest and open to the strongest.'

'Are you a honeybee now?' The question was rhetorical. 'Look,' she said offering him a polo-mint. 'Suck on this instead of flirting with my petals. It will help to keep your mind focused until we can come up with a rationale for your predicament.'

'And after the rationale, do we suck on something else?' Quercus grinned, making headway, he thought.

'I can see I shall have to watch my step.'

'Good, I shall watch with you. Can you explain this device?'

'What? Have you never seen a laptop?' To the shake of his head, she continued. 'Basically, I can store all my files on this. I can also connect to a server and get information.'

'The server, will he tell you who I am?'

'Crikey, where on earth have you been all these years? The server is a...never mind, it's complicated.' Tapping in a few keys, Nina brought up a picture of the library. 'This is where I work. See that window there. That's my office surrounded by a mountain of books.'

'Book? I recall something of a book.'

'What sort of book?'

'A book on plants, I presume.'

She typed plant specifications into Google and from thereon he journeyed a voyage of discovery about the world around him, an abhorrence of tragedies and advancements that made him feel utterly isolated and totally out of his depth.

'There are many wars, Nina of the Atlantic.'

'I want you to know, I was against the war in Iraq.'

'Where is Iraq?' Changing screens, a world map came into view, where he finally admitted, 'I am not conversant with these land masses.'

'This is where we are, on a tiny little island that's forgotten it's British. Some of the most densely populated areas can be found in Europe and Asia. The existing inequalities in both the availability of resources and distribution of population will need to be addressed because every year we see fewer natural resources and every year we see vast increases in birth rates. But what the hell, by the time this planet is killed off, I'm positive the eggheads can find another to do it all over again.'

Quercus was now classifying her species. They were not really mammals, he thought. Every mammal on this planet instinctively developed a natural equilibrium with the surrounding environment but humans did not. They moved to an area and multiplied until every natural resource was consumed and the only way they could survive was to spread to another area. There was another organism that followed the same pattern. A virus.

'With so much knowledge, why has your society digressed?'

'Unfortunately, Governments change but the lies stay the same.' She closed the screen. 'We need the liberal parasites to be thrown off our backs for justice to be done. There is no democracy in this country. We are supposed to learn from our bad habits but men are still men. They keep their brains in their underpants.'

'It would seem you have a dislike of men.'

'To the contrary, they are handy for cleaning the car and mowing the lawn. I knew a chap once who mowed the lawn wearing his crash helmet. He smelt like Christian Dior. I don't go a bundle on men who smell like walking perfumery.'

He sniffed inoffensively at himself. 'Am I walking perfumery?'

'I think you spent a long time in a wood yard before you were dumped. There is an earthy smell about you. Actually, it's very nice. It makes me feel as though I'm in a patch of meadowland. Who knows, you might be a tycoon, shipping Brazilian trees to England, though that could be the trouble. Not a very good occupation. You might have been attacked by Friends of the Earth. I did think about joining. Michael said it would jeopardize my job. I don't really know the answer, so I just give up.'

'Never give up, Nina of the Atlantic.'

'Never give up?'

'A moral dilemma only becomes so by the lack of response. To pursue the right path regardless of its uncertainties does make a difference, however slight.'

'But it may land you in trouble.'

'Far better to stir the pond than let it stagnate.'

Their eyes locked for long moments but it was she who looked away first, clearing her throat. 'I could do with some fresh air. Shall we go to the harbour?'

By the front door he stayed his journey, contemplating the wonders of nature. Between the cotoneaster and the window hung a cloud of silver composed of floating seeds and spiders. 'The seeds will only take if the web is destroyed. Though in its destruction, the spider must build a new home. I feel no differently.'

'Then I shall help you to build yours.'

She offered a notion that held a definite appeal, giving him the confidence to explore and extend the boundaries of her world. And in her world, he discharged through the air like a colourful colossus, viewing a different perspective to this sea-side port than of yesterday. All details were different, a little kindlier where sounds and actions held less threat. A man went by and asked politely for directions to Newbury Street, while saw-toothed chatters of mowing machines drifted from gardens. Two hundred yards further, folk were grouped al fresco style, drinking coffee and eating cakes.

Looking out upon the glistening water with the wind playing havoc with his hair, he said, 'All these vessels, they are strange, yet that appears gracious.'

'Oh, that's an old frigate. Lord Nelson once said, 'Frigates, was I to die this moment, want of frigates would be found stamped on my heart.' Smithe-Jones claims it was part of Nelson's fleet during the battle of Trafalgar but everyone knows he's a liar.'

'Who did this Nelson have grievance against?'

'Well, the battle itself was the culmination of a long campaign. After the treaty of Amiens, Europe was at peace for fourteen months. But across the channel in France, Napoleon, another war lord was planning the next stage of his domination. He needed to control the English Channel but his invasion went pear shaped so his next step was to ally with the Spanish fleet. In effect there was this chase going on across the Atlantic. From Cadiz, Nelson followed the enemy towards the West Indies, masts and sails shot away, fleets drifting slowly about each other, looking for targets through clouds of smoke. Slowly the British ships gained the upper hand. Captain Hardy reported to Nelson that the battle was won, 'thank God I have done my duty' were his last words before he died.'

'Who died?'

'Nelson, he died I think at 4.30pm on the 21st October 1805.'

'Your knowledge is impressive.'

'Michael's hobby is sailing; he has his own ketch.' She pointed into the wind, a gap between rhetoric and reality. 'He keeps Michaelmas anchored beyond the harbour mouth if he cannot get pontoon space. There was a time we would go sailing. I was his first mate before Long-legs came on the scene.'

The day's dying light had been replaced by the glow of the port where they were heading back to the pink-washed cottage. It was then Quercus took in a deep breath, thinking he had made a mistake, something he could not possibly have envisaged, but it happened just the same. Nina had been trying to steer him in the wrong direction because of the inexplicable route of a biological transformation. Now only two important questions remained. How long had he been rooted in the woods and who was his nemesis?

In the living room he kicked off his borrowed tight shoes and watched Nina slip out of her tweed jacket then press a button to a black box. He cocked his ear. 'This is nice music.'

'It's one of my favourites, Every Breath You Take by Sting. I think tea and biscuits are in order then we can assimilate.'

In her absence, he surveyed his surrounds. Low ceiling, rough cast walls, mostly hidden by the fuss of cosy cushions and dark wood furniture. There was something about this room, something important. His brow furrowed, white teeth gnawing at his lower lip as he viewed the open hearth, convinced this major centrepiece was far more familiar than the cottage itself. He drew close, caressing the ornate carvings as though they held a hidden story and then without a second thought, he liberated a panel beneath the mantle with one hefty pull, working his fingers inside, probing a cavity deeper than that suggested. This was his major turning point. The moment he retrieved a small cotton pouch containing two seeds, he had established his status.

'Proof I am a botanist!' Quercus voiced as Nina walked in.

'Quirky,' she said concernedly, placing the tray on the coffee table. 'What have you done to my fireplace?' She peered inside. 'How on earth did you know that was there?'

'Did you not know yourself?'

'Not the foggiest. This puts an entirely different light on the subject. You must have been tracing the Farrow history.' She took a seed out of his hand. 'What's this?'

'Commonly known as Broom. It will only grow where two lovers have met in private and pledged their troth. But this, the rowan tree, should be planted near the home to keep witches away. It is said if you have an ash tree in the garden and you wish to cut it down, you must ask its permission.'

'But if the tree cannot speak, how would you know the answer?'

'You speak the truth; how would you?' He let suggestion roll off his lips, longing emit from his eyes.

With music running through his mind, he placed the contents aside and took her hands to feel the same pulsing magnetism that had drawn them close as she bound his injury. In her arms he could believe he was just like any other man with a place of his own, could dream that relief and resolution were only minutes away.

But then the front door slammed and Michael came into the room with the key ring twirling around his index finger. 'I sent you a text.'

'Quirky found a secret hideaway.'

'Well good for him.' Michael switched off the music and looked curiously into a void, his mouth a tight seam.

'Michael, I think Quirky was tracing the history of James Farrow. Someone was trying to stop him from finding out about this secret hole.'

'What the hell are you talking about?'

'Permit me,' Quercus interjected.

'No, permit me!' Michael scowled with a finger to the face. 'You have the damn audacity to break into our home, steal my clothes, inveigle my sister away from her job and punch holes in our fireplace. Your resume reads like a graveyard and it's still in working progress. What is wrong with your eyes? Are you on drugs?'

'Michael! Will you stop being so discourteous.'

'Short of lying down and sprinkling parsley on yourself,' he angered doing up her top buttons, 'could you make it any more obvious?'

'Oh, how ridiculous,' she said, smacking his hand away.

Quercus sighed, unable to hold his inviting smile. 'How would Nina fare were your love and concern be absent?' He had Michael's attention. 'We are different but share the same goal. I wish to establish my memories. You wish to establish my departure.'

'Okay, carrot top, I'm listening.'

'My name is Quercus Coccinea.'

'Carrot top or tree what's the difference?'

'A carrot is a root vegetable; there is the difference.' Now Quercus went on to explain the situation as he saw it. 'Yesterday, shortly after a rainfall, I sucked my body from earth, void of memories. Not so convinced then as I am now, I existed in the form of a tree.' He paused to the narrowing of eyes. 'Yes, my friend, you may think me mad. Whatever else, I have a key and it is not an initial to boost my ego. The key is the gateway to my earth and sea.' His statement was complete and true.

'I need a drink. What do you want? Weed killer?'

GATES TO EARTH AND SEA

Through the night and beyond, Quercus walked by himself, or kept still while snores and whistles shook the old cottage. His mind was veering in different directions, things were certainly not tickety-boo with Michael and, to some degree not with Nina. Apart from establishing he had been a tree and that he held a key to another world, he neither knew where to go to use the key nor why he was there in the first place.

He journeyed to the bottom of the garden in those crippling shoes, shifting away as if he wanted to escape, going beyond but escaping to what? Did he believe what would come upon him? A thorough search revealed nothing, no more memories, no hidden doorway, just the same old empty space where he had rooted.

A cropped bearded face with brown tightly curled hair like the pelt of a terrier popped up above the dense shrubbery. 'How easily trees can be felled, their limbs removed, their trunks chopped, their roots poisoned. But we survived, my brother.'

Fagus Sylvatica, Lord of the Beeches was a man of great stature with beech-nut eyes wearing sackcloth, something found in a state of emergency. It outlined his muscled whiskered arms and legs making him look like a landlocked Viking. His grinning pleasure weathered his features when they embraced hard, a love of a brother for another.

For Quercus, his memories were returning like snowflakes gently falling from the sky, bit by bit, able to go back in years. He glared direct into the eyes of his dearest friend. 'My memories were lost, Fagus. How did you fare with yours?'

'I had no problem though mine are not so complicated. Do you have your key?'

'Recovery was late.'

'I feared something was wrong when you spoke to Nina of the Atlantic. I heard the details, the projections, kept my profile low lest you had motive or insanity. But we are one again, my brother.' Fagus paused to the resistance upon his arm. 'What troubles you, Quercus?'

'I cannot leave without bidding farewell. Wait here.'

The dawn felt cruelly light as Quercus set off. He remembered on reasonably sound grounds, how he and Fagus, two strong men, swam through a portal in search of a green leather-bound book. This was a relatively high risk gambit but, given the current chaos and uncertainty surrounding their destinies, they did what they had to do. And that cannot simply be wished away by hindsight. *'I am perfectly aware of the consequences,'* Quercus told Fagus in the firm belief their cause was left in safe hands. The irony was palpable.

Against better judgement, Quercus swung into her bedroom and startled. Her head was partly submerged under a pillow, the swell of her bosom open to view with her arms flayed out. It was a vision he would take with him, always. He lightly pulled the sheet over her naked breasts and whispered upon her lips, 'Nina of the Atlantic, I must speak with you.'

'I must sleep with you too,' she mumbled in dreamy confusion.

'Fagus has come for me.'

'Huh?' She propped herself up on one elbow, pushing away her tangled hair. 'Did you say come for you?'

'I must return to my world, Nina of the Atlantic.'

'Are you a member of a secular order?'

He shook his head and went on in a detached voice. 'A century ago it was my duty to destroy a man who walks against the will of Hortus per se on the brink of success I was cajoled to come here. By unkind fate I transmuted into a tree akin to my own kind. Now I must return to fulfil my duties.'

'Wow, that's some story, Quirky. But if you've been away for a hundred years, none of your friends will be alive.'

'We generally live twice your life span, some longer.'

'That was quick thinking. So, this world of yours, what's it like?'

'Two continents split apart by the ocean without your method of advancement and sprawling population, the likes I have seen through your eyes. We have a natural method of communication, though where you covet and create warring factions with weapons that can blow people apart, we seek to live by the will of Hortus, advised by Council Members, a political circle of Ambassadors who represent their tree kind.'

'So you're all walking trees?'

'Nina, we are all part of Hortus and her creations, a subject for debate or discussion under different circumstance. Simply, one may look upon a tree and know it is there to serve another purpose. We turn into trees at the whim of a mad man.'

'So when you popped into my world you were human, and this chappy turned you into a tree…and then what? He turned you back again or did you grow out of his spell?'

'Only he can release us.'

'Ah!' She nodded in amusement. 'So how come he released you after being a pain in the rectum? Surely, he wants to keep you here.' A question he would ask of himself. 'Quirky,' she said taking his hand, caressing the fingers. 'I can see why you have created this utopia. Hell, even I would love to live in a land of magic. But your story doesn't hold water. It's not possible to turn into a tree. If that were so, you would be growing leaves out of your ears. Lots of people are born with red hair, some even as bright as yours.'

'In this untainted cradle of the universe there are mysteries beyond comprehension. But they do exist and I am living proof.'

'Then show me this world. I can take a two week leave.'

'The gates will reject your presence unless you have a key.'

'Okay, we can have a key made.'

'The gates cannot be deceived.'

'You see, Quirky,' she said frustratingly. 'This is what I mean. You cover all angles to overcome the objection.' She swept a sheet round her body and tussled out of bed going to the window. In this new dawn she could see nothing but the whisper of nature swaying to the tune of a breeze. 'Where is this Fagus?'

He came to her side and gently prized the face round. 'It is neither your fault nor mine. Let us bid adieu, remember the time we shared.' Fake, was her heartless expression when he could see in her eyes a depth of pain, so significant he wondered if he had caught a tear duct filling. He laid his hand, palm open along the side of her neck, and for a moment she covered his with her own, a gentle fleeting exchange before he said, 'I engage where I must. I will remember you, Nina of the Atlantic.'

Upon his approach his direct gaze pinned Fagus, who hastened towards him. From the hinterland they proceeded to the harbour, strolling along wind-harried pavements feeling the cold suck of sea air in their lungs. It hardly seemed worth mentioning, but Quercus knew how his companion felt.

'My brother, do you recount your memories?'

Fagus shot a sideways glance, sadness was there. 'I have memories of Syringa, her creamy skin and lilac hair. What has become of her? Shall my mouth taste sweetness or the bitter fruit of evil? How unwise to be trapped for one hundred years. Acer was not to be trusted.'

'Acer was my Father's closest ally. He is no betrayer of us.' By the tone of his growl, by the look on his face, Quercus felt ashamedly guilty. 'Fagus, I cannot help my position, no more than you.'

'I will not presume to question your allegiance. But remember, when our purpose is served, I shall challenge Lord of the Maples.'

The tide was coming in to fill a dry harbour where they waded into the shallows and stole a solitary dinghy bobbing in the water. Indeed, Michael will be displeased to learn that his little craft had been stolen, his transport to ferry him to Michaelmas anchored in deep waters.

They rowed to the furthest-flung promontory where hundreds had sailed before totally oblivious to its importance. This huge rocky edifice that milked the sands and sky with sprawling dispassionate brush-strokes of crags hid a chasm covered by prostrated evergreens that drank salty water for tea. The oars were brought up as the wet sticky climbers drew back like a set of stage curtains. The dinghy drifted forward into a fusion of sapphire waters, bubbling and swelling, pushing them along where they emerged into sunlight, the sky scrubbed blue.

Here was Daylily Port, a picturesque place of unimaginable colour and vibrancy, but it was also the very citadel of Cedrus, enshrined in the politics whose faculties were grouped beneath the unsullied scenery. The language had been forged and was still being crafted by the Juniperus Pirates, current and past who used the gates to steal from the other side. England had its uses.

'Do we row to the harbour, my brother? Or row to the sands?'

Quercus contemplated his whip. 'To the sands.'

They clambered out of the dinghy then Quercus dashed to his remembered spot and dug furiously like an anxious dog retrieving a bone. Miracles do happen. Coursing the whip round his chest, they scrambled the dunes, forward to his house on the wooded clad hills. It was something he had time to inherit, to inherit and dimly know, the blood and beliefs of generations who had been in this world since the time of Hortus. There were ghosts in some of the trees, and each field and hill had several. The Elders knew about these things and would refer to particular ones in personal terms, clumps of trees that bore separate names, certainly far older than Quercus, those who did not retreat at the point of a sword. But the anticipated scenery had changed. Further copses had grown, dotted and grouped, suggesting these were not grafted or seeded trees but planted comrades who joined in battle that night.

Quercus slumped to his knees, he had no real answer, was uncertain if he should petition Hortus for forgiveness or for war and permitted himself the indulgence of tears in a world he knew and loved, a world that was his mother, and he was her spirit.

'My brother,' Fagus broke the moment in a simple act of fellowship. 'The cause is fortunate to have you. I am fortunate to have you. This must not go unanswered. Speak to Sage. Ask why she intervened at a delicate time.'

'Men rise and fall like the winter wheat but their names will never die. Let us say they lived in the time of Hortus, let us say they lived in the time of trees.' Quercus returned his gaze toward the uplands, his anger welled and he bellowed with all his might. 'Hear me, Cedrus! One hundred years does not make a man forgive or forget! It will be in this darkest hour that I shall spread the greatest light!' The wind travelled his voice across the port, over pastures old, up and down valleys to the palace on the highest peak so Cedrus would hear the return of a legendary hero. He stood, wiping his eyes, emotional austerity reasserting itself. 'My Father ignored the wisdom of Sage. I should have done so that night. Will you stand by my side again?'

'First you must gather an army, my brother.' Fagus walked on. 'We shall meet soon. I need to find my Syringa.'

The handle turned with a heavy clung, expecting any moment someone to shout angrily and when it did not happen, Quercus proceeded inside his old home.

Cobwebs and dust did not matter, only his copper kettle hanging over the stove and the grandfather clock that would tick loudly in the hall once the mechanism had been wound. Ordinarily he would whistle while he worked, ordinarily he would rejoice but his heart hung heavy as he dressed again in comfortable cottons, silks and high boots.

News soon spread of his arrival, gossip rode of the wings of White Tails and within days he was enjoying the taste of tart lively beer and to talk of crops and rain, of new acquaintances, of deaths and misfortunes to Jubaea, Lord of the Palms. It was a long leisurely time in the home on the wooded clad hills before they came circumspectly to the pressing issues.

'So it was Acer,' Quercus reiterated, the words faltered in his throat.

Jubaea nodded, his palm green eyes fixed upon Quercus, his maroon woody hair tied back, his trailing forked moustache catching the rim of his beaker, eager to confirm what Fagus had suspected. 'He rallied to his cause. Many were turned then chopped after rooting.' He saw Quercus stiffen and his jaw clench and went on, quickly, 'but your names lived on.'

'What of Syringa?' Fagus held hope.

'There is rumour she was turned but none have seen her. Let us hope she was not chopped. If this is the case, perhaps you may find a way to appease him for her release. Did you find the mouthpiece?'

Quercus shook his head. 'What other changes?'

'The home of Hortus has become a fortress. It occupies his minions, no longer a stately building but a palace of inequity.'

Conversation was interrupted when a stranger to Quercus but an ally to Jubaea, walked in unannounced. He sniffed at the gloriously cooked meat then took a leg of lamb from the table. Before a bite, Jubaea snatched it out of his hand.

'I see your manners have not improved.'

He was Captain of his own vessel, a Juniperus Pirate among others who controlled the seas, slovenly clothed with his tongue exploring his jagged front teeth. Then he drew his dagger.

Jubaea smiled. 'That pint sized blade is no bigger than you.'

'It can cut off your fancy curls to stunt your growth.'

They laughed heartedly, a greeting of similar minds. 'My brothers, may I introduce you to a Juniperus Pirate, willing to take risk. Call him Captain Twist, a man who earned his title for hugging hazardous shorelines.'

'No hazardous shorelines will be hugged unless we can build a large army,' Quercus said.

Twist chewed contemplatively. 'I hear you are Lord of the Oaks?'

'I am.'

'A noble name for such an ignoble fate, to go against Cedrus seals your fate.'

'My destiny was written the moment he fell to his own. If our brothers are to risk their lives they should risk them in search of their own destinies.' Quercus paused to titters. 'You mock my expertise then you mock your fatality, Twist. What reason do you give for taking risk?'

'You forget why Hortus made the Juniperus Pirates. Risk runs in our veins. Did you know Cedrus sends his minions to snatch your women?'

'What has Council to say?'

'They bicker among themselves.' Jubaea rose to advance with Fagus. 'He rejoiced at your absence, quelled the uprising by a political manoeuvre to keep them busy. You will soon discover your own irritations. We shall see you tonight at the palace.'

Twist threw the bony leg on the table and licked his fingers holding his gaze at Quercus. 'I am curious as to why Cedrus should release you?'

'I too question his motive.'

'He does not do things without reason.'

As Twist left him with that thought, Quercus stood to reach his whip hanging on a hook by the fireplace pondering on the mystery. How different his tool of war looked in this light, dark and glowing from who knows what arms of heroes. He remembered his stalwart father settled grave by the stove, a fearsome figure eating carrot cake, brown eyes distant, content to linger in the moment of his tale before steadily rising to his feet to wipe the crumbs off his cotton tunic then sat back down. And when he finished his tale, his chin was resting in his cup and his features were abstract and bright. Could he have ever been that strapping warrior Quercus remembered?

In trying to recapture the presence of his father, Quercus donned white pantaloons and open neck shirt with billowy sleeves, bent down to put his foot through a knee-high black boot, almost ready to feel the rush of wind on his face. Faithfully and strategically, like his father, Quercus had gathered supporters and allied himself to Acer, Lord of the Maples. Considering he was his father's friend he treated Acer with love and respect, shared bread and promises as well as pain. In fragmented groups Quercus planned attacks to precision, weakened the opposition's defences and became a force to be reckoned. His name was spoken on the lips by many. They chanted the tales of a legendary hero that would rid the world of a despot. Women loved him, and he took advantage. Nothing, he thought, could be more exciting than this. He existed for battles and short-lived romances. Tomorrow he may die or the day after that.

Before stepping out to the night, he tied a green sash round his waist leaving two flowing trails to fold against his thigh then hesitated. Should he take his whip? To bring such a weapon would insult Cedrus, so he hung that limply to his side.

A magnificent Palomino, well over twenty hands high and steely grey was waiting to be seated by a new master. The horse was the product of a gift by his old friend, Lord Jubaea who had grown older in his absence but still he was the Jubaea he knew, the brother that had fought by his side long ago. He swept his hand over the steed's neck and saw its nose flare. 'You are a proud and handsome steed, neither dark nor light. Shall we call you Shadow?' The horse whinnied and snorted, as if drawing upon his affection. 'So be it, Shadow it is.' He placed his foot in the stirrup, the mounting went smooth, the bond instant.

Now the fog smothered the ocean. It undulated and seethed as the last eddy washed inland and covered Daylily Port, leaving the upland untouched as though it were part and parcel of the starry night sky. Quercus was nearing the palace in casual canter, beginning to notice the abhorrence built into the scenery and understood what Jubaea had said. It was a dominating physical feature to keep out the populace, a high wall surrounding a once stately building that welcomed men on equal terms. Its summit rose to screen the entire façade, leaving the relatively loose characteristics of a green dome available to the onlooker. The home of Hortus, now the home of Cedrus was no mere veneer of wealth but a fortress of evil.

Here, there were the blue cloths of Ministerial Firs and the green silks of Ambassadors. Close by were others, those who bore no allegiance only to their trade; the Astronomer, Zelkova and hopeless forecaster of weather, and the Juniperus Pirates who controlled the seas between and beyond two continents. There was nothing like it, the hypnotic throb of political madness where unsurpassed wealth was sickeningly rife. In the century of his absence, inner courtyards and floors had been adorned in lavish furnishings, moulded in gold, touched with gems, no sense of restraint.

And all this appeared celebrated by those who paid homage to a ruthless supremacy who was about to make his grand entrance. Young Cedrus started out as a handsome and noble crusader for the forces of good but grew arrogant in the extent of his self-regard, became corrupted by a lust for power and was ultimately lured to the dark side. Once his countenance was pleasingly open and relaxed but a facial derangement had taken place. One eyebrow was yanked almost permanently upwards and the other screwed downwards, while a majestic sneer frequently played upon his lips. He emerged resplendent in silk robes and peacock feathers to show he was the living embodiment of divine authority; his writ and influence were all.

Then the hall drew interest when Quercus approached, one hand on the handle of his whip. It was a mere charade to intimidate and conquer by illustrated means.

'Are we agreed to forget, Quercus? Let the past be a sorrowful memory?'

'One hundred years does not make a man forgive or forget.'

'Lest you need reminding, who released you?'

'I bow to your mercy.'

'Then it would be wise to hold on to that thought before you challenge me again.'

His statement was complete; it served its purpose. Sentimentality played little part in this tyrant's nature but he felt a flush of triumph as he looked upon Quercus who returned, not as a conqueror but as a supplicant without much weight. To his delight, the people did not give Quercus a thunderous welcome or cheer when he appeared in the grand hall. And unreal and self-deluding as his reactions were, they sustained his tenacity and power.

Fagus modulated his voice to Quercus. 'Every day we are denied victory is a day closer to our death unless you can hold your tongue.'

'He would not remind unless he too is flummoxed by our arrival.'

'Do you believe we were released by another?'

'Logic dictates this is so.' Mingling among others, momentum carried them on. 'I cannot remember the threat, Fagus.'

'Farrow was after your balls.'

'Were you bedding his wife?'

'You were bedding his wife,' Fagus corrected, passing over a glass of wine. 'I went in search for the mouthpiece. It was not where she said.'

Another voice interrupted their ruminations. 'You see how he manipulates, my brothers.' Jubaea told them.

'So you too are convinced it was another to release us?'

'Why would it be him? The world is his oyster. Surely you are the last thing he requires, to stir the hearts of our people again.'

'Perhaps he has an agenda.'

'Perhaps like Sage, who sent you unwisely through the gates? Perhaps the mouthpiece does not exist, a fairy tale for the camp fires.'

Fagus spoke. 'It exists.' And he moved on.

'He pines for Syringa,' Quercus said. 'Surely there must be word of her whereabouts.'

'There was no word of your whereabouts.'

A soft woman's voice drew his interest. His past caught up, Quercus turned to meet red berry eyes and holly green hair flowing in a long plait to her waist. She was Ambassador for the Hollies, now married to an infertile man and conscious of her position.

In the customary manner, Quercus bowed. 'Madam.'

Lady Ilex stared at him blankly for a full five seconds, her eyes flared wide open then slowly the fire in them faded when he seemed to have nothing else to say. 'Do you intend to take up your position?'

'I had given it no thought.'

Ilex linked her arm in his. 'Walk with me, Quercus. I feel a little overwhelmed in this stifling hall.' She looked back at Jubaea. 'Please ask Lord Juglans to join us on the terrace.'

Here, the glow and flicker of the harbour lights threw hope into chaos. When Quercus peered down into her face, he could see the small, weathered lines around her mouth more clearly defined, the maturity of age had diminished her infantile youth but not her beauty. 'I understand you have married, Lady Ilex.'

She sighed, her head bent to the perfumed gardens below. 'I had two choices, to wait for your return or marry Aquifolium. I fear I made the wrong choice. He has the mind of a commoner. So much has changed, Quercus, such discontentment.'

'Why has Council not acted?'

'Council is threatened by his Ministerial Firs. They have grown in number and multiply so rapidly it is hard to avoid them.'

'I take it you would welcome change.'

'It is not too late for me or for you.' She turned when two came to her heels. 'May I present Lord Juglans, a man after your own heart, holding weight in his country.'

Juglans dipped his yellow-cropped head. His wide and ragged walnut eyes held Quercus in vast esteem. 'Your reputation precedes you. I heard many great things, not least your expertise as a botanist. I too am a seed collector but leader first.'

'You do me honour, sir.'

'My people are suffocating in his quicksand of madness. It is, as Lord Jubaea pointed out. He has created an order of discontentment to keep us at each other's throats. I understand you were once allied to Lord Acer. Perhaps you can hold weight to his reasoning.'

'I have not seen him.'

'He rarely visits Daylily,' Jubaea confirmed. 'He rests his aging bones on Coniferous land. Meetings are not held in the palace anymore. It is now a leisurely pursuit in the Harbour Winery. Are you going to take up your rightful position among Council Members, Quercus?'

'I am not a politician. Let my counterpart argue for useless causes.'

'You have no counterpart,' Ilex said. 'No-one stepped into your shoes for fear of being turned. The same applied for Fagus and Syringa. No-one represents the beeches and lilacs.'

Indeed, it had become quite political and unnerving. For a few moments Quercus leafed through his thoughts then spoke without looking up. His boots appeared more interesting. 'I would like to digest the matter at leisure. Meanwhile, may I take leave and dance with Lady Ilex?'

Smiling, she held out her hand. 'We left so much unsaid when last we parted, Quercus.'

Holding her, he remembered with a twinge of nostalgia how they stole hours before battle commenced. 'Words do not encompass all, madam.'

'It did not make it easier to be left behind.'

'What do you wish me to say?'

'Give me this night in your arms.'

'Are we not dancing?'

'Would you have me beg for affection?'

'Last time it was I who begged.'

She was among his favourites, a treasure house of erotica. He watched as she licked her lips provocatively and his loins swelled with the prickle of temptation. He felt every plane of her back, the smooth curve of muscles on each side, following the ridge of her spine until he could go no further.

It was a slow process of leaving the glitter and her youthful octogenarian husband, to seek the stables, the smell of hay masking a secret liaison. The adrenalin of lust was like a drug in his blood. His nature and standing were forged from elements that induced others to follow but he was weak for the want of affection. They locked together breathing each other's breath, their tongues twisting, pressing so deep that they threatened to choke each other with their fervour. One hundred years does not make a man forget the pleasures of flesh, the need to plunge and rock and thrust, to still that empty ache.

WISE OLD SAGE

'You will not touch me again!'

'So I have heard for the fifth time.' Quercus laughed.

Syringa went to retrieve her weapon. The whip cracked, she yelped and his audience applauded.

Jubaea and Fagus were leisurely sprawled over a patch of green grass recently tended by Quercus. His land had grown a century of sprouting vegetation, a maze of small traps and snares, climbers gnawing an orgy of borrowing over rampant branches, thistles and weeds claiming their spots and blundering shrubbery claiming theirs. It took hours of hard graft to bring some semblance of order.

'Be quick on your feet, my sister for I will catch you every time.'

She rubbed her backside and pouted. 'You cheat.'

'Better to cheat than feel the bite of death.'

With a suspicious eye, she picked up her staff and circled him. 'Without your piece of leather you are vulnerable.'

An eyebrow arced and he threw down his whip. 'Come, my pretty lilac, do your worst.'

She adjusted her footing and flanked his side, one thrust and he ducked. A return of the staff and he ducked again. He danced back, coaxing and chiding. Enraged, she came in pursuit and struck out again but he snapped at her heels and she stumbled.

Cheers and applause, Quercus bowed to his audience.

'Show off,' she said.

He tilted his head. This ungracious loser needs a lesson. He swung round and flipped her to the ground, keeping her pinned. 'Admit defeat.'

'No!' She howled.

'No? Then I shall drink my wine where I sit.' At once he felt the strength of Fagus pulling him off by the scruff of his neck. 'You are a sore loser, my sister,' he voiced hoarsely.

Prior to this day, Fagus had kept aloof from almost everyone. Yet his sudden appearance with Syringa spoke volumes. Rather than question detail, Quercus spent informal overtures before challenging Syringa to a light-hearted duel.

Now, bowing dutifully to a beautiful springy mass of lilac hair, Quercus sprawled on the grass beside Jubaea directing his question at Fagus. 'Now that Cedrus has given you back Syringa, has our friendship strengthened or weakened, my brother?'

It was Syringa to rush out her words under the sweat of her brow. 'We have taken our positions as Ambassadors. Come to the next meeting, Quercus and take up yours. Let us return strength in Council.'

'I do not engage in politics.'

'Then what do you engage?' Jubaea enquired.

Quercus held a grape to his lips. 'My own affairs.'

'I was allowed my freedom to appease Fagus in the hope of quelling his anger towards Acer but what of freedom for others? It suits the celebrated firs and condemns our people.'

'And you expect me to take on their troubles. I think not.'

'What is this, Quercus?' Fagus gave his heels a friendly kick. 'When we returned you had the fight in you.'

'Acer's allegiance to Cedrus strikes a different chord. He has strength in number.'

'Then you side with me,' Fagus argued his point. 'Listen to me, Quercus. I am not fooled by Syringa's release nor is she. We could easily slip and hide yet conscience overrides personal gratification. There are scores to settle. Our borders meet; it is a good allegiance. Jubaea offers his allegiance and so too Juglans and Ilex.'

'Only five countries, a poor commitment.'

'Six if you join. It is a good commitment. But we must proceed with caution this time. Join Council Members who see sense, here, tonight.'

Another route was contemplated in the arms of Lady Ilex. She had pursued him to excess and he had no complaints. 'Must it be tonight?'

'My brother, to your advantage it must be tonight.' Fagus hunkered down on his heels, muscles bulged at the thighs. 'Sage will come. She will listen to our plans and advise accordingly.'

Quercus sent his eyes away and stared ahead, reminded himself how he had become more circumspect of late. 'If Sage deems this so, then I shall be ready.' Smiling at Fagus, he jumped to his feet. 'Would you like me to teach you how to spar?'

Fagus chortled, a far happier man now he had Syringa. And this made Quercus happy too. He remembered the time when he felt a curious intrigue for delicate Syringa. It was through her that he got into trouble and received the first shock of his life. Without spite or passion, he came up to her in the playground with a stick in his hand and hit her with it. Her lilac hair was springy, so he hit her again and watched her mouth open up with a yell. The experiment might have ended there, and having ended would have been forgotten but under the savage eye of a tight-lipped teacher, he craned his neck and grinned. It was a marvellous gritted teeth expression, adapted to suit those occasions when he was clearly lost for something to say. He was subsequently told to let her do the same thing to him. She picked up a stick far bigger and whacked him on the head, twice. No experience could matter more.

When the sun dipped in its spring heat and crushed down upon fertile lands, it also crushed down on this clandestine night where six were about to meet in the home of Quercus, presently in the stables, vigorously brushing Shadow with straw.

'Juglans has arrived.' Fagus appeared.

'Where did he keep Syringa, my friend?'

'In the palace grounds.'

'Then it would explain why she was unseen.' Quercus rubbed his hands together, ridding bits of straw. 'Did she mention what Cedrus expected?'

'You have no need of concern. Cedrus was tired of her blooms, she served little purpose. She has given him a false pledge to persuade me not to pursue a vendetta against Acer.' A slap to the back sent assurances. 'Burly beeches do not surrender to tides of treason. Come, my brother, we must go inside before Sage arrives.'

Quercus paused in the doorway, his eyes adjusting to candlelight then crossed to where Jubaea crouched on a stool, stroking his trailing moustache. There also, Lady Ilex for the hollies, Juglans for the walnuts, and Syringa for the lilacs, were now his closest allies. All sat in silence for a full five minutes waiting for Sage.

An old woman, inconvenienced by age, took her time to cross over furnished floorboards, her face covered by a dark veil. It was smooth, silky, and when she breathed it drifted out like a feather. The rest of her body was also sacrificed to dark and without uttering a sound she sat on a hard chair by the stove turning her head towards the copper kettle puffing out steam.

Quercus opened up with his thoughts. 'Our forebears spoke of the earth trembling when Cedrus killed for the Book of Hortus. They knew change was on the horizon. As the years infected Cedrus with primitive hungers, they had to learn the ways of war where many were blighted by the disease of ignorance. It was not until my Father had the whip of Hortus did he draw weight behind our cause, to claw back what was taken. Here is where he counselled others. Here is where he crawled to die. Here is where the whip passed to me. So it is perhaps ironic I stand under the same roof to speak of lost dreams.' He stood to the floor and eyed each one with quiet desperation. 'Before Fagus and I were rigidly confined to the other world, we were strong in our resolve, had great weight behind us to usurp this heathen whose only defence was his sprawling fat Ministerial Firs licking his boots. Why did Council Members fail to forge ahead and complete their destinies?'

'Acer should never have been trusted,' Syringa spoke. 'It was him who murdered your father, so he could continue in the guise of an ally. Cedrus knew you would pick up the whip.'

'How do you know this?'

'Was I not his prisoner too, trapped in my rigid confines? My branches heard his voice. Neither Cedrus nor Acer expected you to go through the gates. They expected you to die alongside your army, the whip to be thrown into the seas to rot in its salty element.'

'It was fortunate a good number managed their escape,' Jubaea said.

'And because of this, you grew weak,' Quercus told them at last. 'Rarely abandon your position at the point of a sword. You gave Cedrus licence to do as he pleased, to build a high wall round the home of Hortus, to turn more of our brothers into trees, to furnish the palace in a grotesque manner, to corrupt those with envious eyes, to let our continent be swamped with his kind. I have heard from your own lips how your women are shuffled. This does not bear good fruit. It keeps our number down.'

'We have tried negotiation.'

'You cannot negotiate with a bringer of death.' Quercus glanced sideways at Sage. 'Perhaps I was ill advised to search for the mouthpiece when I was needed to lead.'

Her veiled head turned into the room, her voice unsympathetic. 'The moment your mother was seeded, I knew you would be the cause of change.'

'I have changed nothing.'

'Beyond the gates lies your answer.'

'So once you said. It left me as a tree. You did not foresee that in your wisdom.'

'It was your fate.' She would speak no more.

'We must plan, not argue,' Syringa voiced anxiously. 'We must send word and call for our people to return to the sword.'

'Distant words will not re-ignite their interest.' Fagus spoke harshly. 'We will be like sitting ducks upon a still pond. We should go to them as their Ambassadors, and locate a safe place as we gather in number.'

'All of us cannot vacate Daylily. It will arouse suspicion.' Quercus paused for a moment. 'Fagus, our countries abut. It would be acceptable if you were seen to leave with Syringa. Cedrus will assume you have distanced yourselves from me. I shall give you my key to show to my people we are at one in our thoughts. Likewise, Syringa will hand her key to Ilex. While Ilex gathers the lilacs and hollies, I shall gather the oaks and beeches, and any willing to fight.' He turned to Jubaea and Juglans. 'Is there one you can trust to act in your place?' They nodded. 'Then likewise, my brothers. Keep within the boundaries of Daylily, your ears to the ground. We must act stealthily. Large movements cannot be seen to cross our continent. Each of us will liaise with Jubaea who shall liaise with Twist. Jubaea, how fast and secure is his vessel?'

'Very fast, very secure. His knowledge of our coastlines is second to none. It will be an epic endeavour.'

Quercus looked back at Sage and remained still.

'The wheels turn for the prophecy,' she said, always ready to remind him. It was a myth, he thought, a myth to inspire the weak, to encourage war upon Cedrus who killed for the Book of Hortus and dominated their continent. 'One is able to pass through our gates without a key, shall clear the path for Quercus, and shall control the seas for there, within its bed of mystery awaits Sea Winger. This creature will rise from a mist, wings pure white, breast sapphire to offer protection.'

'So we fight to win on high seas?' Quercus asked.

'To speak of destiny is to alter destiny.'

'Then what words will you speak to aid in our cause?'

'We are in the season where the hearts of your people spring open, even on the greyest days. Acer awakes to look upon faceless men as he stands on land which is not his own. With your followers, you will enter among the tall populus on the west shores. There, you will greet summer to brighten your darkest hour. Your course will change as summer intensifies, so shall your body and spirit, the duration will depend upon rain. Be selective, otherwise the effect of the whole shall be overwhelming.'

Her thoughts were of such distinction that they absolved her from ridicule. Only a few ever understood her meanings entirely, importing moreover a kind of inspiration that it remained unanswerable.

After a long pause, Quercus asked Sage. 'The mouthpiece was beyond my reach. Is it my destiny still to go to the other side?'

'Permit yourself one night in those arms before entrusting your key to Fagus.'

It left Quercus speechless. Abruptly the atmosphere changed. The seriousness in the room became brittle and forced by the wariness in their faces.

Fagus understood. 'She was his saviour in times of need. Let him have his fun for one night. Sage has spoken and agreed.'

Outsiders were considered a greater threat than Cedrus. It was an irredeemable fact how the other world advanced at cost to their environment, had weapons of mass destruction and polluted their seas and skies, contaminated their earth and captured or killed their wildlife. So much damage, so much pain, it was unimaginable. But Quercus had seen a little good, just a little from people like Nina who survived by their humour and hopes.

When most had disbanded, Lady Ilex held back. Her eagerness apparent. 'Quercus, why do you run from me?'

'I do not run,' he answered diffidently. 'Tonight was the subject of planning, not seducing.'

'Now that our planning is over, seduce me rather than seduce a piece of lettuce.'

His brow arced. 'A hanky is a good substitute.'

Their parting was like a merciful guillotine stroke. He walked off smiling, was pleased he had mastered a metaphor that even Ilex would understand. His steady pace carried him towards the shores. Clothed in his usual attire with his cherished whip coursed round his chest, he rushed into the waves, his boots left in the dunes. The key that hung round his neck submerged as he buried his head to swim through the gates of earth and sea, the water cold and biting. There were no limits now, no borders nor boundaries. Everything was possible.

From out of the secret chasm, the port he saw was crowded with yellow trawler men in rubber boots and roll neck jerseys. They were roaring with delight and excitement from their catch, their sounds carried over the night sea that shone from the harbour lights. Blinking the salty wet out of his swelling eyes, he swam in another direction and hit the sands on the other side of the promontory. From there he padded bare foot over the grassy dunes and up the craggy rocks to reach the hinterland of this bay. It would ultimately lead to a little pink cottage nestled among others more salubrious.

There were no bright windows shining on an unkempt garden so he picked up a pebble and aimed it at her window. With no response, he picked up another where it shot the distance and broke a pane. A light came on, the window flew open and a dishevelled mass of dark hair poked out.

'Quirky! What's wrong with the doorbell?'

He went to speak but she was gone in that instant. Moments later, he viewed through the glass her smiling face, her body wrapped in a pink towelling dressing gown, her feet shuffling in pink fluffy slippers.

'How is your world?'

'Troubled.'

'So no chance of taking a holiday there?' She looked down, moistened her lips and blinked. 'Where are your shoes?'

'On the shore.' Smoothing his wet hair back with both hands, he walked in. 'Have I been in your thoughts?'

'Hum, just give me a moment to think about that,' she said, switching on the kettle. 'I mean, was it your debonair way or perhaps your idiotic stories or maybe, and I say this lightly, it might have been the thought of a kiss before we were so rudely interrupted.'

'Perhaps a demonstration may offer a clue?'

Catching her off guard, he settled his mouth upon hers. She tasted sweet like blueberry pie and he lingered to the intoxicating moment until he could breathe no more. Upon his release, she just stood there, eyes closed with an upturned face. Temptation was there to kiss her again.

'Yup, it was definitely your stories.'

'You jest.'

'I jest.'

'I have one night to spare. May I spend it in your company, Nina of the Atlantic?'

'Can you elaborate on that?' She responded with her head in the fridge. 'I mean, it looks as though you're in a pair of pyjamas. Have you escaped from a mental institution?'

'In a sense I am a fugitive. But be warned, I shall invigorate your mind with tall stories.'

'Oh, Quirky, I have missed our conversations. I don't really care if you're a bit loony. I honestly thought I was never going to see you again. What changed your mind?'

'Sage deemed it so.'

'I see, but Sage is not a tree. I normally put it in my casseroles.'

She was dark-eyed and slumberous and it sparked through with agonizing passion to match his. 'I am gathering an army,' he said. 'Five Council Members have signed up for the cause.'

'These Council Members, are any of them women?'

'There is Lady Ilex, Ambassador for the Hollies and Lady Syringa representing the Lilacs.'

'I suppose Lady Ilex is beautiful with red berries in her spiky green hair.'

'There are no red berries in spiky green hair. She has a long silvery green plait to her waist and red eyes that grow wild when she is happy.'

'And Syringa, what is she, a social climber?'

He shook his head, smiling to the ever sceptic Nina. 'Syringa has springy masses of short lilac hair. She captures the heart of my brother, Fagus. She is light on her feet and good with a staff. Often, she tries to outwit me yet I have her measure.'

'I suppose they wear leotards over their voluptuous bodies.'

'Their robes cover their curves and are made of pure silk.' He put forward his arm. 'Like this, made from silkworms.'

'It's damp. Why are you damp?'

'I came from the sea.'

'You must learn to get your story straight. The gates are not in the sea but in the woods, remember?'

'I beg to differ. The gates are not far from your shores.' He unfurled the whip. 'And this is my weapon.'

'I suppose that turns into a poisonous snake.'

'Come, my little sceptic. I will show you.'

In her fluffy slippers and dead of night she padded behind his tall and wide frame until he stopped at a flowering Camellia. He looked back once with a grin plastered on his face then sized his target before cracking the whip. She jumped on the spot when the tip snapped at the shrubbery. He bent down and picked up a blossom, delicately placing it behind her ear. Such a smile, such sweetness, such warm acceptance, the mere touch of her would satisfy his needs.

'Did you work in a circus?'

'Indeed, a circus of monstrous lions. The whip has many advantages. Without killing my opponent I can bring him to the ground before he reaches my person. In war it is preferable to crack necks.'

She gulped. 'You can do that?'

'I can and have but not at my pleasure.' He coaxed her back to the kitchen. 'Tell me, Nina of the Atlantic, what have you been up to?'

'My proposal got turned down. Now I have to revise it again. Honestly, I think my boss is bonkers. One minute he wants a criminology section and next a video collection. I mean, we are not a damn video store. How can Batman and Harry Potter be educational?'

'Who are they?'

'Well, one is a cape crusader and the other is a wizard. It's all fictional nonsense, a little like yours but very entertaining. Would you like to see a film? I have my own collection. You might like Phantom of the Opera. The music is wonderful.'

'I would like that.'

'Oh, goodie, we can eat popcorn and Michael's jellybeans.' She padded in her fluffy slippers to the front room. 'How was your world started?'

'No differently to yours, by Hortus.'

'Hortus did not start our world, Quirky. You should read about Charles Darwin and-'

'Nina,' he interjected sinking deep into a settee. 'We know the works of Charles Darwin. We had discussions long before he submitted his paper. Perhaps you should read his works more thoroughly to understand Hortus.'

'Okay, who is Hortus?'

'Hortus is the machinery that generates the sunlight that makes life possible, to the gravity that glues us to an earth that would otherwise send us spinning off into space, or to the atoms of which we are made and on whose stability we fundamentally depend. She is the air we breathe, the light of the stars, the dirt of the planets and all living things. To respect Hortus is to respect what she provides.'

She slipped in the disc. 'I see, so Hortus is in effect Mother Nature. You certainly go about it in a peculiar way. Michael believes you are a schizophrenic, a severe mental disorder characterized by loss of contact with reality.' She looked around. 'Oh, I forgot the tea. Be back in a mo.'

Quercus puffed out his cheeks. There was no convincing her or was there? When she emerged, he said, 'I acquainted myself with James Farrow and-'

'Farrow is dead, unless of course you can communicate with the afterlife.'

'You forget I was here one hundred years ago.'

'I stand corrected. So what did he say?'

'Too much for his own good. I dispatched his body in the woods.'

'I see. So now you have solved the riddle, just like that, which has been haunting great minds for a century. Why on earth would you want to do that?'

'A good question,' he replied, reluctant to say, skirted the issue of taking his wife as though it mattered how Nina should view him. 'He required vast sums for a book he claimed to have had in his possession. His good wife indicated it was hidden in the mantelpiece. When Fagus looked it was not there so he left two seeds at my request.' He paused to watch her thinking about it. She was nibbling at her thumb, eyes enquiring. 'Hortus created a book of her secrets. Cedrus killed the Keeper for the want of it. Hortus bit into the spine, the bite swift and precise. Fagus and I were after the mouthpiece, the reason for entering your world at the behest of Sage.'

'How can nature make a book?'

'Imagine a young lamb slaughtered for the table, its skin hung to dry, cured for the use of gloves, the type of gloves Jubaea likes to wear when holding the reins. Then imagine the wind stealing the hide, like it would steal bark off the birch, the flimsy turning of outer wear to show the trunk glistening like white marble. And with the rain to soften the folds, to bind sticky resin, a leather bound book with pages has been constructed with colourful pictures etched by snowflakes falling from the sky.'

Nina shook her head. 'All fairy tales have secret books. I suppose you have to slay a dragon before you can win fair maiden and rule a kingdom.'

'I must slay Cedrus, in return I shall gain immortality.'

'Oh, that's even better.' She sat beside him with the controls in her hand, totally oblivious he was actually telling the truth. 'Not sure I would want to live forever.'

'Why?'

'Well, what happens about loved ones?'

'One can have many loved ones.'

'I see, so your attitude is that a change is as good as the rest.'

'Not necessarily. One can have their favourites.'

'I am not entering into this discussion. We shall have to agree to disagree. It's nice to watch movies with someone. Don't pay any attention to me if I start crying. It doesn't mean I'm sad, it just means I get very emotional.'

She clicked the button with her thumb then halfway through, slowly, very slowly, so as not to disturb her, Quercus tilted his head to watch her gentle breathing. The opening of her dressing gown gaped with a view straight down to her naval. Then a tiny crumb of popcorn fell into her cleavage, and negligently she licked her finger to retrieve it. Tautness crawled from his loins to his brain and for the first time his conscience kicked in. There would be no future with Nina, not in that way. Apart from occupying two different worlds, she would never be able to enter his and he would detest living in hers.

She looked up. 'Would you like a jellybean?'

He crossed his legs, awkwardly clearing his throat. 'No thank you.'

Now he was mentally conjugating Latin verbs, multiplication having worn out its welcome. Back to her face, he watched her lips glowing with a half radiant smile that sometimes quivered. There was no doubt at all about her hidden beauty, or the naturalness with which she wore it, and appeared quite unconscious of the rarity of herself.

She stirred with misty eyes. 'You're missing the best bits, Quirky.'

'I think not, Nina of the Atlantic.'

'Are you flirting with my petals again?'

He shook his head. 'I am.'

She giggled. 'Are you hitched to anyone in particular?'

Having viewed the relationship null and void with Lady Ilex he brought Nina into his arms. Where he would normally take in ritual and lust, he took in care and fondness. With his tongue, he snaked wickedly over her body, his skill undeniable, controlling the pace, attentive and affectionate. Honour, the thought blazed in his mind and he groaned silently as on the other side of his brain another word burned just as fiercely, love. But love was new to him as a mobile phone would be to an old age pensioner keeping change for a red telephone box. He knew without prompting, this young woman who dressed so conservatively could lead him from solitude, could take him to a place where nothing could harm him. But he forgot in his intensity that there would be the torment of simultaneous discovery and loss becoming exposed.

Much later they sat side by side, nakedly on the settee with a pink towelling dressing gown draped over their shoulders, leaning together and watching the gas fire flicker along the rough plastered walls.

'Nina, the book I spoke earlier. Would you have seen such a book in your library?'

Her cheerful face belied the seriousness of the situation. 'The only fairy tale books we have are in the children's department. Quirky, are your parents still alive?'

'My mother died giving birth to me, my father slaughtered by Acer, a traitor and spy for Cedrus. In my world there are two continents, two very different societal. Cedrus now dominates all but I shall reclaim what is rightfully ours.'

'I see, so you've had a pretty rough time of it. I never knew my Father, not really, not as much as Michael did. I was very sad when Mum died. I sort of lost my way a bit, so I understand how easy it is to reject reality.'

He smiled, shifting her onto his lap, spreading her legs either side of him. 'This is reality.'

'Quirky, I'm not on the pill.'

'Explain?'

'I know it's a bit late to mention it. But I run a risk of getting pregnant.'

'My seeds will not drop until autumn.'

'No seriously, Quirky. We must try to be responsible.'

He swept back her hair. 'Nina, I shall not waste words on a closed mind. Trust me. I am unable to seed you.'

She opened to him again, let him slide inside, taking him deep with a shuddering whimper. They were moving slow, and feeling their way, sexual union unbounded. He was swollen with new desire, the need to sweep through her in waves, his hands clutching her buttocks like a newborn clutching at sheets.

Nina made no terms, no bargain but had simply given. Rather than demanding his vigil, she had insisted upon his freedom. Yet he was staring at her with troubled gold eyes, the thought he might never see her again. It was almost as though he was about to walk into hell.

'Don't be sad, Quirky,' she said at dawn's early light by the back door. 'Perhaps you can forestall your war and we can go out for a picnic.'

'I shall have no key,' he replied holding tight to the one round his neck. 'It shall be given to Fagus for him to gather support.'

'Then let's make another. There's a shoe place near the tackle shop.'

He placed his finger under her chin and raised it so that they looked into each other's eyes. 'The gates cannot be deceived. I promise you a picnic among sweet-scented flowers. Weeks will pass before Fagus returns. Wait for me, Nina of the Atlantic. Do not give your heart to anyone else.'

He left Nina with her mouth open, ready to give vent to all her loneliness, and drifted off with despondency, his head bent low as though he was finding solace in his feet, could feel that she wanted to run after him, to try and comfort him at the same time be comforted too. The close of the door was cruel. It actually hurt so bad he was afraid she had placed him beyond the realms of common sense.

When he slipped into the sea, he glanced back as though, by some miracle, she might be there to hold his hand, to swim alongside him. It was no different in war. He remembered Fagus looking back at Syringa as he sat in the saddle ready to lead his men. Some had perished, some had lived on and some had turned into trees.

Now in the promise of a new dawn, like a movie starlet who always looks lovely in her pictures, he swam to his shores. Such a different place, the endlessly unravelling hills and greenery was an understated beauty of this most ancient world. The deep inlet of the port was like so many ports of its kind holding on to some functionality but to the craggy side, where he left his boots, a quiet, uninterrupted bay with Lady Ilex scorching the sand.

'Why are you here?'

'To remind you Sage permitted one night in her arms.'

He was swamped with a sense of guilt, and guilt was followed almost immediately by anger. Quick words leapt to his tongue. 'You are not my keeper. You would do well to remember this, madam.'

FACELESS MEN

Astride his mount, Quercus ambled his way along a comprehensive web of dirt tracks lined by trees, whose cool green colour appears in spring but truly spectacular in summer. He was nearing the first remote township, fifty miles north of Daylily, when his sleep-starved mind barely registered a shout. There followed the echoing clash of steel.

Leaving a thudded trail of dust behind him, the scene came gradually into view, a scattered chaos of conflict, and louder shouts of frustrated men trying to unseat their attackers. One, two, and counting, Quercus registered four horsemen garbed in black robes, wielding axes on an ebbing foray of swords, tirelessly moving in for a kill. It beggared belief these brutish bastards on brutish steeds continued to fight with some limbs lost, foot or leg it made no difference, their strength of mind steadfast. Moving in for his first taste of blood in a century, rediscovering the thrill of the chase, Quercus raised himself up on the stirrups and sent the tip of his stinging leather towards an advertised axe. It detonated in the air. Another crack, the brute was plucked from his saddle then a maelstrom of waving swords took advantage to finish the bastard off.

Behind you!

Quercus ducked. An axe skimmed over his head, felt the hard rush of steel clip his hair. He seized a pike from a settler and let it fly the distance, skewering his attacker through the chest, yet still the man carried on without screams, without sense of restraint. Shadow reared, raking his hooves, unseating the skewered black robe, to be finished off by a sweeping sword coming down hard on the neck. Quercus had not anticipated such events, had understood less of what he was dealing with until it was clear that necks were their only weak point. He facilitated, cracking his whip fierce for decapitation on the last two. What had once been so strong had since become so weak.

Spent and panting, letting the feel of victory surround them, Quercus dismounted by the water trough and slapped Shadow affectionately on his flank. Wiping the sweat off his forehead with the back of his hand he crouched down to observe something he had never encountered before. It had a round faceless block of weathered skin, smeared in its own peculiar dark blood and he wondered how these strange fighting creatures were able to see their opposition. A hand came upon his back.

'My brother, you are our saviour. I am told you are Lord of the Oaks.'

'I am.'

Sheathed in chalky white leather, Betula had brilliant gold hair bouncing against his yellowish birch eyes that often spoke volumes for their openness 'What brings you to these parts, Lord of the Oaks?'

'Affiliations and allegiances. Who are these faceless creatures?'

Betula came down on his heels to join him. 'They are the makings of Cedrus, the devils raiding our settlements and stealing our women. Without intervention, we would have been lost, half this settlement destroyed. The necks you snapped are his latest product, hard to unseat. Unlike the old days, his families of firs prefer to fatten rather than fight. They are not grown from wombs but the seeds of monster conifers found in the warmest climate.'

'How can this be achieved?'

'I have been told,' a new settler, past fighter, said, 'the seed is buried in liquid dirt where it grows into a large thick pod before splitting to reveal a thick fibrous creature. Thereafter, the growing time is short.'

Quercus rose. 'I heard nothing of this.'

'My lord, Daylily is a resting place for the blind. I have yet to see my Ambassador.'

From every quarter came a torrent of ceaseless sound. A successful win encouraged high spirits. With an upward glance to a sky scrubbed blue over early perennials, Quercus was encouraged to sit among the brave away from the blinded centre, served with a flagon of wine by a young lad eager to please.

With a ready laugh and happy disposition, Betula held up his beaker for a refill, his face crunching on pride. 'This is my son. My wife runs the inn. You are welcome to stay for as long as you wish.'

'You do me honour.' Quercus flexed his fingers, stiff from the whip. 'You fight well.'

'If that is well then you have my sword, you have most of the swords here.'

They spoke of the past, the revolution after Cedrus took control of Daylily, which had not been immediately perceived as a threat. With control over both continents, Cedrus had become the greatest power by land but not by sea.

'His Ministerial Firs are his lap dogs,' Betula said, puffing his pipe. 'At every turn a devout minion serves his needs while others argue behind his back.'

'You appear to have a finger on the pulse, my brother.'

'I have my contacts. When next you meet Council Members steer clear of Lord Alnus. Not that I claim him a spy. He was the first to kneel at his feet and kiss that ruby red ring. Have you seen him? Lord Alnus, have you seen him?'

Quercus folded his arms. 'My business is to gather support not to survey Council Members.'

'His body is weighed down by gold, his house weighed down by glass. He calls it a conservatory. We call it a greenhouse made of rubber sticks. He follows the same wanting attitude as Cedrus. No doubt you have entered the palace.'

'I have and agree. It has become an abomination.'

'He has a chamber without windows. I know a man who has entered. He spoke of two different walls. One side, Cedrus had painted obscene pictures to heighten his libidinous cravings, explicit sexual acts to smack in the face of Hortus. For on the other side is something quite different…a large circular pattern of amazing flowers, new species, so I am told.'

'And who told you this?'

'A man who calls himself a Handsome Thief, a Juniperus Pirate who rides twenty foot high waves. He may be a brash and wily adventurer but he is well admired among his kind. They look up to him, a man who follows the ways of Hortus.'

'Yet he tallies with Cedrus.'

'No, my brother. He does not tally with Cedrus. The Thief is ashamed to be associated with Cedrus. His curiosity got the better of him. He slipped in the chamber when Cedrus was entertaining the likes of Lord Alnus.'

Quercus held out his hand. 'May I try?'

'Have you smoked a pipe before?'

'No but I am curious as to how it makes your eyes change colour.'

Betula laughed, passed over his pipe and tobacco pouch. 'Smoke at your leisure. It shall not kill you. Tonight we shall speak of our dead and hear their stories through the lips of their loved ones. Are you a good teller of tales, my lord?'

'I am.' Quercus rose. 'I shall speak of a phantom who wears half a mask to cover the shame of his past. Until then, I shall take advantage of your hospitality.'

Pushing open a door, Quercus made his way up the rickety stairs to a room above the cascading cheers, grateful his name lived on, and more than grateful at the dramatic gains of supporters. Yet he was worried and contemplated upon those worries soaking in a tub of perfumed waters. Why would Cedrus create such abominations? For Cedrus was not a man to do things without reason. Had his kind become so fat and lazy that a fall-back position was required? Certainly Syringa never hinted at such abominations where she claimed her branches offered a silent audience to his plots and ambitions. It was open to speculation, something he cared to place at the back of his mind but had to be addressed. Cedrus was good at employing spies, Acer being a prime example. The water cooled while his ruminations continued, shaving with the edge of a sharp bladed dagger.

Betula's wife entered, her eyes dipped to the floor. Without a word, she laid his clothes on the bed and then said before leaving, 'My lord, food will be served in one hour.'

'Madam,' he called rising from the bath, wrapping a towel round his waist. 'Your husband, is he prone to exaggeration in his good humour?'

'He speaks as he fights. Good and true. Why do you ask?'

'For no reason.'

Standing demurely by the door, her fair hair swept up and pinned in a pleat, she challenged his answer. 'There is reason, or else you would not ask.'

'He praises a Juniperus Pirate.'

'The Handsome Thief,' she said in amused affection. 'A rarity, I know for a Juniperus Pirate to have principles. Did my husband tell you he too was born with a key?'

'He did not,' Quercus muffled as he shuffled into his silk shirt. 'Has he never considered becoming a Council Member?'

'Lord Betula is still alive. My husband would not step into another man's shoes before he dies. He too has principles.' She left him with that thought.

He sat on the bed and puffed out his cheeks; new legends were everywhere on this continent. It was a land mass of vast proportions with countries identified by the name of a tree, presided over by Council Members born with keys and expected to represent their kind and country of origin. Before Cedrus, before he made himself purveyor of both continents, people lived and died in their country and rarely travelled beyond their community. Among such communities, legends proliferated, but the strange thing was that among all the many tales that abound, everyone without exception knew the legend of the Book of Hortus. Now that Quercus had spent an hour in a stupefied state from smoking Betula's pipe, he descended the stairs where a child's face appeared, his blue eyes huge and swimming. Quercus bent down and picked him up. 'Where is your father?'

He tugged at the hair. 'Mine is not as bright as yours.'

'That is because you are a pin oak, my little infant.'

The boy struggled loose, ran to his father propping up a food laden bar. 'Do not expect me to rally to your side,' said the pin oak. 'I fought in the last uprising. Cedrus punished me by slaughtering my eldest son.'

'Then vengeance should stir your heart. I saw how you fought with the devil inside you. What devil is that if not revenge?'

'When your turn comes to sire a child, you may understand the need to protect.'

'And who will protect you to facilitate your need?' As such, Quercus laid a comforting hand on the shoulder, patted twice and whilst chewing a chicken leg he ambled among the growing company.

Women, men, children, wives and husbands, old and young, all with smiling faces shining from the candlelit walls. His tale better be good.

It was a tale new to them, a tale that also brought back memories for him of Nina, left clinging to the hope that one day he would complete his promise of a picnic among sweet-scented flowers. Lately, his thoughts had gathered more keenly on his objective, to hopefully add to a swelling number that would give him an army greater than anyone had ever seen. As the end drew near, he was absent for a finale, due to the fact that he made love to Nina without paying attention to the last act in Phantom of the Opera.

'A good tale, my lord,' Betula said, taking a seat beside him. 'I too have heard this story. The end never fared well for the phantom. Lady Ilex brought it back from the other side. She went in search of you.'

'I did not know this.'

'Neither did Cedrus. When she returned, he threatened her position. It was due to her marrying that imbecile she saved herself. The gates are rarely used by Ambassadors. What has their world become like?'

'It has extraordinary foolishness. They pave their earth with acidic material, ride in noisy chariots, speed when their destination is without threat. Money is still their divinity. Everything which Hortus has provided is taken not in kind but in payment to another.' Quercus sipped at his beer and then licked his lips. 'I have seen through electronic eyes how they have advanced to the detriment of Hortus. Already fear is growing in their hearts at her revenge.'

'Then we must be thankful for small mercies,' the pin oak intervened.

'It is no small mercy to see your home destroyed, loved ones taken.'

'You ask too much of me.'

'I ask you to join your brothers in the same cause.'

'That same cause which lost me a son in your absence.'

'That same cause which can lose your other.' Quercus glared direct into the eyes of the older man. 'I make no promises save one. I shall not leave your side, regardless.'

The pin oak made a cast at Betula. 'Who will be here to protect the women and children if all men leave?'

'Our women are resourceful creatures. Already my wife makes a plan with others to create an underground system of escape. Come, my friend. Join us. Leave the seniors to supervise and protect. Their strength is not yet done.' They watched him shuffle away, still in two minds. 'He will come.' Betula was confident.

It was approaching dawn as Quercus slipped from the inn and padded through shaded streets pregnant with the noise of activity. He had slept little, in part through the energy-elation of supporters, in part through concern of black robes. Already women were pulling up flagstones outside homes to dig secret tunnels. Blacksmith hammers and stonemason mallets were beating out time, counting down. There was armour to make, horseshoes to fit, and blades to sharpen.

'I will come,' said the pin oak.

Quercus smiled. With thirty good men, by far not enough, the faithful few journeyed by day and slept by night under misty stars. More townships were visited and the hero inflamed some hearts but not enough as he would like. Was it the frightening thought of black monsters?

Among the dust carts and horses and men, a White Tail screeched and circled above. These were bearers of news, elaborately plumed eagles that criss-crossed the skies, able to effortlessly home in on their mark to deliver a message. It landed on the square shoulders of Quercus. Fagus was due to anchor off the west shores sweeping the populus forest. They travelled on. One hundred good men behind Quercus, it was better than nothing.

The full moon stood high above the glistening shores silvering their sheer ravines and plunging gullies into deepest black. Supporters from the far west were climbing the slope of the glade, for they were the elite, and their expressions were proud and solemn as they watched Quercus on Shadow march out of the populus forest. He dismounted and greeted Fagus with a bear hug.

'I had visions of you lost, my friend.'

'Not under the Captain's helm.'

The burly beech stood aside and introduced Fraxinus, Lord of the Ashes, a Council Member that once had bravery cornered. He was an imposing figure with a craggy weathered face and hard jutting jaw, thickened round the waist. His ashen eyes and ashen hair were somewhat dulled by age though he had many years fight left in him. He stopped only a pace in front of Quercus, his hand gripped tight on the handle of a sheathed sword.

'I pledged my allegiance to the cause, sixty-two of my best.'

Indeed this was good news, a new ally, now there were seven Ambassadors. 'Welcome, brother Fraxinus.' He turned to Fagus. 'Where is Syringa?'

'She stays on board with Twist who must sail to pick up the palms. Jubaea has pledged fifty of his own.'

Fagus and Quercus exchanged keys and then followed the fighters into the forest and met one hundred others, faithful to the cause. It was a natural amphitheatre, screened by the dense populus yet to bear their silky white hairs round their pendent seeds. This was a secret place, hidden from curious or hostile eyes, perfect for the purpose.

Around the camp fire, Quercus asked, 'Fagus, were you aware of the faceless black robes?' He watched the head shake. 'My brother, I have crossed paths with these monsters. Cedrus has been nurturing these from seed to faceless beings. The firs no longer fight, so I am told. The new settlement to the north of Daylily showed no fear of these warriors that wield axes. These beasts offer a frightening sight.'

'I have not seen them.' Fraxinus said.

'Perhaps not, but they are real. Methinks their place of manufacture is across the sea on Coniferous land. This would explain why Acer remains aloof.'

'It makes no sense,' Fagus puzzled. 'For what purpose are they needed unless Cedrus was the instrument of our release, had envisaged war, an excuse perhaps to rid our species.'

Quercus nodded slowly coming forward on his elbows. 'You may well be right, my friend. As Captain Twist said, he does not do things without reason. Methinks of Sage and her words. Acer awakes to look upon faceless men as he stands on land which is not his own. I am surprised Acer and his men would live among firs. Whatever is there must be a strong inducement to keep them pinned on those shores. The warriors we have will be nothing compared to my thoughts. These brutish beasts need little nurturing time, easily replaced unlike our own.'

'The change has come,' Fraxinus claimed. 'I felt the change on our leg. What I glimpsed upon the seas was no mirage, a span of ninety feet shining against the night sky. It was Sea Winger.'

'Rum swilled your brains.' Fagus chortled. 'Our mighty Lord of the Ashes had his head over the side the entire journey. Twist certainly plays with danger along our coastlines. Have you word from others, Quercus?'

'Ilex has gathered fifty between the hollies and lilacs. They will arrive shortly, bringing additional steeds and supplies for our camp. Juglans sends a mighty three hundred. Their journey will be arduous round the cape.'

Fagus slapped his back. 'Then we have the makings of an army. One hundred and eighty joined up to your key, one hundred and fifty of my own. Syringa too gathered fifty between the hollies and lilacs.'

'All told, a little fewer than a thousand. Against faceless men we have a daunting task.'

Fagus went quiet, looking at Quercus, his features frozen it seemed, like an ice-block without colour. 'These faceless ones, are they hard to fall?'

'They take to steel like eating paper. Their only weak spot is decapitation.'

'Then we must advise the men. What is a camp if not to practice decapitation?'

'It is not so easy.' Quercus tried to dampen down his ghoulish enthusiasm. 'They wield axes upon large steeds. I have been in the midst of their fury. They strike quickly and never tire. To get close with a sword will present difficulty.'

'They must learn your ways, my brother. Are you not here to tell the tale?'

Quercus stood and at that moment, men paid attention. He paused to survey the scene. In their eyes was loyalty, a fire of recognition that here was a legendary hero to end their suffering and he had seen this look before a century ago. This time he would not leave them. Instead he would lead them into victory, a better world, a world where their women would be safe, where their children would be safe, where there would be no threat of turning into a tree, either to be felled or to live in black noises. Never before had he felt such a weight on his shoulders.

'My brothers,' he voiced in a meaningful manner, walking among them. 'Before this night is out, each will hear the tale of Betula, the birch from north of Daylily. A brave warrior who saw his brothers hacked by axes from the hands of faceless creatures garbed in black robes. These are not men, they are abominations created by Cedrus and nurtured on Coniferous land by Acer, a traitor no less. Now he and his men live among firs. Perhaps our weather was not to their liking.' The men enjoyed his joke. 'If we do nothing we are just as guilty. We would be guilty to give them licence to plot our destiny when we should plot our own. This is what Hortus gave to us, the freedom to live without fear, the freedom to love, the freedom to roam our deciduous lands. This is our continent, not theirs. This was the will of Hortus, the will Cedrus stole from our Keeper. Now he puts fear in our hearts so we capitulate on his terms. I have seen the world through the gates of earth and sea. You hear stories told by the Juniperus Pirates who steal from this world. Soon, it will not be necessary incidentals they steal or black robes to beat at your doors but explosions and gases to appease a mad man that seeks to rule unmercifully. Here, among tall trees we shall nurture our own campaign and fight until the last breath is drawn. I shall be, not behind but in front of you. Follow my lead and I can promise you victory.'

A lone man stood. 'Similar words voiced a century ago, yet you abandoned us.'

Quercus remembered the man. 'You are my namesake, the young hero who rode by my side.' He walked up to him. 'Your wound has healed on your neck, my brother. Unlike my own, the wound I bear is locked in my heart. Yes, I left but not to run and live another day. Sage advanced me on a journey of importance, a journey to search for the mouthpiece. I was turned by Cedrus for one hundred years. Had Acer been the man he claimed to be, we would not be planning a campaign; we would be living by our own determination.'

'Did you find the mouthpiece?'

'Alas, I did not. It was my mistake and will not happen again. As surely as I stand before you, I shall lead you. You shall see me in front of you. You shall see me behind you. Each way you look, you shall see me cut and thrust the enemy, even in sleep I shall continue till the last of the enemy falls!'

Hail Quercus Coccinea, Lord of the Oaks.

It was, perhaps, the best he could offer. To tell it like it was, to embed the truth and the urgent undertaking not to falter in the cause.

'A thought, my brother,' Fagus said moving towards the camp fire. 'If we assume another released us, what other reason can there be for black robes?'

Quercus frowned and scratched his head. 'I am hard put to answer.'

'From what you say, these are not men, not flesh, blood or bone. Like the seeds you once brought through the gates, they too can pass through the gates without a key.'

'Why did I not see this myself?'

'Perhaps your mind is elsewhere?'

Alone he would agree. He felt the key close to his chest, a key that would one day be used to complete his promise of a picnic. 'Cedrus requires control of the seas. Yet the black robes appearance will alert those through the gates.' He wagged a finger. 'No, my mistake for they would not be alerted. I have seen men with covered hoods, women shrouded like Sage. Cedrus must know this. Their presence would not be alarming but accepting. It is as Nina said. They have all sorts.'

'Are we to assume Cedrus intends to take their world? If so, he is mad. What is there to gain? Control over idiots? We have the Juniperus Pirates to steal what we need, or do we? If Cedrus takes control of the gates then we shall be without steel, without glass, without those things we cannot manufacture lest we spoil our lands.'

'Fear not. There is one who holds great weight on the seas. True he is full of himself but I am told he has principles. A man who has principles with great weight is a true adversary.'

'Who is this man?'

'He calls himself a Handsome Thief.'

A HANDSOME THIEF

That very same night, the night Quercus and Fagus were ruminating around a camp fire, Nina was hunched over the breakfast bar reading the gardener's encyclopaedia. She was wearing tight grey leggings beneath a long loose T-shirt with the words *has it been a while since you rubbed up against a woman with a brain* printed on the back.

She looked up when Michael came into the kitchen. 'I got you some fish and chips. They're in the oven.'

He slipped out of his chalked-stripe jacket, placed it on the back-rest of a stool and crooked his neck to see what she was reading. 'Are you going to tackle the garden?'

'Not exactly,' she replied, turning over a page. She scanned it quickly and flipped back to the prior page. 'Michael,' she said. 'Quirky was telling the truth.'

The oven door slammed. 'That man is a schizophrenic as well as a damn thief!' Resentment, aggression and certainly lack of sympathy, Michael had it all. 'Where's the salad cream?'

'I forgot to buy some. I suppose Miss Social Climber will be coming round?'

'Nope' He pulled out a drawer. 'You should try a little harder to like her.'

'You should try a little harder to take your brains out of your trouser pockets.'

Michael shrugged off the rebuke and sat down. It appeared that no further communication was occurring between them. But five minutes later, he looked up above his rimless spectacles. 'It was him, right? Him that pinched my jellybeans.'

She slammed shut the book. 'I ate your jellybeans if you must know.'

'I knew it! I bloody knew there was something up with you.' He popped a chip in his mouth, chewing contemplatively and then swallowed. 'What makes you think he's not a pathological liar?'

She held up two fingers. 'One, there is room for a tree in that spot. Two, he did find the secret panel.' She picked up her notes. 'The first thing I tackled was species. Did you know there is a difference between conifers and trees?'

'A tree is a tree to me,' he muffled.

'That's what most people think. However, conifers are distinguished from trees because they produce seeds exposed or uncovered on the scales of fruits…whereas trees produce either by grafting or covered seeds, which in Quirky's case, his seeds fall in autumn.'

'So let me get this straight. You had unprotected sex while eating my jellybeans?'

Nina flushed.

'Perhaps you should take your brains out of your leggings.'

'That is absolutely typical coming from you. Has anyone ever told you education and imagination open the mind otherwise closed to the common man?'

'Okay, Miss Clever Dick. What proof do you have?'

'Err.'

'Ah, none! Only speculative theories.'

'You cannot deny his looks. His hair is not dyed, I know because his bodily hair is the same colour. And his eyes react, depending on his mood.'

'Had you considered he was on drugs?'

'I know it's hard to place feelings aside but try to be a little bendable. Try to imagine a world just like ours but without commerce or industry, a world with two continents…he did mention two, so I figured one could be a coniferous land mass and the other deciduous. Is it worth exploring anyway? The point being, let us assume this world really exists. Where we choose to sabotage nature, they embrace nature. He was familiar with the works of Charles Darwin, conclusively agreed with his theories. Okay, we evolved from primates but we cannot preclude the issue evolution sent them on a different path…and why not? We know there are some carnivorous plants in tropical places. We also know there are plants in the sea that actually walk. You only have to switch on the Discovery channel to be informed of creatures that have incredible attributes.'

'So what's his story?'

'There seems to be some sort of war between the two types. The kind Quirky talked about was a member of the conifer family, called Cedrus. Whereas his kind are considered as trees, such as Fagus and Ilex. He mentioned Syringa, which has me a little confused because she's considered a shrub.'

'Does she look like a shrub?'

'Quirky said she has short bouncy lilac hair. According to him his people are very colourful, which begs the question what do the conifers look like? Anyway, he claims he came here a century ago to find one half of a book which Hortus created, Hortus being Mother Nature. She or this Keeper was angry at Cedrus for killing someone. He mentioned something about his father being killed by Acer. I wish I had paid more attention.' She passed over her pad. 'It seems a bit confusing but I made a diagram to show how each family tree works, the genus and its species.'

Michael glanced down. 'How can nature make a damn book?'

'It's complicated. Let's just say she can. Cedrus got wind of Quirky coming into our world so he followed him and turned him into a scarlet oak because that is part of his genetic soup. He never found the mouthpiece. James Farrow's wife claimed it was hidden in our fireplace.'

'So what was he doing with Farrow's wife?'

'Why must it always come down to sex with you?'

He shrugged his shoulders. 'I thought sex was the fundamental basis for evolution. Of course, correct me if I am wrong.'

'Well what do you think?'

'You really don't want to know what I think, Nina.' He slid off the stool and switched on the kettle. 'Okay, I go along with the concept of DNA mutations. Does it explain how this biological transfer takes place? No, because magic wands don't exist. Coffee or tea?'

She shook her head. 'We accept telekinesis. Why not accept this Cedrus has discovered a way to connect with matter? Perhaps this book holds the very secrets of matter.'

'Tell you what, sis. Next time he comes round, I shall have a word with him.'

'Consider what happened last time. You were very rude.'

'My interest is looking after your interests.' He pulled a face, wrinkling his nose. 'Come on, sis, try to keep your feet on the ground. Has he been round since?'

'He's busy gathering support.'

'Or busy with a wife and kids in a tree house.'

'Oh, I give up.' Nina sighed. 'The truth is you're still irritated because he got one over on you.'

'I was half asleep!' He shot back. 'All you had to do was send me a text. Instead I'm confronted by a large carrot in my clothes. Not on, Nina. I was defending our castle, yes, man's basic instinct. I promised Mum I would look after you. We both knew you had a gullible tendency and that was proved many times over. Something happens in your brain. It goes cock-eyed when you see someone in trouble. And look at you. What woman in their right mind wears their mother's old suits and buys stupid T-shirts from charity shops.'

'Why should I keep up appearances just to fit in? Besides, Mum's clothes still have the wear in them and it makes me feel she's still around. Like Quirky, he has his father's whip.'

'So his father was a lion tamer?' He made her smile and continued. 'Okay, let's just start on an even keel. When he comes round, we'll take him out for a drink and go on from there.'

'Can you take me sailing tomorrow?'

'Why?'

'To see if we could find his gates to earth and sea.'

'You have to be kidding me!'

Conversely, Nina kept her discovery close to her chest. Her goal was in sight but she needed the assistance of Michael who was not exactly enthralled with the idea. 'I have never asked you for anything.' She padded behind him into the living room. 'You took the afternoon off the other day to go sailing with Greg. Why can't you do the same for me? It has to be close, maybe a mile or two out or as far as a man could possibly swim.'

'I have sailed out there a hundred times. There is nothing remotely resembling a gateway. It's a shipping lane not the Bermuda Triangle.'

'Well that's because you weren't looking for one. It could be the simplest of signs one can easily overlook.'

'And if we find this simplest of signs then what? You need a key, don't you?'

She dangled one in front of him. 'I have a key.'

He moved towards her. 'You had that made.'

'No I didn't,' she said smiling.

'His was a Q so why a C?' He shook his head. 'You had it made for a laugh. QC, Queen's Counsel.'

'No I didn't,' she repeated in the same amusing tone. 'All I want to do is to confirm it.'

'Like hell you do. If you saw it you would drop into it.' Walking back to the kitchen, he checked his watch. 'I need to go.'

'Go where?'

'To see Sonja.'

'You never said.'

'Look, we shall go this weekend…make it a foursome, me and Sonja, you and Greg. Greg's a decent fellow. You might get to like him.'

'Oh whatever,' she irritated. 'Why not invite the entire surgical team.'

Michael was silent for a moment and she watched him for any sign of misgivings. There was none. But she was not one to give up that easily. If Michael could handle a fifty-foot foot ketch then so could she.

In her bedroom she foraged at the bottom of her wardrobe and brought out the green leather bound book in a half-penny shape, nodding her head. It was so simple to work out. Once she had established Quercus was telling the truth, all she had to do was trace the contents taken from the mill before the tower was demolished. The curators of the museum, unable to establish its provenance and unable to comprehend why the pages should be blank, tucked it away in a dusty old cupboard little realizing a key was hidden in its lining. It was left to Nina to provide the single spark of illumination, claiming it was intended to be used as a diary by James Farrow. And with one lie pressed upon another, she managed to secure an item she knew perfectly well was the mouthpiece.

Slipping on her trainers with the key hidden inside, she tied back her hair with a simple kerchief, grabbed her blue anorak and slipped the book inside its pocket. Then she went downstairs into the kitchen and picked up the photograph of her mother, realizing for the first time how the picture had faded.

'Mum,' she said, wiping a tear away. 'If all goes pear-shaped, I might be joining you. If not, look after Michael and do something about his stupid girlfriend.'

She kissed and placed the picture aside, took a long hard look at her surrounds and sighed. Deep within her there had always been an empty aching feeling of something, like a picture painted in lemon juice that would only come to light with heat.

Everywhere there was water, glistening and shining in the flat glare of electric lights, running back in channels each side of the teak deck. She slipped the vessel's ropes from the bollards and jumped on board. The very air was wet seeming to fill her lungs like treacle as she negotiated out of the harbour, a diesel engine turning a single propeller. Now she was chasing legends, cruising along a dark coast with a spotlight rigged on the uppermost part of the main mast.

She had half a dozen heart faltering moments before the engine coughed, spluttered and then died. The spot died too. All around dark waters merged with dark skies and gradually despair overwhelmed her. Michaelmas was running the current, edging painfully towards hazardous rocks. Then a deluge of waves swamped the stern and dispatched her headlong, tumbling like a tightly rolled up piece of paper blown in the wind. Beneath her, the hull reverberated and before she could adjust her footing, she was thrown again. Her reprisal had been brief. In blind anger she had stolen Michael's cherished possession and now she was feeling the backlash of her adventure without principle.

Hours passed before she heard lapping waters and laid there on the edge of consciousness feeling closed fingers lightly on her hand. Her eyes flickered.

Could it be she was looking at the most striking man on this earth? His features were angular and strong, his hair brown, his eyes green, and his lips parted to show a straight row of white teeth. She must be in heaven.

She came up on her elbows. 'Are you Michael's friend, Greg?'

'Eat, you need vitamins.' He placed an orange on her stomach and left.

How odd?

On deck, her horizons visibly improved. Michaelmas was fast and steady, cutting through a blue and white carpet of waves and the skies were overcast and grey. But the sails were rolled and it seemed she was being towed by another much larger vessel that appeared to be coming her way, or so she thought. It carried one central mast with the bow and stern identically shaped so it could reverse its heading by the flip of its sails. Men on deck were scurrying among swooping eagles. It all seemed wrong somehow.

Almost as if she had posed the question, he said, 'They are White Tails delivering orders.'

She turned to face him. 'Do you catch fish?'

'No, my pretty, we steal from the gates.'

'Gates!' She clasped her hands. 'Did you say gates as in gates to earth and sea?'

His response was cut off by the wind but she knew she had achieved her ambition. She clung to the remnants of her memories; the stories Quercus had told and how there was always an element of doubt. But now it was true. She was sailing on seas in another world. It did exist and it excited her.

'So where are we?'

'North of Inbetween.'

'In between what?'

'Inbetween is an island between two continents.'

'Oh, I was right! I bet the gates are there.'

'No, my pretty, the gates are in Daylily on Deciduous land.'

'If you can give me the co-ordinates, I shall sail to Daylily.'

'You cannot sail in a vessel you do not own. Can you not see you are in tow?'

Such complications should be avoided. 'Under Mariners Law you cannot claim salvage rights with a person on board.'

'Your laws do not apply in my world.'

Then suddenly it struck her. 'Let me get this straight. You go through the gates, steal what you like and bring it back here? That's a damn cheek. M&S put ten percent on their goods to cover for theft. It's us, hard working people that pay through the nose. I suppose you're a gun runner as well?'

'We disapprove of war.'

'Oh, me too,' she replied enthusiastically. 'I never agreed with the war in Iraq.'

He was a sea veteran with few weathered marks, a true ancient of a confer species that pillaged and raped the other side, feeling no conscience or remorse. He waved his hand through the air, visibly trying to reinforce a point. 'All this is free from war, my pretty. No-one is burdened with taxes. No-one is forced to labour for another, not on my watch, a utopia to envy.'

'Well of course it is,' she said, poking him in the ribs. 'You steal everything from us. Not very democratic, and you, what are you, some sort of twenty-first century pirate?'

'Permit me to explain.' He bowed extravagantly, his webbed feet placed together. 'I stand before you as a humble veteran cast precariously as both victim and villain by the vicissitudes of fate. I am a Juniperus Pirate, no mere veneer of vanity from a bygone era but known as a Handsome Thief roaming these seas to meet the needs of others.'

'And what exactly is a Juniperus Pirate, seaweed?'

'Why do you insult me when I give you safe passage on my vessel?'

'This is not your vessel. It belongs to my brother.'

'I think not.'

'I think yes.'

'You are hardly in a position to argue.'

Mmm, she thought, this is a wily character. But she could be wily too. She went to the stern and looked down, realized at once from the crumpled rail she had been pushed through the gates. It was a fleeting glance but already she had caught his interest. 'Do you see this?' she said pointing. 'You cannot possibly have this vessel unless you get the bilge pump working. We are taking on water.'

With a worried expression he came to her side and bent over the rail. Look, there, she continually voiced until he could stretch no more. A little push and splash! Men are so gullible. She made haste and raced to the bow, slipped the towing rope from its cleat and watched the vessel ahead make distance.

'Have mercy!' His garbled plea was hardly audible.

She raced back, ducked under the boom and looked over the stern. 'I could leave you there for your men to pick you up.' She glanced back. 'Oh dear, they seem too busy to notice your absence.'

'You own the boat!'

She threw him a line, grabbed the flare pistol then watched him grabble on board to stand in his own puddles of confusion, his hands raised.

'Give me the co-ordinates to Daylily?'

'Why, when you can sail to Inbetween?'

'I don't want to be between continents. I want to find Quercus.'

'There are many with the same title.'

'You know it crossed my mind that was rather strange,' she said waving the pistol like a baton. 'I mean, how does one differentiate? If you don't have an individual name, how is one able to address the other without everyone turning round thinking it's them.'

'We address each other face to face.'

'Well how do you know which Quercus I mean?'

'Usually,' he replied, his eyes following her cavalier attitude. 'We speak about absent brothers from their achievements. For instance, I am known as a Handsome Thief, the most feared pirate on the seas who can out-manoeuvre waves twenty feet high.'

'Eh, twenty feet, not only are you conceited but you exaggerate.'

'Do you think you could point that pistol elsewhere?'

'It's interesting though, introducing people with a piece of their history. I know two women with identical names. When I speak about them, I always have to say, it's the Penny Brown with rosy cheeks.'

'There, you have the drift,' he replied, moving a cautious step closer. 'What of your achievements?'

'I am Nina, the one who works in the library but has so far failed to get her proposal passed by her idiotic manager.'

He edged forward again. 'I never saw your vessel, Nina, the one who works in the library but has so far failed to get her proposal passed by her idiotic manager. I was just as surprised when my vessel hit your stern, pushing you through the gates. However, the gates never deceive. Each one who passes must have a key. Where is yours?'

'Obviously you searched me.'

'It was a good search.'

'Does everyone carry keys?

'Chosen ones carry keys, such as handsome me.'

'Oh please,' she said, rolling her eyes to the sky. 'Have you no modesty?'

Her guard dropped, he retrieved the pistol in one deft move. Now the boot was on the other foot, again. The Thief turned the vessel to its original compass heading, locked on automatic pilot and hoisted the sails. For all her display of optimism, she had her doubts of what had really been achieved.

'I suppose I'm going to be sold off as some sort of slave.'

'Inbetween is a good place. There you will be safe.'

'Safe from what?'

'Everyone, my pretty. Outsiders are considered a threat.'

'Do I look as though I'm a threat?'

'You wish me to answer when you tricked me overboard?'

She slid down against a plastic buoy, loosening the tie from her hair. What could she say or do to make a difference? Twirling the scarf between her fingers, she looked back at him, aware he was observing her. 'Have you ever been in love, Handsome Thief?'

'This Quercus without history, how did you meet him?'

'He was rooted for one hundred years in the woods near my home. Of course, I thought he was utterly barmy until I got to know him. Now he has to kill Cedrus.'

'I know him. He is not in Daylily.'

'Do you know where he is?'

'No-one but his men know where he is. But there again a spy may know where he is and since I do not know the spy then I do not know where he is. Although a White Tail would know where he is but White Tails are unable to speak. Now if you could fly with a White Tail, you would know where he is but you cannot fly. Alternatively, you could send a White Tail to let him know you have arrived but in so doing you make him come out of hiding and then everyone will know where he is.'

'A simple no would've sufficed.'

'So shall we settle for Inbetween?'

'Is there any other choice?'

'Come, my pretty. Such a sad, sad face…can you tell a good tale?'

'One of my favourites is a story about Moby Dick. Do you know it?'

The Thief quickly sank beside her, squeezing her knee. 'I shall be the first to hear this tale from the lips of an outsider.'

So there, perched against a plastic buoy, a whisper away from a handsome pirate she related the story of Captain Ahab, the way this embittered peg-legged man sought his revenge. She described the sounds of his cold panting breaths, his sailors driving their harpoons into blubber and the last cries of agony as he and his crew drowned in the wake of a white whale inexorably drawn to the ocean bed.

The heavy humid winds carried from the south had brought rain. Water teemed over this luscious large island of mixed greenery, and teemed over them as they docked against a wide wooden berth stretching from a white sandbar that folded upon itself to form a secret lagoon.

'Here we shall wait.' He told her dropping into the cabin.

'Where did the other vessel go?' she said, towel-drying her hair.

'To drop my cargo of fabrics on Coniferous land.'

'I thought silkworms manufacture your clothes.'

'True, there are silkworms and cotton farms. But fabrics with gold threads and sequins have been in much demand of late.'

'What will happen to Michaelmas? Do you intend to sell her?'

'We barter.'

'Sell, buy, barter…it's all the same.' She rattled the kettle. 'Do you want a cup of tea?'

'No,' he replied opening a bottle of wine. 'We shall drink to your vessel.'

'Say that again?'

'Yes, you earned your freedom by a good story.'

'Wow,' she exclaimed. 'Are stories that valuable?'

'What else is there to offer? Tales are good entertainment. It stirs the imagination.'

She chinked her glass against his. 'Thank you, Handsome Thief, may your imaginations stir. I have never known a man who owns an island. Who else lives here?'

'No-one. I do not step on land. This is my mooring place to escape bad weather or, in this case, to hide an interesting find.' He sniffed. 'You have a lasting scent of blueberries.'

'It's my Mother's concoction. I make my own soap and shampoo. Perfume is so dear nowadays. Tell me about yourself? You mentioned you were cast precariously by the vicissitudes of fate.'

'Like many of my contemporaries, I was born to steal from the gates. We blend easily with your surrounds so our presence goes undetected.'

'Had you never considered it's wrong to steal from the other side?'

He sat down beside her. 'It cannot be wrong when Hortus shows one way. Consider…we have no need for commerce, no need to build dirty factories, no need to pollute our sea, no need-'

'Yes, I get the message. Our world becomes the dustbin and your world becomes a haven of beauty. So who else has keys?'

'Ambassadors of tree kinds have keys. They are many countries on Deciduous land, some larger than others. I will recite. Alder, Ash, Beech, Birch, Elder, Holly, Lilac, Lime, Maple, Oak, Palm, Walnut, Willow, and not to be forgotten the last surviving Elm called Zelkova, the Astronomer and bad forecaster of weather. His country is shared by neighbouring countries.'

'These countries, is there nothing but the same type of trees and people? For instance, if I was to fly over Lilac Country would I see a mass of lilac trees?'

'I understand. Let me explain it simply. Plants are planted where people want to plant, and people are people and live where they want to live. The firs act no differently on their continent and left us out because we are the Juniperus Pirates owning the seas.'

'Well, that seems clear enough. So what about the keys held on Coniferous land?'

'Ah, there is a continent much larger where only three kinds occupy, Abies, Cedrus and Ginkgo. They do not have keys. Only the mighty wicked Cedrus has a key. Many moons ago key holders would enter the gates for knowledge. There is no point to enter now since there is nothing worth learning.'

'Why don't you step on land?'

The Thief rolled up his cotton sleeve to show a burning scar cutting across his forearm. 'This is from the scimitar of Cedrus. Had my feet touched ground, he would have turned me into a dwarf conifer. That is why I never set foot on land. I do set foot in Daylily, only as far as the Harbour Winery ten paces from the harbour wall.'

'But surely you are part of his family. Why would he do that?'

'I respect the will of Hortus,' he said shuffling his sleeve down. 'Cedrus killed the Keeper of her secrets. The men who serve on my watch share my values.'

'So what's wrong with your island?'

'Nothing is wrong. There are no people to talk to so I do not step on land.'

'I see, I think. So who was the Keeper?'

'You have a deeply enquiring mind, Nina, the one who works in a library and has so far failed to get her proposal passed by her idiotic manager. To understand, one has to return to the beginning.'

'Unless you have a previous appointment, I have the rest of the moon to listen.'

'In the beginning there was Hortus where she made one land for all. From the surrounding seas there were curious little fishes.'

'Little fishes with legs, I presume.'

He turned his head briefly and smiled. 'I tell the tale prettily.'

'Okay, pretty is good.'

'Her seas grew wild and impatient, split the land apart but not equally. The biggest was claimed by the conifers, the smallest left for the trees. Pirates claimed the sea, willing to take risk against mighty storms, one such storm threw open the gates. The disgruntled conifers made boats and crossed the dividing waters to take control of the gates. Hortus was displeased and created a book of her secrets, to be read by her Keeper. The Keeper, being a fair minded man, banished the firs to their homeland and gave control of the seas to the Juniperus Pirates, willing to take risk. For centuries we all respected the Keeper's laws until Cedrus killed for the want of her secrets. How it was achieved, is left to speculation but the consensus of opinion is that Cedrus gained immortality by killing the Keeper. For one thousand years, Cedrus has presided over two continents but he shall not have the seas. The seas were promised to us.'

'Why would he want the seas anyway?'

'To control the seas is to control the gates. Man or woman with a key may pass for knowledge. Only the Juniperus Pirates go through the gates to steal. Only the Juniperus Pirates have the wherewithal to keep our presence low. We keep our ear to the ground, our eyes ahead, dark or light we see and hear like a cat.'

'Like a cat,' she mused. 'Would that be with or without whiskers?'

He kept his expression inscrutable but lowered one eyelid at her in a furtive wink. 'Without looking at your shoes, tell me what you see?'

'Err…um…shoelaces?'

'You do not see the weevil poking his elongated proboscis into your left shoe?'

'So there is.' She leaned forward and flicked it off her trainer. 'So how did you own this island? Was it given by the Keeper?'

'It was acquired by custom, passed from father to son. Though there was an occasion it was passed from father to daughter. She suffered sea sickness.'

'You know, a thousand years is a very long time. Why has it taken so long to get rid of Cedrus? Okay, so he's immortal and can turn men into trees but surely-'

'No,' he interjected. 'The firs have an aggressive and invasive disposition. Many sided with Cedrus. Trees were hard pressed to resist the mighty firs; the insurgencies were easily overcome. And then they grew stronger, more resilient. Your Quercus caused a big headache for Cedrus.'

'What does he look like? Cedrus, I mean, what does he look like?'

'His self-delusion considers himself the most handsome man on this planet. Yes, he is taller than most. His hair is black, like yours. His eyes are very black, pools of evil shine from them, shafts of malevolent smiles pour from his fleshy lips and his chin is square like a chessboard.'

'So he's tall, dark and rugged?'

He studied her, wiping her hair from her face. 'There is a legend that one will pass through the gates without a key and take control of the seas with the aid of the Juniperus Pirates. For there within its bed of mystery awaits a magnificent creature to fly over Deciduous land and drop its shit on the firs.' In her laughter he topped up her glass. 'Are you the one, Nina?'

'I very much doubt it. If you live by the will of Hortus, why don't you lend a hand and help out the trees?'

'It is not our war.'

'That's not a very nice attitude. Cedrus is making them suffer. All they want is their right to live on land which was promised by the Keeper.'

'Did you not disagree with the war in Iraq?'

LEVITY BROWN

SUMMER CHAPTERS

In early summer, more colours are added by a profusion of perennials and biennials, often lasting until autumn. Shrub interest diminishes as this season progresses, which is when the annuals make their contribution, brightening up the heavy green face of summer.

ENROLMENT

Quercus rushed him. It was a brief clash, the easiest of deflections for Fraxinus, a traditional ancient, the last of that dignity of warriors to whom age was its own embellishment.

Around them, others were practising. The men were learning new techniques. Each crack of the whip was fresh agony as it stretched the torn muscles and ligaments and burned the soft tissue of their lungs. Some had been constructed from hide, others by the soaking and plaiting of tree bark. A very effective tool if used wisely. Though in the use of such a tool, it wreaked havoc on their out-of-conditioned limbs. Soon they would be skilled in the art.

Done and dusted for the evening, Quercus picked his way across camp under the last practised sounds and knelt beside recumbent Fagus. In the balmy night air, a different sound joined the faint murmurs of men settling down for the night. It was the loud purr of a green leopard that edged between them. So while Fagus, outstretched, looking at the stars with his hands behind his head thinking of Syringa sailing with Captain Twist, Quercus was sharing his meat with the wildlife.

'Did I not inform to keep Syringa by your side?'

'On water she is safe.'

'When our campaign begins, what do you intend to do? Keep her with Twist?'

'Keep her with me,' Fagus crustily replied.

'There is no logic to your reasoning. I am surprised Syringa agreed to keep on board.'

'She acts in our interests. I do not trust Twist.'

'Ah, now we come to the heart of the matter. Jubaea vouched for him.'

'We must take precautions where necessary. There shall be no traitor in our camp.'

Quercus was caressing the leopard's belly, her paws paddling the air. 'Look, my friend. Is she not beautiful? She gives herself freely like the wind in our hair.'

'Like the woman who sails with a flat stern.'

'It is Sea Winger.' Fraxinus joined them, affectionately patting the leopard.

'Sea Winger is not a woman.'

'How would you know, Fagus? You have not seen it. I have.'

'Who spoke of what you saw was true?' Fagus paused. Fraxinus remained quiet, his face blank. 'Then you make my point. Sit and eat before your mouth fills with more nonsense.'

Fraxinus considered the advice, a wise man in company with others. 'Quercus, speak of your tale on the other side.' There was so little to do but wait and tell tales. 'I hear you watched a story.'

'It was on a flat box called a television. Actors played their parts. They sing while they fight, sing while they make love. I cannot do either.'

'You can shout and grunt, is that not the same?'

In the midst of their laughter a rider came storming into camp, going directly to Quercus. 'Thirty robes on fast steeds approach from the east!'

Quercus picked up his whip. 'Fagus, sweep the perimeter. This might be a trap.' With a stuttering heart, he worked his way across camp and leapt upon Shadow who felt the give on his back.

The scenery changed with dramatic suddenness as he emerged from the forest into the shallow valley covered with rushes and grasses, their silver and pink seed heads brushed his stirrup irons as he forged onwards in a mild canter. Ahead, it was as the runner explained.

Jubaea pulled down his hood. 'You have been a devil to find. Where is our camp?'

'If you are lost so too will the enemy.'

'Have my men arrived safely?'

Quercus turned his reins. 'Indeed they have.'

They flung their horses forward and broke into a thundering gallop. No trap here, no confusion but the common bond of a cause. Blasting into camp, brothers greeted brothers save one.

Jubaea removed his gloves. 'Quercus, we have an outsider who claims to know you.' He turned. 'Come, you have his attention.'

The robed swept off and Quercus immediately recognized Michael, astounded and brought forth his hand. The return came by a fist to his chin and once again Quercus staggered back, caught unaware. An audience gathered. Now pride over-ruled his curiosity.

The aura of conquest sat easily on Michael's broad shoulders. The fight was on amid chanting. They called for their leader to win, Quercus, Quercus, Quercus but the lightweight challenger paid little heed, his confidence brimming, his anger simmering. In the blood roar of the enveloping crowd they weaved and ducked until another hard punch landed on the mighty Lord of the Oaks. Had he not been warned by Nina? Grunting like labouring bulls at punches thrown and received, the heaviest impact came when Michael soared through the air, swung round and sent his foot into Quercus who subsequently landed three feet away in the dust. Twice caught off guard by this man from the gates, he got to his feet and smiled. There were other ways to bring down a cocky opponent. In a fluid instant, he dodged a fist and struck at the legs. It had simplicity about it, a rhythm and defining end.

'Now, my brother,' Quercus said, his foot to the chest. 'What are you doing here?'

Jubaea replied. 'He claims you took his vessel and sister.'

Quercus removed his foot. 'Explain, Michaelmas.'

'Nina wanted to find that bloody door.' Michael brushed the dust off his jeans. 'I came home and she was gone, no note, nothing. I walked to the harbour and no boat. I hung around and waited for her to return. By morning, I'm thinking that perhaps there is something to this invisible gateway. So I go home, make a few calls just to be sure then I snatched a dinghy and the next thing I knew I was sucked into a damn bubble bath. I thought I woke up on the same shoreline. Everyone was looking at me as though I had the plaque until I bumped into this guy, Jubnuts.'

Jubaea let the moment pass, feeling slightly besmirched. 'Quercus, he spoke of Nina having a key.'

'And where did she get this key?'

'She refused to say,' Michael volunteered.

'Where is the one you hold?'

Jubaea answered. 'That is my point. Michaelmas entered the gates without a key.'

'Michael, my name is Michael. It's my boat that's called Michaelmas.'

'And my name is Jubaea.' He pushed a beaker of wine into the chest. 'Here, we respect our fellow men regardless of status.' Jubaea turned to Quercus, anxious to give other news. 'Cedrus is questioning the Ambassadors. He rooted Lord Sambucus. And Lady Tilia is in a poor state. She was stripped of her clothing, humiliated in front of his Ministerial Firs, flogged until blood coursed the ground upon which she stood.' The jaw clenched. 'We must strike now before he comes here.'

'Strike where?' Quercus said sharply. 'We must wait for the walnuts.' He held his head in his hands then swept them back over his hair before letting out a sigh. Matters were coming to ahead. He swung round. 'Fagus, what else was said in the rumour?'

'The vessel was heading for Inbetween. But the rumour is old and unfounded. Sage mentioned one to pass the gates without a key.'

Quercus nodded. He looked sadly at Michael. 'She would not be able to fool the gates with a key made in your world. Did you see wreckage?'

'Look, I saw that key. I stake my life she never had it made.'

Quercus was fidgety now. He rocked from one foot to the other whilst cracking his knuckles. 'How long, Michaelmas? How long has she been gone?'

'Nearly three weeks.'

'We must assume it was Nina. Do we assume the Thief is keeping his prize? What better place than to stow her there for her own safety.'

'We cannot divert Twist,' Fagus said. 'It will put our position in jeopardy.'

Quercus looked up to the stars and permitted himself a foolhardy hope, to nurture an idea that might just work. He cupped his hands to his mouth and let out a piercing shriek.

'What's he doing?' Michael asked Jubaea.

'Watch the night sky and see how we communicate.'

Nina, mark your bearing due north. Quirky. He rolled up the note. 'Michaelmas, how good is Nina at bearings?'

'Bloody good.'

'By the time she draws close, Twist will be ready to intercept.' He held up his hand to interrupt Michael's concern. 'She has not been harmed, not if she stayed on his island.'

'How do I know he's kept his thieving hands off her?'

'Since I have little knowledge, we do not. Let us hope she has the mind to barter for your vessel.'

Above, a shrill then eyes rose to a White Tail spiralling cosily down in the dim light of camp fires. After the bird collected the note, Quercus sized Michael up with interest. All things considered, there may be something to this man. Sage had said in spring, the wheels turn for the prophecy.

'You held yourself well,' Quercus told Michael. 'You will become famous. Your endeavours will pass the lips of brave warriors around camp fires.'

Michael shook his head, vigorously. 'No way, I have no intention of staying. Once I get my sister back and my boat, I'm off.' He motioned with his hands. 'Back, just like that, the same way we came in.'

'But you are a healer. We will have great need of your services. Your destiny has been written, my brother.'

'My destiny is on the other side, my brother…my job, my girlfriend, my house, my sister, death and taxes…that is my destiny, my brother.'

Michael was possibly the wrong choice, possibly a mistake but Quercus saw him playing an important role. He was a breed apart, a healer with scant regard for his company, for the men who recoiled at his hostile sarcasm. Temptation was the answer for enrolment.

'Here, you can have a house, a better house and instead of removing tonsils, you can gain expertise elsewhere on the body. But more importantly, you can have a better woman, one with greater claws, brighter hair and swelling breasts.'

'You pay too much attention to my sister.'

'Do you claim to be in love? A man in love would sacrifice his name at the altar. Is that not so, my brothers?'

It is so.

'We are getting married when I can get round to it.'

'Then congratulations, Michaelmas. I am sure your name will be read aloud with pride.' Quercus walked around him, stroking his chin. 'What would she say if she could see you top in your field, an eminent man who lays claim to the greatest scientific discovery in human history.'

'No-one would believe this place exists, so forget it.'

'I was not referring to our world.'

His interest had been drawn. 'What scientific discovery?'

Quercus placed an arm about his shoulders, drawing him close to the camp fire. 'My brother, think what may be gained with the knowledge of our longevity. Do your people not yearn for extended youth? Do you not have a little curiosity as to how we can turn into trees and live twice your life span?'

'Twice our life span, are you sure about that?'

'Am I not living proof?'

'You spent a century in a state of suspended animation.'

Quercus indicated to Jubaea. 'There is a man who was the same age as I when last we fought side by side a century ago. Does he look like Rip Van Winkle to you?' He paused at the encouraging signs. 'And what of our unchartered waters, treasures to discover, glistening diamonds and gold fields.'

'How do you know if they're unexplored?'

'He makes a good point, Quercus.' Fraxinus said, offering Michael bread and cheese. 'But he has a vessel. He can sail the seas without hindrance. I hear your shipping lanes are crowded.'

'How long will this uprising take?' Michael asked Quercus.

'How long is a piece of string? I will personally ensure your safety.'

'So I don't get to kill?'

'Only to save.'

'I will need medical supplies.'

'You shall have it.'

'Not just band aid but the whole kit and caboodle.'

'You shall have it.'

'And I want my boat or equivalent.'

'You shall have it.'

'And I want my sister.'

'As we speak, her rescue is under way. Do we have an accord?'

Michael glanced down. Incredulously, he was stroking a leopard, caressing the soft anvil of creation as though it was the most natural thing to do. 'Why is he green?'

'He is a she. Her colour has mutated to accommodate her environment. She is your friend, like so many here, they are your friends. However, be warned, turn against them and they will eat you.'

'You have a deal.'

Quercus kept a tight grip on the proffered hand, his words issued deep. 'In future you will show some manners and address us with respect.'

By now, the camp had found its own calm. Men were resting on their straw beds, their curiosity fed. Fagus, Jubaea, Fraxinus, Michael and Quercus sat by dying embers telling tales before closing their eyes to dream of better days.

'Our inspirations hang in tattered shreds, Michaelmas.' Quercus relayed. 'For one thousand years the Book of Hortus has been lost due in no small part to the revengeful Cedrus. He grieved for this book. Hortus grew angry and bit into her own spine just like a hungry child would bite into a slice of bread. The pieces were separated, lost in different worlds, the mouthpiece in yours, the other in ours.'

'So what made Hortus angry?'

'Cedrus killed her Keeper, the Keeper of her secrets. From what we know, Cedrus claimed to have the gift of reading the pages and manipulated the Keeper to divulge certain knowledge. It is that knowledge which gave him the faculty to turn men into trees.'

'So this Keeper, who was he?'

'A man of great wisdom and fortitude,' Fagus replied. 'Hortus choose him to guard our dominion when the firs tried to take hold of the gates. He was given her secrets, the power to banish them to their homelands. All was well until that heathen was born. We do not know for certain if we shall ever return to the old ways save for the wisdom of Sage.'

'We will, my brother,' Quercus confirmed. 'Do not lose heart. Our Sage speaks of a prophecy, one who is able to pass through the gates without a key, shall clear a path for me, and shall control the seas for there, within its bed of mystery awaits a sea creature. She will rise from a mist, her wings pure white, her breast sapphire and her presence will offer us protection. At present, Cedrus holds us to ransom. His family is untouched whereas-'

'Ah!' Michael interjected. 'Nina found a distinction between firs and trees in her gardening book. Firs produce seeds exposed or uncovered on the scales of fruits, whereas trees produce by grafting or covered seeds.'

'Yes, there is a distinction between the two but unlike gardening books we breed the same as you, the difference is slight. Firs are fertile year round; we are fertile in autumn. That is the way of things. Cedrus favours his family, he does not favour ours.'

'Before Cedrus we all shared in the old ways,' Fagus reminded Quercus. 'Now, many of the Juniperus Pirates dare not step on land for fear of being turned, their allegiance is to themselves.'

'Fagus, we must not forget many refused to condone his actions.' Quercus looked at Michael. 'You will soon understand our history.'

'Tell me what happened when you popped into my world?'

'A Juniperus Pirate informed Sage he had knowledge of a man called James Farrow, a smuggler owning a windmill on your coast. Farrow boasted of an unusual find, a book that looked like a green leathery pancake folded in half but much thicker. At the behest of Sage, we went through the gates with great optimism. We first encountered his wife, presenting ourselves as wealthy buyers of old volumes. She confirmed her husband hid the book behind a secret panel in the fireplace. While I entertained the wife, Fagus went in search. It was not there so he placed two seeds as our calling cards. Regrettably, Farrow materialized at a delicate-'

Michael interjected again. 'You were screwing his wife.'

'I would not put it so bluntly but yes. There was a measure of discourse, a fight ensued and I snapped his neck. His wife became hysterical, calmed only when we presented her with flowers. She suggested we bury her husband in the hinterland of your bay. And there, no sooner had we buried him, Cedrus appeared. I was struck first. Fagus managed his escape, or so I believed.'

'And now you're back to square one.'

'Square one would suggest we have not advanced any further. We have identified the spy and for that we must be grateful. Sage believed it was not my time.' Quercus stood to show a remarkable thing. It was no ordinary entwined leather lash that could crack a man's neck but instead, by a flick of his wrist, the limping weapon became a rigid instrument of steel that glistened fatality in the glow of embers. 'It is the whip of Hortus, passed to me upon my Father's death. From birth I have been given the skills to use it. I shall not fall short where others have failed. I shall use it to pierce his heart and crack the necks of our enemies.' He paused. A piece of the puzzle fell into his lap, or so he thought. 'Fagus, it was as Sage forecast, my destiny to wait so I may train others in the use of the whip upon the faceless ones.'

'Had Acer not betrayed us, there would be no faceless monsters.'

'What faceless monsters?' Michael asked.

'Creatures, who bleed dark blood, stand after falling unless their necks are broken or if we can get close, decapitated.'

Michael let fall his beaker. 'Hell, you could have mentioned this before!'

'Do not be afraid,' Quercus said. 'My promise stands, my life before yours. We each have our destiny, Michaelmas. Perhaps Nina has her destiny too. It has become clear, it was our destiny to meet, her destiny to come here as an incentive for you to enter our world. But why did she find it necessary to sail the seas?'

Jubaea, man of little words threw a stick in the fire, ready to bed for the night alongside snoring Fraxinus. 'Perhaps she sails to charter her own course.'

'That sounds like my sister. Once she gets a bee in her bonnet, nothing changes her mind. After all, this is a great adventure for her. Ever since she met Quercus, she's been like a cat on a hot tin roof.' He paused in his yawn, rubbing his tired eyes. 'She's never really had much of a life after Mum died. I took her for granted, sad to say.'

'Explain?' Fagus asked.

Michael shifted his position, lazed back on his elbows, crossing his ankles. 'Mum died when Nina was about to go to university. The problem was that she mortgaged the house to give me the financial support I needed to complete my internship in London. Bottom line, Nina left her studies to work as a librarian until I took up residency at the local hospital. She had an opportunity to go back to her studies. Instead, her crafty boss offered her promotion so he could use her brains. She did have an opportunity to go to Australia. To be honest, I didn't really want her to go.'

'So she acts as mother rather than sister.'

'Look, Quercus. She loves the house, it was Mum's house and she likes working at the library. The problem is she has a soft nature. On the one hand she can be the brainiest woman in Britain but when it comes to men, she acts very naive. Take you, for instance…you dipped your wick and buggered off. If you had just eaten my jellybeans, I wouldn't be here worried sick to death.'

Fagus puzzled. 'Dipped your wick?'

Quercus coughed. 'You see, my brother, how your destiny has been written. I suggest we follow the sounds of Fraxinus and get some rest.' He proceeded to the bushes, Fagus by his side. Nature called.

'What does this woman mean to you, Quercus?'

'My Achilles' heel. I have loved her flesh. But fear her brother will not love me when he hears of my reputation.'

'A man who has no commitments can please himself.'

'And for certain I have pleased myself. If Nina meets Lady Ilex, my adventures, no doubt will be exploited.'

'Have you spoken lies?'

'I have remained quiet which in itself is a lie.'

'Why did you not eat his jellybeans?'

Quercus smiled and shook himself. 'My brother, there is no competition between jellybeans and Nina. Would it be unreasonable to keep her to my side in times of solitude? What chance for me now? Here she will hear my tales, here she will see others and here she will be cast asunder because she is an outsider.'

'Then she will ask for your succour and protection.'

'She has Michaelmas.'

'He cannot be the one. He thinks only of himself. For certain he will return after he takes our spoils.'

'I am not convinced. The gates cannot be deceived. If he entered without a key then he is the one. But I am puzzled by Nina's key.'

Their parting was a gradual process.

Quercus lay with his face cradled in the crook of his elbow, the other arm by his side, clutching his whip. His eyes closed to the night sounds but his thoughts came alive and buzzing. It raised such frightful images that he opened his eyes and stared across his sleeping army then transferred his attention and turned on his back to look up at the stars, drawn to their brilliance. Hortus will always be there in the garish day or the darkest night, always he will feel the breath of her on his cheek. Finally he went to sleep.

The silence afterwards was not truly silence. It was the murmur of sounds, the sea heard at a distance, the snoring of nature and man, all this until dawn's early light. Then a different sound joined those soft folds. It came from the shore and carried the footprints of Juglans warriors dressed in tawny shirts and bloomers, rigged by cords and leather straps that held a number of weapons. They appeared like a spreading ochre virus, their hair yellowish-brown, faces brutishly sharp, eyes wide and round. The walnuts had arrived.

Men were rising from their straw beds, yawning and stretching and anticipating the newcomers. Quercus buried his head in a clean bucket of water then re-emerged, raking his fingers through his wet hair, charging it back. After wiping his eyes, sharper focus came. Thereafter it was the customary bear hugs and greetings between men from all corners of their continent. The amphitheatre had grown to fill its vast void. There were now near a thousand strong.

Michael was looking at the whole picture with an apple in his hand, the other in his jean pocket, leaning against a tree with a green leopard by his side. Men of great stature were debating about almost everything while feeding their bellies and quenching their thirst. Had he found new friends? Were some of them going to cross his scalpel? There was no certainty that any of these souls would be seen alive or uninjured. A minute later he looked back at the sound of hooves. Lord Juglans and Lady Ilex were dismounting. Quercus had not exaggerated the female species if she was anything to go by. He stood motionless as Quercus approached.

'What thoughts do you carry, Michaelmas?'

'I used to think if two powerful men could just battle it out between themselves there would be no need for war.'

He clamped a hand on Michael's shoulder. 'My sentiments entirely. Unfortunately, Cedrus is far stronger than I. It is true he can turn me into a tree in the time it would take to run four paces towards him. To get him alone and unawares is the answer.'

'Is that your plan?'

'If it were that easy, this would be the plan.' He glanced down. 'I see you have found a new friend.'

Michael caressed the jowls. 'She must have been in a fight. Her left ear has a piece missing.'

'We all have our enemies of nature, Michaelmas. It will please you to know Captain Twist has left with Lady Syringa to meet with Nina.'

'Let's hope she received your message.'

'Unless the bird has suffered a malady, she has received it. Come. Meet Lord Juglans and Lady Ilex. They have travelled from Daylily to greet their subjects.'

Ilex looked beyond Quercus and smiled. Her beautiful red berry eyes widened and sparkled when Michael paid her respect. He turned to Juglans in the same manner, the warning heeded.

'Why is he positively captivating,' Ilex declared. 'I hear you came through the gates without a key. Are you the prophecy, Michaelmas?'

'Quercus seems to think so. I came in search of my sister Nina.'

Ilex shot a glance at Quercus. The telling and receiving translated into silence.

'Michaelmas,' Juglans said. 'My brother has informed us you are a healer.'

'I like to think my experience stretches beyond tonsils.'

They spoke for a full ten minutes before Quercus tired of their fascination, called for the map. Fraxinus rolled it out on the ground and said, 'If your assumption is correct, we need to find the breeding ground and destroy it.'

'We do not know how Acer intends to play his cards. Will his men rally to his cause or will they stand adrift.'

Their gathering and ruminations round the outstretched map intrigued Michael. He was no fighter, had no experience of war, had no concept of strategic movements or seen the enemy that made them shudder. 'I say chaps, had an idea,' he voiced aloud. 'Why not pop next door and pick up some bazookas?' If looks could kill he would be dead.

Quercus took him to one side. 'My brother, do not speak of such weaponry. The concept is abhorrent.'

'I thought I was the chosen one?'

'Chosen to make a path and-'

'At least let me look at the map.'

Quercus nodded and they walked back. 'My brothers, please allow the prophecy to study the map.' He pointed. 'This is our position, Michaelmas. One hundred miles west of Daylily…sixty miles due south of Inbetween. With any luck, Nina will be here by nightfall.'

'She was right. You do have two continents. We had two continents 180 million years ago, Laurasia and Gondwanaland, although Gondwanaland was really in three parts. Of course tectonic plates caused both continents to drift apart and then about forty-five million years later they drifted northwards. Africa and South America began splitting apart to form the origins of the South Atlantic. India continued heading northwards to Asia. The southern part of the North Atlantic had widened considerably. Perhaps this planet is not as old as next door. The rift zone between your two continents appear to have created a fully fledge ocean. Do you have any Dinosaurs?'

Quercus offered a gritted teeth smile to the impatient audience. 'One has to make allowances, my brothers.' He regarded Michael. 'Now is not the time to discuss geophysical investigations or evolutionary comparisons. Do you have a point of reference to where the sea creature will rise?'

'Not a dickey bird.' They sighed. 'Look chaps, this might be familiar stuff to you but it's all knew to me. Has anyone made a survey of sea depths?'

'Is there relevance?' Jubaea asked.

'Yes, there's relevance. It's like the legend of the Loch Ness Monster. It dwells in deep cavernous areas. If I had some diving gear, I could explore.'

'There is no time for exploration,' Fagus said. 'Our seas are vast. Our coasts are vast with dangerous inlets and shoals.'

A runner burst into camp, breathless, racing his words in wheezing panic, near two thousand approaching the valley. The camp broke into life, shouts and bodies raced for their weapons and steeds, scrambling to saddle up.

Quercus boomed, 'HOLD FAST!' He paused for silence, watched as colourful heads grouped tightly around him. 'Remember that neither you nor your horse must break ranks. Keep the circle tight. Be swift and accurate. Aim for the necks. Saddle up and wait for my lead.'

Ilex went to his side. 'Be careful, Quercus.'

'Ilex, go to the nearest settlement, bring medicines and instruments. Take Michaelmas with you.' He turned to Juglans. 'Brother, lead your foot soldiers, take the stragglers to cover our flanks. By tonight, you shall have the pick of the enemy's steeds.'

They emerged from the populus forest leaving a wake of dust, a rage that descended into a thundering acceleration of hooves and howling men towards the shallow valley covered in a sea of black robes. The consequences were almost too appalling to consider, the developing scene almost too unbearable to watch. Axes glistened against the new day sun, their faceless heads a fearful sight. This was no accident, no casual encounter but a precision led force to take Quercus by surprise.

Shadow foamed at the mouth, his eyes rolling, his ears flattening. He was part of the stampede. Then, at a timed moment Quercus and Fagus led their own charge, splintered into two detachments. Their tactics were simple; herd the enemy like wailing sheep and keep them pinned in a tight knit circle. They met and worked from the outside in, rising up on their stirrups and cracking their whips, the enemy slowly falling one by one, no easy task against powerful mutants wielding axes.

To your rear, my brother! To your death you faceless bastard!

Brandishing a whip, Quercus braced himself against a stumbling black steed, rendering a black-robe in half, beheading two more in a single sweep. Others followed. There was no give, no respite. The heavy dust of ramming hooves, the cries and shrieks from willing men and the unrelenting energy from soundless black robes carried on into the bloody afternoon.

It took six hours before the enemy number weakened to a greater extent. Shouts and cries with hope in their voices could only mean a successful kill. Quercus struck them high and hard, propelling them from their saddles. One down, another easily replaced. He saw a flash of movement from the corner of his eye, men running forward in a short burst. His attention had been drawn for a fatal second and it was in that fatal second, he felt a sudden give to his back. The axe had bereft him of energy. Changing tactics, he flicked his wrist for steel. It was perhaps the best he could do.

On the closing part of success, urgency inflicted greater damage and spirits soared as the sun plummeted against the depletion of black robes. Cracked or cut, their throats tore open, their heads rolled but still they managed one last thrust before their bodies slipped under the mire of hooves. It was a miracle anyone still fought, a greater miracle many men survived and an even greater one the yellow hairs on foot had out manoeuvred the stragglers. Horses and men were snorting for breath but celebration was muted in the count of their dead.

Quercus, slumped on his sweating steed, slowly ebbed through a tide of bodies, the earth bathed in red and black blood. Dotted among the fallen were dying colours of heroes. He was gazing at the stumbling wounded that were themselves looking for their dead then saw Fraxinus favour his arm. Pain showed in his weathered face.

'Are you hurt, Fraxinus?'

'A mere cut,' he said so bravely. 'A good fight, my brother, one that was encountered with stealth and precision.'

Fagus rode up, his mouth turned down from the stench. 'They are abominations, a grotesque smell to sicken the stomach.' He turned back in his saddle and watched Lord Juglans wield an axe, chopping off dead heads, still in the throes of heightened kill. 'Someone should tell our brother his blows are wasted.'

'Make a fire and burn their bodies. Let Cedrus smell his creations.' Dizziness came upon Quercus and he slumped further.

'You bleed, my brother.'

'It is not my…' His voice trailed. It was not his time to die, not now, not here.

For Quercus, the long days had been full of doubts and foreboding. There was so much that could go wrong, so many details that had to mesh perfectly to ensure success. And even though victory came in this first battle, he knew it came at a price. He lost too many good men for his liking, and remembered the feats that had assailed him on the eve of other battles and desperate endeavours. Surely, he thought as he felt himself give to unconsciousness, there must be another way to end this madness. There must be another way to stop Cedrus.

Cedrus would be unable to see the spiralling smoke from a funeral pyre that sent its acrid smell towards the east. His horizons from the stone-clad balcony of his stately building were limited. But within the hour of defeat, a White Tail flew to the skies, landing to deliver a traitor's message. Blood curdled in his pumping veins, his eyes grew vengeful as he felt the bite of defeat and turned on one of his Ministerial Firs.

'Did I not command sufficient number?'

'Twice their number sent, Divine Majesty.' Alas, a poor reply.

He stared without pity as the headless body slumped to marble then went to the next. 'What is your answer?'

In abject terror, the man dropped to his knees and rushed out his words. 'The enemy is weak and low in number, Divine Majesty. The next wave shall have armour to their necks.'

Cedrus leaned on his scimitar, watched him look up for approval. 'Send word to Acer.'

'Sire, do you wish him to lead?'

'No relief has been sent, no reinforcements. They stand alone and lick their wounded under misapprehension.' He paused and gazed below to an inner courtyard where other Ministerial Firs radiated calm and authority while those about him argued. 'I do not wish him to lead and do not fail me this time.'

'It will be done, Divine Majesty.' The Ministerial Fir straightened and with due ceremony retreated backwards until no more could be seen of him.

'Why did you release them?' Another voice, a different kind stirred in a seat.

Cedrus stood perplexed for even the answer had eluded him. 'Perhaps,' he finally concluded to the man who married Lady Ilex, 'the smog they breathed in the other world has potency. What of Council Members?'

'They act no differently.'

'How do you know when you are distanced?' His tone was gently chiding as he poured himself wine. 'If I am to crush this uprising I need to know the traitors in Council.'

'You have turned one, despoiled another. To get rid of Council Members will only promote his sentiments. We fight the same enemy for the same cause.'

'Do not presume to think your cause is the same as mine.'

The aftertaste of insipid wine was sharp in his mouth. From his vantage, overlooking the seas, Cedrus understood the meaning of strong opposition. A sound, a smell, a taste in the air, the clouds maintained their gossamer course yet the atmosphere had altered. He could sense the upturn, the surge of optimism and their craving for change. There had been a ground mutiny to the north, and there was incipient rebellion due east though not enough to warrant action. Rather than deal direct, he sent black robes to quell the trouble brewing, prepared to shed every drop of blood in order to restore his kingdom. In a bloody and deadly melee of slashing and stabbing, Cedrus had gained another layer to his invincible reputation yet what he failed to realize that his actions were indeed promoting Quercus's cause. Thus, every atom of logic and military insight of which there was none, spoke against the wisdom or necessity to do such things. Far better to appease than slaughter, far better to offer terms rather than act like a spiteful child pained by his losses.

DARKEST HOUR

Laid on his stomach, his head to one side, Quercus blinked twice. She shadowed the early sun-rise where behind her formed a nimbus and it took an effort to concede this was no mirage but flesh and blood. Quirky, she spoke his name and the pain diminished. Her long dark hair glistened to a hint of midnight and he felt her hands delicately working their magic to his wound.

'Where did you find the key?' Ilex asked.

'I had one made.'

'You cannot have one made.'

'Just goes to show how wrong you can be. If you had cared to study the books your lot steal from my world then you would know we have great technology. We can create duplicates of most things, even humans…'

Quercus slipped into unconsciousness again. When later he woke he was hearing the exhilarated voices of victory lingering over the smells of sizzling food. Here, their staple diet was fruit and vegetables with the occasional leg of lamb or roast pork, generally farmed by settlers on their small acreages.

'Four days past we showed our measure,' Fagus related treading ground. 'This very hour Cedrus angers at our success though we must not be complacent. Our camp has been marked. One hundred and eighty good warriors lost. Others will come to test our mettle…'

Quercus shifted his position, flexed his shoulder and winced, glad he had escaped death, annoyed Ilex was latched to his side. To his left lay a platter of meat, a bowl of fruit and a beaker of wine. He had lost his appetite, was under no misapprehension to think there might be a traitor among them. It was no mere coincidence black robes had descended in the early part of his campaign.

Ilex broke into his thoughts. 'What do you make of Michaelmas?'

'He is the one.'

'His obnoxious sister claims a key can be manufactured. Who is to say he did not enter with a key.'

Quercus looked at her face, waiting to hear his words, could see the expectation in her eyes, not knowing what he would say but knowing he would surely say something. 'This is no place for a woman,' he finally said. 'Now our position has been marked, you should seek safety.'

'There is no safer place than by your side.'

He nibbled at his bottom lip. That never went down very well. Another tactic was needed. 'To the contrary, my side offers danger.'

'We are all in danger.' She plucked a grape from its stalk and placed it to his lips. 'Has it not occurred Cedrus was informed of our whereabouts?'

'It has occurred.'

'Then who amongst us is a spy?' Her eyes wandered over the camp. 'I do not see her, do you?'

'You speak of Syringa?'

Ilex threw back her head and laughed. 'Her blueberry scent has dulled your senses, Quercus.'

'Careful, you are close to accusation.'

'Then listen to the rumours permeating to the remotest corners of our camp. She openly admits to have lived with a pirate, acting the whore. Her smells linger to dull a man from his senses. It does not dull mine. Blueberries are more than for baking pies. You of all people should know this.'

He could not really grasp it but sensed the enormity of what she had said. Now his mood was no better than it had been four days ago.

Not that his smouldering dissatisfaction was visible, Quercus rose to his feet and took the opportunity to wander, to talk among men, to share their thoughts, to quench his thirst. By now the sun had risen and the heat crushed down upon the amphitheatre causing men to claw back in the shade. But distanced apart was Nina, asleep under a tree with her head resting against the recumbent green leopard. He smiled and stared with the sudden realization of his hollow hunger, the need that he had kept suppressed, which now suddenly threatened to consume him.

'You seem a little distracted, my brother?'

'I have things on my mind, Fagus.' He sank down beside him. 'Where is Syringa?'

'She bathes in the pool with Lady Ilex, a place where Nina is prohibited to go. I fear Ilex has a streak of jealousy rather than a streak of common sense.'

'You believe Nina is true?'

'She is a breath of fresh air, Quercus. She bound many men's wounds with tears in her eyes. Unless she is an accomplished actress, I doubt they were false. My Syringa took to her and that speaks volumes.'

'And Michaelmas?'

'A surgeon of the highest order, yet he acts strange of late, will not look you in the eye, keeps his head down.'

'Then I shall speak to him.' A tap on his shoulder and he looked up to Michael wearing a pair of sunglasses.

'We need to talk,' Michael said. Gesturing with his head, he walked on until a lone spot was found. He removed his shades to show Quercus how his eyes had changed colour to sapphire, and not only that, he had no need for his rimless spectacles. 'What's going on, Quercus? Am I going to change into this creature?'

'Do not be alarmed. You are at one with Hortus. This is a good sign.' There was something else, Quercus thought, something Michael was holding back as he just stood there with a vacant expression. 'Michaelmas, whatever reservations you may have, you are the prophecy.' He prodded the heart. 'In there I feel is a good man struggling to accept his new environment. I speak freely to you as I would hope you would speak freely to me.'

'Nina claims to have found the mouthpiece.'

'You jest?'

Michael shook his head. 'I kid you not. She told me she found it in the museum and inside the lining was a key. She claims it was this key that allowed her to come through the gates. Do you know about this key?'

'I do not.' Now the news had sunk in, euphoria swept over him. 'My brother, the relief is overwhelming. Where is it?'

'Ah, we have a little problem. Nina refuses to divulge where she's hid them.'

'Why?'

'Well,' Michael replied with a regretful sigh. 'She's convinced we have a spy in the camp and, to be honest, so do I.'

'Has Nina spoken to others about her discovery?'

'No. She told me in confidence.'

'I appreciate you sharing this confidence. I shall share mine. I too believe it was no mere coincidence the black robes descended.'

'By the way, you recovered pretty quickly. In fact, most of the men recovered pretty well considering some of them were nearly at death's door. Is there something I should know?'

Quercus reached up towards the nearest branch and bent the tip. 'From the moment we enter this world, we are in the flow of it. We measure it, we mark it, we cannot defy it, we cannot even speed it up or slow it down, or can we?' A tiny bud started to open, to blossom into a golden leaf. It was all of nature, all of art. 'Have we each not experienced a beautiful moment when it passes too quickly, that we could make it linger, or felt time slow on a dull day and wished we could speed things up.' Releasing his grip, he continued. 'We are at one with Hortus. That is what you should know.'

'How did you do that?'

'It is no parlour trick, Michaelmas. The air you breathe is her air, entering your lungs. She has given you sight, now use your vision wisely. Did you not stroke a beast without thought of danger?'

'I think I understand. You develop a natural instinct for your surrounds, sort of like a symbiotic relationship.'

'There, you have it in one. I understand from Fagus, Nina made herself busy as soon as she arrived.'

'That's Nina for you. She organized to have my vessel stripped of its sails to make a hospital tent like a North American tepee so I could do some ops, even had my teak decks stripped. It was her that noticed my eyes changing when she assisted me.' He chuckled. 'She said if I changed into a bird, I would be able to fly without a passport.'

Quercus smiled, encouraging Michael to walk on. 'Did she mention her exploits?'

'She was pushed through the gates by the Handsome Thief. Of course, you were right. He encouraged her to stay on the island where she squeezed every last drop of information she could. Is Syringa a tree or a shrub?'

'For the purpose of doubt, she is from the same family.'

'Is Syringa the only one you haven't dinged?'

But this was different, Quercus told himself, and perhaps Michael would understand. 'A man who has no commitments may please himself. Is this not so, my brother?'

'Sure he can please himself but not with my sister.'

'Is there no appreciation for our position?'

'And what position is that? Syringa has told her all about your exploits, especially with Lady Ilex. Now correct me if I'm wrong, but apart from being unable to offer her diddlysquat how do you intend to wind her round your little finger when she's leaving.'

'Leaving?'

'Look around you. She walked into a nightmare. Ilex treats her like shit and she's in danger of being killed by a monster. Not on, Quercus. Be the man and make her see sense.'

Quercus was silent for a long time, his head turned away, then looked back at Michael and said, 'How can she leave with no vessel at hand?'

'Send a White Tail for this Twist character to pick her up, drop her through the gates.'

'How do we know he is not the spy?'

'Then question everyone, find out who's been sending postcards to Cedrus.'

'A traitor hides behind a mask of sincerity, therein lays the problem. There was a time when I believed Acer was my closest ally. Now I must set aside my feelings and consider all.' Quercus settled on a log where there was an abundance of a very unusual dwarf hardy perennial that flowered at night. At present it was still in its stages of sleep, but soon it would bring its cheeky colour to the eyes of those that looked on. 'I am worried,' he admitted, placing his elbows on his knees. 'Our cover has been exposed, likewise, wherever we may go that too will be exposed. When I read Nina's screen of wars, there were parts that intrigued me. I think you refer to them as elite combat groups.'

Michael settled beside him. 'The system only works if the enemy is earmarked.'

'Sage forecast summer would brighten my darkest hour. This is my darkest hour, Michaelmas. I am desperate for enlightenment. Without doubt vessels are heading this way with more black robes to arrive on our shores, probably thrice our number. If we can find a way of surprising them, we may have a chance.'

'Before you can plan anything, you have to stop the mail, right? And if you can do that, he's going to know you've worked out there's a spy in your camp. So while we're here waiting to trap them, they'll be creeping up behind trapping you.'

Quercus nodded. 'Indeed a paradox, my brother. I do believe I have a way of ceasing mail, in which case we must vacate and locate their landing point.'

'How much do we know about these black robes? Not a lot, except they have no faces which may suggest they have little nuance. That may go in your favour.'

'They are not so lissom on foot. I have seen their bulky weight tread apprehensively on land to suggest they need steeds to give them manoeuvring capability.'

'Okay, what sort of vessels would transport horses and men?'

'Not the kind the Juniperus use.' Quercus paused until he finally said, 'Perhaps Cedrus has built his own vessels. It would make sense if his aim was to take over the seas. Their landing point would probably be a sandy covered shore, free of rocks, a slope or a wide path to easily climb. There are many hazardous reeves along our shores yet further west the coast softens.' He reflected on the problem, chewing a blade of grass between his teeth. It had been fate that brought the spy to his door, now it would be a fatal outcome if he never took action. 'We must break camp and ride west, send scouting parties ahead. The odds, I know are probably four to one against. But a man can kill swiftly by surprise. Do you think the method logical, Michaelmas?'

'The method is logical.'

A leaf dropped on his head. Quercus looked up. 'Are you leaves dropping?'

'Your metaphors are improving,' Nina replied. 'There's just one thing you've overlooked. Since these men have no faces, they must use basic instincts. So the probability of smelling you a mile off is high.'

Quercus opened his mouth then closed it. It was something he had overlooked.

'If we could capture one,' Michael said. 'It may be possible to process their amino acids then the men could cover themselves in the same stink. In fact, if you could also dress like them, you could virtually walk among them without being noticed.'

'Why are you climbing trees?' Quercus asked Nina.

'For two reasons really. First, I understand if your feet don't touch earth Cedrus cannot turn you into one. Second, I'm trying to escape prickles.'

'Prickles?'

'Yes, Lady Ilex. My money is on her as the traitor.'

'Would there be a particular reason for that thought?'

'Err…I need time to think about that. I mean, it could be her hoity-toity attitude, or perhaps her conciliatory grin or maybe it might be her motive. After all, she needs to get rid of her husband. Since he's a boot licker, one might follow the other, if you get my drift.'

'Perhaps your thoughts are like your position at this very point in time, pie in the sky.' He watched her claw back among the leaves and turned to see Ilex approaching. He stood. 'Madam.'

Ilex regarded the sky. 'Do you have foreboding, Quercus?'

'I feel a change in the weather.' He tugged at his ear. 'Perhaps we shall have rain.'

Ilex turned to Michael. 'May I have a moment alone with Quercus?' She waited for him to leave before saying, 'Truly, Quercus my patience has been tried. She pays me no respect and her manner of dress is deplorable. When is she leaving?'

'I can hardly ask her to leave when her brother is the prophecy.'

'You know she cannot stay. Her place is to go back from whence she came. Sage has deemed it so.'

'I do not recall that mentioned.'

'Sage gave you one night for your conquest. No more. Tell me this is not so?'

'It was so. But-'

'Her brother admits to entering the gates without a key yet I have been informed a key can be duplicated. Is this not so?'

'Is it so. But-'

'No buts, Quercus. It is time to take your head out of the sand. One enters without a key yet fails to raise Sea Winger at a point when we most needed protection. The other enters on the pretence of a key she has yet to show.' Her voice softened. 'Quercus, can you not see what they are doing? They are allied to Cedrus. It is he who has spun a web of deceit in this camp. I ask you, no, beg you to send them away before it is too late.'

'I can only heed wisdom from Sage.'

'Then release yourself from duty and go see her.'

'What you ask, I cannot do. My place is here, my destiny written.' His eyes were understanding, their gentleness at odds with the severity of his feelings. 'Remember your place too, Ilex. You swore allegiance to the cause yet you tail my feet, watch my movements.'

'I seek only to please.'

'Then you will please me to leave.'

She bridled at his remark. 'You will not find me so willing when your ardour pushes to my pelvis.'

Their simple discourse could not have come at a worse time. Ilex was constantly at his side and upon each turn she would be there to interrupt his efforts to win Nina's favour. Now he had no favour at all. Had he not spoken to Fagus about this? Looking up to lush silvery greens, darkened by the coming of night, Quercus chose his words carefully. 'My heart and soul benighted. I would far rather be a tree to hear your happiness than live as a man fragmented.'

'Choice words for someone who adds notches to their whip handle.'

'Nina, my neck is straining. Will you come down so I may speak with you?'

She dropped to her feet in front of him. 'Michael warned me of men like you. But do I listen? No…no because I was the idiot that opened her petals to a hornet.'

He looked down into her face, a face meant to smile but she was frowning. 'I proffer the truth. I was given leave by Sage to revisit you.'

'For what? To conquer me?'

'No, my Nina, not to conquer but to be in your delightful company.'

'You failed to mention your personal involvement with prickles.'

'I have no personal involvement with prickles.'

Nina folded her arms, tapping her foot on the ground. 'That is not the impression I gained. Did you or did you not use your broomstick on a married woman the night before you made love to me?'

He felt a flush of guilt. 'My broomstick did sweep. But,' he held up a finger. 'Not after I swept with you.'

She burst out laughing.

War was taking its toll, treason in the uppermost part of his mind and matters of his heart were being torn by the mere presence of a woman he could hardly take his eyes off. 'Did you write those words?'

'You mean this?' She pulled at her T-shirt. 'I bought it for 50p in a charity shop. I thought it was very apt at the time. Obviously, it doesn't account for the odd stupidity.'

Taking her hand, he gently folded his fingers with hers so neither hand could be distinguished and coaxed her to sit on the log where the dwarf hardy perennial was opening their buds, masses of small yellow daisy-like flowers with chocolate-coloured undersides.

'The plant is called berlandiera lyrata. Every evening, they bloom. The following morning, they shed their petals and the plant produces another crop ready to open twelve hours later. Part of my promise I keep. The food is but a mere stone's throw away.'

'They are lovely.' She picked one and brought it to her nose. 'They have a chocolate scent. Can you eat them?'

'They serve no purpose other than their heady aroma.'

She kept her eyes to the flower. 'The Handsome Thief told me you have been left a pretty hard legacy. This Cedrus is a very mean character.'

'No meaner than the black robes.'

'You don't sound worried.'

Quercus drew in a deep breath. 'Yes,' he said slowly exhaling. 'I have lived on the edge of apprehension for so long, I ignore the bridges that assail me. In these hands I hold life. Not just yours but others. I cannot afford to sound worried. True, I may die in my endeavours. I may also survive in my endeavours. In the latter respect, I would hope to celebrate with you beside me.'

'And if you are left with immortality?' There was such a silence that she looked at him. 'I understand you have been very amorous in the past.'

The uncertainties of war were easier to negotiate than the uncertainties of feelings. 'Nina, I could not help my cavalier ways. I looked upon life as one day at a time. The women I chose were of the same mind. It was for comfort of lonely nights. Admittedly my interest was brief. It had to be. Then I met you at a time when I had no memories. Anything was possible. You stirred my senses, made me laugh as though I had never laughed before. When my memories returned, regrettably there was no other choice. My duty was to return. Ilex requested one night in my arms. I was a man without commitment and furthered the nights until I returned to your shores. You filled my empty soul with warmth. When I am with you, I feel drunk, giddy.'

'Actually, to have anything to do with me is foolish. You even mentioned it to Fagus. I am your Achilles' heel.'

'Achilles slaughtered for fame, not for Hortus.'

'Teach me to handle a sword, Quirky. I shall slaughter for Hortus.'

'No woman fights in a man's battle. It is our burden to bear.' He pressed his lips to her fingers. 'Why do you hide the mouthpiece?'

'Let me assure you it's in a perfectly safe place. Besides, what good is half a book without words? Did you know the pages were blank?'

'The pages are blank for good reason. When two halves are joined, only then shall the pages be read.'

'But you have yet to find the other half.'

'It shall be our quest after I have rid that heathen. Does that suit?'

'Oh yes,' she said enthusiastically. 'Tell me about your home, what's it like?'

In his mind he was building castles that were not castles, mountains that were not mountains. 'It sits with views to the east, to see the sun rise and know another day brings a new destiny and to the south the magic of water, a reminder of the gates where I often crossed in my youthful years to seek knowledge of plants. My garden has many plants that grow in different seasons. I can pick flowers to brighten my home, even in winter. There is a copper kettle over a stove, always ready to welcome my brothers and a grandfather clock in the hall to hear time in my ears. It lacks a woman's touch but still the nature outside provide curtains to my windows and sometimes, when it snows, wildlife enters from the bitter cold.'

'Do you have a lounge and bathroom?'

His lips curled. 'I also have a bedroom with clean sheets.'

She bobbed the flower on his nose. 'That's the ticket, keep your pecker up.'

Here, among the berlandiera lyrata, they dined on chocolate scent, laughing and talking. He touched her face, gently outlining her eyes and lips, and she pinched the thick hair of his eyebrows between her finger and thumb, tugging it into little tufts. Was it enough when the cause weighed so heavy in the moment, when hopes were left so fragile.

It was in the closing part of the evening that Quercus was ready to address the men, convinced of the way forward, remembered Sage and her words, how his course would change as summer intensified. He spoke with clarity and force, his eyes suffused with a fierce mandate.

'My brothers, tonight we shall not sleep lazily on our straw beds but take to our heels and advance further west.' He paused to their musings as he walked among them. 'Acer, by command of Cedrus will no doubt send greater number of black robes. They will land on soft beaches, gathering their wits, seducing their minds into believing they can come here and slaughter us like sheep. We herd them! They do not herd us!'

Hoo-rah, hoo-rah, hoo-rah.

'My brothers, our swift retreat from this camp is justly recommended for among us we have a traitor, a person who wears a mask of sincerity.'

Fagus stood, sending a growl in his voice. 'Who is this traitor? Let me be the first to disembowel his whimpering guts!'

'My own hands would have alleviated this traitor's presence had I an inkling.'

'It is the outsiders who have charmed their way in with false stories.' Ilex was quick to suffocate the moment. 'Neither one can produce a key yet one claims to be the prophecy. Do you see a creature rise from the sea? No because they are the minions of Cedrus and his crafty dealings.'

Quercus held up his hands to their dissention. 'Lady Ilex has her own views. I too have views.' He bent down and removed Michael's shades. 'Look into his eyes. Tell me if he is not the prophecy.' There was a moment of gasps and shuffling as they came to inspect. 'If I had to mark a spy, he would be last.'

'Would I not be last?' Fagus asked.

'My brother, my heart is sickened, my mind set. Was it not you to teach me the errors of my ways with Acer?'

Jubaea spoke. 'How certain are you?'

'Do you think the black robes were a chance encounter?'

'Cedrus has other ways of detecting our presence.'

'Not in these woods, Jubaea, not here where the populus protect our presence from prying eyes. The black robes were advancing before the walnuts arrived. They had not anticipated their arrival so soon. His objective was simple, to wipe us out then they too would be taken. He knew our number, used the black robes to pick us off before he walked among the weak. No, my brothers, be certain of this, we have a traitor in our midst. We cannot identify that traitor but we can forestall that traitor and keep our methods secret. Are you willing to obey?'

Hail Quercus Coccinea, Lord of the Oaks.

'Then heed my words. Each one shall marry with another, let there be no moment in time for separation. No White Tail shall be summoned. Nothing must pass your lips unless served by your own hand. As one sleeps, so shall the other bound by their wrists.' He turned to Council Members, one in particular. 'Forgive me, Fagus. I cannot bind you to Syringa for reasons obvious, therefore she must be bound to Ilex, and Nina to Michaelmas.'

'Surely Michaelmas and his sister should be separated,' Ilex voiced sharply. 'You said yourself to Fagus, for reasons obvious.'

Quercus had banked on this. 'Lady Ilex is correct. Michaelmas shall be bound to Fraxinus, and Nina shall be bound to me.'

'You take favour!' Ilex scowled. 'It should be her bound to Fagus!'

'Are you that cruel, madam, to see Nina sleep with a stranger, a man, no less? At least she has comfort in the knowledge that I am no stranger.' He held up a finger. 'No, madam, the decision has been made.' He turned to Michael and smiled. 'You shall like the sleeping sounds of Fraxinus.' The men enjoyed his joke. 'All else, find a partner and stick fast. We must break camp.' He saw a hand raised. 'Yes, Michaelmas, what troubles you?'

'May I ride in the cart? It would mean Lord Fraxinus would have to ride with me.'

'I do not object,' Fraxinus said. 'I would appreciate the comfort of a cart.'

'Then make haste, my brothers. This camp must be cleared. Take everything, leave nothing but nature.' He went to Nina. 'Have you ridden a horse?'

'Never,' she answered with alacrity. 'Do you think we can go slowly?'

As the camp came alive, he walked her toward the horses. 'First acquaint yourself then we shall see his reaction.'

She held the cheek strap. 'My name is Nina,' she said and kissed the soft nose. The steed blew through his nostrils and shifted his weight. She glanced up at Quercus. 'I don't suppose you have anything smaller?'

'Lord Juglans,' Quercus called out. 'Send me twenty of your men who have horses taken from the black robes.'

'What's on your mind, Quirky?' Nina asked.

'A thought that might possibly work,' he said, stroking the flank. 'Horses are creatures of habit. They act no differently from us when we recognize our surrounds.' He transferred his attention to Lord Juglans. 'My brother, allow your men to ride in advance and give their steeds head. You and Betula will cover their flanks.'

'What shall we look for,' a warrior asked.

Quercus switched his gaze. 'Fresh water. Two thousand steeds needed watering. Once you have found that, you will no doubt pinpoint the bay. Be watchful, there may be black robes guarding the surround.'

'That's very clever thinking,' Nina said. 'Of course, if it had been left up to me, I would have re-fitted Michaelmas and sailed the coast.'

'And you would be none the wiser.'

'I wasn't thinking of being wise, just of an easier ride.'

He mounted Shadow. 'You will enjoy this one. Give me your arm.' She came to his stirrup, he leaned down and they hooked elbows. Swinging her up behind him, she sat astride, sliding her arms round his waist. 'Is this not cosy,' he said, turning the reins.

'The only time my legs have been this far apart is when we made love.'

'Perhaps I should ride backwards.'

'What an interesting proposal.'

Behind, he led a long stream of traffic that wended a snaking outline on a faint dirt road. At times he was visible to the night sky, at other times leafy branches slapped gently against his thighs. Asleep, Nina was pressed hard against his back, her arms clutching tight round his midriff. She was soft and warm, her hair a whisper away from his ear, her blueberry smells lingering. Suddenly he was all but immobilized by a calm euphoria, aware of a benign feeling, yes of love, as though he were being held by someone that cared for him very deeply. His thoughts were too big for utterances, words were incapable of conveying his feelings and even though he may not have known it before, he certainly knew it now. She was his destiny as surely as he was hers.

As the sun clawed pink to a new dawn, two riders approached. Their speed and smiles indicated good news. 'We have found the bay, my lord,' one said turning his reins to amble alongside Quercus. 'It was as you said. A clear water stream travels through a wide gulley to meet an open bay. There were remnants of dark patches on the sand. It smelt of black robes.'

Quercus held a fist in the air and the line came to a halt. 'Seek Fagus and Jubaea.' He craned his head round. 'Nina, hold tight. We are about to ride with the wind.'

On the spur of his heels, Shadow took flight accompanied by the outcries of Nina. The rigidity of her body worked against his ride. He leaned forward and shouted duck on the approaching low branch and then kept his position so she could feel the wind in her hair. It was the sharp end of a lesson. Slowly her confidence supplanted her howling cries, her body relaxed into his and they rode as a unit beside four others.

This resplendent part of the west coast breathed in the balmy air as if there was no tomorrow. But tomorrow seemed to promise even more expansive times for the complex super-rich shores, hitherto untouched, growing wild and frantic with fierce coastal inlets and flowing streams. The beauty of this grand scenery offered a crescent of gloriously wooded highlands where they petered out on a small gradient towards a sandy bay. It was here that Quercus dismounted, cocking his leg over Shadow's mane and then held out his arms for Nina to slip into them.

'Did I not say the ride would be enjoyable?'

'Yes, it was great but I have an itchy bum.' She pulled the crotch of her leggings away. 'I think I have accumulated horsehair in my knickers.'

He gestured to the sea. 'The remedy is simple.'

'Are you coming?'

'Later.' He watched her throw herself at the sea fully clothed then turned to Fagus on a more serious note. 'We do not know how much time we have…perhaps a day, two at best.' Taking in the surrounds, his gaze held at the sloping dunes then tracked them towards the cover of greenery. 'There we shall camp. No fires.'

'No fires, no woman, my body will be cold at night.'

'Nonsense,' Jubaea mused. 'I shall keep you warm, brother Fagus.' His green eyes went to Quercus, his query festering. 'I mystified at your coupling with Nina. How was that accomplished?'

Fagus understood. 'By the nature of a jealous woman.'

'Perhaps a threesome would quell dissention.'

'I cannot manage two,' Quercus replied.

'A poor statement to make. I can manage three, perhaps four if given chance.'

They turned to Jubaea and sent a disbelieving laugh.

Humour was rife in their voices yet beneath their tones they carried a faltering note of uncertainty. All three had fought alongside each other in the past where a traitor existed. So many men died that day, a day when Quercus left with Fagus to seek out the mouthpiece. To be mutually in league and to leave a traitor in charge was one thing but to discover that the frightful disparity caused a century of torment, was another.

A VEIL OF TEARS

'**Do** you see anything?' Nina asked.

Stood on rising ground towards the west, Quercus struggled to see anything save for the sun sharing its sparkle with the sea. He turned the binoculars nearer to shore and smiled. 'Methinks, I see the daisy making a chain with my men.'

'Anything is worth a try, Quirky. Who knows, the creature might be lurking on the bed.'

'No doubt Michaelmas will find himself a turtle.' He shifted his gaze, was content to eke out these minutes, to watch Fagus, paired off with Jubaea, help gather cockles beside the woman he loved. Not ten feet away, Ilex worked her silvery green hair instead of working her supper. 'Methinks Ilex is not very hungry.'

'Considering she steals when nobody's looking, I'm not surprised.'

'Have you seen her do this?'

'It stands to reason. She never foraged for food last night.' Nina climbed from a carpet of blue-bells. 'It's not right to keep Syringa tied to Ilex. She's been without Fagus for one hundred years and misses him.'

'How can she miss him when he is there to be seen?'

'You know exactly what I mean.' Nina took the binoculars out of his hands. 'Last night prickles never stopped ranting on about Michael and me. Poor Syringa could hardly sleep a wink, and Fagus spent his night plaiting Jubaea's beard.'

'And this is what you do, listen and look in my arms?'

'Now you're being silly. I couldn't sleep for feeling guilty.'

'Nina, I must protect my men. What proof can you give as to the spy's identity? Give me proof then we shall all sleep peacefully.'

'So you heard her too?'

'In war a man sleeps with his ears tuned.'

He resumed his outlook, troubled. Ten days had passed since that bloody encounter in the valley, surely time enough for Cedrus to have sent more reinforcements. Had he miscalculated? Was the cunning Fir too cunning by half? Acer knew his tactics. Acer may have advised a new strategy. As if Hortus had heard his doubt, he could make out a speck, the flickering outline of a billowing sail coming into focus. He remained unmoved, expecting more sails to accompany that which already splintered the horizon. But the tardy vessel coursed alone, unsuspecting and unlikely to carry more than three hundred black robes. The challenge of the unknown had faded, replaced by the symbol of impending combat this night.

'Do you see anything?' Nina asked again.

'To be certain I see my efforts rewarded.' Sending a screeching whistle, Fagus acknowledged the call. 'Nina, keep close to Michaelmas when battle is joined.'

'I shall climb a tree.'

'Cedrus cannot turn you.'

'Well hello, I can take a fall-back position.'

'You take a running position.'

She frowned. 'And where do the likes of me run to?'

'Into my arms.'

Before she could think of an answer, Quercus moved on, the taste for a kill now uppermost in his mind. The tapestries of war, once again, hung over his head. No matter the heroics, this was improvisation and opportunism on a grand scale.

How circumstance could change, the traitor thought. One moment Cedrus was in the throes of success, next, his army was heading into a trap.

'My brothers,' Quercus addressed the men. 'Soon we make our first wave of silent attack. Every black robe must be skilfully slain, their garments kept. We must approach stealthily. If we are detected too early it gives them chance to mount their steeds. That cannot happen for we shall be at their mercy. Our strike must be quick and fatal, one blow is one less to worry, one more to give us victory. Let us trust in this night their senses are limited in distance...'

Syringa, aided by Nina, and behind the backs of their men countenancing war placed a live crab at the hem of a tunic. They giggled when the pincer took hold.

'Do you like crab, Fagus?' Nina kept a straight face.

Fagus turned with grinning pleasure. 'Far better to eat cooked than raw.'

'Alas, we cannot have fires,' Syringa teased. 'What say you, my love? Is it possible to heat one by the flame of your passion?'

'My blood boils in rage, not in love.'

'So your ardent desire lacks the capacity to fulfil my wish?'

'I am tied to another, Syringa.'

In the fit of their laughter, and by observation, Quercus cracked his whip in jocular fashion making Fagus jump, thoroughly familiarized by now with the scope of Nina's shenanigans. Nothing could have been in greater contrast to what they might face this night, that which would demonstrate consummate skill and confidence.

Thus, in concealment and silence men waited and watched on their bellies in the brush, on the brow of the crescent shaped scenery, looking down at the black robes disembarking, wading in the shallows, pulling at the reins of their steeds, urging them through the surf. The vessel weighed anchor, and the tempo of muted activity charred on the beach like clock-work toys, slick and animated, tutored in regimented action.

'I count five hundred,' Fagus whispered close to Quercus.

'As do I, though I expected far less. Still, we can take them.'

'When this is done, may I take comfort for one hour with Syringa?'

'Do you think me cruel?'

'I think you wise.'

'Then my answer is no.'

Quercus motioned to begin their slithering descent in the grasses, closing distance their sight adapting to the dark and grainy images. The black robes appeared catatonic, sat in some kind of stupor, would be caught unawares, overrun before they could gauge the direction of their threat or the magnitude of their calamity. All was going well until one turned its wooden-block head. Quercus knew. He knew it had scented the kill, could trace the elements of humans.

Sensing the urgency, with an upward glance, Quercus came to his feet shouting the charge, a ripple explosion of men meeting monsters. Some pushed forward, others fell back, their clamour and apprehension rising. It did not take long to realize the enemy wore protective guards round their necks.

Slice their extremities!

A piteous cry, Fagus had fallen but with him the answer. Without hands there could be no axes, without feet there could no stance. Grim pictures played out within the hour. It was a bloodbath of oozing black liquid spurting from dismembered parts, all throwing themselves without tactics or heed, still alive but unable to fight. Such a sight would render an ordinary man speechless.

They stood back panting, liberating their voices looking at writhing creatures, worming and squirming on sands without sound. Quercus threw himself into a small gathering, shouting disbelief, falling to his knees beside Fagus, his eyes to the night sky, the sliding and dying energy of a dear friend.

'Weep not for me, Quercus. This is my destiny.' Grasping the chain at his neck, Fagus husked his last words. 'My key to Syringa.'

Gently kissing the forehead, a final farewell to Fagus, Quercus removed the key. It now belonged to Syringa. The victory was solemn. The beeches rallied to mourn and weep, felt the loss of a good warrior, their Lord of the Beeches with tight curly hair and a short-bearded face.

A voice spoke softly. 'Quercus, the tide is coming in fast. What shall we do with these writhing monsters?'

His throat had closed, he could not reply. His eyes were streaming, wishing the earth would swallow him whole, wishing he could take it all back and give Fagus his due.

Jubaea leaned to the ear, his voice more urgent. 'The tide is coming in fast.'

'What is our loss?'

'Forty-five to their fate and many wounded.'

Quercus shook his head. It was an unexpected loss. 'Take their robes, remove their neck bands and chop off their heads save one. Give him to Michaelmas. For the rest, dig deep in the dunes so their corpses may rot in the salty elements.'

They had become the killing dogs of the night.

Rising to his feet, Quercus spat out the dust of guilt threads. It was hard to expel the sour taste in his mouth, harder to erase the searing flashes from his thoughts. The final moments haunted him. He had chained his brother to another these latter days for the sake of his own needs, had refused him one hour of happiness, precious moments that could have been spent with Syringa. His head hung low and heavy in the passing of a precious key.

'Syringa, my heart shares your grief.'

Such a statement would have impelled her into an impromptu reply but she simply walked away, her destination to the body of a man who fought so bravely.

Standing there, feeling totally alone, encompassed by grief and guilt, Quercus watched forty-five good men carried to their place of burial, one his dearest friend. They would be honoured, each laid to rest against a tree whose bark would open for a day long feast. It was one of the tricks of age, a protracted meal of body and soul, to be at one with Hortus.

Then a touch of warm fingers melded into his. He looked down beside him and Nina said nothing. She was there but not really there. Her face was full of solemnity, her eyes so close to tears, her bottom lip quivering, resisting the urge to cry. How he so desperately wanted to hold her and be held in return.

'Do you understand what is happening, my Nina?'

'Not really,' she faintly replied.

'Hortus will take them into her bosom. She will caress their thoughts and deeds and let them spill to the air so we may take in their fulfilled life. The song of Hortus will be sung one day. I hope to be alive to hear this song, to hear my brother Fagus once more.'

A drop of water fell on his head and he looked up. One, two, three drops at a time and they all looked up. After these first kissed hints there was the full embrace, the sheer wetness pouring down, bouncing upon dusty surfaces, hammering insistently against anything left to the open sky. Men embraced the rain, shaking their heads like bath-time dogs and turned to each other in amazement. Then it petered out, the noise dropping away, leaving the air suffused with a smell of fresh blueberries.

Quercus felt his body and spirits lift where Sage had told him this would be so, the duration will depend upon rain. Be selective, otherwise, the effect of the whole shall be overwhelming. Now Quercus knew what to do.

'My brothers,' he said under the brow of wet hair. 'Jubaea shall marry to my side. Nina will pair with Lady Syringa and Lady Ilex and have her ankles and wrists bound at time of sleep.' He paused to their ovations and knew he had pleased them. 'More vessels will come. Of this I am certain but when? It can only be answered by logic. Keep your eyes peeled to the sea. Lord Fraxinus will pick the men who choose to dowse themselves with the enemy's stench. And while this wave fools them on the sands, others will take the vessel. We shall add to our fleet and use their creature comforts for a change!'

Hoo-rah, hoo-rah, hoo-rah.

His teeth and hands clenched, his knuckles rose hard and white when he saw a condescending smile. Ilex had succeeded where he had failed. Striding past her without formal recognition, he went deeper into the greenery towards the hospital tent accompanied by Jubaea. When he ducked through the flap, there were the injured, their wounds bound and partly asleep. Michael was on his knees trying to examine a writhing specimen on the planks that were once his teak decks.

'I say, this chap is amazing.' Michael looked up above his surgical mask. 'He has no internal organs. His whole system has independent nerve cells so when a piece of him is chopped off, the rest is unaffected but this is interesting.' Pointing to the base of the spine, Michael made a valuable comment. 'This is his central core, like the main tap root of a tree.'

Quercus poked his finger through the hard black flesh. 'His core stem is strong.'

'Nina was right. If you look closely, its body is covered by minute follicles.'

Jubaea took a magnifying glass off the trolley. 'On our approach one head turned before others.'

'I too noticed this.'

'It's possible they communicate by these follicles,' Michael continued. 'So when one picked up the scent it passed it on to the others but don't quote me on that.' He pulled down his mask and washed his hands in red tainted water. 'I'm bit short of equipment. If you want a detailed analysis I would need a microscope. Pity I can't have a computer, still, never mind. Sorry to hear about Fagus. I really liked the chap. Let's not make his death in vain.'

'Thank you, Michaelmas,' Quercus said. 'Your words are comforting. Fagus saved the moment. There would have been greater loss. I had to pair Nina with Syringa and Ilex.'

'You did the right thing. Now she feels she can help Syringa in her time of need.'

How Quercus hated looking at that writhing dark grain on the floor. One crack from his whip and the head rolled. 'I noticed she cries for others.'

'That's Nina for you; she always cries a lot. Hell she even cried the day you came on the scene.'

Quercus sat on a stool, folding his arms, his legs apart. He had new thoughts. 'Did I upset her?'

'No, it was me who upset her. I fixed her up with a date, told her Greg would be at home ready to take her out for a meal. She blabbed down the line so I had to cancel the arrangement. That's why there was a mix up. When she bumped into you, she thought you were Greg.'

'Ah, she did not want to go out with a man of your choice, regardless of appearance or circumstance.'

'Greg is a decent fellow. He would have measured up if only she'd given him a chance.'

'What kind of man requires another to find a woman?' Jubaea asked.

Quercus answered. 'One who is scared of his shadow,' then quickly added, 'Michaelmas, it rained on the day of my release. Here too, it rained with a taste of blueberries.'

And Jubaea agreed. 'Nina smells of blueberries.'

'So what are you saying? That she makes it rain when she cries?' He smiled, shaking his head. 'Hell, if that was the case, England would be flooded.'

'But she is not in your world, Michaelmas.'

'This key she speaks of,' Jubaea asked. 'Where is it?'

Michael shrugged. 'I have no idea. She was always good at hiding things. You store a lot in this destiny lark, don't you?'

'Destiny is our creed,' Quercus said. 'We are each entwined, each responsible for the other's course in life, to make that life a good journey, to watch each other and serve dreams rather than nightmares. I served Fagus a nightmare. My heart is full of regret.'

'I lost a patient once on the operating table. It took me a long while to stop blaming myself. Nina kept feeding me cup-cakes for tea. Said for everyone I ate, I was consuming guilt to fatten my desolation. She was right, of course. I got sick on chocolate cup-cakes and-'

Fraxinus interrupted their conversation, a hint of doom in his voice. 'Quercus, another vessel approaches.'

The second wave of black robes disembarked in the sure knowledge that five hundred of their kind were sitting on sands waiting for their counterparts, the look, and the smell inviting until a sudden rush at their feet. Indistinct shapes moved fast and furious and pounced. When one tripped and toppled, a replacement was in position but more kept coming, streaming off one vessel. The Captain grew cowardly and nervous and ordered to weigh anchor but immediately below the shallow depths of the keel, Quercus was readying his assault. He kicked his heel into a wooden face then vaulted the rails, shouting, 'Join forces with me!'

'You have no hope, no future. You put this vessel in jeopardy, my crew in jeopardy.'

'Then you are a traitor to your own destiny.'

A second voice rang out. 'Why should we suffer and die when it's your cause?'

Quercus leapt on a barrel, drew back his whip and cracked off a leg, his mission almost complete. 'You carry the black robes to these shores.' He met with resistant again. 'Why not keep them on your own shores if you are so inclined.'

A sprightly pussy willow cracked a jar over the damn Captain's head. Quercus smiled, surprised to see a Salix Caprea on board. She had been taken captive by the black robes, hauled on deck for distribution elsewhere but the Captain had other ideas, and so it would seem had his crew. They were a small and wretched band of firs, barely comprehending the horrors of their plight. But they fought to save their vessel and refused to believe they would inherit a desolate and blighted place if Cedrus continued to rule.

Quercus walked among the dissidents, stripped of their weaponry and garments. 'You are no Juniperus Pirates.' He prodded an overfed stomach. 'Where are his creations manufactured?' He paused against muted sounds. 'Your choice is simple. Be hung by your balls or be free to return to your homelands.'

The Captain performed as spokesman. 'We act as sailors upon his vessels.'

There was no surprise shown. 'Where are his creations manufactured?' Quercus asked again. The head shook vigorously so he leaned close to the ear. 'Your fear is wasted on Cedrus. See my accomplishments before you next speak.'

Quercus did not delegate. He took a brother's sword and cut a man open with a single deft stroke, left him alive long enough to reach inside and liberate the warm and beating heart. There was an intake of breath when he held the dripping organ to his mouth. No hesitation as he took a firm bite and chewed at a man standing in his own puddle of piss.

'Abies Bay!' The Captain spat out. 'They board at Abies Bay! That is all I know!'

'How many vessels head this way?'

'Three were sent.'

'Why fifteen hundred when two thousand came before?'

'I beg you. I do not know. We act as sailors upon his vessels.'

Quercus wiped the blood off his mouth and gestured to his men. 'Throw them overboard. Let them swim home.'

In a ragged spray they collided with water, their sounds diminishing replaced by the victory chants that sung the red head's name, Quercus, Quercus, Quercus but their reverie was short-lived. The third vessel was sighted. The battle was unfolding as it had before.

But it soon became a head on clash, on land and on vessel because of a damn crew that had the capacity to intervene. They fought on the black robes side with might and vigour, brandishing knives and cutlasses intent on retribution. They would not be spared. Quercus would see to that.

They were desperate scenes played out in the art of survival, every clash leaving strewn innards and more dead as the black robes fell under a welter of blows. Enemy deaths littered the decks, littered the sands, left to the tide. A once beautiful bay, it was now a terrible place with two vessels in their capable hands.

Quercus, heavily grazed, walked in the hospital tent, his clothes so sullied one could barely distinguish skin from cloth. He winced at the number of wounded. There could be no doubt, war was a bloody affair. Men were stacked shoulder to shoulder, their faces lifting, their hearts reignited to see their leader. He went to each one. A nerve tugged behind his eye when he saw an amputee, his arm removed from the elbow down. Axes were the trademark of the black robes.

'We could do with some help here, Quercus,' Michael spoke through his surgical mark. 'Is there anyone else who can sew?' He quickly glanced up then down at his patient. 'That looks like a bad cut.'

'It is nothing,' he said wiping the blood from his eye. 'Where is Syringa and Ilex?'

'They went to investigate the rumour. Apparently, someone was claiming to have seen a number of trees reverting into men not far from here. It happened while it rained.'

His heart jumped through hoops; his mind worked on the scenario Nina had been the instrument of release. 'Are you well, Nina?' He asked, picking up a needle and thread.

Behind her mask she nodded, her space limited, her fingers delicately working through skin. He could tell she was fighting back tears, unwilling to display grief, her breathing a little erratic. If his theory held true, he wanted her to cry again. More than that, he wanted her established in his world, to be accepted and become part of it like he was part of it too.

Then a point had been reached, a moment poised between earth and heaven, mortality and oblivion. There was a smell in the air, sprung like an electric tingle winding from the ground to the sky, a smell without a name but easy to recognise and everyone knew it smelt like blueberry rain. This time it doubled, impossibly, a blind blanket of water falling across their continent. How far it stretched was left to imagination but most certainly the impact was dramatic.

And even more dramatic was Cedrus. Absence of news from a traitorous pen did little to surmount his growing frustration and his latent fury erupted, gripped in anger bent of achieving a single kill. His foot stamped down on a ministerial neck; the whirling scimitar claimed a life. Before him, he was witnessing through rain, trees turning, one by one, falling into the welcoming arms of their brothers and sisters. Across the horizons he could see all that, vacant lots unfolding. Even he astounded at the number. It was an unacceptable gain for them, an unacceptable loss for him.

A Ministerial Fir was dressing him, fearful and quaking, his hands trembling believing any moment his head would roll too. He had been careful to appease, to watch his tongue and straightened the black leather tunic, requesting Cedrus to lift his right arm.

'What news of my creatures?' Cedrus asked.

'No news, Divine Majesty.' The minister paused, waiting for repercussions. 'Perhaps Lord of the Oaks led his army to meet with yours, Divine Majesty.'

Cedrus threw a tantrum and kicked at a table pointing angrily into the room where other apprehensive ministers stood. 'What news of Acer?'

'He will be here before sun-rise, Divine Majesty.' Falteringly, the minister bent down to offer up a pair of black boots. 'Will you require anything else, Divine Majesty?'

'I want Quercus Coccinea you blithering fool!' Cedrus glanced at the Astronomer. 'Where does this rain come from?'

Now the Astronomer, although anxious, was hardly panic-stricken by the thought of death, for he being the only forecasting agent in the sciences of heavenly bodies. He was tall, absurdly rotund and absurdly bright.

'One lonely cloud suffers a bout of emotional distress.'

'What nonsense do you speak?'

'A prophecy spoken by Sage.' The Astronomer came further into the room. 'She foretells the coming of an outsider who can enter the gates without a key to bring forth Sea Winger.'

'Yes, yes, I have heard this prophecy. I was informed a man claimed to have come through the gates without a key, his sister with a key. What is this Sea Winger creature supposed to be? Where is it? All I see is rain and vacant lots.'

'All I see is a veil of tears for those who stand as trees, where the dead are no longer dead, the living not necessarily alive.'

Was Cedrus hearing some new and disjointed way of bringing down his empire? Or was this Astronomer ever ready to outwit Sage? 'Which is it to be, the woman or the man?'

'Consider Lord of the Oaks has deceived his army. With the aid of Sage, two were found to promote the prophecy. When last informed, the woman appeared unkempt, her brother eager to find riches.'

'Then neither can claim to be the prophecy, nor outsiders. It is a false rumour to unsettle me.' Cedrus looked at the conventional minister still on his knees. 'Why did you not proffer the same thoughts?'

'I was under the same misapprehension, Divine Majesty. Is there possibility someone close can remedy this ill, a quick kill for two pretenders, Divine Majesty.'

'I have received no word. One must assume he has gathered a traitor lies in his midst.' After stepping into his other boot, Cedrus straightened and walked onto the balcony feeling a little calmer, more devious, stretching out his hand to soak in the rain. His eyes followed a slow moving stream of lanterns in the harbour. Rain did not bother them for they were celebrating the coming of change. 'Perhaps they rejoice too soon.' He turned back into the room. 'This shall work to our advantage. Send for Lady Tilia.'

'If you send her to Quercus, he will know her disposition.'

'That is my point, Astronomer, a challenge indeed for his mental abilities. His army bathes in false hope one of these sub primates is the prophecy. How Sage achieved the release of my prisoners, I have yet to consider.' He irritated at her meddling. 'She is a Labiatae, a repugnant menace created by Hortus. She speaks in riddles to make of it what you will. Not even the mighty Oak can interpret her meaning.' He waved his hand. 'Bring me the Lime.'

Cedrus looked conceitedly at himself, observed in the mirror he was by far the most striking man on this earth. His eyes paid homage to a tall invincible figure dressed in black from head to toe. Apart from the red flash of silk banding across his chest, he would forge himself against the black of his stallion that, until now, had seen days of peace rather than war. He was anxious to leave behind the suffocating ruminations of his Ministerial Firs, the hollow emptiness of news and the reckless attempt to reach a traitor where a word would have put him at ease. But now he had to course another devious plan, a plan of manipulation. He would forestall his journey to the west shores.

As the rain gently lifted, petering out to the flush of a released moon Cedrus sat in silence at his solid gold table drinking lemon tea, the wide doors open to the fresh night air. His mind raced, finding his imagination working when he saw a stricken woman approaching. She had been unmercifully stripped and lashed, her beauty cruelly taken, her body scarred with deep welts. Once her complexion was of cream and pink petals, almost too perfect, yet redeemed from insipid vacuity by the brilliance of dark lime eyes and hair.

'Lady Tilia,' he said offering a potion to drink. 'You do not look at your loveliest.'

'Indeed not,' she said barely above a whisper.

'Drink up, it will not kill you.' Cedrus did not favour her with a smile, but his stern authority had dissipated. 'Such beauty should not be wasted. There is so little of your kind. Why, indeed, the lime is a heady scent at the best of times, lingering to a man's soul, if man has a soul.' He demonstrated once again the swift and sweet onset of life, watched with amused forbearance as her skin took on change. 'I, for one, claim my soul is in a predicament. So will others without your help. I do not ask much. In return you shall live out your life knowing you have saved our kingdom.'

'Saved our kingdom?'

'A woman not of our world but a great pretender has entered our gates.'

'Do you speak of an outsider?'

'Most certainly I speak of an outsider, one that has entered as a spy and stands beside Lord of the Oaks. To let her stay will bring destruction and open the floodgates for others to enter unless she is halted.'

'But the gates cannot be deceived. Is she not the prophecy?'

His eyes narrowed. 'What do you know of this prophecy?'

'I know very little, Divine Majesty.' Her voice was penitent but her mind active to the thought of what he could do. 'It is said one will come and bring forth a Sea Winger.'

'Do you see a Sea Winger? For certain I do not. Do others claim to have seen it? Do you even know what it is?'

'No, Divine Majesty. But word is spreading we are on the cusp of change. People have been released from their confines. Perhaps this outsider is a Sea Winger rather than the monster you portray.'

'It was I who released them in the hope of stemming this uprising.' A lie?

'Forgive me, Divine Majesty, it did not occur.'

'I cannot sate the madness of Quercus Coccinea. He has slaughtered the black robes, has taken away our army built to protect our kingdom from outsiders. Do I place worries on my subjects? I do not do things without reason. I find myself in a position where good men must be sacrificed in order to suit the whims of that mad man. Acer has been my loyal servant. Do you think he would offer his men to my calling if there was no real threat to our dominion?'

'But how did this outsider gain entry, Divine Majesty?'

Here came another convincing lie. 'The gates have remained open from the day he returned. If you do not believe me, then speak to the Juniperus Pirate that hugs these twisting shores. He can tell you she came in without a key, her brother too. Proof enough the gates have opened. Now they stand alongside Quercus to dull his senses and he will bring others who have weapons greater than ours unless those gates can be sealed. Did I not offer a hand of friendship and ask him to forget?'

'Yes, Divine Majesty.'

'And what was his reply.'

'One hundred years does not forgive or forget.'

'So what is your answer?'

'Do I have a choice, Divine Majesty?'

'If you cannot avail yourself at my disposal then you are free to go.' He waved her on. 'Go, before I change my mind.'

Tilia was in a state of unrest. Never had Cedrus shown mercy or remorse for his actions and yet he was prepared to let her go, had claimed he was the liberating agent for those who had been living their lives out as trees. And all other things he spoke appeared logical yet illogical to what she had known and heard. Was he the greatest illusionist of all time? She made a full curtsey and turned, hesitantly walking, wondering if her redemption was just another ploy designed to see her writhe in agony again.

And when she disappeared from view, Cedrus sipped his tea and held up his hand to refrain the Astronomer from speaking. His final act was now in play when she re-emerged. 'Have you changed your mind, Lady Tilia?'

'Are there not others far more worthy to kill an opponent?'

He replaced the cup in its saucer and got to his feet, wending his way round her rigid stance. 'For two reasons, Lady Tilia, both are obvious for you are a woman who is able to get close to another. I have seen your actions in the play pens against Lady Syringa and most assuredly you are, by far a better opponent. Quercus will consider you a spy in his camp for without doubt he has had news of your past disposition. At this very moment he revels in false hope on the west shores.'

'What would be my excuse, Divine Majesty?'

'You will give no excuse. You will go to him and only to him and say I gave you a potion to cure your welts in exchange for spying but that you had a change of heart and rally to his cause. Speak now if you feel unable to follow my command?'

She dipped her head. 'I will do what you ask.'

'Your lips must be sealed about the gates. I cannot reinforce this enough. Such information to the populace would create panic.'

'I give you my word, Divine Majesty.'

He clicked his fingers. 'Take Lady Tilia to her wardrobe, give her choice of weapons and make ready a fast steed. Remember you do this for your kingdom. Set aside emotions as I set aside mine.'

Tilia curtsied and kissed the ruby red ring on his outstretched hand. She was so far removed from her experience of Quercus that she knew she would have little impact upon him but her choices were made. Would the dramas interest her? Apart from the scenery changes, where screens of mountains and animals or rippling oceans or even battle scenes full of brave men would suddenly whisk to reveal starry night skies, Lady Tilia was more heartened by her restored beauty and planned to keep it that way.

His cheeks were rough and a little loose around the bones, the day's stubble already itching through the skin as he strolled through his rambling empire, his footsteps echoing to the tune of design. He looked ahead, a strange figure garbed in the green fur of animal skin. A leopard no less with its tail still attached, sweeping the floor. 'What news?' Cedrus asked, always asking for news, always anxious to be one jump ahead.

Acer was not past his prime by any means yet he had the scars of weathering, his features set with the confidence of a veteran under a mass of bright green hair. He stood still for a moment, scratching his jaw line watching Cedrus disappear through a door, his voice just as menacing as his appearance.

'He took them by surprise.'

Cedrus kicked off his boots. 'A White Tail could have told me as much.'

'They have taken command of two vessels.'

'So we drown them at sea.'

'From my understanding his quest is greater than ours. I hear vacant lots have sprouted across this continent due to a woman who came through the gates without a key.'

'You have been misinformed. She claimed to have a key. It was her brother who claimed otherwise.'

'Then it is him your informant must destroy.'

'It is the woman who must be destroyed. I was told she was his Achilles' heel.' Cedrus went over to an elaborately gilded cabinet and poured out wine. 'I want your army here. They are to spread rumours it was I who released men from their confines not this pretender and make it known they are androids from the other side.'

Acer took the glass. 'It would be wise to bring the black robes here. This is where he will come.'

'He takes vessels for a reason. The reason is simple. He wishes to cross swords on water to protect his own hide. He knows I cannot turn him on the seas. Let him cross swords with the black robes, his number will deplete then he will come here and you shall finish them off. This time he will not escape so easily.'

'He left in search of the mouthpiece.'

'A useless cause when the other half is destroyed. It will serve him no purpose.'

'Did you see it destroyed?'

Cedrus sniffed the air. 'My roses are stripped for my chambers. Remove your animal hide.'

This made it even more surprising when a few moments later Acer stood naked. 'Which is the better, the smell or the body of man needing a woman?'

MOUTHPIECE REVEALED

Quercus and Michael had toured the divisions of these two schooners, coming to the conclusion they were no ordinary vessels but something else. They had deep sunken flat bottom hulls yet above they conformed to the two-masted fore-and-aft rigging. Space was the obvious functionality to their design. Even so, there was a grave disadvantage that to venture rapidly or hastily would be like turning a lump of iron in watery custard, and to be caught in a storm, the chances were slim for recovery.

So stretched out in the midday sun on the quarter deck, Michael was in conversation with Quercus.

'Even I would feel sick.'

'Do I take it these vessels are not to your liking?'

'Nina mentioned the ketch that towed mine had a deep keel with the same fore and aft shape. Now that sounds more like my cup of tea.'

There was a quiet pause while Quercus stroked the skin of his right hand with the fingers of his left. He was feeling the calluses from handling the whip, remembering details, the time when Nina felt their softness between throes of breakfast and laughter. He looked at the small cuts and blisters and turned his hands over to examine the unharmed areas of skin.

Michael was watching him. 'So what are you going to do, Quercus? Stay here until the next lot arrives?'

He removed his shirt. 'To seek their breeding ground would be better than for us to stay here and fight.'

'Well you can count me in. I can sail one of these bathtubs, mind you it won't be that easy if Nina keeps crying. We might land up in a tempest storm.'

His lips curled. She cried for his people and it warmed his heart, no greater love could a man have. 'For someone who entered without war in mind, you offer your services.' He turned in the balmy air, his wound still raw. It was a cut from temple to cheek, narrowly missed the eye. 'You are a good man, Michaelmas. You are my brother even though you are a seasoned daisy.'

They laughed and continued to talk idly. Strange how these two men from different worlds, who showed immediate hostility, should now become the closest of allies, the closest of confidantes. Each, in their peculiar way had been drawn together by fate through hard circumstance, destined to share life's turmoil, destined to trust in a single cause.

In the background, men were regaining their strength, either sleeping against the rails, playing Monopoly on decks, telling stories, washing their blood stained clothes, calling out from one vessel to another and all manner of things warriors do in their free time. Elsewhere, four women, broken in pairs but serving on the same ship, were keeping themselves busy. Salix was admiring Michael and sometimes when he sat up to get cool, he would return her gaze but quickly she looked away and carried on stitching a tear in the mainsail. Nina, plaiting rope, sat next to her. Often her eyes would lift to the sun beating down on her shoulders and then across to Syringa who was crouched on the main deck in a world of her own. Her face was a picture of gloom, a breathless yearning for Fagus, catching memories in her mouth like the dust blown from unused textbooks. Beside her stood Ilex, her back to the sea, her elbows resting on the rail keeping her eyes suffused on Quercus.

'He's handsome is he not?' Salix asked.

Nina spoke with a loving sigh. 'Oh yes. He's my hero.'

'I was speaking of Michaelmas.'

Nina hummed and hawed, tightening the frayed ribbon holding back her hair. It was a struggle to keep up appearances in the midst of war. 'Do you want me to introduce you?'

'And what would you say?'

'Let me see. I would probably say you're the one who came out of nowhere and cracked a jar over the Captain's head. Or I could say you fancy him rotten. By the way, what were you doing with the Captain?'

'The black robes descended and killed my brother, left my mother for dead then took me.' Salix paused, sending her silky grey eyes to the sky. 'Every night I prayed destiny would sink the ship so all men on board would drown.'

'Rotten bastards,' Nina scorned. 'At least you had the chance to get even. So what species are you?'

'A pussy willow but you can call me Pussy if you like.'

'Wow, Michael is going to love you.'

Salix giggled and went back to her sewing. 'He might not be interested. My hair is colourless grey, not like Syringa's lilac.'

'Oh poo bear, look at me. I'm like a zebra crossing but Quirky finds me attractive.'

'Why do you call him Quirky?'

'At first, I thought he was from a mental institution. I mean, it was difficult to believe he was a tree. He came to my home and I bumped into him thinking he was my brother's colleague. I thought he looked different. To be truthful, it was ever so exciting. Then I found him in my shed, bleeding all over the mower. If anything, it was his eyes. I could swim in those golden eyes…Oh, but his hair is so gorgeous…look how it glistens as though he could set the world on fire. It saves on Christmas tree lights.'

'You have a romantic nature, Nina. It is not very wise to love so deeply in war. I have read about wars in your world. You not only destroy people but destroy your environment too.'

'I want it known I was against the war in Iraq. I am against all wars but Quirky makes a valid point. If Cedrus cannot see reason then you have to fight for what you believe in. Anyway, better to have loved and lost than not love at all.'

'Lady Syringa would say otherwise.'

Nina glanced across the decks. 'Oh she looks so sad. She really misses Fagus. I try to make her feel better but prickles keeps getting between us. Would you look at her now, standing like Miss Congeniality? With any luck, if her nose gets any higher a swordfish might jump up it.'

'She has her eye on your man.'

'Yes, I sort of noticed that too.' Nina could see Ilex scheming and plotting, her eyes and ears tuned to catch the words between Quercus and Michael. 'I think we should invite her to come and join us.'

'Lady Ilex will not associate with me.'

'No, silly, I was referring to Syringa. We can try and cheer her up by talking about Fagus and his bravery.' Nina called out. 'Syringa, join us for a chin wag.'

Quercus alerted. He looked to see Lady Syringa struggle to her feet; Lady Ilex pushed her down. Words were exchanged by which time Nina was stomping towards them. Now he was on tenterhooks listening to a fresh deluge of sarcasm hitting the air, the usual clamour, the customary snapping which resulted in Ilex stamping her foot to the deck. It offered a challenge. There was the absolute, almost belligerent pause, after which nothing would come unless in response to her threat.

Quercus was quick on his feet. 'Nina is not accustomed to our ways.'

'If she claims to be the giver of life then she must know our ways.'

'You test my patience, Ilex.'

'As you test mine,' she said spitefully, pointing to the other vessel. 'She and the common willow should be there. That is their station yet you choose to antagonize me by placing her under my nose.'

'I see no antagonism other than your own. Perhaps it would be wise for you to remove yourself since she displeases you.'

It only took a moment for Ilex to gain attention from those around her, to dampen his spirits, to dampen all spirits with her accusation. 'She should displease all who look upon her. Lord of the Oaks claimed it was she who released our brothers. Yet she shows no key. No such prophecy exists.'

'You forget the words of Sage when we forged alliances,' Quercus reminded. 'In spring she said the wheels began to turn for the prophecy.'

'She spoke of one entering the gates, one to release Sea Winger. We shall have no success if we keep our eyes closed. There is only one man who can release us and he is Cedrus.' Men were gathering. She had their attention. 'Listen to me, brothers. We accept there is a traitor but that traitor is not hidden, that traitor stands there making a mockery of us.'

'I was released,' Quercus claimed. 'Not by Cedrus but by Nina of the Atlantic.'

'The night of your return you claimed it was him.' Ilex was quick to say.

'It was convenient to let him think so.'

'Like it is convenient to let us think it is her!' Behind Ilex, Nina made a finger-down-the-throat gesture and Quercus tried to withhold his smile, which only encourage Ilex to continue her malice. 'Look at her, she has no colouring and is unkempt. Why, she even smells like Cedrus.'

'That is untrue.'

'The rain, it smelt of blueberries. Do you deny he likes blueberries?'

'I like blueberries. We all like blueberries.'

'Then let her show us the key. Let us see some truth. Let us see if she really is what you claim her to be or one of his new creations? She admits things can be duplicated. If she holds a key to the gates we shall know if it is real.'

Mumblings were thrown into the arena. Dissention was upon him. There had been so much emotion on these shores, victory and loss, rain and release, hate and love. He knew the feeling all too well, aware how the darkness played tricks on the mind, how desolate it felt to be a tree. He regarded Nina whose eyes were to her feet. She bent down, took off her trainer and worked her way through the lining until she produced the object Ilex desired most to see. Immediately, it was snatched out of her hand. It was that litigious smile Ilex wore to worry Quercus. The key passed from hand to hand.

'She did not enter the gates!' Ilex rejoiced aloud, had the attention of others on the vessel moored alongside. 'She is the product of Cedrus!'

Jubaea passed the key to Quercus. 'It is not a key to the gates, my brother. The prophecy only speaks of one passing through the gates without a key. Michaelmas is the prophecy.'

'Is he?' Ilex said, holding her hands in the air. 'Where is this winged creature to afford us protection? I do not see it. Has anyone seen it?'

'I saw it fly over the Atlantic.' Fraxinus claimed.

'And who can back up your story?' Ilex snapped harshly. 'Men have died when they could have been saved. I would have been the first to rejoice if the prophecy came true.'

'Listen, my brothers.' Quercus walked among them, the key clasped in his hand. 'Has it been discomfort to marry with another? More discomfort for Nina who sleeps bound by ankles and wrists. Soon we shall see another wave of black robes. Instead we ready ourselves in accusations upon two people who have served our cause.'

'Fagus would disagree.' Ilex scorned. 'He died with days lost, next to Jubaea instead of Syringa. Would you say otherwise, Quercus, or has this woman stolen your senses?'

'Oh listen to Miss Know-it-all,' Nina said, unable to hold back her feelings. 'Quercus has scorned her, her husband suckers to Cedrus and she prances about in her green satin robes stealing food where she can and stirring up trouble.'

'You,' Ilex poked Nina in the chest, 'kept the key hidden because you knew it was false!'

'Halloo…where are your brains? If I was manufactured by Cedrus, would he not have given me a real key?' The pause was long as she surveyed blank faces. 'Am I missing something here?'

'Nina,' Quercus conveyed glumly. 'Each who has a key is for their passing alone through the gates. The gates cannot be deceived. I can no more use Jubaea's key than he could use mine. Our keys have our initial shaped. The White Tail hatches the key with a newborn in sight. It is they who choose the people to have keys. Unless you were born here and a White Tail delivered you a key then one can only assume you came through the gates without a key.' His gripped tightened on the key, convinced there was more to the prophecy than met the eye. 'We all know their shape and distinction. This is not a key neither hatched by a White Tail nor given to Nina by Cedrus for he would be a fool to carve his initial on a false key.'

'But it was in- Ouch!'

Quercus stood on Nina's foot, sent a disapproving look. It was imperative to keep the mouthpiece a secret, imperative she was kept safe. 'Nina, perhaps Lady Ilex is correct. It would be wise for you and Salix to stay on the other vessel.'

He was aware how his words had affected her, for she tried to control the reflex stiffening of her body and simply shook her head. 'No,' she said. 'Let smarty pants move.'

They were silent again, and he started a trail of thought that was unpleasant but had to be followed to the end. 'When we feel insulted, we have the right to challenge,' he told her. 'Ilex threw down her gauntlet by the stamping of her foot. You have a choice to accept her wishes and move to the other vessel. Alternatively, you may pick up the gauntlet in the hope of victory. In our world most women choose to improve their dexterity and muscle formation by sparring in the pen. Ilex has proved to be a resourceful and worthy opponent among the best. It would be her choice of weapon.'

'What weapon does she want?' Nina asked.

'I choose the dagger.' Ilex responded.

One could die for any reason, Quercus thought. It might be the axe from a black robe, the infection from a wound, or a matter of principle. Taking her face between his hands and turning it gently so he could look into her eyes, he said barely above a whisper. 'Nina, I beg you to go on the other vessel. I will follow.'

'Remember what you said to me? A moral dilemma only becomes so by the lack of response. To follow and pursue the right path regardless of its uncertainties do make a difference, however slight.' She turned to her audience. 'I pick up the gauntlet.'

Gasps! The sound of expelling surprise came in different forms where men could see the notable difference in stature and build. Quercus wiped his face with an open hand, unable to speak, unable to calculate the extent of damage Ilex could render.

The shallow dry wind kissed sun-baked shoulders and sweated brows, closing some faces. As two daggers passed, men on the other vessel hopped over and joined their counterparts making a tight circle on the main deck. Now it was sport of a different kind.

'The rule is simple,' Quercus announced. 'The first to draw blood is the victor.' He turned to Ilex. 'One cut and one cut only.'

'Then I shall make my cut deep.'

Unquiet shadows clouded his eyes. Yes, she would make her cut deep, make it count.

Ilex ventured forward and puzzled at Nina regarding the sky. She looked up. Bizarrely, everyone else looked up too. In a dazzling instant Nina administered a left hook! Ilex went hurtling in the air and landed spread-eagle on the deck with a bloodied nose. What an ungainly climb-down.

'I win! I win!' Nina jumped up and down to their cheers. 'I win! I win! Toffee nose can move next door.'

Disbelievingly, Quercus shook his head. 'Your sister has unknown qualities.'

'Who do you think was my sparring partner?' Michael said proudly.

'She made no cut!' Ilex screeched, rising to her feet.

'She drew blood.' Quercus claimed. 'Now remove yourself from this vessel.'

Bruised physically and mentally, Ilex was ignored in the uproar of applause, her mind in the thought of settling a score. The moment turned. A blade traced the air and caught the corner of Quercus's eye, was within his peripheral image but he reacted too late. Nina crumbled to her knees with a groan, holding her abdomen, painfully aware of her costly mistake. This was treachery of the worst kind.

Provoked, his hostility towards Ilex had reached its zenith. Quercus deftly drew Jubaea's knife from the waist band, ran Lady Ilex through, watched as her eyes focused on the impaling, waited as the hands clenched the blade and pushed it deeper. He kicked the body off and threw it overboard. Act over he began to weave a steady path.

Forging quickly ahead, Michael had Nina in his arms, her blood spilling its sorrowful trail, coursing his denims, her wheezing words echoing in his ear. Urgency was in mind. Behind him Quercus, questioning detail, demanding answers but Michael had no answer other than to say, 'I need saline solution and a drip feed.' He laid her on the captain's table, grabbed a needle, clenched and unclenched his fist to pump the vein in his arm. 'Salix, keep your hand compressed on her wound while I draw two units of my blood. Syringa, get her prepped for surgery.'

Quercus bent over her pallid face. 'Nina, it is not your time to die.'

Syringa edged him away. 'Come, Quercus, let Salix and I prepare her.'

Reluctantly shuffled from the hospital cabin, once the salubrious captain's quarters, a man who had offered information in return for his freedom, Quercus was unable to clear his mind, to make sense of the absurd and leaned over the rails, head bent. Nina, he mouthed, live through this so I may hold you again. It was such an unforgivable act on such a wonderful undeserving day. He never gave thought to Ilex. If anything, it will please him later to remember her death, but not now, not when his mind was elsewhere, scribbling the memories of Nina and how fate had brought them together. He believed, like many, what was true in this life was true in another, that each man and woman played an important role with Hortus. For certain he knew it was his destiny to bring down Cedrus and whether he would survive or not, he also knew there would be victory. Of a single fact, he knew this to be true.

Occasionally, the faint proximity of his closest brothers could be heard, the glimmer of Fraxinus, Jubaea and Juglans, all three outlines detected until he blocked them out and kept his eyes transfixed on his tarnished boots. Ingrained blood splatters from earlier battles were forged in leather and he wondered if by any remotest possibility there might be one of hers to cherish.

'Good news, Quercus,' and he craned his head round to Syringa. 'The danger is past. She is resting at present to regain her strength.'

A moment of relief. 'I did this to Nina as surely as I did for Fagus.'

'Fagus completed his destiny as I will complete mine. We know how it is to be dead yet not dead. How it is to be alive yet not alive. For one hundred years I heard the teasing voice of Cedrus and the pain he inflicted upon others.'

'Then surely your world was darker than mine.' He turned to brighter waters with a lighter heart. 'I had no memories whatsoever. I heard nothing, not even the sound of wind rustling through my leaves.'

'It was dismal and lonely yet when I thought of Fagus my spirits lifted. I should have intervened. Nina was fighting my battle; Ilex was mocking me.'

'Has Nina been a good agony aunt?'

'She spoke of a way to overcome my sorrow, that to look at the worst and weigh it against the best, invariable the best is such a blessing. She once said that to live without principles is to live as a zombie. I do not know this word zombie but she explained it as going through life without caring, not even caring enough for flowers grown in your garden. She said her plants kept dying at the bottom of her garden but she never stopped trying and that is the point, is it not?'

Quercus felt similarly but did not say. 'Fagus once believed you had been chopped for firewood. No-one knew for certain, had not seen you.'

'I was rooted in his secret garden,' she sighed. 'It matters not. I am here barely alive in my heart. The prophecy you spoke mentioned one through the gates, instead it was three. Nina was with child.'

'The Thief?'

'It was not the Thief, Quercus. It was your child. Please do not ask me to explain, but Michaelmas has confirmed it. He is in no doubt.' Now his eye twitched and she held him back. 'She needs her rest.'

Asking himself why it should come to this, he felt another presence. 'What is it Fraxinus?'

'We have a visitor, my brother. Lady Tilia.'

He sent his eyes ahead. 'Has she brought support?'

'She is alone and requests a private audience.'

'What are your thoughts?'

'The spy that hides in this camp frustrates Cedrus so he sends another.'

Quercus nodded. 'Then we share the same thoughts. Bring her over.'

Lady Tilia curtsied. 'My lord.'

He sighed, reason and reasonableness in his voice. 'Why have you come? Certainly with no support, certainly of no help in battles unless you are prepared to die alongside your brothers.'

'Cedrus has sent me to spy.'

His eyebrows rose. 'Such truth and directness, should I be astounded?'

'I do not wish to live in fear, my lord. I was unmercifully beaten, left scarred then called upon and given a potion to remedy my ills.'

'No such potion exists. If so, why has it not come to light sooner? Perhaps your scars were unfounded, your tale exaggerated.' He held up a finger. 'No, madam, I am in no mood for fairy tales. Return to Daylily.'

'I do not wish to be sent back to Daylily. I wish to fight beside you. Show me no favours. I expect none.'

'What news of home?'

'Men have been released from all four corners of our continent. Rain such of the likes we have never seen or smelt made people rejoice in their soaking. There is mention of the prophecy. Is there truth in this?'

He beckoned Fraxinus. 'Do you wish to see the truth?'

'I do.'

'My brother, align Lady Tilia to whomever you think fit, give her no favours. She will fight in our next battle and that is the truth.'

There was a long pause, after which Fraxinus said, as if to himself, 'a woman in battle, what heartless bastards have we become.'

As it would, Quercus realized, anyone if willing. He returned his gaze upon the glistening waters against sunlight blackened by his mood. It was much later that he felt a cold chill upon his skin and slipped on his battle weary shirt. Shortly thereafter he was summoned.

Nina was looking somewhat careworn, pale and withdrawn, lying there on a wide berth in a semi-prostrate position, able to manage a smile. 'Quirky, are you alright?'

He took her hands, taking them to his lips. 'My Nina, it is I who should be asking you.'

'Michael told me you killed Lady Ilex.'

'Her name is not worthy of our conversation.'

'I'm sorry, Quirky.' Her loving fingers ran through his hair. 'I should have told you but you would never have believed me. I was so frightened you might have sent me away.'

'I have no explanation. It has never been known.'

Quercus fought to keep control of his emotions, laying his head upon the bedcovers, lightly felt her belly, his throat dry and choked. It was a moment between them, a private affair, and another casualty of war.

And he never left her side, not this night, not for anything, not even when Jubaea received a message from a White Tail, anxious to convey news. Occasionally, Michael popped in, saw how Quercus slumbered against Nina when she slept, they both slept, hers heavier, his lighter. But try as he might, Quercus felt his attention drawn to Lady Tilia and why she was really here, to the unanswered questions why three came through the gates, and why the creature, Sea Winger was still absent.

'Have a cup of Harrods tea,' Michael said.

Quercus yawned, flicked his eyes to sleeping Nina, pulled his legs over the edge of the bunk. 'Thank you, my brother.' He inhaled the drawn features of Michael whose eyes were puffy from tiredness and worry, his black hair strewn over his brow and his body suggested he needed comforting too. 'She never told me, Michaelmas. For certain I would have sent her home.'

'But where is her home, Quercus? You know she feels a little left out in this place. She's desperate to fit in.'

'She will be stronger. I will teach her our ways.'

'Quercus, this might sound a little weird but I think Nina may be the prophecy. For some peculiar reason I'm the one who has physically changed but she seems to be the one who can make things happen. I have no clue how to raise this sea bird.'

'When we ride the waves, it will come to you as surely as Nina's tears came to her.'

Michael's eyes were still on Nina, his voice suddenly grown nervous, as if he were divulging information he was not authorized to provide. 'I know where she kept the mouthpiece,' he said and rummaged in his medical bag. 'Nina stowed it in the boom of my yacht then hid it in here between its base and lining.'

Quercus jumped to his side, fell speechless, in awe, fondling the green leather bound book as though it was more precious than life itself. Given the fact it had been in his thoughts forever and given the fact Nina claimed its discovery but failed to disclose its hiding place, holding the mouthpiece, feeling its presence between the creases of his blistered hands proved it was no hallucination.

'How long have you known?'

'It was her last words before she passed out.'

'Her heart was not for herself but for my people. She spoke in the belief it would be her last words. She thinks so less of herself, it makes me feel humble.'

'Why are the pages blank?'

'Until the joining of pages, they will remain so.'

'It must be highly explosive material in there?'

'I have never been fortunate to read the Book of Hortus let alone have the contents explained. It is for Hortus to choose a new Keeper.' Quercus sent his glazed eyes to the porthole, the dark shimmering shine of waters calling for something else, a different point of the compass beckoned. 'We do not sail to destroy the breeding ground. We ride to Daylily and seek out Sage. How soon can Nina be moved?'

'We can make a good bed up in one of the carts and cover it over in case she starts raining on our parade.'

Quercus smiled and looked back at him. 'Your wit is good. I have one.' He held up the book. 'Her bite is greater than our bark.'

Michael nodded. 'Not bad, remind me to tell you about the Genie who put a cork up an Irish man's arse.'

'I have read about Genies. They grant three wishes.'

'Exactly, so when the Irishman saw one, he said no shit.'

Humour had its place.

On the rising deck, the walnut's face was red and sweating, his stately habit not so stately now. Like others gathered round him, the ravages of war wreaked havoc on clothes.

'We have been warned,' Juglans announced. 'Acer anchored in the harbour at Daylily with four hundred of his men yet they are nervous and some are questioning his authority.'

'News of our success was expected.' Quercus turned to Fraxinus, his ashen hair catching the glints of a full moon. 'Lady Tilia failed to disclose this. Then would she have known?'

'What does she know?' Jubaea asked.

'She offers nothing save her allegiance as a spy. Did I rid one and gain another?' He looked at their faces, three worried expressions in the attentive pause. 'We are leaving these vessels to take the road to Daylily. He expects us to fight on sea.'

'But the sea will bring forth Sea Winger, aid in our victory,' Juglans argued.

'To fight the black robes bring down our number. He makes no sacrifice where we make many. No brothers, heed me well. We have learnt to be stealthy, to be the killing dogs of the night. I have been told by Lady Tilia there are vacant lots across our continent. On our way to Daylily we shall pick up good warriors, men who will be anxious for revenge, no greater weapon.'

'If we strike at the heart, Cedrus will turn many.'

'Can you turn in the rain?'

SEA WINGER

The influx of men had swelled their number, the chatter of anxious voices and the press of ambling steeds created a torrent of ceaseless sound. Darkness had fallen eight times.

Sat huddled in large groups by camp fires, eyes staring into the flames, newcomers listened to the stories. And there were many to tell. But Michael was talking and gesturing in a manner befitting the style of courtship. Quercus watched them, loath to puncture the moment.

'Michaelmas, I would welcome your time.'

'I'll get back to you, Pussy.'

Salix squeezed between three other women. 'He said I was like a cure for a hangover. He will have to do better if he wishes to set my heart on fire.'

'I should have warned you,' Nina said with girlish giggles. 'He's not very romantic. I understand from Sonja, he's a wonderful lover. It lasts as long as it takes to cook a casserole.' Their eyes widened. 'Of course, you must remember we have microwaves so the cooking time is a little less.'

'How less?'

'Oh, I would say about two hours.'

They rolled about laughing, curled up in a ball.

It drew his interest. Quercus looked back, uncertainly.

'She's doing okay. Pussy thinks the world of her.'

'Pussy is not a good name to address a woman.'

'Lighten up, Quercus. Pussy is a great name.'

'But it refers to a woman's anatomy.'

'Well you should know considering you've had plenty.' Michael would push him no further. 'Look, James Bond had a girlfriend called Pussy Galore. None of the women took exception to that. Now what's on your mind?'

Quercus edged to a quieter spot, kept his voice low. 'I am going to pin down the port and storm the palace.'

'Sorry you lost me. I thought we were finding Sage.'

'We shall, my brother. Shortly thereafter I will join my killing dogs. All will become clear. A day's ride and we shall be there, at her door by which time my men shall gather a half mile from Daylily. There I shall make divisions and wait for the signal. The attack must take place tomorrow night before the hour strikes a new day.'

Michael nodded. 'Sounds good, so what's the signal?'

Quercus rushed his hands through his hair. This was going to be difficult. 'My brother, speak the truth. Inform me how Nina fares?'

'She's quite full of herself, as usual.'

Indeed this was good news. 'How can we make her cry?'

'Eh? Are you some sort of sadist or what?'

'Hard rain will protect my men, disguise our coming. This I feel certain is Nina's true destiny. What thoughts do you have?'

'The thing is,' Michael replied scratching his head, 'you never know when. Sometimes she gets the hump if you upset her then cries later. Now it could be two hours later or even the next day. It all depends what else she has on her mind.'

'What would make her cry immediately?'

'She would cry if she saw you kissing another woman.'

'I will be readying for battle while she is ensconced with you, distanced apart.'

'Oh, I see.'

'What if you informed her of my death?'

'That should do it. On the other hand, it might not. She's built up immunity to losing you. Think about it. Your life has two extremes, either you're going to die before your time or you're going to live beyond your time. It doesn't worry you, does it? Death, it doesn't bother you like it bothers us.'

Quercus looked down at his boots. He always looked down at his boots when he felt uncomfortable. 'Death holds no fear. It is our destiny to make room for others.'

'And if you kill this chap, how do you make room for others when you gain immortality?' The silence drew out. 'I see, so you will live a sort of lonely existence, watching your friends die, one after the other until eternity, sounds a pretty naff prize to me.'

'If truth be told, I gave the matter ill consideration. I have lived in the knowledge my life may be short. But I feel I am close, Michaelmas. In my heart, I feel I can make a difference in these coming times. Without her tears we have no protection.'

'I'll think of something.'

Away from the fires, Quercus led Nina among the delphiniums, the most attractive of tall perennials, with their snowy spires of flowers making a spectacular display in these last days of summer.

'Nina, will you stay with me this night. I ask no more than your company.'

'I might not be able to stay awake.'

'Awake or asleep, I shall find comfort.'

'Can Lizzie sleep with us too?'

'Lizzie?'

'Yes,' she said fondling the leopard's ear. 'I named her Busy Lizzie because her nose is in everyone's lap, especially mine.'

'That is because you keep feeding her sweets. Do you have one for me?'

They lay on a mattress of delphiniums, crushing the stems and leaves beneath them, enveloped in the aroma of their juices and the perfume of their blooms. Her head went against his chest and he stroked the hair from her temple.

'Nina,' Quercus spoke softly. 'What was your strongest motive to enter the gates? Was it your pregnancy?'

'I never knew I was pregnant until I spewed up over Perry's foot.'

'Perry?'

'Yes, the conceited Juniperus Pirate who calls himself a Handsome Thief. Of course, he has a tendency to exaggerate, although I must confess, he's very handsome. Actually, underneath his bravado he's a kind person. He let me have Michaelmas back, stocked her with fresh food and made sure my compass heading was right. He speaks very highly of you. He told me you were the greatest warrior on land.'

'So will you tell me or shall I be left wondering?'

'It was you, Quirky. I wanted to be with you.' She lifted her head. 'Though had I known about your amorous adventures I may have thought twice.' She laid her head back down. 'I want to fight by your side.'

'Women do not fight men's battles. It is our burden to bear.'

'Yet I understand from Lady Tilia you expect her to fight.'

'She is a spy; there is the difference.'

'I don't believe that for one moment.' Her head came up again. 'What makes you think she's a spy?'

'Cedrus sent another because we stopped his fan mail.'

'Michael and I are a bad influence. Every day you sound a little like us. Sometimes I think every day I sound a little like you. I have a joke. An Irish man walks up to a blacksmith. The blacksmith says have you ever shoed a horse? The Irish man said, no but I have shooed a donkey. Yes? Shooed as in shooed away?'

'Ah! I understand. You mock different kinds. Is it because they have created wars?'

'It has nothing to do with wars. The English have a dry sense of humour. But it doesn't go down well, not lately because some foreigners get tetchy. They take it the wrong way. The problem, I think is that they come over in droves, some unable to speak our language and expect to practice their religions and preach their own laws. I wouldn't say this if I was at home but I rather like the idea of different kinds being separated. What will happen to the firs when you kill Cedrus?'

'It shall be as before. They will keep to their lands and we shall keep to ours.'

'I see, so no mixing then?'

'We do fear them, Nina. They have an inbuilt mechanism for aggressive behaviour. They seek to own at any cost, a little like those through the gates. They have greedy eyes and forget Hortus when it suits. No, when I kill Cedrus, the firs that survive shall be returned to their homelands. And so it should be. We do not want to see their faces or smell their habits. Only the Juniperus Pirates will serve both continents and be the go between of two nations that strike different chords.'

He lay awake long after she was asleep. Holding her close like cold hands upon a warm teapot, he nurtured his thoughts for the battle to come, to fight for the men who died at his side, and to foster cruelty towards Cedrus. It was a way to empty fear. He could see himself from afar, was transported to the days when his father stormed the palace and men carried the points of their swords to the throat of their enemy. Their deaths would not go unpunished. Nor will the death of Fagus.

Dawn clawed grey across the still-dark, and he was awake to greet it. It felt similar to the rest, neither good nor bad but a twilight in which he killed black robes and loved Nina. She slept on beside him. Such moments helped soften the trauma of combat. He climbed to his feet and stretched, splashed water on his face to rid himself of sleep. It might be his last, could end with great consequence. Any outcome was possible.

'Let me come with you.'

'I cannot.' He knelt on one knee and removed the chain from his neck. 'Nina, take my key to remember me by. Keep close to Salix until Michaelmas returns.'

'Come back to me, Quirky.'

He stayed motionless to appraise, to admire then kissed her goodbye, rose to his feet and picked his way to Shadow. Michael was there, already mounted. They said nothing to each other. There were too many pressing concerns.

A little more than two hours after handing his key to Nina, they had found the two valleys snaking south towards the sea, further on they followed the tracks leading to nowhere other than a sharp sunken lake where the magical wings of bubbling life skimmed and settled on water. Trees relaxed in their branches, shrubberies sculptured and in this green geography a trail of choking smoke from a red-brick chimney clawing its way out of a wooden cabin. Both dismounted and followed the path with their steeds in tow.

'Are there fish in this lake?' Michael asked.

'Do you like fishing?'

'I prefer sailing.'

Their idle words seemed to make the crooked door open. Here, rustic simplicity in a weird and wonderful way. Stacks of books sleeping on floors, silver framed photographs taking up their shelf space, china bowls full of flowers, vases holding dirt, and cowslip cushions scattered on tapestry chairs. This lip of chaos all pulled together under candlelight fantasy.

Quercus placed the mouthpiece in the folds of her lap and watched her numinous actions. They were ancient hands fondling green leather, her character infrequently changed. She showed no excitement nor bellowed any sound except to say, 'Ask your question.'

'Why three and not one through the gates?'

'Two came as one for they share the same blood. The child served its purpose at the hand of a traitor.'

'You failed to disclose this.'

'To open destiny is to close destiny. What is your plan?'

Quercus remained quiet for a while, assembling his thoughts. 'Possibly,' he said, 'I have swayed more toward one than the other. Nina of the Atlantic shall cry to offer protection when we storm the port. Is there a side to the prophecy which has not been spoken?'

'A woman is not afraid to cry. A man is not afraid to die. She releases a veil of tears. He releases Sea Winger. Come to me.'

It took Michael a moment to realize that the words were directed at him. He came forward and went down on one knee. It was a gradual process. And now, in the slow yellow light of the candles, he kept still with spent words in his ear. For him, he had never experienced anything like it, nor would he.

'Now go and prepare for the blooms of late summer. The self-seeding will emerge in a random way.'

Both men flung their horses forward, aiming for Daylily. It was for Michael to volunteer those secret whispers not for Quercus to ask. But something was different. Michael was well on the way to realizing, intellectually as well as instinctively, that the variables involved were such that battles could not be fought by a method of centralized command and control.

On rising ground, from a pair of night-vision binoculars Quercus wondered if he had merely won an extension of time, a prolonging of their agony. In the distance, five schooners were approaching, a world away and their water displacement spoke of heavy cargo, black robes no doubt. Elsewhere, Acer had the port locked down. Against the odds and overwhelming numbers, Quercus still held hope. For a little more than three hundred of his men slain, Cedrus lost thousands. He squinted back, looking up to his cherished spot. It was there, a light blinking periodically in the dark. His home was on fire. The sight churned his stomach until he found intestinal fortitude. Other homes had been torched too. The scene did not bode well.

At the last moment, he side-stepped behind a tree and looked at his camouflaged forces crouched on their anxious heels. 'We are expected.'

Jubaea, Fraxinus, Juglans and Syringa followed his line of sight. There was not much to see, her face and hair lost in the shadowy packages. Lady Tilia stood, pushing through the lines, keeping fixed on his attentive pause.

'I was sent to kill Nina of the Atlantic.'

'You failed to disclose this.'

'You failed to listen.'

'I am listening now.'

'I was told the gates were left open when you came through them, that Cedrus readies himself against outsiders who will come with greater weapons than ours. It was an absurd tale to disturb my senses. It served my purpose to act in his play so I could win my beauty and see for myself.'

'And what do you see?' He motioned beyond. 'We are expected and greatly out-numbered.'

'White Tails have been criss-crossing our skies, news of your army and gatherers have reached his ears. He brings his army to his doors to crush you. You now know the enemy number, their location but you leave Nina behind. Bring her here and give her something to cry for so we may be protected.'

His eyes squeezed, unsure if she was too clever by half. 'You try to place yourself on our side, madam. Whichever the victor you have your bed made.'

'It would have been easy to poison her drink by the camp fires, easier still to slit her throat when she laid by your side, both in the land of dreaming. But you left her well this morning. Does it speak traitor?'

Quercus shifted his gaze to Syringa. 'Why did you fail to tie Lady Tilia to your wrists?'

'Why not tie us all to a tree?'

There was still a little hostility there. He paused for a moment and looked at his men. Their eyes were like pin-pricks on green velvet bands, shiny and eager to please. He would not let them down. Raising his hands in a gesture more suited to ward off spirits, he said, 'The veil of tears shall descend and protect you, greater than any shield you hold, greater than any armour you wear. Before this night is out, you shall feel the truth of the prophecy.' He turned to his aides. 'You shall not proceed until they feel the wet on their backs. This port must be taken before the black robes descend. I shall lead my group on horseback into the palace gates. It shall be them to hack down the blue cloths and give me a path to Cedrus. Juglans, you shall wait here in the east, Jubaea to the west, both shall stealthily tread their way into the port and pick off Acer's men. Fraxinus, we need Acer's vessel with the smaller crafts to log-jam the entrance to the harbour so the captains cannot enter to unload their cargo. And Lady Tilia, your cunning may be as wise as your words. Go with Lady Syringa and rally the women and children, ensure they are beyond his reach.'

These killing dogs shuffled in silence.

Quercus had demonstrated once again his desire to continue the battle, that his fund of aggression was one of heroic proportions, that he was a professional of violence of the highest order going beyond that element necessary to fulfil his destiny. He adjusted the harness of Shadow, bent again to check its saddle-straps and felt his tension. It had been many weeks since they last galloped together in search of a fight. He patted his neck before mounting and glanced back. His own division was assembled, ready to go. Until they struck, they would be silent and unseen. But his thoughts were on Michael coming up trumps, not too far, or so he believed for that is where he told him to stay with Salix and Nina.

At first, Michael was blind to their whereabouts until the green leopard came from the trees, two women constrained by their positions and worry. He cantered over and dismounted, leading his horse under cover.

'Sis, I want you and Pussy to come with me to the far shore. I need to pop home.'

'Pardon?'

'I have to get Smithe-Jones frigate.' He grinned, explanation about to come forth. 'What does he call his frigate? Ocean Flight vis-à-vis Sea Winger, get it?'

'Is that what Sage told you?'

'She speaks in riddles. I never understood at first then it twigged. Remember what the Thief told you about the Juniperus Pirates destined to drop their shit on the firs?'

She gasped. 'Oh, Michael, you are brilliant! You see, you are the prophecy. Quirky never doubted you for a moment. You must contact Perry. Got a pen handy?'

He patted his pockets. 'A pen, a pen my vessel for a pen.'

Salix stuck a twig and leaf under his nose. 'We use these when there is no pen.'

'I have no idea how this works.'

'It is simple. By pressing the stick like a pen you have bruised the leaf. The words will appear by the time it reaches its destination. Do you wish for me to call a White Tail?'

Nina was in another dimension as these two chatted over her head. She had tasted love and longing where fate had conspired to snatch it away. What did he say? Not much, she thought. He said very little but gave her his key. She clasped it tight as though she was carbonizing the metal into her skin. For however long she stood in contemplation, the White Tail had been and gone.

In taking the long way round, they avoided any chance sighting by one of Acer's men. The Handsome Thief had sweated in the brief interim, had already made careworn tracks in the sand. Their meeting was pleasurable, recognition immediate. Nina gave him a hug.

'Oh, I'm so glad you could make it,' she said in a rush. 'Perry, we need your help desperately. Michael has to steal Sea Winger from the gates.'

'Sea Winger,' the Thief acknowledged. 'Sea Winger is a vessel?'

'Look,' Michael interrupted. 'Sorry to break up the meeting and all that but we need to get going. I'll explain on the way.'

'Not so fast, my friend. We do the stealing; we own the boat.'

'Okay, you can have the boat when I'm done. Now we must get going.'

'Not so fast,' the Thief said again. 'Who are you to keep the contract binding?'

'He's the prophecy,' Nina replied. 'He's the one who came through the gates without a key. I did have a key. You just never looked in the right place. But you were right in one respect, the Juniperus Pirates do aid the prophecy.'

'The prophecy claimed to be a bird dropping its shit on the firs.'

'Oh for certain it will be dropping its shit.'

The Thief proffered his hand. 'We have an accord.'

'Where is your boat?' Michael asked.

'In the harbour, I cannot reach it because Acer has the port locked down.' The Thief clicked his fingers and his crew popped up from the dunes. 'You should know five vessels are approaching, the likes I have not seen before.'

'Five? Hell, that's a bummer.' Michael turned to Nina. 'Now listen, keep in the dunes, both of you.'

'Wait,' the Thief said. 'We do the stealing. Where is the vessel moored?'

'I should come because-'

'My prophecy, we can stand here all night and argue. We do the stealing.'

'But I live through the gates.'

The Thief pointed to webbed feet. 'But I swim fast through the gates.'

'Do you know the old lifeboat station?'

'Yes.'

'Go beyond that and you'll see a frigate called Ocean Flight.'

'Why not called Sea Winger?'

'Look, just trust me. That is Sea Winger.'

'Ocean Flight is not a good name.'

'Well paint the bloody name out. Time is short, chaps.'

The Thief beckoned to his men. They stared at whatever it was they held then made a dash across the sands, quickly escaping into the cold and dark folds of a watery grave. Even at that distance and in the deepening dark, the swim was hard and exhausting.

A little over an hour and from the near dunes a shadow emerged. 'We had to anchor next to the promontory,' the Thief said.

While keeping a wary eye on the time, that precious commodity, with only fifteen minutes to spare before midnight, Michael propelled into the water, followed by Nina and Salix. The adopted green leopard stayed on the beach, watchful.

His mind on tactics, Michael kept Nina pinned on the poop deck, his fingers crossed behind his back. 'Sis, if you knew something about the woman I was involved with, would you say in a time of crisis or would you wait until the crisis was over?'

Spitting out salty water, she wiped her face with her hands and said, 'Pussy is not a spy.'

'Just answer the question?'

'I would probably wait until the crisis was over.'

'Then I'll tell you later. Come on, we've got work to do.'

She forestalled him. 'Did Sage tell you something about Quirky?'

'It can wait until the crisis is over.'

'Michael, stop fluffing about and tell me!'

'He's our grandfather.'

Nina felt dizzy with the sensation of loss. It was like slow moving images, small things that played on her lips before opening up to a greater possibility of pain. She let out a howl of unimaginable proportions and then an angry outburst of tears, so acute it made him shudder to think.

There seemed to be some uncertainty, Michael thought, the slim chance of making it happen but when it occurred it was ferocious and sudden, so sudden as though a camera flash had exploded into his face. Everything went white, ghostly white for a second and silence dropped down, the briefest of silences, like a falter between heartbeats before the whole sky lit up again to make this night, no night at all.

Elsewhere, and for a while, it rendered Quercus speechless. He held himself tight in the saddle pinning down Shadow who pressed against others trying to buck the ripping fork of streak lightening. Not once, twice but endless, a rupturing sky with unsettling interludes. Constant flashes followed by claps of thunder, so dense and loud it made the port grumble. Men braced their positions, framed in fighting eagerness, carrying their own thoughts, cloaked in their own dread, anxious for the feel of rain. And then it fell like a blind blanket of water so intense it cropped twigs off trees.

Now, my brothers!

For Cedrus, the point had been reached, the critical instant he knew would come. It would be written in the blood of Quercus, not his but wherever he looked, wherever there was engagement outside the walls of his palace, all he could see was a choking curtain of water and all he could hear was a harsh sound like marbles thrown on a dustbin lid. It seemed his entire world was decomposing. Ministerial Firs were falling left, right and centre, misfits were scampering, half their limbs lost. One hundred years does not make a man forgive or forget.

Quercus moved forward like a wet roller coaster running through men, cutting off their high-pitched cries, no finesse, no quarter given. He threw himself into a raging pulse of ferocity, weaving between pillars and openings, from one chamber to the next, up and down marbled staircases, onwards, oblivious to anything except for a kill. Shadow shied, his front hooves drew history at the sight of a leopard jumping out from a grim abyss. Such an act could render a man off balance, could have afforded the enemy a chance for a single blow but Quercus was quick to his feet.

'I knew you would come.' Acer snarled.

'I come for a traitor!'

The sword unsheathed, rising to the bait. 'I did for the cause as you did for your people, abandoned for a better prospect.'

'My mistake to depart in trust!'

Acer was quick to dodge the snaking velocity, which was surprising because he wielded his sword like a nuisance. From hand to hand, he indulged in the theatricals keeping his eyes fixed on Quercus who was timing the tempo, readying for another strike.

Perhaps it was best this way, yet he was no leopard and this was no cage. This was the magnificent hall that had people dancing not killing. Quercus remembered the night shortly after his return, how Lady Ilex coaxed him towards the balcony and played him like a minnow, fresh into the pool of politics. Was this the moment when she turned traitor or was it later? Was it when she learnt about Nina? Did it matter? He smiled to her demise, was glad of it. Also glad he was going to bring down another traitorous bastard.

Instead of the whip, his foot pummelled the leg, rejoicing when he heard the bone crack. Acer looked up disbelievingly, a different perspective now, the sword thrashing thin air from a cripple.

'How do you feel facing death?'

Acer hobbled backwards, shouting defiance. 'I did no more than you, Quercus! I protected my family as you protected yours.'

'I do not hide in the shadows, sneak behind walls and strike unarmed men. You slaughtered my Father as surely as you aided in the slaughter of Fagus.'

'You would do no differently. I have seen your tactics.'

'I do not share bread in two camps. Show me the honour in that?'

'There is no honour in war.'

Acer was there for the taking. A sorry sight indeed to think he could wheedle out of his predicament; to think he could call upon favours when there were none to give. Quercus had no more patience to pretend otherwise and let rip with a flush of hate. Now Acer lay in a heap, his neck broken, his terrified eyes left with the vision of a man that had more than a cause written on his face.

On his steed, a warrior advanced. 'Cedrus has fled. We cannot find him.'

'What is our position?' Quercus swung himself into the saddle.

'Our brothers have gone to aid others. Do we follow?'

There was no question about it.

Within minutes Quercus was deep in the element of rain, a welcoming pour of protection. Afar, smouldering fires extinguished. Some homes had burnt to the ground, some left standing with their outer walls, some saved by the hour. Ahead, the sounds of clashing steel and clamour of war cries. These were the extremists of Acer's men. Quercus changed tactics, flicked his wrist, the whip now steel ran a man through. A spear flew overhead. It was quickly followed by another. He leaned against the neck of Shadow, willing it on, cutting and thrusting. They seemed to be coming from nowhere. Behind, another and so it went on, death and eternity, plunging into the chaos of the falling and the flailing while the rain soaked men and blood.

And the battle wore on till the light of a new dawn that showed the extent of the mayhem, the colour, the shape, the way it all joined into one another, capturing an architectural blunder, trying to get the correct perspectives and elevations under a sky that showed no mercy. Daylily Port was no longer a pretty and picturesque place. It had become a war zone, a terrible site, hell and damnation by the killing dogs of the night.

The vessels have broken through!

Beneath his exhausted breath, Quercus dismounted and raced to the harbour wall, the barrier broken. On deck were black robes, so thick in number they were barely distinguishable, cloaked in the same kind of animated state. He looked back, his eyes resting on the weary. He too was weary.

'Look!' A voice bellowed. 'It is Cedrus!'

There was no mistaking the stature, perched on the forward section in the leading vessel, his hair stuck fast to his face, his silk red band crossing his chest. Even in the curtain of rain one could see the outline.

'He will not fall for our tricks this time, Quercus.'

'Indeed not, Fraxinus. We must hold our positions here. Take them as they disembark and pray to Hortus the rain continues.'

'But the harbour is wide and generous. And we have too few.'

Give us strength, Quercus mouthed then closed his eyes to think he had wanted to make a difference, and now it made no difference, reminiscent of former days. Where Acer's men had failed, they would succeed. Is this how it must end?

At the very moment of disbursement, a sudden explosion blurted the air. A prodigious sheet of flame shot skywards, taking swathes of black robes to their end. There was barely an interval before the rushing wind of displaced rain and air, and then the cataclysmic roar. The debris which shot upwards, had no time to fall before another then another and then another, a constant detonation bursting upon the enemy's seams, cascading in a brilliant waterfall down the sides of the port. Steeds drew their hooves in the air, dismounting men, fearful of its merciless sounds. Incinerated wreckage kept leaping upwards, hung high as it could manage among shrouds of smoke and sickly sweet smell of charred flesh. The whole harbour was engulfed in a blazing début. Parts collided with masts and sails, with cloth and wood, wave upon wave, endlessly unravelling the threat until the harbour itself was a glittering carpet of timbers. Nearby there were some muted cheers.

The noise had subsided to a crackling hush of burning wreckage, spitting and spewing out cinders. Nervous men peered over the rampart, spellbound. The sight was incredulous, a dying, disintegrating netherworld. Skittering movements of burning debris, impossible to differentiate, mutilated and charred extremities floating, black blood spilling like oil as though life still existed somewhere in their cells. Limbs beat among the wreckage, bodies kicked and twisted, faces rose and sank. Gone in minutes were the aspects of five vessels and yet, still, men stood in a breathless pause of disbelief, unconsciously aware the rain had stopped, replaced by the choking breath of smoking decay.

Quercus jumped on the harbour wall. His vision limited. Confused, he blinked, wiping his streaming eyes. There, masked in the smoke an outsized shadow cutting flotsam, pushing forward through the hellish nightmare, scarcely noticeable until it blocked the smouldering daylight with its huge white sails. It was conceivable he forecast another skirmish yet seconds later his musings changed when a three square rigged masted frigate emerged with figures on the apex of the bow frantically waving, their shouts inaudible.

Jubaea looked on. 'My brother, why is the vessel still in motion?'

'Methinks Nina is at the helm.' Quercus leapt for his life. He had sensed she was coming in too fast and without him realizing, his voice had grown louder, more impassioned directed at men who remained mind-numbingly on the harbour wall.

It was merely a matter of judgement, a different approach. The jutting bowsprit rammed through a window above the baker's shop then the wall corrupted, a confluent impact, the head held in the jaws of masonry.

'What did I tell you?' Michael angered. 'Turn to port, not go into port!'

'I couldn't see a damn thing!' Nina retorted.

'We're bloody stuck in the rampart!'

'Oh poo bear, it's only a few blocks. No harm done.'

'By the way, I lied. Quercus isn't our grandfather.' The arc of her eyebrow rose no more than a millimetre. 'You had to cry to protect our brothers.'

'Look at me!' She yelled, slapping his shoulder. 'My eyes are like ink blots!' She pointed to her foot. 'My toe is twice its size!' Then she pointed to her hair. 'This! What am I supposed to do with this?'

'You offered to help!'

'I thought my life had come to an end!'

There ensured the customary exchange of heated words but what a beauty, what a steal. Sea Winger was a fifth rate frigate, was one of the Navy's glamour ships with their main armament on a single gundeck, searching out enemy merchant ships. This one carried 24 twenty-eight-pounder guns and could accommodate a crew of about 150.

At a loss what to do, Nina turned to leave and bumped into Quercus. All of the last few months trapped in the bottleneck of this moment. She held up her finger. 'Say one word and your dead meat!'

Quercus shot back, watching her hobbling gait. 'What have you done to Nina?'

Black-faced Michael handed over a can of beer. 'Have I been put through the wringer. As soon as I told her, she went berserk, the whole sky went berserk so I took her mind off things and ordered her to help load the cannons but she forgot the bloody gun recoiled and then we were short of fuses. Pussy refused to cut her hair, so I got Nina to cut hers.'

For now there were just a few lines, vaguely etched and erased and re-etched, between their scattering sentences as they wandered over the various decks of an early nineteenth century frigate, a marvellous steal, even Nelson would have been jealous. Michael spoke so proudly of his sister's achievements although he never had an opportunity to tell her, and he also spoke of the Handsome Thief who mustered men to aid in his cause. Some thought them brash, impetuous but others believed them adventurers without principle.

'What is his price?' Quercus asked.

'I promised him this vessel. I needed them, Quercus. It would have been impossible to do it on my own. There was no problem in stealing her. Perry said he just slipped the lines and silently drifted until he could raise the foremast to give him a bit of wind. As soon he got through the gates he had to drop sail in case he was spotted. The problem came when Nina lit up the sky.' He parked himself on one of the ship's cannons. He too was weary. 'We can clear these out, no problem. All weaponry dismantled, pity though, they're part of a brilliant frigate. Boy, does she respond to the helm.'

'We have need of this vessel.' Quercus walked on, counting the number, twelve aside. 'What is the range of these monsters?'

'Might get a thousand yards on a good day, why?'

'Strange how we use the feminine to describe a ship.'

'Are you going to tell me why or is it another secret?'

'No secret, my brother. We must advance as quickly as possible to get to the breeding ground of the black robes. Did you not heed Sage when she said the self-seeding will emerge in a random way?'

Michael caught up. 'Can we at least take a break? There are wounded men who need…'

'My brother, we have our own surgeons.' Quercus strode out on deck and looked into the streets, the smoke wafting over his head. 'How did you make Nina cry so angrily?'

'I told her you were our grandfather.'

Quercus remained blank. 'Did Sage inform you of this?'

'No, it was a joke. News of your death wouldn't have worked because she has been expecting the worse, sort of building up a resistance ready to handle it. But let's be honest here, your job isn't over and Nina's been put through enough.' It was evident from his manner that he had something further to add, so Quercus stood quietly, the look of intense interest still on his face. 'You saw what happened with Ilex, and the baby, and now look at her. She's a bloody mess.'

'Do I take it you would prefer me to leave Nina here?'

'Hell yes, that's exactly what I'm saying. Can you tell me categorically this guy you're after is dead? After all, he's supposed to be immortal.'

Quercus gave an understanding nod. 'It is told by Sage, Cedrus dies by the whip of Hortus. Yet how can a man survive such a holocaust?'

'It seems to me this bloke has certain attributes. Now if he's still alive, the chances are he would be anxious to gather an army and the only army he has left is where you want to go. She will want to come, you know that. Make her stay here while we go traipsing for these pods.'

There was an awkward pause. Quercus thought of what he could offer her. No guarantees, only a few hours of his skin pressed against hers. 'One cannot choose whom we love.'

'As I understand it, you never gave her a choice when you dipped your wick.'

'If my wick, as you so impolitely refer had not been dipped, the prophecy would be on the other side of the gates and my men slaughtered.'

'So now you have an opportunity to make good.'

Quercus puffed out his cheeks and strode on, destination Harbour Winery. 'She will not be easy to convince, and to convince I may have to lie and to lie is abhorrent.'

'Look, you lied to those blokes when you promised them freedom.'

'I did not lie.' He smiled. 'I gave them freedom. It is not my jurisdiction to show them how to swim at length.'

'Still, it was a crafty move. Like that heart business. I bet you swapped it for a piece of raw meat.'

Quercus halted. 'Your imagination is as vivid as Nina's.' He made his point and carried on. 'What do you propose?'

'Give her something she would enjoy, something she can get her teeth into. By the way, where are we going?'

Among the crafted oak tables and benches laced with the spills of beer, Quercus stepped into the assembled. The news had provoked consternation, was bound to.

'The prophecy came true.' Quercus radiated calm and authority. 'Within the bed of our seas she rose from the mist, her wings pure white, her breast sapphire and her presence offered protection. Sage forecast such a coming.'

'The prophecy fulfilled, the vessel must return through the gates.' More weasel words from a Council Member.

'No!' Quercus demanded. 'The vessel must stay to take me to the seeding ground of the black robes. Every trace must be obliterated if we are to be free in our thoughts.' He laid a hand on Michael. 'This man has cared for our wounded, has shown great courage and fortitude, brought forth a weapon that saved us this day. You have closed your hearts for long enough. Open them now to what you know.' He ambled among them, the unsure and the frightened. 'In his world he speaks against such weapons yet he used one to aid in our cause. He did not know our ways, so we must look upon this as part of our destiny. We must not be afraid of the vessel which holds weight in these waters, instead be afraid of the users.' He pointed to the Thief. 'Only one who owes allegiance to himself would argue otherwise. The vessel was promised and the promise kept, not before I locate the seeding ground and the vessel stripped of its weaponry.'

'Where is this Nina of the Atlantic, why is she not here if they are as one?'

'She hides in shame of her appearance. Nina gave her hair freely to light the fuse.'

They were mumblings. Michael was curious. 'Is that important?'

'For certain it is, my brother. Women cherish their hair, worn proudly like peacock feathers. Length establishes strength as well as fertility.'

'Crikey, I never knew that. I was a bit sharp with Pussy.'

Quercus looked into the room. 'Tonight we shall open the doors to the home of Hortus and feast on our good fortune, hear tales by the faithful, those who journeyed through hell and back. Men with firm sea legs will accompany me to the other continent.' His gaze held on the Thief. 'Will you join our expedition?'

'It is not my war.'

'Then my point is proven.'

After the Council Meeting, there was an element of disquiet about Sea Winger that traced its bows into the harbour wall. It drew quite an interest where many climbed on board to witness the kind of weapons they feared the most, though conservatively speaking they had no concept of what twenty-first century England could offer.

It was a strange sort of day, a day that promised change, the kind of freedom spoken in whispers on the wind. For a thousand years they had been slowly subjected to the impulses of Cedrus, and for a thousand years they spoke of a forgotten legacy given by Hortus.

Though the streets were well lit with torches and lamps, the dirt roads led away into darkness, the port hung like a heavy black coat. The palace was a shadowy hump which glowed dimly in the pleasantries happening within. It was here that Michael and Nina made their first debut, were treated more like avenging angels than menacing outsiders. Michael was garbed in the customary clothing of white pantaloons and white billowy sleeves, a sapphire sash to his waist and took to it well, even the boots made him feel like a highway robber. He had enjoyed stealing Sea Winger mainly because Smithe-Jones was a pop-belly pompous idiot with a lot of cash.

Quercus was searching. 'Jubaea, have you seen Nina?'

'I have yet to see Juglans. Perhaps he has gone to supervise the loading.'

Michael sidled up. 'Hell, this place is full of Pussies. I can't see mine anywhere.'

Jubaea smiled. 'Pussy, by that I take it to mean Salix Caprea who cracked a jar over the captain's head?'

'Yes, have you seen her?'

'No, have you seen Nina?'

'Yes, she's easy to find. Did you see her?'

Quercus irritated. 'Jubaea would not ask if we had. I need to see her before we depart.'

'Same here, I need to see Pussy. Last time I saw Nina, she was talking to Fraxinus.'

Each candle suspended a ball of light, a luminous fragile glow, which swelled and contracted to the spluttering wick or leaned to the moving air. Against the bright swathes of silk, Nina hung a distance from the candlelight like a sleeping beauty in a simple black gown. Her hair was trimmed to a short back and sides with a heavy fringe but even so, there was something strangely different. She stood among the tall, her hand to the hollow of her aching back, curving her face upwards to Fraxinus. Then she had become aware of Quercus, observed his oncoming.

'You are a vision of night and day in this light, Nina.'

'You look pretty smart yourself. Fraxinus was telling me we are going to seek out the pods, how exciting. Do we have to leave tonight? Can we go in the morning?'

'My brother, may I borrow Nina?' He coaxed her from Fraxinus, anxious to convey his thoughts. 'Nina, I wish to discuss-'

'Oh, Quirky,' she interjected. 'I'm ever so sorry. I never meant to be mean with you this morning but I was hardly a sight for sore eyes. What do you think to me now?' She gave a twirl. 'I can fit in. Unfortunately, there are only ball gowns, not very suitable for day wear, especially for a sea voyage but I can take one for the evening while we tell stories.'

Away from the shadows, further into the candlelight where her face lit up, Quercus noticed the difference. Her eyes, they had turned liked Michael's and danced with a spirit independent of breeding.

'Nina, your eyes are wondrous, a beautiful sapphire.'

'Are they?'

'Can you see beyond, like Michaelmas?'

She shook her head. 'I never noticed anything when I dressed.'

'We must talk, somewhere private.'

'Let me show you a room full of dresses,' she said grabbing his hand.

'No, let me show you a room full of pictures.'

He led her through a sprawling, lavishly furnished edifice where rooms had no ending, where whispers would echo into loud voices and where walls created a voluptuous gloom, excessive opulence by obsessive nurturing of wealth. And it set Quercus predictably lonely, reminiscing of his home near the wooded clad hills. Proceeding down the grand marble staircase, he continued popping his head round doors until he found what he was looking for. Here, in a windowless chamber, apparitions rose, striking postures of shadows.

'These are his creations,' Quercus said, holding a candle to the wall.

'Golly!' Nina exclaimed. 'They are dreadful. Does he actually practice this?'

'He has unrestrained libidinous cravings.' He coaxed her to the other wall. 'This is my interest. Betula from the North told me many flowers had been painted in a circle revealing new species.' He ran the light over one. 'He does not exaggerate. This flower is exquisite.'

'Quirky, do you think they really exist?'

'I do hope so, Nina. When all is done, we shall seek out these new species. I shall go down in the history books as a great botanist.'

'Surely you're already there as a great warrior.'

He smiled, going on to the next. 'Perhaps one of these flowers has been discovered by Cedrus. Lady Tilia spoke of a potion to restore damaged skin.'

'Wouldn't that be something? If you did find it, do you know you would be the richest man in the world next door?' She paused for a moment then said, 'Is Cedrus a botanist?'

'Cedrus is a troglodyte. Look around you. Does it appear he loves flowers? He loves himself and his frescos, I think. If such flowers do exist, they exist for a reason. Why keep a wall of beauty against a wall of shame?'

'Do you think this has something to do with the Book of Hortus?'

'I do not know but most certainly they are exquisitely painted.' He bent down and pointed. 'Look here, my Nina. See the tendrils defined in detail.'

'Do you think there is one to make your hair grow faster?'

The door creaked open to the weight of a man, the light of a lantern swinging in behind. Michael's face appeared, disturbing in the glow. 'What are you doing with my sister?'

'Michael!' Nina voiced sharply. 'You really must change your attitude. Sex is always on your mind.'

'I say,' he said coming further into the room. 'Cedrus has certainly got some imagination. Not sure about goats…sheep, yes, but not goats.'

She waved a hand in front of him. 'Halloo, these pictures are not for public viewing. These are far better.'

He pecked her on the cheek. 'We have to go.'

Quercus irritated. 'I have yet to inform her.'

'Then be quick about it.' Michael walked off.

Such complications. 'Nina, I cannot allow you to come with us.'

'Why not?'

'It is far too dangerous, a place where women cannot go.' He saw that look again, a sorrowful face and lifted her chin. 'You are needed here.'

'To do what?'

'Why, paint the wall, of course. Such pictures must be obliterated. Think of it as your destiny.'

'My destiny,' she murmured.

'Destiny, Nina. You are as much mine as I am yours.'

'You think so?'

He took her hand and walked on. 'Leave the pretty flowers. And organize a window to be created in the room so we may look upon them in the light.'

'Quirky, I'm not a builder, I'm a librarian.'

'I shall ask Betula to gather some men and help you.' He would also ask them to protect her. 'Keep to the palace, do not wander. We cannot be certain of our enemy.'

'So you think I might be abducted?'

It was a disturbing thought, a grimly evolving one. 'We must all take precautions.'

'All the more reason I should come with you.'

He opened his mouth to speak then closed it, trapped in his own argument. She showed no trace of fear, no trace of sadness. Slowly, he ran his fingers through her deep fringe, imagined she could hear the pounding lies across his chest.

'Here you go.' Michael galvanized him into action, thrusting the reins of Shadow into his hand. 'No wandering, sis and-'

'Yes, yes, keep to the palace. Quirky, do you want your key?'

Quercus mounted, shook his head and spurned Shadow on. Keeping promises were hard, telling lies, even harder. On the way to the port, he pulled up the reins and turned in the saddle looking at flattened woodlands where single bare trees stuck uselessly out of the desolate soil like dead men's stiffened arms jabbed accusingly at the sky.

'What I took before in kindness, I will take forever in revenge.'

'Meaning what?' Michael asked.

'My Father planted those trees. It will be a number of years before the soil heals for replanting.'

'You think you've got problems. Did you see our garden? It's like a damn jungle.'

Aiming their steeds towards Fraxinus, Juglans and Jubaea who were among a thinning crowd of workers, they were greeted with a bellow of approval.

'Good news, Quercus,' Jubaea said. 'The vessel was unharmed; we can sail tonight.'

'And where are we going exactly?' Michael asked Quercus.

'A place called Abies Bay on the northwest coast of Coniferous land. It is a sheltered area among tall snowy mountains…rather like the French Alps, this is called Abies Alps.'

'We have a prisoner in the hold,' Fraxinus said. 'One I think will be of interest.'

Quercus and Michael followed in their footsteps two decks below, and there, to their surprise was a surviving black robe held in chains behind bars. They studied him as he rushed them, admiring his focus, his nerve, his single-minded commitment to the kill.

'Take a closer look, my brother.' Fraxinus held up a lantern. 'What do you see that is different?'

'There is something impregnated into his chest.'

'My brother, other black robes did not have this.'

Michael clicked his fingers. 'Of course, what an idiot…he's a unit commander. Orders from headquarters get relayed to him then he relays the orders to the fighters. That would probably explain why they remain static. They don't budge an inch unless this guy tells them to, which means he has probably got more nuance.' Poised to move inside and condemn the prisoner, Michael held Juglans at bay. 'He might be useful. If we can find out how to control him, he can lead us to others.'

'We have a bitch on board. She has a good nose.'

'I hope it's a husky because it's going to be bloody cold. I don't suppose you have ski suits by any chance?' Michael walked on, more like talking to himself. 'You know I am really getting to like this world. Not sure about the candles but we could rig up some windmills to give us electricity…'

'Perhaps he needs a lesson in comfort,' Quercus said with others agreeing. 'We should let him sleep on deck with the wolf.'

AUTUMN CHAPTERS

As summer fades, the greenery starts to flare into the fiery colours of autumn. The intensity of the colours and their duration depend upon the weather.

ABIES ALPS

Quercus looked out upon the snowy peaks, the rough and dense growth of forests and the huge dramatic spaces beneath where it required a cavalier attitude towards time and distance. The anchor dropped.

'What do you think? Do you think he's here?'

'There is no certainty, Michaelmas, apart from one. The breeding ground is near. I feel it as surely as I feel the wind in my hair. We shall start in the morning. You will stay here and I shall lead the assault.'

'Waugh! What's the point of traipsing up a mountain when you have these cannons?'

'Do not get carried away with a gung-ho attitude. This is the road to damnation. The prophecy complete, we fight our way.'

Quercus walked off, closing his ears to the last of Michael's protests *but they're bloody plants, not men!* By the very nature of their different trades and attitude, there would always be a difference of opinion, especially on board a vessel like Sea Winger.

'What are you thinking, my man?' Michael said in the hold. He lifted the lantern to gauge how the light may affect this abomination. 'Can you understand my words? 'The silent wood, smelling of oil, held up a grainy hand to the lantern. The answer had been found.

Later that evening, Michael was languishing against the main mast on the quarter deck eating fruit, surrounded by men and wolf. He was quiet, weighing up moods. All were toughened, single minded warriors who kept their feelings deep rooted. They never elaborated upon their homes or their wives or their lovers but sometimes about their children, and how they would grow to follow by example. And there, he had to agree with Nina, men on the other side had become fragile, self-reliant on technology, growing weaker in body and feeble in mind. He studied Juglans in his stately habit with walnut eyes and yellow spiky hair, how he held himself proud even in the most relaxed position. Then he viewed Jubaea, a man with palm green eyes who would speak less but take everything in while he toyed with his forked moustache. But there was no mistaking Fraxinus with a craggy weathered face and hard jutting jaw. It was possible this old warrior could hold his own with Quercus, a tie-breaker if they were ever to cross swords. However, if one had to place bets, Michael would place them on Quercus. Most assuredly he was a man that even stood out from his own kind. Everything about him promoted confidence, the capacity to make and take chances, pushing forward with intelligent resolution.

During Michael's ruminations, his ears pricked up when he heard his name. Quercus could not resist the opportunity to promote his tale and directed his last remark at him. 'Was it not a head lock, my brother?'

'I was in the land of nod. I had a bad night with Sonja and never got to bed until two in the morning. Awake, I seem to recall giving you a couple of black eyes.'

'I seem to recall my foot on your chest.'

'I was taking a breather.'

The men laughed.

Quercus stiffened. 'Perhaps I should try repeating this?'

Michael popped a grape in his mouth. 'You don't have to prove your worth in front of these men, Quercus. Look about you. Everyone is prepared to follow you right to the bitter end. You know your trouble; you have a death wish. Some old biddy tells you it's your destiny to rid an immortal man so you go through life with nothing else on your mind, expecting to die, expecting these men to die.'

'You insult me.'

'You insult your intelligence.' Michael goaded him further. 'See this ship. It can expel cannons faster than you can swing your whip. Up there, you're going to lead these men into another assault all because you have a hang up about weapons of mass destruction.'

'We have no need to promote such weaponry. The Elders saw the greedy thirst of men for greater armaments in your world so they could gain control of lands and shipping lanes. Now they sit on their laurels drinking their world dry of resources.'

'I seem to recall a couple of days ago these guns saved your sorry arse.' The tip of a knife rested hard against his throat. 'I see,' Michael wheezed, 'so there's no free speech anymore.'

Quercus laid a hand on the blade. 'Put it away, Jubaea. Let us hear what this daisy has to say before we throw him overboard.'

Michael had now gained their interest, motioned them to come closer, to heighten their curiosity, a mere charade to invoke their senses. 'Look, if destiny plays such an important part, then why are we here, on Sea Winger with me on it? Think about it. No-body gets hurt unless Quercus feels he wants a one on one with a tree bark.' He paused to their lenient smiles, looked about, sending his eyes beyond, playing a good part in the drama of suspense. 'All we have to do,' he said in a whisper, 'is to set wooden top loose. I have watched him. He has a pea brain but he's hungry for oil. They feed on it, were raised on it that's why they're so bloody tireless.'

Juglans spoke, his voice also down to a whisper. 'Does he tire now?'

'He needs a top up. If we let him think he's escaped, he will go to the oil refinery.'

'Where is this oil refinery?' Fraxinus was confused.

'I am speaking metaphorically. He will go straight to the breeding ground. That's where he was born and raised. That's where he'll go for food. There are probably thousands of these guys. After he's fed, his next instinct will be to communicate with others. Then the whole lot will come to us. We make up dummies on the shore. Let them think we're having a party. Puff the magic dragon.' He paused for a reaction but there was none. 'So what do you think, guys?'

Eyes rested on Quercus nodding slowly. 'He speaks a good plan, my brothers.'

'How can we be sure all will come?' Juglans asked Michael.

'Hey, that's how they operate. They're thick as two short planks. They're primed to attack not to run away. And afterwards, we can climb whatever we have to climb to see how their breeding ground works. If my assumption is correct, there is crude oil up there.'

Juglans pushed a beaker into his chest. 'We shall not be considered good warriors by Council but I will drink to your plan.'

Quercus smiled but, on the whole, there was not much to smile about. He was missing Nina's laughter and optimism, was anxious about treading new ground, and was also aware animals in this neck of the woods were not so inclined toward humans. And beyond all that he may fall into a trap laid by Cedrus. He eased himself back into the padded comfort of cushions and began to think idly of the unknown flowers painted on the wall in the windowless chamber. If they were new species, what was their significance? Failing that, why should they be there in the first place?

'What troubles you, Quercus?' Fraxinus asked.

'Flowers,' he replied and glanced at Juglans. 'You are a seed collector, my brother. Tell me if you have ever encountered a flower with red angled wing stems, the crowns banded white and deep purple, or perhaps one with heart shaped leaves and large funnel-shaped, sky blue flowers?'

'I recognise the first as a passiflora quadrangularis.'

'No, my friend, the wing stems were much larger and the flower had long tendrils.'

'Then I cannot say. Where did you see such flowers?'

'In a windowless chamber below the main hall. There is a large circular pattern of exquisitely painted species quite new to me. I find it hard to accept Cedrus would appreciate such beauty unless they hold some significance.'

'Perhaps these flowers grow on Coniferous land and do hold significance. Lady Tilia claimed she was given a potion to redeem her skin.'

'You may well be right. If this is so, I doubt if we shall ever see them.'

'Why not?' Michael asked.

Juglans explained. 'With exception of present circumstance, we do not encroach upon their continent, nor would we wish to. We are not welcome nor do we welcome them on ours. In point of reference, we do not wish to see a fir. The exception to the rule is the Juniperus Pirates. They step on our land to unload their cargo and quench their thirst at the Harbour Winery.'

'So no mixed couples,' Michael said, grinning at Quercus. After which there was a pause in the air before changing the subject slightly. 'I gather they don't have keys except for the Juniperus Pirates. If that's the case, how did Cedrus go through the gates without a key?'

'Cedrus has a key,' Quercus confirmed. 'It was because of this he was looked upon by his kind as an elected leader by Hortus. You show doubt in your face, Michaelmas.'

'I wake up each morning pinching myself. Is this all a dream? People living beyond anything I've ever known, wounds healing in double quick time, birds as messengers, wild animals strolling at ease, etcetera, etcetera. There must be some divine spirit to give Cedrus a key just to stir things up or perhaps another kind of intelligent direction. Take the gates, for instance. If you can only go through them with a key then that suggests the key has your own DNA fingerprint. But then that doesn't explain why I came through the gates without one. Nor does it explain why Nina came through with a different kind of key. By the way, what happened to that key?'

'I have it,' said Quercus. 'We are not poles apart, my brother. Just because we chose to respect Hortus does not mean we lack the curiosity of Hortus, her building blocks of life. Scientific exposition is not like reading a novel where events unfold in a simple linear fashion. We ask ourselves, how could something so extraordinary and so special emerge from lifeless slime? Indeed, what is the crucial component of things that endows them with life? When our scientific eyes burrowed below the surface of appearance and discovered the molecular basis of the web of life, we discovered the whole universe is life itself. And there is the difference between your thinking and ours.'

'Can you elaborate?' Michael asked.

'Consider this. Do we not share her elements in our body? As she is a free thinking spirit, so are we. When we feel pain, she feels pain. When we feel joy, she feels joy. It is no different for other life forms. They feel pain and joy. Sometimes we must feel pain in order to appreciate joy. To assume there is divine intervention is like suggesting Hortus is manufactured as a stage for actors to play their part. Why not accept we are at one with Hortus, we are her intelligence. It is free thinking radicals choosing their direction in the evolutionary path of life. Cedrus and his kind were choosing theirs and over time the evolutionary path provided their wishes. As to your curiosity about the gates, then your assumption is correct. Our DNA is imprinted on the key. Why both came through the gates without a key, including an unborn, we can speculate scientifically for months and return to the simplest answer. It is us choosing to open the gates for assistance. There was no magical sea bird but your capacity to end our sorrowful days. There was no magical rain from an angel but Nina's capacity to reach out and be at one with Hortus. When you can separate the difference between black and white, you will come out of your grey area and realize it is life itself pruning and cutting the evolutionary path, planting and seeding with their thoughts and actions, not a magic wand orchestrated by divine intervention.'

'We see the degree of abstraction represented by Quercus neatly captures the empirical laws that portray two different aspects of our world.' Juglans said. 'Life's energy and requirements…in the latter, my present requirement is sleep.'

That night, one hundred men slept on deck. Occasionally the faint proximity of howling wolves could be heard, the glimmer of shaded stars and a cool confession that autumn had finally arrived. For Quercus, he was under no illusion to the immense and urgent undertaking. At best he would drive his weapon into the heart of Cedrus. At worst he would eradicate every last drop of black blood.

In dawn's early light the plan was set in motion. The crew swam into Abies Bay, made out they were camping on the sands then on the command of a flag, the black robe was placed in a rowing gig with two other men. Michael was looking through his binoculars. It was habit rather than visual aid. The gig heaved in a swell, tipped over, throwing them into the sea. Deliberate shouts and splashing as though drowning, enough theatricals to allow the black robe to submerge and disappear unhindered.

'He's fallen for it.' Michael passed the binoculars to Quercus. 'Best guess he's swimming a little to the west.'

Quercus adjusted his sighting until he caught a wooden body clambering into the undergrowth. 'You are right, my brother. We must allow him time to gather our moves before we set the stage.' He brought the binoculars down to his chest. 'Have you calculated distance and trajectory?'

Michael shook his head. 'You sound like a naval captain. Go on, be honest and tell me if you're not enjoying this, just a little bit.'

Quercus offered his gritted-teeth smile. There was a certain symmetry to it all, a logic.

Preparations were rapid when the signal was given. Men threw off their clothes, making up dummies to create a scene reminiscent of those days on the crescent shaped open-necked forest, so life-like it even fooled the critical eye. Upon their return, Michael gave the order to hoist foresail and took Sea Winger into deeper waters so it could negotiate its position for a quick turnaround. He radiated personal commitment and enthusiasm, charging the spirits of those he would lead, personally supervising the buoying of waters, seeking the views of others as he measured the facts of the tactical situation. The distance calculated, less than half mile to target, better still quarter mile for full impact. Men were readying the cannons. The game was afoot where the waiting brought its own sounds.

'Did you ever think about using the gates to share your knowledge?' Michael asked.

Quercus nodded. 'Many never returned. It was later discovered they were tortured, thrown to the lions or crucified. Some of our women were raped. Time showed your world digressed.' He sighed. 'A thousand years has given Cedrus the opportunity to corrupt good minds. He demands lavish things and in turn uses the glitter of gold and power to drain the strength of Council Members. We do not require the theft of unnecessary incidentals, only that which avoids commerce and industry.'

'Do you have any industries?'

'We use false light when there is need to enjoy night. Mostly we go to sleep in the dark and wake to ancient sunlight. There is no rush, far better to steal from the gates so we all benefit.'

'So I take it the answer is no?'

'My brother, do not make the mistake our world would fall apart if the gates should seal. We have true craftsmen among us.' Quercus motioned with his head. 'Jubaea can craft a saddle greater than any machinery. Fraxinus can mould wood to any angle without reference to drawings. Juglans can seed an acre of land and be certain to bring healthy food to our table. Such crafts were once abundant in your world. They are now forgotten, replaced by steel and fumes, chemicals and acids.'

'See, the trouble is we have a lot of people on our planet.'

'You have a lot of people with limited resources on your planet.'

'We can hardly cull the population, can we?'

'Instead you increase the population.' Quercus made a valid argument. 'I read the miracle cures by genetic engineering. In the seeking to cure one problem, you make two more.'

'Hell, Quercus, we are not built like you.'

'You are not built like us because you ignore Hortus. Your bodies have grown weak in the time she has given you, your minds argue over petty differences. Nina spoke of different men, the acceptance of human rights so you allow the guilty to suppress the innocent. You accept this as you would accept a loaf of bread from a baker's shop. Here, we would feed stale bread to our chickens.' Quercus picked up the binoculars. 'My words may seem harsh yet here we truly respect our brothers and sisters.'

'So are you saying no-one commits any crimes?'

'The Keeper turned wrong-doers into trees and gave the axe to the victim. Since your world is unable to do the same, I would have thought a gun more appropriate.'

'So this Keeper, where did he get the faculty to be immortal and have unusual gifts?'

'The Book no doubt will reveal this.'

'I see.'

'What do you see?'

'Well, since nobody has read this Book, nobody really knows what's in it. Do you know how Hortus chose its Keeper?'

Quercus was unable to answer. He looked through the binoculars again and saw movement. 'I believe they have learnt our ways.'

Michael followed his line of sight. 'Hell, have we got a big pie to bake.' No time for discussion. 'Hoist mainsail and prepare to come about!'

A thick black wave moved slowly, had learnt new tactical measures gained from their last encounters on the west shores of Deciduous land. They were spreading out, circling the perimeter of the bay where the vegetation was at its thickest making sure there would be no escape. It was magical yet frightening.

Michael swung the helm hard to starboard. Sea Winger picked up wind in full sails, and rolled, ready to train guns on the shore. Then in a maelstrom, the black robes poured through wielding their axes, rushing at dummies. Their education was still in working progress.

Hold your wind and hold your water! Fire one!

There was a droning sound then the deeper crump of explosion swelled upon impact. The target shot in the air, an ignited surge. No time for delay. No time to watch a moment of glory. The next followed just as succinctly, precise intervals, starboard guns fired, one after the other, crashing, smashing, embedding and hitting gunpowder barrels. The vessel shook from a continuous barrage, toughened by its overlapping and tarred planking. Above the heads of men, all around, the solid and consuming noise of thudding, whistling and explosion. The work-gangs toiled until the ship moved out of range. Sea Winger made a hard about turn to portside, throwing the amateur sea legs off guard.

Steady, steady, steady…fire one!

Strange that Michael had transmuted into a sea lord, stranger still Quercus felt the adrenalin rush of kills without whip or sword. He now understood the actions of sails in times of stress, how the wind was employed for the purpose of war, to out-manoeuvre and train the weaponry on the target. It was another curve in his learning cycle. By the time Sea Winger finished invalidating nature, nothing was left except scorched sand and black extremities.

'I still have the fight in me, Michaelmas.' Fraxinus felt the limp bicep, no competition. 'Do you think yours will grow by yelling out commands?'

Michael made a fist to pump more blood into his arm. 'Now feel it. You don't get that from taking out tonsils. I got that from working out in the gym.'

Fraxinus flexed his, twice the size. 'Do you see this? I got that from wrestling with bears.'

Camaraderie heightened his spirits. 'I say, Quercus, can I have a whip?'

Now he wants a whip. 'Do you know how to handle one?'

'Show me.'

'Keep your eye on the target, throw as if throwing the handle but allow the whip to ripple. Fraxinus, place a bottle on the rail.'

For Michael, the whip felt heavier than anticipated. He flicked it a few times to get a feel of its length before sending his arm wide back to unleash an almighty crack. It recoiled and shot out of his hand, landing at Jubaea's feet. The men laughed.

'What about a sword?' Michael asked.

'My brother, if you cannot wield a whip, you cannot wield a sword.'

Fraxinus brought out his dagger, indicated its advantages. In one fluid action, it coursed a straight line and clipped Jubaea's ear before impaling wood.

Michael pointed to Fraxinus. 'He did it!'

Jubaea's eyes turned dark, smearing the blood on his fingers. 'Was your aim off, my brother, or was I an intended victim?'

'My apologies,' Fraxinus said. 'Your gait was as quick as my throw.'

'Perhaps it should be me to teach Michaelmas how to throw a knife?'

'Look guys, I think I better stick to something else. I can put a plaster on that.'

Quercus roared with laughter. 'Michaelmas, climb a tree, it will be safer for my men.'

In the broken husk of the bay, one hundred naked warriors were emerging from the sea, each one shaking themselves down, their eyes peering bloodshot and lips slightly blue. It was the sharp end of their journey. The rowing gigs carried their weapons and clothing.

Quercus picked out two bundles of white and green heavy linens, throwing one to Michael. Aware he was being observed, he slipped on green pantaloons, tucked the hems into the top of his high boots then slipped a green long-sleeved vest over his head. Over that he wore a white robe falling short to his knees. But he smiled when it came to making the head-dress. Michael was having some difficulty.

'My brother, allow me. It goes round like so, from side to side once and round again then we go under the chin and tuck the end in, like so.' He stood back. 'Now you are a pumpkin without a weapon.'

Men chortled. Their tanned, strong featured faces against white made an impressive sight, a cross between a Turkish sheik and a Sultan.

As they picked their way across charred sands, Michael asked Quercus, 'Don't you ever wear underpants?'

'What is the need?'

'It gives support to your testis.'

'The only support a man needs is a woman's hand.'

In minutes they were indistinct shapes, pressing onwards and upwards into a sprawling blaze of greenery. Steeped in timber lore, here was another side to Coniferous land, the magic of the magnificent conifers growing on the borders of the bay. The beauty of this sloping forest was enhanced by clear streams and pretty cascades, and by a wealth of wildflowers refusing to die in the shade. Further on, the vividly coloured rocks bit deeply by the action of freezing rivers, forming splendid gorges where intensely cold water gathered in pools and where surprisingly lush vegetation flourished. Even more luxuriant plants were a feature, nourishing the shrubbery of a relict rainforest. But within two hours it began to change. They met a carpet of alpine wildflowers, unrolled where the snow retreated. It formed a puzzling and frustrating barrier to the dazzling snowy mountains, the highest peaks and the most extensive snowfields.

Michael gazed up, his mouth open, his breath a plume in the ether, his eyes squinting. 'I have never climbed a mountain let alone tackled anything like this.'

'And you think the black robes can?'

'Not really, they look too clumsy.'

'Then you have it in one.' Quercus pointed. 'The wolf sends us to the ridge. There we will find our answer.'

Quercus moved forward, his men pulling softly behind as they executed a hazardous trail over steep rocks towards a gulch. It was a steady slow pace until they came upon an opening, cavernous within. They kept their bodies low, looking in all directions, going deeper, growing more perilous and late.

Wolf growled. Everyone froze. In the distance, shapes, shadows of dark outlines. It was merely a few steps to the killing zone. Wolf reached it first, seized an arm, its jaws locking deep, pulling with the effort until the arm detached. Elsewhere, the attack came, thick and fast, cut and thrust, the killing dogs had grown accustomed to their enemy's ways. One by one, they scythed them down, transformed them into shapeless scraps. Here was confirmation of stunted growth, stumps for their feet and hands, their outer shells hardly weathered and their heads like rotten melons. They just kept coming, timely falls and trips by their own clumsiness, content to be hacked in pieces. This was no battle; this was easy pickings.

Michael called out. 'Hey, chaps come and look at this!'

Their rushing footsteps echoed in the hollowness and there, before them a pool of black liquid with spent pods in abundance, huge swathes dotted along ledges, some yet to hatch.

'This is crude oil. I think it's the kind we refine for generators.' Michael lifted a sickly, sticky tube, followed it to the rim of the basin. 'Okay, I see how it's done. This is the feed line with independent branches directed to each pod. There's some sort of mixture in the pod, perhaps you might know what it is?'

Quercus approached, dipped his finger into slime then sniffed. He shook his head. 'I am at a loss. Where does this heat come from?'

'We are actually over a sleeping volcano. I suggest we torch the lot.'

'Oil is usually found in the ground. Why does it lay here in the basin?'

'Leftovers, Quercus. I reckon on the last eruption, the oil kept within the linings of fissures and seeped into the basin when the volcano settled down. There is not much of it left. You have to consider this might not be the only place for a breeding ground. If all you need is crude oil and heat plus that mixture then you have the perfect recipe.'

Quercus took the torch out of Jubaea's hand and picked his way through the minefield of pods. Men pulled back when the first one was lit. Some pods crackled, some burst open. It soon became a cauldron of burning pitch. At the last moment, he side-stepped and threw the torch into the basin. The whole cavernous region instantly came alive. He paused and ducked at the scudding rush of air, equally lethal. Flames danced around him, acrid smoke filled his lungs, searing his eyes. His focus was on destruction.

Now, where the snow retreated, they watched and bore passive witness to the inevitability of total obliteration. It did not matter if there were any more stragglers, their food supply cut off, their home destroyed.

Michael fell into step beside Quercus. 'So where's Cedrus? Escaped again or dead?'

Beyond reach. 'You never speak of your father.'

'We never had much time with him. He was in the Navy serving as an officer when the Russians sunk his submarine. The Admiralty never admitted it, which left Mum in the lurch. Had they admitted it she would have received compensation. Anyway, Mum packed his photographs away. It was too painful to look at them. I take after Dad. He was a brilliant seaman, liked to take me sailing when he was on leave.'

'Why did you not follow in his footsteps?'

'I was tempted, no doubt about that. In reality, I prefer to save lives. My hobby was collecting frogs and dissecting them until Nina put one in the stew. Did you see her eyes? They changed colour like mine.'

'She is a far happier person.'

'Maybe so, but we're still classed as outsiders. Any chance of altering our agreement or do we have to return?'

'I have never contemplated otherwise, Michaelmas. This is where you both belong.'

Whilst other men talked idly, relaxed in their gait, Quercus was beginning to feel the release of strain, the days, the weeks and months of waging war. Now his mind was on a single kill, to be quick and artful, to judge the moment that would bring him victory without injury. But where was Cedrus? Was it possible Sea Winger's guns had obliterated his existence? Was it possible Cedrus survived and remained in Daylily? Or had the tyrant gone through the gates to get hold of a greater weapon?

'Michaelmas, what weapon is the greater in your world?'

'It has to be nuclear, nuclear warheads.'

'And a warhead, can it be easily stolen?'

'If he's gone through the gates to steal one of them, he'll need more than a band of pirates. Those things are rigged in guided missiles.'

Hue and cry broke out, the clamour of angry men coming into view on foot, their faces contorted in rage. Quercus held up his hand, a leader unmoved before a swathe of four hundred. 'Do not hinder our return journey, gentlemen.'

They were tall and strong and garbed in rich cloths with swords drawn. They were one of three kinds, Abies on Abies territory. Their hair and eyes shone dark forest green, their skins deeply tanned, their wrists covered in leather bands. One in particular wore a leather band round his head studded with diamonds and he spoke angrily in deep baritone.

'This is our land, our right to hinder your journey.' He pointed to the bellowing smoke. 'Your ship has gone the same way.'

'I very much doubt that.' Another voice, another kind worked his way through. It was the Handsome Thief. He flicked his finger at the man's nose. 'Sea Winger is mine.'

Abies smiled and returned the action. 'See how easily it bends.' He looked down at the point of a blade stuck at his ribs. 'You take sides, Handsome Thief.'

'I take precautions. Now run along and play cowboys somewhere else.'

They did, grumbling in their wake.

Quercus spoke. 'I am indebted to you. The fight would have cost many lives.'

'No need,' the Thief replied returning his dagger to its sheath. 'You should have kept a watch on my vessel.' He walked on signalling to his men. 'Make sure you leave it tidy.'

'My brother,' Jubaea said. 'That was remarkable.'

Quercus smiled looking on at the man who never looked back. 'Indeed, we have a strange alliance.'

'What's with the flicking of noses,' asked Michael.

Jubaea flicked Michael's. 'Keep your nose out of another's affair.'

ROSE PETALS

People were cheering, waving, their hearts jumping like seismographs, caught unawares in the time it took for the eye to see and the mind to understand Sea Winger was entering harbour.

For Quercus, everything was tipped into the centre of this moment remembering how different things looked before, the bloodied streets, the flotsam of black extremities and wreckage, the moment of departure leaving Nina behind.

On ground he kept his speech short. 'Not one man lost, not one man injured. The black robes are no more!' His statement true, he paused to their cheers then held up his hands. 'Rejoice in your freedom, open your hearts to the men who fought bravely and give them a fond farewell.'

'Is your quest at an end, Lord of the Oaks?' A man shouted from the crowd.

'My quest will finish when Cedrus lies at my feet.'

Their tones singed with excitement, Quercus, their hero thread through the well-wishers and proceeded to the stables. It was while he and Michael were saddling their horses, he became aware that the tension had returned to his shoulders.

'We have lost Nina,' Betula said, his face hung heavy. Trapped, his eyes went to the left and fell upon Michael. 'We do not know where she is.'

Quercus moved around Shadow. 'Did you see her leave?'

'We did not. We stood guard for a week and saw her well. She had visitors, many came to pay respects. We sent White Tails and riders to comb the settlements and still we have no word.'

His foot in the stirrup, Quercus spoke no more. The thudding hooves, the pounding equine muscularity pulled him on. He was scarce able to breath in the half-mile distance. At the palace steps, he fanned out with impatience, looking for clues. Here, conversation was subdued, he could see the beginnings of change, seating arrangements disturbed, a hardened paint brush stuck to a paint-lid, and altogether it spoke of sudden departure. Up another flight, the tale spoke the same. There was nothing. And if that was not enough, he did it all over again, just to be sure, just to be certain, looking in wardrobes and boot closets, just to be in no doubt.

'She would not have left.' Quercus was adamant.

Michael spoke angrily at Betula. 'Perhaps one of your men fell asleep.'

'You question my loyalty?'

'You were meant to keep an eye on her.'

'If you seek to lay blame, look to yourself.'

Michael turned with a flourish. 'He was the incompetent bastard left in charge!'

Quercus struck the first blow. Michael ducked on the second incoming, returning one in the gut. In this fashion they carried on knocking each other senseless in a windowless chamber where Cedrus once connived, where the secret panel blended seamlessly into the licentious frescos, and where on the opposite side of the room a different perspective. These were the pictures of petals and storks that were always there to be looked at.

It took four men to separate these raging bulls, their faces and knuckles grazed and their bodies weary and pummelled, their eyes full of sorrow. Now, upstairs in the grand hall with clearer minds, they stood side by side on the balcony sharing a bottle of rum, watching the dim remnants of light fade in the west.

'Do you ever change your clocks?'

'We change no locks.' Quercus dropped a consonant, sending his tongue over a swollen lip. 'Would Nina return through the gates?'

'Why would she? It makes no sense unless she wanted to collect some personal items.' Michael turned into the room. Four men were seated with begrudging respect, waiting for the next move. Betula looked on, his eyes fixed on the man who insulted him. 'I was out of order.' Michael went over. 'Nina keeps telling me I have a short fuse. Will you please accept my apologies, no harm done, I hope.'

The golden haired birch shook his hand. 'My brother, more harm done to your face than my pride.'

'Was there any time a man may have left his post, like taking a piss for instance?'

Betula shook his head. 'We piss on the spot.'

Michael corkscrewed to Quercus. 'I have to go through the gates to see if she's there. Maybe she recognized those flowers in our garden.'

Garden! His heart sank. 'Lady Syringa mentioned a secret garden.' He motioned to Betula. 'Dispatch your men in sections to scrutinize every wall in every chamber one level below. I will look down from the balconies with Michaelmas.'

'Hell, Quercus,' Michael said, rushing to keep up. 'Why didn't you mention this before?'

'It was a sorrowful time,' was all he would say.

The configuration and enormity of such an edifice required a cunning mind, as well as architectural knowledge of which they had none. Of course, it never helped in the fading light that soon transmuted to dark, a cruel and desperate exploration, too many chambers and not enough knowledge to limit the search.

As new dawn approached, Quercus and his men heard unusual footsteps, the tapping of metal and they turned to an approaching Michael, his hands behind his back, his face a picture of satisfaction.

'What is wrong with your boots?' Quercus asked.

'I pinned aluminium to the soles.' They instinctively laughed at such foolishness, a short-lived foolishness when considering the application, although untried, might just work. 'By my reckoning,' he continued, 'roots are unable to penetrate metal and if Cedrus is hanging about I would rather take precautions.'

'And why do you wear precaution when you cannot be turned.'

'Hey, remember what you said, we're in your world now. I had an idea. Come with me, chaps.'

Changed into outsized boots, no doubt from the palace wardrobes, five men followed Michael. Ahead, there was a stack of crates balancing on top of a cart so he could reach the rampart of a high wall that encompassed a seven acre plot.

Michael glared at the west façade where balconies grew like oversized platforms. 'Right, chaps,' he said. 'The sun rises in the east and sets in the west, so this invisible garden needs to get light on its plants, right? If we follow the arc of the sun as it travels due south there has to be a point when we might be able to see shadows, because shadows can form perspectives. Of course, the problem we have is to wait for the sun to take its course.'

'We do not have to wait,' Quercus said. 'Use your eyes.'

Michael was almost afraid to say why. 'I can't see through walls.'

'Have you not noticed your sight is greater than ours? You saw the black robes descending on the beach without the use of binoculars. Now use your eyes to see beyond the illusion.'

Out on the landward wall of the palace Michael walked the rampart, searching the balconies as though he was trying to gauge the trajectory of the sun at different times of the day. Amazed, he pointed. It seemed to them as though this balcony jutted like every other where underneath was part and parcel of the ground floor structure. At least it gave a reference point. It identified the windowless chamber.

Under lamps, hands swarmed, fingers worked across the frescos, not minding their space, trod on each other like birds in a hole, elbowed their ways without spite, all mumbling at once or all silent at once but never feeling overcrowded. Occasionally a cry or a gasp, a significant breath dying upon a false alarm but still they conceded or accepted parts were smooth and flawless until a panel flew open and brought in the light.

Taking the lead, Quercus gingerly stepped forward, his apprehension rising, his lungs filling with a heady-scent, daring not to glimpse, forbidding himself a moment of weakness among men, but he had to look for there was no comforting outcome. All he could see was a carpet of thorny black roses.

Michael brushed by, demanding answers. 'Is one of them Nina? Is this one my sister? What about this one?' He tapped Quercus on the head. 'Answer me, damn it? Which one is my sister?'

'I do not know!' Quercus angered mostly at himself. The infection of war was gone, and in its place was grief, the heavy tiredness of a tainted core. He wanted to sleep. He wanted forgiveness. He wanted the solace of Nina and her arms about him. 'Can we assume she is one of them, all of them or can we assume he has taken her?'

'Hell is too good for him!' Michael raged, kicking at dirt. 'Wait till I get my hands on that bastard!'

A promise instantly undermined. 'It is I who will get my hands on that bastard.'

A shout and Quercus alerted. Betula had discovered a secret passageway. They rushed down the tunnel where it led to a rocky vista overlooking the sea. But Cedrus had shown so far, the wit to escape serious ill. Neither Quercus nor a fresh commitment to gather more men would alter his predicted course.

'Hell, it was a bad call,' Michael said at the tunnel's mouth. 'It was either her chopped into bits or some hope here under guard. Now she's probably been chopped up anyway.'

'We do not know for certain.'

'Well is she black roses or not?'

'Can you cry, my brother?'

'It's women who cry, men who die, remember?'

'She would have been safe on board Sea Winger.'

'Would she? You had this crazy notion to go charging into the breach without using her guns. What would have happened if I never managed to persuade you to use them? What would have happened if the Thief never turned up to protect Sea Winger? Those men would have set light to the vessel with Nina on board.' He walked back the way he came, his voice dampened by the barricade walls. 'I don't know which is worse, here or through the gates. I gave an oath to save lives, not to see my sister turned into roses. I mean I thought he turned people into trees. Would I be turned into a daisy, I wonder.'

'We shall visit Sage.'

'Oh yeah, let's see the herb. Maybe she's got some fairy dust to sprinkle on her petals.'

A foot into his back propelled Michael into flight. He landed hard and did not rise to an angry voice. 'Your tongue wags like a bitch on heat! The *what ifs* are irrelevant! They will never solve a problem, only enhance acrimony.'

For Michael, he was to near-despair.

Two men facing the same quest mounted their steeds, their ears tuned, their eyes searching, their sixth sense reaching ahead and hoping nothing would stand in their way, only an answer to their immediate predicament. And the whole thing crept back to them, and they wondered how such important memories became veiled, like the dip in two valleys, moon beams bouncing off a lake and smoke churning from a chimney.

Their attachment to Nina was still fragile when they walked into the cabin, drawn and melancholy, paying no heed to the fuss of furniture that seemed never the same. A fireplace crackled with beech twigs, the mantel was littered with fine old china and freak tomatoes, and of course, there sat the old woman in her usual attire warming her hands.

'You cannot release what is now bound to earth.' Both men slumped, a disastrous outcome indeed. 'Unless,' she continued 'you rid the engineer of her fate.'

There was hope. 'Cedrus is like a wriggly customer,' Quercus said. 'At every turn he is one jump ahead. You forecast his demise by my hand yet this did not happen.'

'You assumed it to be at the place and time of your determination.' Her veiled head turned. 'Take back what you promised before her sails leave harbour. Keep one cabin vacant, place the rose petals in cloth and provide silk sheets.'

'Why?' Michael asked.

'You do not question wisdom, my brother. What is the purpose, Sage?'

'What is unseen by day will be seen by night. The last of autumn is your time, Quercus Coccinea. Your colours will never shine brighter against a heart of gold yet both shall be challenged in a season not of your choosing. Now make haste.'

Outside, with his foot grappling the stirrup, Michael asked, 'How come you can ask why?'

'I requested what not why, there is the difference.' Quercus was such a quandary at times. 'Her wisdom must be taken to your heart. Without changing destiny she warns of destiny. We must split at the palace. I will collect her petals. You will take back Sea Winger.'

'What can I offer him?'

'Your fist may be a good starting point.'

Quercus noticed there were always small magical patches of time between being completely in limbo and becoming close to his desired goal. It had no prescribed duration, always felt tantalizingly short since it began to fade the moment he became aware of the next hurdle. But this patch was more like flying in some sunlit element and discovering his wings had melted. If the devil was in the detail, Quercus was prepared to sell his soul for Nina.

On rising ground towards the palace, the nodding manes of three horses and riders indicated their progress. 'My brother!' Betula shouted, the face composed of urgency. 'Thank destiny I found you. Cedrus was sighted on a pirate's vessel.'

'Do we know his destination?'

'It was a chance sighting by Lord Jubaea. He spotted the vessel heading west.'

Quercus urged Shadow on, through the palace courtyard, straight ahead to the ground floor chamber. He slipped off his saddle, looked about and found a linen tablecloth then picked his way through the open panel leading to the secret garden. Time being of the essence, he made haste and forcibly gathered the petals, speaking his thoughts aloud.

'Sage has told me to rid the engineer of your fate. This I intend to do. I shall extract retribution for your misery and degradation. As destiny is my witness, I shall use my last breath to gain your freedom.'

He wondered if this gesture would bring her scant reward, wondered if she was able to hear. Having something to look forward to only served to emphasize the featureless desert he felt his life had become. But sometimes, as now, with heady scented petals gathered in cloth, clutched in his hand, he raced outside and spoke to Betula with a vision in mind.

'My brother, I sail on Sea Winger. I do not know for how long or destination. I do not know if I shall return or if Cedrus has contrived another ruse but I must ask one thing.' He paused to look back at the building he had come to despise. 'Here was once the home of Hortus, where her doors were open for her people, where her walls were as one with the fields, where the wildlife showed no fear to visit and feed off this land. We have no need for such trappings to alter men's minds. For you, for our children, rid that grotesque wall which has become the blight on our landscape and remind Cedrus he has no place in our world. Bring light to the home of Hortus.'

'It shall be done.'

'If not you, ask another to supervise.'

'I shall stay.'

'Do you not have a wife and son in the north, running an inn?'

'They are not forgotten, my lord. My place is here until word of his death then I shall return to my family and tell them with truth we course our own destiny.'

It required no answer. His look was enough.

After that, Quercus placed the scented petals in his saddle bag and mounted Shadow. The hooves thudded dust, the steed strained, his sinews and breath working to open the distance, to carry his master toward the harbour.

Dismounting at the stables, he threw the saddle bag over his shoulder and placed his arms about Shadow, pressed his face into his soft nose. 'This is my time, dear friend.' The steed snorted. 'If I do not return, one of my brothers will care for you.' Picking his way across the street, he made haste to the Harbour Winery. Inside, he spotted Jubaea. 'My brother, I have need of your services.'

Jubaea was quiet for a moment, looking into his beaker. 'Do I detect the cause is Cedrus?'

'I understand you sighted him.' Quercus called for wine then drew up a stool. 'He has turned Nina into black roses. To kill him will release her. I need fifty to manage her sails.'

'Men have returned to their families. If we make haste now, we may gather the last on their trail.'

'There is no time. We must sail before midnight.'

'And Sea Winger?'

'As we speak, Michaelmas has control of her sails.'

It was a misguided thought.

Michael was having a problem. 'I'll even throw you in a pair of these specially made boots.'

'Do you not see my feet? I have no need for steel boots when my feet are for swimming.' The Thief refused to keep still, was floating from helm to mid-ships, organizing his raffish men.

'What about your very own flag of independence.' Michael gestured with his hands. 'I can see it now, the Juniperus Pirate who challenges twenty-foot waves, the Handsome Thief who sails with a skull and cross-bones.'

'I have no need for a flag to show my independence.'

This unrewarding negotiation and fuss about the whole thing, Michael became more and more helplessly irritated. 'Look, we need Sea Winger.'

'Why?'

'To go after Cedrus, kill the bastard and set my sister free.'

'He has your sister?'

'Well actually she's a bunch of roses.' Now, plan two came into effect. 'Okay, if we cannot negotiate, I shall place an embargo.' For a second, he looked at him, and the face showed signs of pallor. 'I mean what is the point of going through the gates to steal when you cannot bring in the goods?'

The man beside the Thief sighed and slumped, he was anxious for a decision but suddenly things dramatically altered and he tapped his captain's arm. 'Handsome one, look what travels up our gangway?'

'You don't want to be messing with that guy.'

'This vessel was promised.'

'But promised without guns.'

'You halted my progress to dismantle.'

Quercus coughed. For the occasion, he adopted a slightly different posture. This Thief needed friendly persuasion for a crew was needed. 'The matter can be easily settled,' he said. 'Join us.'

The Thief shook his head. 'It is not my war.'

'I do not ask you to fight, or your crew. Just be adventurous in her sails, your sails. Watch them balloon to their fullest extent. See how she handles under your command.'

The Thief gave him a wary look. 'So you require my crew as well as my ship. What do you have to barter?'

'Michaelmas, a great sailor who can see beyond anything imaginable, let him be your eyes to the farthest flung corners of the world. He still has good years left in him.'

'I say, Quercus. I'm not for sale.'

'Be a man, do the right thing.' Quercus smothered the smile and turned to the Thief. 'Come, Handsome one. Is it not a good trade? Consider the tributes to your navigational skills, consider the first-hand tales from a brave outsider and consider your name as legend.'

'As legend, you say?'

'As we speak your name has entered our history books as the pirate who challenged Abies ready to advance with his thousand strong warriors.'

'Four hundred,' he corrected.

'Four hundred is still a great number. Do we have an accord?'

'No, we do not have an accord!' Michael irritated. 'What happened to the part where we all look after one another, to make our journeys less painful?'

'I shall make your journeys less painful,' the Thief said.

'Look pal, slave labour was abolished a century ago. Now here's the deal. My eyes only for this trip and I'll throw in some dirty jokes.'

Instant silence as the Thief's eyes darted to his crew, a hesitant crew waiting for the captain to agree or disagree with this bold proposition. 'We have an accord,' and the crew gulped. It would be a challenging voyage.

In the dim and unsettling night, at the point of a deal being struck, a familiar dark figure in silky black folds processed the gangway. In one hand she carried a basket, in the other a map. They looked on in stupefaction as she processed the deck, her stooping gait heading for the captain's quarters.

'Would you look at that?' Michael said. 'Did you remember to bring sheets?'

Indeed, Quercus thought, this was a significant move to have Sage accompany them on this voyage to wherever. He carried forward and with his knuckle made a slight tapping sound on her door, waited for what seemed an age then rapped a little louder. Within a few seconds the door opened as though by itself. She was sat on the bunk looking ahead as if she were in a world of her own, a rolled-up map by her side. Quercus took it and left. If it were mystery and wonderment he required, she could provide it.

Under a lantern held high by Michael, the Thief rolled out the map in present company and traced his finger along the line of the equator. Hazards aplenty presented themselves to mariners negotiating these waters.

'Has anyone been to this place called Nepenthes?'

'It is not a question of whether anyone has been there or rather what is there.' Quercus told Michael. 'Nepenthaceae is a genus of evergreen, insectivorous, mostly epiphytic perennials.'

'Come again? You lost me?'

'Their leaves are adapted to form pendulous, lidded, coloured pitchers that trap and digest insects. They require a humid atmosphere, partial shade and moist.'

'Hey, that doesn't sound too bad. At least we won't get bitten.'

'In truth, you may get eaten before you get bitten,' the Thief said. 'I heard a tale by an old pirate who claimed his grandfather came across such an island only visible at night. He and his crew were lost to their pitchers.'

'Who was left to tell the tale?' Jubaea enquired.

'Before the captain fell to his fate he called for a White Tail and wrote his dying last words on a banana leaf.'

They nodded. It was acceptable.

A splodge dropped on the map. Michael looked up. 'I suggest we make sail.'

'I give the orders.' The Thief annoyed rolling up the map. Then he walked on and shouted to his men. 'We make sail.'

'Cocky bastard,' Michael disgruntled. 'Woe betide him if he flicks my nose.'

'Woe betide you if he does,' suggested Jubaea. 'Did you not see the point of his blade tickle the rib of Abies?' He unsheathed his sword. 'I shall teach you how to duck and weave, splice and cut from chest bone to pelvis. Here, take it. I have another.'

Michael accepted the light-weight sword while Quercus continued to stand and observe a scene reminiscent of former days. Would his friend carve a name for himself or would he die and leave his sister to cry?

It rained towards the closing part of dark to the opening part of light, a drizzle and that was all, there was nothing else unusual or unexpected and somehow it seemed wrong that there was no build-up, a feeling in the air, a premonition or a warning or a clue. Actually, if there was something, it was missed because they were not paying attention.

It seemed such a daunting task. No such island called Nepenthes or otherwise had been recorded, either in this world or the next, but to ignore Sage was to ignore trueness and veracity. For two weeks she remained aloof with meals supplied on a tray, by a rap on the door then left on the floor. She never spoke, never wanted for anything and never indicated she would leave her station, so it was to some surprise when she emerged in the closing part of an evening. She went beyond the foremast, the wind playing with her skirts. Was she their outlook? Did this have meaning, they wondered.

'A bit of fresh air might do her some good,' said Michael at the helm, not particularly disturbed in the aura she created. 'Do you think she's left for a sheet change?'

Jubaea smiled. 'You speak in metaphors.'

'Hey, blame it on Shakespeare. He's the one who increased our vocabulary.'

'I am sad to learn of your sister's confinement. Were you not able to cry?'

'Women cry, men die.'

'Shame on you. Your tears would have released her.'

'Not so, only Nina does the releasing bit.'

'How do you know if you do not cry?'

'Look, I cried bucket loads but nothing happened.'

'That is good, my brother. Did you leave the buckets by her stems in case there is a dry spell?'

It had taken Michael that long for him to acknowledge Jubaea was a lot smarter than he made out to be. He looked his way, but the gaze seemed to fall just beyond him, as if something behind caught his attention. It was the relief.

'I say, Jubaea,' Michael asked handing over the wheel. 'Fancy teaching me how to throw a knife?'

From a distance, Quercus shook his head, indeed a good lesson if not. He traced the decks, his mind on what he might encounter on the island but uppermost was Nina. He could fly high in her company because she was the wind beneath his wings but now, she was a bunch of black headless roses, waving her prickly stems over Daylily. Although it was dark, small chinks and streaks of yellow light emitted from the oil lamps in a hopeless attempt to keep the decks intelligently clear but even so, not by design he encroached upon the Thief talking to Sage. He quickly turned in another direction and wondered if she was trying to recruit a captain and his crew to fight by his side. The odds were slim if not impossible.

Days moved on, the climate grew warmer. The Handsome Thief gave orders to veer east and drop anchor off the west coast, the underbelly of Coniferous land. Here they would stock up their larders.

From the quarter deck Jubaea, Quercus and Michael were casually leant against the rail gazing into the distance, each with their own thoughts while the oarsmen were bringing in their stolen harvests. Friends rarely parted.

'If we get through this,' said Michael. 'I think I will explore the seas.'

'In what shall you explore?' Jubaea asked.

'I thought about building a smaller version of Sea Winger.'

'The Juniperus Pirates control the seas.' Quercus reminded. 'They will not take too kindly upon vessels sailed by others, particularly by an outsider. Far better to barter a passage for exploration rather than tempt providence.'

'Hey, you led me to believe I could sail uncluttered shipping lanes.'

'That was Fraxinus. I made no such mention.'

'Yes, you did,' he argued his point. 'You encourage me to search for riches in unexplored regions.'

'That is true but I did not say how and there is the difference.'

'Pity, I quite like sailing.' Michael was resigned.

'Then sail in our lakes with a fishing rod.'

Quercus chuckled, sharing Jubaea's joke. Michael grimaced until an unexpected sighting caught his peripheral vision, close to something familiar. His mouth gaped in wonderment. No doubt about it, Nina was slipping on board, body splashed wet with a peacock feather gripped in her mouth. There was nothing quite like having the last laugh.

'It must have been difficult to pluck the petals off my sister.'

'It gave me no joy. Rest assured I will rid the engineer of her fate. This much has been said to give her hope.'

'Did she manage to flutter a leaf just to let you know she understood?'

Quercus turned his head. 'What would you have me do? Ignore the wisdom of Sage? Dig up her roots and plant them in pots?'

'Hey, that might have been a good idea. We could have popped in some compost and brought her on board just to make sure she was watered every day.'

'My brother,' Jubaea intervened. 'Michaelmas goads. Do not rise to the bait.'

'And why does he goad?' Quercus irritated, fragile still for the want of Nina. 'He blames me for her circumstance. I was not his acceptable choice. What do I have to offer her? Diddlysquat, is that not so, Michaelmas?'

Michael puffed out his cheeks. 'Actually chaps, I think my joke just backfired.' He paused, unsure how to phrase his next statement. 'You're never going to believe this but Nina's on board.'

'Methinks your sword play has thickened your senses.'

'I kid you not. I saw her slipping on board in just her knickers.'

Quercus felt utterly at odds as though he was on the brink of madness. Why the duplicity in her modest simplicity? He brooded darkly, leaning over the rails, not speaking for a while among the tempo of preparation. Men had boarded with their supplies, the anchor weighed, the sails hoisted and the clamour of voices grew loud as Sea Winger swept away from this headland. Every thought took him back to the secret garden, to Cedrus, to black roses, to Sage and her counsel. *You cannot release what is now bound to earth* and then she added *unless you rid the engineer of her fate. Take back what you promised before her sails leave harbour. Keep one cabin vacant, place the rose petals in cloth and provide silk sheets.*

'What do we know,' Quercus finally said. 'We know the roses were not Nina. Sage had said we could not release what was now bound to earth. So we assumed the roses were Nina. What did she mean by us ridding the engineer of her fate?'

'Search me.' Michael said. 'Do you know, Jubaea?'

'I know less than you.'

'We know Nina was in disguise. We know she was talking to the Thief. Therefore we must assume he knows what we do not know. And what should we know? If we know too soon it may alter destiny.'

'I know I'm confused.' Michael glanced at Jubaea stroking his trailing moustache. 'Are you confused?'

'I admit I am confused.'

'Well then, let's find out what we don't know before we should know.'

Quercus held them back. 'I shall go.'

And go he did but not the way they expected. Picking his way to the stern, Quercus vaulted the rails as the waters rolled heavy and then he edged his way along timber ledges until he could see through the leaded windows. Suspended in the afterglow of curiosity, he watched her towel-dry her hair wearing her beauty like a kind of sleep, a composite of inner light and outward perfection.

'Is she there?' Michael asked in loud whisper.

Quercus looked up and smiled. But still he did not move, preferring to spy on the woman he loved. She slipped on her T-shirt, popped a piece of gum in her mouth then sat in a soft leather chair at a desk to shape the hollow point of a peacock feather until it was razor sharp. Among other things, he spotted a mortar and pestle, assumed she had pummelled the black petals Sage had asked him to gather. Next, she poured a measure of black liquid into the hollow spine and sealed the end with her chewed gum. Then movement betrayed another presence. Busy Lizzie brushed to her side and she stroked her head before moving to select a peppermint from a bag of boiled sweets lodged against a bottle of wine. It was a perfect moment to take a picture if only he had a camera.

'What's she doing?' Michael's curiosity considerably enhanced.

Quercus gestured obscenely as he hung on the precipice of life and looked back as she looked at him shaking her head. He offered his gritted teeth smile.

The window flung open. 'What is wrong with you?'

'I would ask the same.' He climbed in.

'As well you might ask. I must have Miss Gullibility written on my forehead. Whose bright idea was it to leave me behind?'

He ran his fingers through his mutinous mop of lengthy hair. Indecisiveness was not one of his shortcomings. 'I am to blame,' he said at last. 'Far better to be safe than chopped up in bits by the black robes.'

'Oh what rubbish. I bet it was my idiot brother.' She poured a glass of wine. 'Never mind,' she said handing it over. 'Give me your whip.'

'Why?'

'Because I have to doctor the tip. Do you want a sweet?'

'Wine, sweets, what else shall you offer?'

'It depends upon your behaviour.'

He hung over her as he sipped his wine, watching the application of black liquid brushed on the tip of his whip. 'I hazard a guess and say they are his black roses.'

'Listen carefully, Quirky. This is your time and we must make use of what we can. Cut his skin three times so the agent can be released into his blood stream. It's the only way to slow him down, to give you an equal fight.'

'The roses, why did he grow them if they act as poison.'

She blew upon the tip and applied some more. 'The roses secrete an aphrodisiac to make his women comply. They grew in the earth from the blood of your brothers. It dulls the senses but used in their undiluted form will work against him.'

With a combination of wit and charm he knelt down beside her. 'Nina, my heart is gladdened you are not pot bound but safe and well where I shall take it upon myself to ensure no harm will come to you.' He paused to her laughter and it gladdened his heart. 'Truly, I am sorry we have missed good nights but why the charade?'

'There I was up a ladder painting out his obscenities, a frugal excuse you used to keep me there if you must know. Remind me to tell you to stuff your silly ideas next time.' She looked back at him and smiled. 'I am going to Nepenthes with you to fight by your side.'

'No! Here you will stay.' He held up a finger, ready to extrapolate when she surprised him by placing it in her mouth and he groaned. 'You take liberties, madam.'

'Hark at the kettle calling the pot black?'

'Nina, why do you make life so difficult? I am on my knees begging for attention and you play with me like a child would play with a toy.' He sat back on his heels. 'Do you play the same game with the Thief, I wonder.'

'Jealously is too petty emotion for a man of your stature.'

'Do not credit me with too much nobility.'

'Look, it's very simple. Lizzie came in with some other friends. They might have been weasels or maybe some kind of squirrels. Anyway, it was hard to find time to make lunch and supper for all my visitors let alone paint a wall among a collection of wildlife. So I got up early, climbed the ladder. Lizzie started to make funny noises. I climbed down the ladder, put the brush on the paint lid, the lantern went out then a panel flew open to let in some light. Naturally, I was curious. I walked through and there was Sage. She told me I had to leave, pronto because Cedrus was heading my way. Do you know he was actually looking on at the battle from that tunnel entrance? I mean what audacity the man has. He dressed up one of his men to be blown sky high and if-'

'Nina,' he sighed. 'Where were you?'

'Where else but with Shadow. I slept with him and Lizzie until you came home.'

He shook his head. 'You were not in the stables.'

'I beg to differ. I was in the stables under a pile of straw. Sage had given me strict instructions what to do. I followed them to the letter. And no, to tell a destiny is to alter destiny.'

He placed his empty glass on the desk and rested his head in her lap. 'Would you stroke me just as lovingly as you would Lizzie?'

STORMY MOMENTS

Quercus woke with a thirsty agony in his throat. To the sound of a gentle murmur, he snaked his head round and studied a sleeping beauty. If he could just get through this, if he could weaken Cedrus, render him powerless and hand over the kill, his future would be starkly different from what Sage had proposed.

With a new leaf frame of mind, he wriggled away from her side, swiftly dressed and padded bare foot to a relatively calm deck to a relatively warm dawn. Michael was slumped against the helm, his eyes shut. Close by, Jubaea lazed on cushions propped against a barrel, his eyes shut but always at the ready. The Thief was strolling among his half-asleep crew. But there was such a thirst and arid taint in his mouth, he sank his head in the water butt and gulped in quantity. Satisfied with that, he slapped his good friend on the back.

Michael jumped into life, involuntarily shouted, *who goes there* and then his woozy eyes fixed upon Quercus before they flicked to the compass. 'I thought I was done for. Obviously, things worked out last night.'

'Indeed they did, though Nina cried a little before we slept. I wonder if my overtures of love had a profound effect. What do you think, Michaelmas?'

'Far be it from me to squash your ego, pal but don't you think being left behind had something to do with it? So what happened?'

'Cedrus was waiting for an opportune moment. Sage intervened to protect Nina. The roses had to be pummelled to extract poisonous liquid so my whip could be doctored. To cut my enemy thrice will afford me an equal fight.'

'That's interesting.'

'Nina is of a mind to fight by my side. She will be safe on Sea Winger. Now it is your turn to convince her to stay on board.'

'And how am I expected to do that? Tie her to the mast?'

'If necessary, anything will do.'

'So you don't pay too much attention to what Sage tells you?'

'To ignore wisdom is to ignore trueness.'

'I seem to recall her exact words. What is unseen by day will be seen by night. The last of autumn is your time, Quercus Coccinea. Your colours will never shine brighter against a heart of gold yet both shall be challenged in a season not of your choosing. Now I may be wrong but I figure what is seen by night must be the island of Nepenthes. Since that is on the equator, it's going to be jolly hot, ergo a season not of your choosing. So whose colour will never shine brighter against a heart of gold?'

'Your heart, my brother. Both of us will be challenged in a season not of our choosing. My season is autumn, as a daisy is for summer.'

Michael chuckled, foraging in a barrel of fruit. 'Remember what you said to me when she was fighting for her life.' He paused, reluctant to argue his case because Quercus seemed in such a good mood. 'Look, I don't like it any more than you but maybe she's the one to make this happen.'

Quercus wiped his face with his open hand, from forehead to chin, in an agony of indecision, torn between two duties; the killing of Cedrus and the woman he loved. At last he sighed and conceded Michael was right. 'So I must agree and take off my blinkers. It shall be the four of us.'

'Not so. Last night while you were doing whatever it was you were doing with my sister there was a lot of tapping going on. It turns out the Thief went ashore for aluminium pots. Two guesses as to why. Whatever Nina said, she managed to persuade him and part of his crew to come with us.'

'Indeed, this is good news.' Now his thoughts veered to his next hurdle. 'Michaelmas, since you fear death would you like to escape it? Live for eternity and love beautiful women.'

'Excuse me?'

'I shall bring Cedrus to his knees and pass the kill to you.'

Michael vigorously shook his head. 'Not me, my man. I shall stand by your side and probably poop in my pants but to live for eternity, no way.'

'I want to be with Nina.'

'Well that sticks out a mile. Have you discussed this radical plan with her?'

'Not yet but I shall do so. She once gave her views, which were not compatible with my own at the time. But things have moved on, Michaelmas. Would it be unreasonable to ask if she would give me her years? Would a woman in love give her years to a man that never grows old?'

'From the sound of it, you have answered your own question.' Michael proffered an orange and began peeling one himself. 'Oh sure, it might work for a few years. But it will chip away when those wrinkles start appearing. And remember, we don't live as long as you so that makes it even worse. Jubaea is a good target. He's brighter than he looks and single. On the other hand, who is to say that by passing your weapon to someone else the trick will work? I mean, if you're into this destiny lark then it has to be you to finish him off. Do you really know how you gain immortality?'

Quercus shook his head, popping a segment of orange in his mouth. 'My Father,' he said after swallowing, 'found the whip of Hortus the day I was born. He said the writing was on the bark, that to kill Cedrus would render the victor with immortality.'

'I see, so you only have his word for it?'

'My Father was no stretcher of lies.'

'Hey, I'm not suggesting he lied. I'm suggesting no-one seems to have the full story. For instance, take the Keeper. How did he become immortal? Do you see what I'm getting at, Quercus? Perhaps some of those answers are in the Book. After all, Nina found the mouthpiece. Who knows, she might be able to find the other half and maybe when it's put together you can both live happily ever after and watch me grow old.'

Quercus smiled. And as though his mood had reached out and summoned her, Nina emerged, stretching her bare arms to the sky, breathing sea air into her lungs. The Thief greeted her with deference, bowed and smiled. They talked for a moment then she approached.

'Did you sleep well, my Nina?'

'I was given an excellent sleeping pill.'

'Did Sage give you this?'

'Sometimes I don't know whether you're pulling my leg or not.'

'Nina,' Michael asked, 'got any ideas as to where the other half of this Book might be?'

'Not really. In fact, Perry heard through the grapevine it was gone forever. Somehow, I have a tendency to think he's more in tune with legends than anyone else.' She paused in the uncertainty. 'Quercus, I know it's not what you want to hear but he said the other half of the Book was destroyed. He heard Cedrus claim it was destroyed.'

'Cedrus is unable to differentiate lie from truth.'

'Well ask yourself this. Why hasn't Sage indicated where it might be? A hint or something…after all, everyone knew the mouthpiece was through the gates and that's because it served a purpose to turn you into a tree for one hundred years.'

If anything, Quercus hid a hint of concealed stupidity, a man frittering it all away in search for something that never existed, wasting it on impossible dreams or burning it up in despair and despondency. 'We must keep our minds focused on the future, not the past.'

He left to walk into life as it stirred on deck and wondered why Sage had placed severe limitations upon him. She was, he thought, as susceptible to analyse as the human body itself. Was it by craft and manipulation? And for what purpose other than to spend a lifetime of servitude.

Twenty of the crew had crafted and nailed aluminium soles to their boots. The process was simple but the invention untried. It was a strange affair to see boots strung round necks yet it was nothing more than a defence position, the act of keeping another weapon to hand.

'Did things go well, Quercus?' Jubaea asked, the Thief closing to his side.

This man, Quercus thought may be up for it. 'Tell me, brother Jubaea. Is there no greater pleasure in loving beautiful women?'

'Have you forgotten your own so quickly?'

'Imagine eternity loving beautiful women. If you claim to love four in one night, you would find time to rest and love again.'

The Thief snorted. 'Four?'

Jubaea ignored him and asked Quercus, 'What are you proposing?'

'To render Cedrus to his knees, you take the last thrust.'

'It will not do,' the Thief interjected. 'The truth-'

'Quiet!' Jubaea reprimanded. 'I want to know the truth.'

'It is said, as well you know,' Quercus reminded. 'That to still his heart by the whip of Hortus will offer immortality to the user.'

'Cut off his balls more like.'

'My brother,' Jubaea irritated at the Thief. 'Interruption is not permitted.'

'By whose authority?'

'He is closest to you.' Jubaea told Quercus. 'Chop off a toe if he interrupts again.' He remained silent for a while, stroking his trailing moustache. Two were looking on with bated breath. 'Why the turn around,' he finally asked Quercus.

'Love,' he said so simply. They followed his line of sight and watched her standing beside Michael, picking out pips from an apple. Boyish and untidy yes, smaller than most, intelligent and gullible at times, but still, for him, she was the most beautiful creature on this earth. He glanced back at Jubaea. 'I do not ask you take on my burden out of friendship. I ask you to accept only if you find the proposal appealing.'

'I find the proposal appealing. We have an accord, my brother.'

'Let it be between us three until the time comes. Are we agreed?'

'I am agreed.' Jubaea scowled at the Thief. 'Agree, Handsome one.'

'Ah, I see I have your permission to speak.'

'The proposal was offered to me.' Jubaea watched him walk off. 'He is a grumpy man without a sense of humour.'

Quercus saw the incoming and ducked. Jubaea received the water full in the face. Confused, he blinked, wiping his streaming eyes.

'You are not permitted interruption.' The Thief grinned.

It was hard not to stifle his emotions for it all suddenly clicked into crisp focus. For the first time in his life Quercus was planning a future. He would not be denied his revenge, would make it linger, pass the whip to Jubaea and watch the sweet kill. Then he would marry Nina, rebuild his home on the wooded clad hills and there they would grow old together. A moment later his gaze fell upon

Michael and Nina. They seemed to be engrossed in deep conversation but something was wrong. Michael flapped his arms and strode off, kicking hard a nearby lantern. It was at Michael's pleasure to pay some duty to the sea and never responded when Quercus laid a hand on his shoulder.

'A trouble shared is a trouble halved, Michaelmas.'

'I don't belong in your world, Quercus. So let's just leave it at that.' He turned when Nina shot to his side, clasping his hand with urgency. 'Both of us don't belong in your world. When this is over, we're returning.'

'No we are not!' Nina snapped.

'Nina, would you care to enlighten me?'

'Michael feels a little apprehensive, that's all. It's nothing we can't sort out.'

'Nothing we can't sort out,' Michael snorted his derision. 'What do you think, Quercus? Can a man hold his load on a pair of shaky shoulders?'

'We all have our fears, my brother. My Father was a proud but unwise man. He led men to their death in their hundreds. No one would speak or rally to his cause after that day. For many years I watched him grow weaker, for many years I held my head in shame. I used those years to go through the gates and watch others more foolish. It was a lesson well taught. I am measured for my deeds, as you are measured for yours.'

Michael shook his head. 'This goes beyond measured deeds and regrets. Hell, ignore my ranting and raving. I have a short fuse. Women cry, men die, right?'

'No,' Quercus contradicted. 'My life before yours, remember? My promise still stands, Michaelmas. Should you fall after me, remember the song of Hortus. We shall have chance to send our breath to the living as the living shall send their breath to the dead.'

'Oh stop being so morbid you two. I am going to protect you all.'

'I see,' Michael said with a hint of sarcasm. 'We don't get to wear platform boots but raincoats instead.'

'You two are so wrapped up in your own predicaments you fail to see the most obvious.' She gestured to the Thief and Jubaea. Enlightenment was about to come forth. 'Perry,' she said placing her hand on his arm, 'has agreed to join us with twenty of his men. He does so because I told him what I have and the reasons of why I have it. Immortality is not gained by killing Cedrus. It is gained from a potion; Sage has told me so. She also has given me what she claimed to be the last of white dust left over from the Keeper before he died. It's this white dust which turns people into trees. On my command you must hold your breath and shut your eyes while I atomize the air. Now have we got that?' They nodded. 'Perry has consented to serve under your leadership, Quirky. You must ensure his men know the command word, Hyb.'

'Hyb?' Jubaea enquired.

'Hold Your Breath.' The Thief prodded the chest. 'And there is the truth if you had not interrupted me. No immortality for you.'

'Intriguing, my Nina, it did not occur he uses white dust, nor have we seen such a chemical.'

'If you had seen it, you would have known, wouldn't you? If we plan for the worst, we hold our breath for thirty seconds. I suspect that's as much as Cedrus would do.'

'Did Sage indicate his army number? Are there black robes?'

'She just said I will make a path for you against an army of firs that live on the island. I know it sounds a bit daunting but I can do this. We don't know if the boots will work so we must hold our breath to avoid the dust getting into our lungs.'

'I can throw dust. I am the tallest.'

Nina shook her head. 'Quirky, I am the least suspect.'

Suddenly, without warning, the vessel heaved. They looked at each other for a brief moment then before gathered company could respond, it came too quick and silent to be a tempest but was much as could be described. Against pallid ropes and sails, feet and hands, Sea Winger rolled in its turn, caught in a spinning current. Their sea-cries dwindled in the uproar of waves, wet through and overwhelmed, men were heaved and tossed asunder, clinging to rope or mast, it did not matter just so long as they were self-contained. Yet despite the turbulent and powerful insurgences, the frigate held fast and did not disappoint, giving physical form to the conviction it could outrun this turmoil. Its bows constantly rose and plummeted down in a tumbling pell-mell, crashing upon the sea's furore, a merciless place when angered. This was no squall of nature, no whirlpool of sorts but the violent measures undertaken by Cedrus, whose faculty created a maelstrom.

Quercus lost his footing, slid along the planks and then felt the heave to portside. There was an almighty shatter as part of the deck erupted. The main mast fell horizontal, plummeted down, missing him by inches. Next, he was propelled headlong through a ragged fissure, dropped seven foot, landing on his back followed by a deluge of water. As he grappled to his feet, the vessel rolled starboard, a ship's cannon near dispatched on top of him. By the second, extinction was graduating from possibility to probability.

Consciousness returned, arrived with the sudden impact of seawater to his face. Quercus groaned. In wordless gratitude he sat up, adjusting to his watery surrounds and to the men who crouched beside him, white and speechless.

'How do we fare, my brothers?'

'No man lost, just flummoxed and witless,' replied Jubaea

'Is Nina safe?'

Michael answered. 'She's been in her cabin keeping your weapon dry.'

Quercus regarded the open sky through a splintered hole and saw where the mast had fractured. He shook his head, thinking the rough end would be the rough end for all. He did not pause to feel sorry for himself. His main objective was to keep the men safe; all badly needed in this already undermanned ship.

'What is the damage?'

'It looks worse than it is.' Michael kept pace. 'The Thief reckons he can rig a fulcrum and repair the mast. We lost some sails but we can repair the tear to the mainsail. There's minor damage to the decks but that won't impede us. Apart from that, we have a mess.'

Quercus stopped in mid-stride. 'How was Nina able to keep my whip dry?'

'You know women. They bring everything apart from the kitchen sink.'

That was an acceptable metaphor.

Around them, it looked calamitous but the sea was calm and the day was not yet over. They worked on the main mast, supervised by the Thief. Like Fraxinus, he knew how to shape wood, to cut and mould, to strip and dowel. During all this while they had hardly made headway due to loss of sails, only drifted in a slow slip-stream towards their compass heading. By nightfall they were done.

Now the time was set in motion for a change of scenery, an optical illusion. What is unseen by day is seen by night, a full moon glistening on an island exposed by the reflection of the ocean's bed. The outline of a pirate's vessel showed to be anchored not far, perhaps proof indeed Cedrus was there, though some had their doubts.

Nina appeared on deck in a black leather tunic deeply fringed, black boots shone. Her arms and thighs luminously bare, a leather band round her head with a trace peacock feather, a bead necklace to her throat. She looked like a little wigwam warrior.

Quercus crept up behind her. 'Is the feather to cool your desire?'

She turned and laughed. 'Oh Quirky, can you try and stay in one piece?'

'I shall do my utmost.' The feather held distinct possibilities. 'Do you intend to tickle my fancy?'

'I thought you would tickle mine.'

Men roared with laughter, no sign of worry which had driven them to this point. It was short lived, replaced with unease as Quercus initiated a platform on which to address the crew. Here he would give praise and recognition.

'I have fought alongside courage, men with a single cause, the cause to live by their own determination. In our midst we have greater men for they already live by their own determination yet they choose to aid in our cause. Although twenty-one Juniperus Pirates are to set foot on land, the others are no less brave for they stay to protect this vessel and ensure we have safe passage home. I speak for my kind. Your names will be legend in our history books. Your tales will live on and be spoken in awe. No greater accomplishment shall herald this moment.' He paused in their cheers. 'I shall not waste words,' he said pointing. 'There, on Nepenthes is danger. What danger? The question would be better answered by you. The plan is simple. We make no divisions. We shield the brother beside us. I shall take the lead at all times. No man shall walk in front of me. The Handsome Thief will take up the rear. When time comes, Nina will shout the command, Hyb. You must hold your breath for thirty seconds, the time it takes for berlandiera lyrata to open its buds. Now make haste.'

They threw themselves into the moment, made ready the boats, and cornered the market for bravery. By comparison, they were a small and noble band of men with no weight of artillery against the giants that littered this island.

'Who is she, if not the prophecy?'

Moody, majestic Cedrus stood silent for awhile, observing his freedom but not yet free of irritation. After making two adjustments to his red silk band striking across his black leather tunic, he looked down at Captain Twist. 'If there is one truth in the prophecy it would be his Achilles' heel. I shall need your vessel for my return.'

On the shore where shadows came alive, Twist ran a tongue across his ragged teeth and remembered his first encounter with Quercus. Unsure then, he was convinced now that change was on the horizon. He had helped to ferry an army chartering hazardous reefs around Deciduous land, had seen their number and determination grow but considered it prudent to retreat while able. That was the way of Juniperus Pirates. Now he was one foot away from the incoming tide, content to let Cedrus agonize and wallow in his own belief what his thoughts desired him to believe. Soon the waters would cover his thread bare soles so conversation was merely an interval for positioning.

'This island, will it provide my crew with daily rations of fresh fruit.'

'Fruit of the most sought after.'

'There is the matter of women. Men have been without for many weeks.'

'Is there not one coming, more than enough for a crew of your size?'

'I shall leave you the rowing boat.'

Aboard his own vessel, Twist paced his decks with his men looking on. His face showed concern, his shoulders weighing heavy at the prospect of escaping a maelstrom that only Cedrus could artificially induce. Would it be wise to keep anchored and see the results from the approaching lanterns or would it be wise to join forces?

'What is it Cap'n?' The first mate said.

'We are in the middle of war with no escape.' He placed his foot on a barrel, leaning over one knee, contemplating his options. Ahead, two loaded rowing gigs were making headway to the shore. Was there advantage to pick this side? 'Ask Lord of the Oaks to partake in wine and share our food.'

'What food, what wine or are we to starve and thirst?'

'Not if I can help it.'

The first mate dived in. Picked out by the sporadic movements, accompanied by the ever present Quercus, his hand rose from the murky waters and clasped an oar. 'The Cap'n invites you to dine with him.'

'We do not go to war with our heads clouded.'

'Nor should you on empty ones,' came the reply. 'You may be interested to fill your brains with knowledge before entering the unknown.'

It was a reasonable enough request, a reasonable enticement.

The first man on board, Quercus faced Twist who smiled, generous in his words. 'Your deeds speak for themselves. The black robes destroyed, even their breeding ground, the palace is yours and Cedrus chased to his island.' His eyes glanced over Nina. 'I also gather you hold the prophecy.'

'You choose sides when it suits.' Jubaea said.

'Did I not aide in ferrying your army? Be frank, my brother.'

'I am Jubaea, not Frank.' Nina tittered, others smiled and Jubaea continued. 'What do you know of that place?'

'I can describe a path to avoid Nepenthaceae. From there you will come across the dark forest where tall firs dwell and beyond you will find Cedrus.'

'Show us the way to the forest.'

Twist shook his head and said nothing.

'Then you have a problem. While Cedrus lives he will keep you pinned to these shores. How long will your supplies last, a day, three at best? Perhaps it is your turn to be Frank.' Jubaea indicated to Nina. 'This woman shames you. She offers her heart regardless but here is our guarantee. If you are turned, she will weep for your sorrowful self.'

'And if she dies? I would prefer to take my chances with the maelstrom.'

'Let him course his own destiny.' Nina spoke with mocking amusement. 'We do not need men to soil their pants.'

Disgust creased the Captain's face. 'And I do not need the company of a whimpering female, one who masquerades as one of us!' He did not anticipate the backhanded blow to his face.

Quercus peered into the watering eyes. 'Slight Nina is to slight me. Take us to the forest or I shall pin your balls on the mast.'

Stroking his chin, pursing his lips, Twist regarded his crew. They were a stained and mottled group, subdued in the gravity of the moment. Did they really have a choice? 'Why do you stand there, chop, chop, we go to the island!'

ISLAND OF NEPENTHES

Part of the soft sandstone of this island had been eroded into spectacularly strange rock formations with powerful greenery organized in shapes of wilderness and trepidation. To avoid the pitchers of Nepenthaceae, Captain Twist indicated a steep snaking trail leading to the black forest.

Midway, a clump of twenty foot high, evergreen, palm-like perennials with small, banana-like fruits offered a short rest in the shade. Indicating to Jubaea and Michael, Quercus dumped a coil of rope which he had shouldered and settled against the reddish mid-ribs of Musa ensete.

'I have spent too much time in Daylily.' Jubaea was flagging.

'Nina mentioned you have fourteen countries.'

'Thirteen for certain, Michaelmas. We do not recognise the Elm. His country is shared by neighbouring countries. Zelkova is the last of his kind. He has no people left to serve, no country to serve since he serves Cedrus.'

'And Daylily, where the gates are, does it stand alone?'

'Lilac Country is the smallest, and honoured to have the gates close. Mine is Palm Country, the farthest west where it never snows. If we get through this, I will return for the women. They are beautifully bronzed with green eyes and silky maroon hair covering their breasts. Go there and some will remember a young pup tying his whip round their thighs…'

Nina heard everything, Quercus thought. He felt the impact of Jubaea's words. She moved out of range, her voice carried to the Thief who, rubbing his temples, had detached himself from the men.

'Are you alright, Perry?'

'Can any sane man be alright on this island?'

'You haven't changed your mind, have you?'

'I do not welch on a handshake.'

'It used to be that way in England many moons ago. Now it means nothing, a word means nothing, easily broken.'

He glanced back at Quercus and then at Nina. 'Have you told him?' A pause and he guessed. 'You will only tell if he survives.'

'He will survive, Perry. We shall all survive if we just keep focused on the objective.'

'Twist and his men are focused on another objective. See how they squat on their heels, ready for take-off.'

'Can you really blame them?'

'My Father gave me a good piece of advice. Never put your trust in a man who smells like a fish and struts like a chicken.'

'That's a very good analogy. What if he smells like a fish and struts like a bear?'

'Then he has to be a fishmonger with a headache.'

There was still a little humour to make light of a bad situation.

While the heat intensified, Twist and his men followed nervously behind Quercus, and behind them the Thief took up the rear with his raffish crew. In between, Jubaea and Michael cloaked in their own thoughts. For Nina, she wanted to be brave, a key remaining clutched in her hand, the chain pulling hard at her neck. Their progress was halted as Quercus stared at the forest, dense, dark and depressingly foreboding. Not a place to enter with weary limbs and oncoming night.

'Beyond that ridge is a waterfall, a good place to eat and sleep.' Twist immediately moved to the subject which brought him here. 'I have shown you the way. Beyond the forest you will find Cedrus.'

'Beyond the forest you will find redemption.' Quercus moved on between the crest of wrinkly crags. 'We shall rest for six hours. One hour watches by two men. I will take the first watch with Twist.'

There was advantage in spiriting Captain Twist, a man who showed signs of resistance and fear. But there was also a small element of fear in the Thief and his crew. That too had not gone unnoticed. Tales of the giants were widespread, colossus and naturally aggressive, born to survive in a hell hole where ordinary men might last months, certainly not years.

After his vigil Quercus remained awake, keeping alert, touring the divisions of snoozing pirates until he found a solitary spot, a place where he could watch Nina sleep, curled like a hedgehog against a rock. Under the moon and the crushing sound of water, he sat there touching the skin on his arms, very slowly tracing the contours, pressing against the ridges and lines, running his fingers across all the marks and scars as though he could read his blemishes like Braille. It was not fear that gripped him, only restlessness, the heightened sense of things to come, the sea born breeze coolly kissing the sweat at his chest and neck.

'Fancy a chat?'

'I have no other company.'

Michael crouched beside him. 'Sage was spot on. It's like summer. Mind you, it's a bit eerie in this place. I can't hear any night time noises like you do in tropical places.'

'It would seem good nature is limited in a hell hole.' He looked at Michael grinding the tip of his sword into the ground. 'Do you intend to use it?'

'Must get some practice in.' Michael sounded a shade lighter for being able to say that. It was once someone else's war, now it was his. 'If something should happen to me,' he said edging a deeper channel. 'Will you promise to look after Nina?'

'And if I should die? What can I promise?'

Michael shrugged. 'At least find a way to let her know I never meant to be a pain in the arse. I only wanted her to be happy. She had such a rough ride after Mum died. And I promised Mum to take care of her so I tried to find her a nice chap.'

'Nina understands and loves you. This is all you need to take into your heart.'

There was a tiny movement, not truly a sound, light as the flirt of a White Tail's wing, both lifted their heads and Michael said, 'If Nina had kept her child, I wonder who it would take after?'

'A good question, since Nina is not of this world. If the same kind mate there is no doubt, though sometimes seeding occurs between two kinds, and then it is left up to Hortus. My Father was a pin oak, my Mother a scarlet oak. Fagus took after his Father who married an ash.'

'Interesting, so there's no divergence, no creating new kinds?'

'What is the point of creating new kinds when the kinds we have are strong and established?'

'Err, right. I see your point. How old are you?'

'Half my life lived.'

'So you're a hundred years old.'

'Give or take a few years.'

'So being a tree doesn't affect your age?'

'In some respects it does. A tree is a place of shelter; it is the body put over our body. As our bodies grow old so shall the trees, as our bodies may sicken so shall the trees but the tree can live a far greater life span. For instance, an oak may live for up to a thousand years and in this respect my age has been halted to some degree.'

'I see. That's why those people who were released came out virtually like they went in.'

'There have been a few exceptions. Those confined in the earlier years when Cedrus was practicing his art of torture.'

'Care to enlighten me about your father?'

'My Father,' Quercus began, 'was not chosen by a White Tail to have a key yet he felt drawn to the gates. He spoke of the time when he arrived at Daylily, thousands of miles from a land where mighty oaks grow. From there he rallied support and married, established a home on the wooded clad hills. The influx of warriors had swelled the population. From every quarter came a torrent of ceaseless sound, all beating out time, counting down for a hopeful victory. He told me how he was dry with excitement, tight with dread, how he instilled confidence in men ready to fight under his banner. But his fame turned bad when he led the revolt. Many were killed by the firs, many turned into trees. No-one would speak to him or look him in the eye. It took him years to re-establish himself.'

'I remember you telling me he found the whip the day you were born. Something about the writing was on the bark, that to kill Cedrus would render the victor with immortality.'

'That is so, my friend. But we now know he misinterpreted the words. Perhaps he believed he would become immortal by driving the whip into his enemy's heart. He was not a man to listen to the wisdom of Sage. When I returned from your world, I discovered Acer had killed my Father. Cedrus knew the importance of the whip, anxious for it to be thrown into the salty elements. Syringa told me this. She too was rooted for a century in his secret garden where he spoke of his libidinous cravings as well as his scheming.'

'How long have you known Syringa?'

'Syringa and I were schooled in Daylily. Fagus was also there. His father came over with mine.' He smiled with cherished memories of Fagus then his gaze fell on sleeping Nina. 'Fagus fell in love the moment he met her. She was a little urchin. It took him a long while to establish himself as her suitor. Of course, battles never helped. Fagus picked up the sword before I picked up the whip.'

'So where did your father get the whip?'

'It was hung on a branch in our garden, the message buried deep in the trunk of a scarlet oak. By the time I grew to a sensible age, the trunk had healed. It was not until I reached the age of maturity did my Father hand over my key. He did not want me to become a Council Member, to be involved with politics.'

'So what happens when a Council Member dies? Is there always someone standing by with a key to take up that position?'

'It is often the case. Sometimes a position is left open until one comes forward. The oaks had no representation when my Father took up the cause.' In the long silence, Quercus studied a look on Michael's face he had previously seen before. 'What is really on your mind, Michaelmas?'

'Remember what you asked me? I want to take the final strike, go down in history.'

'You have never killed, Michaelmas. It is a daunting task, one that is levied against amateurs. When a man fights for his survival, the adrenalin pumps the heart and instinct provides the scent of a kill but to kill for killing sake places you last in the history books. This is not you, my friend.'

'Of course, you're right. Can't deprive a man from his honours and all that, no icing on the cake, what?'

Quercus gave him a wry look. 'I do not seek honours, Michaelmas.'

'Course you don't, forget what I said. You're a great guy, Quercus, and I shall consider you as my friend.'

'I am deeply touched.'

'Changing the subject a bit, why would a Keeper want immortality?'

'There is wisdom to immortality. Unlike those through the gates, we do not suffer short-sightedness. If a ruler has an indeterminable age, he will grow wise but not old, he will sew for the future not for the present. He shall see his efforts please generations and shall be held accountable. Alas, without the Book there shall be no Keeper.'

'What if the Book was found? Who gets to be Keeper?'

'Whosoever reads her words shall be Keeper. In the old days before the Keeper, peace and self-expression took precedence until disgruntled firs forged vessels to cross the dividing waters. The legend described a man of great knowledge and power, claimed to be the Keeper of her secrets. When he showed others this Book, no-one could read the pages for they were blank. The Keeper banished the firs from our continent and gave control of the seas to the Juniperus Pirates. For centuries we all respected the Keeper's laws until Cedrus killed for the want of her secrets. For a millennium we have suffered at his hands.'

'So what are you going to do, Quercus? Once Cedrus is killed, without a new Keeper, without the Book your continent is susceptible to another war lord.'

'We shall manage, no doubt.' He was not that interested, not when he yawned for the want of sleep. His head lightly dipped, his eyelids drew heavy and Michael's departure was quiet.

But his mood at that point was as bright as the stars. His cheery optimism matched the gurgling waters swilling into the basin. It seemed strange that the woman he met in spring, the woman who claimed to be a librarian was now part of his strength, where he would go, she would go too.

Midnight passed, light progressed towards dawn and Quercus woke to an appetizing smell and the echoes of camaraderie. He rubbed the sleep from his eyes and focused ahead; such sights were welcome. Skewered fish held horizontal on canes and bathed in smoke above the charcoal flames. Nina was splashing about in the water, her back to the men with Michael standing guard.

'My brother,' Jubaea called out. 'We are blessed with good food. Come and eat.'

'Where is Twist?'

'He took three men to scout the area. Do not concern yourself, he will return.'

'Are you so certain?'

'The Thief tracks their movements.'

Quercus held the cup to his lips, watching an insect swarm round Nina's feather as she approached. 'You take such risk, Nina.'

'Not really. I kept my knickers on.'

What else is there to want, Quercus thought. He studied her as she picked cooked flesh off the bone and popped it in her mouth, murmuring with pleasure as she swallowed.

'What?' she said, mindful of his gaze.

He handed over his beaker and whip then removed his shirt. 'I shall follow your route and take a dip with my knickers on.'

Leaving their titters behind, Quercus dived into the basin, a beautiful hero submerging into crystal clear waters. Rising to the surface, a hand clutched at his ankle, gaining purchase. A face appeared and then another, jovial men offering sport of a different kind. For most of his life, dawn had carried the threat of an enemy assault or involved preparations for a raid. Here, it was a small freedom to escape beyond a nightmare.

In contrast, they entered black-wretchedness an hour later. Here, the weed of evil bore bitter fruit among tall, bulbous trunks that sucked the earth dry and trapped the winds, prolonged agonies. It was a place where only the insane dare to venture.

'Christ, how deep does this go?' Michael whispered to Nina.

'If there are giants in this forest they certainly know how to hide. I could do with cold lemonade right now, the sort Mum used to make. Do you remember the time you jumped off the shed and fell into the greenhouse?' Her pause was long before she said, 'Michael?' Her head twisted round, was she possibly dreaming or really alone?

'Were your intentions to kill the enemy by tales of your history?'

'It has been known to bore people to death.'

Strapped by a rope to his ankle, upside down Quercus reached for her outstretched arms, and together they went high in the air, as high as one could imagine. The rope stretched to the weight of two people, the disturbing dark becoming lighter. It was an old trick of past days when Cedrus stalked the ground to seek out his prey. The deception still valid, a stunt well received in times like these. Up here, it was cooler and brighter, bare foot they advanced on thick branches reaching to other thick branches like a road map. They were veterans with their boots hung round their necks, feeling at ease with the occupants that lived and fed off nature among the grey-green leaves and whorls of rich brown cones.

Michael slapped his neck then examined his palm, pleasure writhing on his lips. 'That bastard has been plaguing me ever since I got up here.' His eyes fixed through the density of blackness where nothing became sacred within seconds. In twilight greyness, creatures moved themselves about, easing into relaxed positions. 'I say, chaps, there's about twenty down there. They don't look that big to me from up here.'

They will from down there.

Yet something troubled him, a little jarring on the nerves, an ominous picture that upon closer examination revealed itself to be women enduring labouring tasks. Wisps of smoke, escaping chickens, running children, the steel of smithies and stockpiles of food were already taking shape in his eyes. The last details were being finessed, the final unpleasant surprise. There, without doubt, among giants, women of different origins laboured as slaves.

Michael addressed Quercus whilst laying culpability at Twist. 'Want to know where some of your women are? Then ask him. I hazard a guess and say there are about eight, maybe more.'

Quercus beckoned Jubaea. 'Our women are left in a hell hole. If we position the Thief's men at four corners, we can haul them up and hope their escape goes undetected. I shall descend to make contact. Michaelmas will be your eyes.' He smiled dryly at Michael. 'There are other ways to confront the adversary. If I am correct in thinking, Twist and his men have leather soles.'

Again the rope was tied to his ankles, and he was lowered down into the abyss. The smell of decayed flesh, the excrement, foulness in the air so putrid he smothered his mouth and nose. Quercus had placed himself where the ground puddle black then lodged behind barrels of rotting fruit, his focus was on a female caked in mud to her thighs. She was a lilac, thin and wasted, collecting an armful of twigs and behind her, something beyond imagination. Tanned dark as an Arab, her eyes were deeply recessed, ears particularly large and seemed even more so because of the shortness of her hair. Her nose was long and thick, her hands those of a labourer. The female species of these gigantic firs had bulging muscles, their torso tight, their hips thin and altogether a sure sign of enduring strength.

'Faster, you oaf, be faster.' The lilac was pushed down, her body pinned by an outsized foot. 'Stupid dwarf, be faster next time.'

It was purgatory, a feeling he worked hard to quell.

'Water, please, water.'

'You will get water when you learn to move faster.'

Thudding steps moved on. Quercus peered over the barrels, locked eyes with the lilac and placed a finger to his lips. 'Syringa,' he whispered loud, 'do not be afraid. Your freedom is at hand.'

The lilac looked about, taking her time to pick up twigs. 'Who are you?'

'Lord of the Oaks. Sea Winger waits near the shores to take you all home.'

'I have heard of Sea Winger. It is the prophecy.'

'You must tell the others we are here. They must remain silent and drift to the four corners of this camp. There they will see the hands of safety. Can you do that?'

'There is one who lies ill. She needs water.'

'Where is she?'

'Behind the shacks where the chickens lay eggs.'

With extreme caution, he snaked round the camp, went creeping through the higgledy-piggledy arrangements, sometimes on all fours to avoid detection, to avoid powerful men and powerful women, some who lingered and basked in smoke to rid biting mosquitoes. It was a strange sound, a welling and droning of wings busying themselves over rotten carcasses. He spotted a water butt and submerged a beaker before travelling on. And there by the chicken coups, a lifeless heap, a doomed captive unable to fend off the flies. Blood oozed from her muddied side, her lips cracked and dry from the want of water. He held the beaker to her lips.

'Who…who helps me?' Her words issued slow and painful.

'Your saviour.'

'I am done.'

He ripped the cloth, studied the infested wound. 'Listen to me. It will hurt when I hold you. Bear the pain without sound. Tell me now if you are done?'

'I am not done.'

The oaf has gone!

Hue and cry had broken out, the clamour of angry firs demanding the whereabouts of their slaves. They raced in many directions, stirring the putrid air with their thumping feet. Sense and reason void. To look up would offer an answer.

With his journey impeded, Quercus pressed his back hard against a bulbous trunk, his heart beating wildly, the stricken lime clutched in his arms, nowhere to run, nowhere to hide without being seen. Then escape dangled by his side. Nina jumped to his aid, tied the rope round his waist and gave one tug. As he ascended, his felt Nina take hold of his legs, the line taking the weight of three people.

Aloft on the branches there was now debate. What to do? Go on and leave the women to work their way back to shore, take their chances, or wait under the canopy for their return. There was no guarantee anyone would survive.

'They are skin and bone, Quercus.' Jubaea remained close to his side. 'They will not last two days. Nor can I see them venturing alone.'

Quercus leaned worried against the trunk. 'To split our forces will weaken our defences. To stay will weaken our defences. Our position has been compromised. We must move on yet we cannot move on with these women.'

'The obvious solution is to let Twist and his men take them back.'

'It was him who brought them here in the first place.' Michael objected. 'Who's to say he won't drown them at sea after he's raped them.'

Quercus looked at Nina. She was holding a canteen to the lips of a lime. This was no place for them. They appeared so fragile, so close to oblivion and it filled him with agonizing concern. 'We have no choice. Jubaea take six of the Thief's men and-'

'No,' he interjected. 'I fight by your side. Let the Thief lead the party.'

'The rest of his men are nervous enough. If they see him leave it will create further anxiety.' He turned to Michael. 'You may lead.'

'Sorry, Quercus but I stay close to Nina.'

'Then take Nina.'

'What is the delay?' The Thief came into view. 'Your women must return to my vessel before they collapse in this heat.'

'We do not trust Twist with the women.' Jubaea said.

'Nor should you,' came the Thief's quick response. 'Four of my men will take them.'

'Take Nina,' Quercus asked.

'You are touched in the head. Once a woman has made up her mind, not even Hortus can change it.'

Did he really need to be told this?

Parting company and moving swiftly on, they were almost at their destination, pulling softly towards their goal. When the canopy thinned, Quercus and the Thief climbed beyond the grey foliage, was aware the sunlight had mellowed and the terrible heat supplanted by a breeze. Ahead, within a large dust bowl, there was a smaller replica to the home of Hortus.

'No doubt the heathen is there.' The words of Quercus were cold.

'This is what we have come for, no? Win or lose, there is no turning back.'

'Let me extend my hand to your courage.'

'I am a thief, a handsome thief, born to take risk.'

'Even a thief may prick the eye of Cedrus.'

His head dropped away. 'Do your worst. I shall do mine.'

One by one, like viscous liquid they slid down the ropes, which was more than could be said for the chicken-walk Twist and his fishy men.

Michael's bare feet touched ground. He followed the Thief's finger and looked up. 'Bastards, bloody slave traders as well as cowards.'

'I ordered my men to scupper his vessel.'

A grin formed. 'Chose the wrong bloody side, didn't he?'

Quercus shoved his feet into boots. It seemed his journey was now coming to an end. He looked up and stretched out his arms to receive Nina. What a place to be in love, what surrounds to lower her into. He cupped her face in his hands, resignation welcomed. 'We all stand together.'

'We stand together.' They voiced in unison.

He smiled with a welling in his heart. All told twenty men armed with steel, one woman armed with a feather, did it matter their death, only their victory? Their names would live on, their stories told. This was destiny, their fates determined. No hero could ask for more.

SECRETS AND BARGAINS

From a balcony littered in greenery, Cedrus viewed the oncoming threat awhile. There was no fear in his mind, no single thought of defeat just the purpose to kill his irritation. There would always be the likes of Quercus, of Fagus and the beautiful Lady Ilex willing to fight or spy.

Sipping his Harrods tea from a gold cup, he carried it through to the anteroom where a small entourage of supporters fell behind. They were the last of his Ministerial Firs. Their gaze held. There was recognition in the eyes of Cedrus, his hatred of Quercus, a constant thorn in his side. He had survived a century of confinement, had defeated two thousand black robes in the valley, had cut his lines of communication, outwitted the second waves on the west shores, and obliterated the rest of his army with cannon shot. Quercus had butchered so many, had reduced him to this pitiful facsimile on Nepenthes. He would pay dearly.

'Perhaps a small demonstration,' a Minister advised, lost, it seemed, in a private race from death. 'She is his Achilles' heel.'

It was a symbol Cedrus recognized. 'She escapes as easily as a ghost. Perhaps she is an ingenious strategy by Sage to thwart my endeavours. Yes, a small demonstration so I may gather information to her skills. Send twice their number.'

Quercus walked on, his white silks tattered and grey with dust, the whip coursed his chest, a sword in one hand, the other, the tender grip of Nina's fingers. They were closer to the enemy here, thrust out in the open. He felt her apprehension. It was no different for him. Behind, men were dutifully keeping pace, their swords levelled, their expressions set, some glancing back, a common rule of engagement.

'Quirky, if you see him raise a hand, don't forget to hold your breath.'

'There is no amusement for him to root us.'

'Quercus!' A man shouted.

He turned to a small army of sequoiadendron giganteum, the world's largest species of the conifer family emerging from the forest. But they were cumbersome, and advanced to the tempo of a slow heartbeat. Even so, their presence and proximity, their physical size rendered him speechless. He looked back and shaded his eyes, adjusted to the scorching glare of white walls and there he viewed the self-deluded Cedrus. Was he testing Nina?

'We must fight them, Quirky.'

'This was not the plan.'

'To root them will not coax the fox from his burrow.'

'But you have no weapon.'

She pulled the feather from her head band. 'Oh, but I do.'

Michael laughed nervously. 'You have to be kidding me. Do you think tickling them to death is the answer?'

As yet neither of them had entered battle, was beyond wildest imaginings and Quercus wanted to scream at the agony of it. But even in this tight spot he choked it off and took a running lead. He was now another man moving with greater speed and commitment to thrust eviscerating blows from chest bone to pelvis. Grotesque figures fleetingly glanced down at their flooding wounds, their expressions changed before dropping.

'You move fast, my brother!' Quercus spun to meet another.

'Jubaea taught me well!' Michael was engaged in his own battle, exploiting tardiness, searching for opportune.

Cedrus gathered their quick response, watched the onslaught of his tardy allies, forfeiting their lives at his pleasure. Before him was the agreeable sight of Nina who seemed lost in the transition against the spray of blood, weaving between bulging legs on hands and knees, stabbing feet with a feather? But one stumbled, to be dispatched by her brother. No more needed to be seen, no second glance given.

When the threat was neutralized, Michael threw up his sickly bravery. It was his first kill, an experience of animal desperation and commitment. All that mattered was survival. A hand came upon his back.

'My brother, do not be ashamed. Each of us has thrown up our dinners on the first kill.'

He wiped his hand across his mouth and stood erect, his sword hung heavy. 'Christ, I don't know who had the best weapon around here, me or Nina.'

They were now a focal point, like gladiators sent in the ring to amuse the audience but the audience had grown from all angles, emerging from the density, creating a barrier for no escape other than toward the building. Sightings of giant reinforcements, ready to act upon their master's bidding, unsettled them. Too few men against the devil and his army, there was certainly little point in challenging the inevitable.

'We have entered the lion's den with our eyes closed.' Quercus made a cast at Nina. 'What chance of turning those monsters into trees?' He saw her thinking about it carefully, an option between gain and loss, and he sighed silently with relief when she nodded.

'Our mettle will be tested. Look who approaches.'

None could mistake Cedrus, a hard face with a mouth pursed in dissatisfaction. A red silk band crossed his chest against a black leather tunic with a scimitar hung to his side, a whip in his hand, an impressive and immaculate appearance against white walls. He approached their faces, blackened with dust, their clothes and skin roughened by the rigours of combat.

'You expect me to quake?'

'No, I expect you to die,' replied Nina.

Cedrus hung immense against her. 'Would a feather cure your ill?' He snatched it out of her hand and she startled. 'You expect me to fear my roses when I inhabit a place of everlasting life. You are nothing more than waste product, a pip in a putrid bowl of apples.' Cedrus allowed his stare to drift along to Quercus, his shadow crawling over the head of his irritation. 'It would seem your kind does not share your sentiments.'

'The Thief fights for the same cause.'

'Have you not spilt enough blood?'

'Every drop counted upon your demise.'

'You live in false hope, Quercus. Rose petals will not defer your fate. I am the true Keeper of her secrets.'

'A true Keeper can read her pages.'

The eye twitched. 'I have long wished to see you dead. Should we save it for continuing endeavour against my army?'

Quercus threw his sword aside and unfurled his whip. 'Are your men so sure of your judgement or perhaps sickened by your machinations?'

Hatred welled in Quercus, obsession in Cedrus who had never been known to suffer the indignity of failure. Any outcome was possible in this ponderous heat.

The eyes followed Cedrus as he tinkered with his whip, wagging the tip like a dog wags his tail. Then with effortless speed, it lashed out, the leather fell short to skin, the sound discharging into the humid atmosphere. Quercus seized the moment and ushered his own, the tip tickled the face. First blood was drawn. There were cheers.

Cedrus traced a finger to his left cheek. No doubt he had misjudged his quarry. Reprisal came fast, a most furious aim, it flew the distance and stripped flesh. In gasps, Quercus clutched at his throat. Another strike and it was damaging. Darting from marble to ground, from cover of pillars to openness, inflicted several times, chased by splintering impacts, hope drowning until a narrow gap of fortune taken on impulse, and deadly meant. Second blood was drawn!

Now there was something in the bearing of Cedrus which suggested a hint of concealed pain. The potion was doing its worst but not worse enough. The whip had corrupted his flesh, not his resolve.

'I see you volunteer for magic, Quercus.'

'I take whatever is necessary.'

'You are under misapprehension. My roses will not kill me.'

'But they will slow you.'

In a raw and spitting fury that mirrored his own, Quercus caught the oncoming flay, had braced for pain. It was a mental struggle between the instinct of avoidance and creating opportune. He reversed Cedrus toward the curving elegance of a pillar, his hate a driving force to be reckoned. The doctored tip flew the distance, impacting with a heavy blow. Third blood was drawn!

'Now it would seem we are evenly matched.' Quercus swung his focus to Nina. 'Perhaps a tap dance would be soothing.'

Cedrus did not seem so lissom or svelte, slithered into reverse, backing sinuously away and shouted an order to his men. A thudding and rumbling backdrop, it needed no explanation upon this invasive swarm.

There were intakes of breath upon Nina's command as she ripped the beads from her neck and threw them high as she could manage. They merely lingered, added to the atmosphere then spontaneously spawned white dust, imperceptible against the sky.

The first invasive wave came to a perplexed halt. Cumbersome feet rooted to earth, from lower limbs and upwards crinkly wood crawled upon their skin. Their howling screams vibrated the ground upon which they stood as rigidity set in. Behind, the second wave cumbersomely crashed into the first, and it happened all over again to become an architectural blunder of the greatest magnitude.

Beneath the lip of the canopied ceiling, Cedrus threw down his whip and brought out his scimitar. 'I will have my day.'

'It is not this one.' Quercus smiled, flicked his wrist to match the steel, could feel and taste the end. Never had he dreamt of such rapture, a crazed thrill that conclusion was finally within his grasp.

As another battle unfolded around him, he was chasing and being chased, deflecting and descending, trying to finish it off. An opening at last, Cedrus staggered and fell. Quercus stabbed at a lower limb then carved his weapon upon his opponent's face in a joyful manner.

'Your fate is written, Cedrus.'

His presence less mortifying, but still he had an element of acuity in his voice. 'I am myself hard put to recognise the fact.' With a sudden foray, his scimitar spun out of his hand.

'Are you hard put now?' Quercus lunged and gouged the knee. Bone and ligament separated. 'Where is your invincibility now?'

Cedrus reached for purchase on a statue, his body grasping for hope. 'There is no immortality to be gained by taking my life. I can give you immortality. We shall share a kingdom.'

Kingdom? Immortality? It meant nothing to him now and he singled out Michael. 'Cedrus is yours if you have the stomach for another kill.' The instrument of Hortus was taken but Michael lingered so Quercus said, 'be quick lest he regains his strength.'

A word whispered in the ear, something which made Cedrus choke, then a downward sweep, the blade was planted through the chest and rammed home with such vengeance it demonstrated Michael had a crusade of his own.

The steel turned to leather, wriggling through a fractured and aging body where the screams carried to the sky, the earth trembled and for a moment it seemed as though other lives would be at risk. This used to be the most feared ruler in the world. Cedrus, giver of life, taker of death had eluded many battles for a thousand years, had exacted misery and degradation, and now he mouldered into the afterlife taking with him the whip of Hortus.

Quercus limped on. The pain quelled by such happiness that at last, he had fulfilled his destiny, had come through alive with the prospect of sharing his future with Nina. Nothing else mattered. Behind him, a skeleton crew, each in the mind-numbing throes of victory. It took a while to absorb and pass back as they settled under this obedient shelter, a complex of beautifully designed spaces, intended to calm the often inflamed tempers of its occupants.

'I say, chaps.' Michael had found his voice. 'Do you think there are any more of those troglodytes?'

Jubaea toyed with a platter of dates. 'Perhaps Nina has more beads.'

Quercus watched her slip away and go through an open door with some towels. A rare grin split his features. 'If you will excuse me, my brothers, I have greater imperatives.'

Following her blueberry scent, he picked his way to an open pool spa and watched her hang out her knickers on a protruding twig, curve her face upwards, and for now the air smelt sort of clean, infused with the shades of greenery. There were no roses, only desert climbers, muffling the hard edges, climbing up the walls, thickening and flowering and spraying out spores to breed in any untouched corners.

Removing his clothes, he slipped into the pool watching her tunic drop to the ground. 'A word, if it pleases you, madam.' Her coolness in crisis had impressed him almost as much as Michael. 'You held yourself well. Are you my Nina of the Atlantic or perhaps an illusion?'

'Have I not led you through my seas?' She slipped in beside him. 'My poor, Quirky, you are such a wonderful hero.'

His finger fed through the chain round her neck. 'Is your intention to keep me pinned in this world?'

It was rightfully his and should be with him always until end of days. She filtered the chain over his head, accidentally catching the deep gash on his neck. 'Oops,' she said. 'I shall bathe you; would you like that?'

'Below the waist is less painful.'

'Below the waist is less dirty.'

'I disagree.' He warmed to her laughter, turned and squatted low so she could sponge his back. 'I am curious as to what your brother whispered in his ear.'

'Knowing him, it was probably some obscene word. I was on tenterhooks most of the time. You took quite a lot of punishment before you could get him the second time round. I remember when you clipped a flower in my garden. I jumped then. Never in a million years would I have ever believed a whip could do so much damage.'

'Strange, but you are correct. Cedrus can handle a whip yet my head never rolled.' He stood erect and rotated, looking down into her worried face. The little things, insignificant at the time but now full of meaning came crowding back; the wine which was proffered, a raging thirst the next day and the feeling of wellbeing that he could conquer the world. He tried to see beyond her lucid intelligence, the surface of those eyes and his own expression hardened.

'I had to do it, Quirky. You would have died.'

'How did you come by the potion? Was it his roses?'

'No, it was not his roses. Sage gave it to me.'

'And you thought not to tell me?

'I am telling you now.'

Her words amplified his anger. He heaved himself out of the pool, a towel wrapped fiercely around his waist. 'I receive more loyalty from my men! Was it too much to ask the same? Instead, you bade me drink under false pretence, cried in my arms hiding your guilt. It is hard to expel the sour taste in my mouth.'

'I would feel angry too, Quirky. I forgave when you lied to me.'

'Ghosts will be my companions, is that what you wish?'

'I wish you to understand how I wanted you to live.' She ventured from the pool, unrepentant. 'The first strike would have seen your head roll. You know that to be true. Look at you now, ready to face the world again.'

Those were wide and open seconds as he surveyed his skin, shiny as iron, worn as a rock, his body unmarked of welts in every quarter. He glanced sideways and, despite his rancour, smiled. 'Give me your years, Nina.'

She shook her head vigorously. 'Now is not the time to discuss these things.'

'Now or later, what is the difference? We have served our destinies. Let us serve outcome.'

'Anger can take you a frighteningly long way, Quirky. Far from those who love and hurt you, far from everything you thought you knew about yourself. It's better to calm down and discuss the outcome logically.'

'Do I look out of control?' He offered his gritted-teeth expression.

'I would say you are in the throes of turmoil.'

He stayed motionless, his mouth half open to the remotest possibility she could be right but he felt utterly confused as though he might be on the brink of being quite out of his depth with also an element of sheer disappointment. 'I understand, my Nina. But I shall not fall like the winter wheat. I will love you until end of days and will love no more.'

'I wish it were that simple.'

'It can be that simple.'

'Things are never simple.'

'It is you who wishes to complicate the matter.'

'You are getting angry again.'

'I am not angry.'

'Yes, your eyes are flaring up. You are angry.'

'Frustrated, not angry, there is difference.' But there was no difference. He was, without doubt angry, desperate to have an answer. 'Nina, do not weave a tighter web. Loosen your thoughts and say you will share your life with me.'

'It's not possible, Quirky. It's not possible because-'

'Not possible! All this has been for nothing! I would far rather have taken my chances than to be told we are not possible! When should this parting be?'

She remained silent and unrepentant.

He picked up his boots and strode out as the mood took him. Upstairs where the air smelt fresher, where the views appeared brighter than his heart he leaned against the balcony and considered he was too hair-shirted to take a relaxed view of the situation, having too much mental and physical energy. Perhaps, he thought, perhaps she found his manner too daunting. Ease back, yes, ease back and allow her time to see reason to his argument. It was some while later he heard his name but he never looked back.

'Here's a nice cup of lemon tea.' Michael placed it on the balustrade. 'I made it myself.'

'Is there an antidote?'

'Come on, Quercus. She was frightened to tell you in case you tried to go it alone. Whatever way you look at it, you were destined for immortality.'

Quercus drank his tea in silence and stared ahead. There was something else on his mind, the whisper, the contorted face encased in a mottle tone of purple upon that whisper. Not quite the warrior's passing, certainly not quite the way of a doctor without much cause. He placed his empty cup in its saucer and said, 'What did you say to Cedrus?'

'Oh man,' Michael responded immediately. 'I wish you hadn't asked me that.' It was difficult not to be ruffled by that flat level stare which Quercus regarded him. 'I said,' Michael finally volunteered, 'Quercus has f*** your daughter and your son has f*** you.' He laughed nervously. 'Now you know our secret.'

Downstairs, men were laughing, eating and drinking and enjoying their tales. Up here, Quercus closed his eyes and considered in this barren place, his soul had been destroyed. He had lost the one thing he desired most in this world and a tear rolled down his cheek. There was no simple answer, probably no answer at all. He waited for his heart to settle then sighed. To him the world was coming to an end, his emotions tangled like a piece of cotton caught in a web.

'I have no Nina,' he finally concluded. 'What was I thinking? Foolish dreams when my choices were already mapped.'

'There are so many confused thoughts whirling around your head, my man. The only way you can prevent yourself from splintering into a thousand pieces is by refusing to acknowledge any of them.'

'So it is your wish I suffocate in my own ruminations?'

'No,' Michael rebuked that concept. 'I'm just trying to tell you to take one day at a time until you can get your head round it.'

'How does my head get round such a revelation? How could such a thing happen?'

'I shall tell him.' Nina answered. 'Quirky, it was not my intention to withhold the truth.'

Quercus craned his head round for a moment to face the woman he loved, the woman who now had discarded her leather tunic for a silk shirt that accommodated its mass to suit her size by rolling up the sleeves and wrapping a blue sash round her waist. It just seemed impossible that she was one of *them* and how he despised *them*. He turned back to the views and leaned once again on the balustrade.

'But withhold you did.'

'It was just important to withhold until Cedrus was gone, dead, pulped, disintegrated or whatever. I wasn't allowed to tell you. Sage told me that to tell a destiny is to alter destiny. Quirky, look at me.'

'No need to look when I can hear.'

'As your people watched a celestial spectacle of a total eclipse lasting for eight minutes, Cedrus was raping a woman of his own kind. She had dark blue hair and very unusual eyes. Instead of black, they were bright sapphire and it made him all the more anxious to have her. In the months that followed she became a distant memory and was cast beyond the palace walls to fend for herself, but Sage was there to help her. Where she would find comfort in birthing twins,

Sage promised her Cedrus would meet his end by looking at the prophecy, knowing he had unwittingly played a part to his own demise.' Her hand came upon his and he found comfort in that. 'I am heartbroken too, Quirky. Michael is heartbroken. Our lives have been a farce. The parents we thought we had were our adoptive parents. Whether they knew or how much they knew is left for speculation.'

'The Thief, he knows?'

'Yes,' she confirmed. 'I told him in order to secure a bargain.'

'What bargain?'

'I told him he can have this island in return for his help.'

Quercus nodded slowly. There was no fool like a fool in love. 'I was led blind by consorting firs.'

'Oh, Quirky, that's untrue. You're getting angry again.'

'It is my right to be angry!' He shuffled past her and strode into the room, opening and slamming wardrobe doors. 'One hurdle upon another,' he growled dispatching shirts to the floor. 'Sage is no different. Why did I not follow my Father's advice is beyond common sense.'

'Excuse me! We have damn fir cones in our DNA and apart from the fact we can't live on Deciduous land, I have fallen in love with an immortal tree! So if you think you have problems, take a hard long look at mine!'

Her eyes, they were fierce and sapphire. He was held by them. Now he was of a mind to take off where they last left in reasonable conversation. 'I am no longer in the throes of turmoil, my Nina.'

'Well I am! What are we supposed to do? We can't return through the gates. Our sudden appearance will reignite a police investigation. And if we manage to get through that, how on earth can Michael practice medicine with a blemished record? He was supposed to operate on a young boy but he was so worried about me, he just upped and left. So what alternatives do we have? Tell me because I would love to know. Do we apply as asylum seekers or what?'

Quercus took a deep breath, a shirt held crumpled in his hand. 'It is true.' The breath extinguished. 'News of your history will, no doubt become a great talking point among both kinds. Your people will see you as their new leader. Mine will see you as opportunists. Council Members will see you as a threat.

Even with the weight I hold, there is no argument against long established ways.'

'So where are we expected to go?'

'Here,' the Thief voiced walking into the room with a plate of cold meat and a bottle of wine. 'Here is a good place.'

'Here is a desolate place,' said Michael.

'Here you can make it a nice place.'

'Your place.' Quercus told him. 'Is there no honour among your kind? How do you intend to rid the giant females who lost their men to Nina's endeavours?'

'I should imagine Captain Twist and his crew are in the process of doing it for me.' The Thief walked to the balcony, took a swig from the bottle and gestured with his hand. 'My island. My island I rent to Nina and Michael.' He looked back with a boyish grin which only enhanced his handsome features. 'In return I ask them to make it a nice place. I will build more vessels like Sea Winger using the large trunks Nina made. Good timbers for ships like Sea Winger and then I will venture beyond.'

'Beyond where?' Michael's interest had been drawn.

'If I knew where, I would not say beyond. I would say to wherever then you would know wherever is and beyond would not be so attractive. You can be my eyes, Cedrus Michaelmas and I can be your transport.'

'And me,' Nina asked. 'What am I supposed to be?'

'Free to build a Garden of Eden with your Adam. Is it not a good plan?' The men exchanged glances and smiled but Quercus was not amused so the Thief extrapolated. 'Come now, my good friend. You can spend your days with Nina, make love under the stars then return to your homelands when she dies and find another to keep your bed warm.'

'Quercus, this is madness.' Jubaea emerged, stealing the moment. 'You cannot while your time growing flowers and making love to a fir.'

'And why not,' Nina retaliated. 'I am the same woman who cried for your people. Michael is the same man who killed for your people. I can see why Cedrus took the view he did against such bigotry. In England there are laws against racial prejudice.'

'This is not England!' Jubaea spoke fiercely. 'Put away your fanciful notions. Fagus believed more than most we shall have a Keeper.'

'Well what if Michael is the Keeper or me. After all, I found the mouthpiece. That would soon put paid to your stupid laws.'

'Some of you would choose to ignore why we have come this far. You, Thief, have you not yearned for a return to our old ways? You, Nina, have you not served your destiny? You, Michaelmas, have you not served yours? Let Quercus serve his. Fagus believed Quercus was destined to be Keeper, to return to the old ways, to make each life a good life.' He returned his gaze to Nina. 'It would not be the wrinkles on your face to sadden your heart but the pain upon his face as he wrestles with his destiny.' Jubaea now looked at Quercus. 'Even when you returned, I still had my doubts but Fagus never doubted. And Fagus was right not to doubt. The prophecy came true and the mouthpiece existed. More than ever now, I believe the other half exists. Tell me, my friend, do you believe it exists? If not, I shall say no more.'

The room fell silent. Quercus bent down, gained purchase of his left boot and turned it on end. The key slipped into his palm. How easily it could have happened, how easily he could have thrown it away. He had stored the key in his original pair for weeks then transferred it to a borrowed pair Michael handed over at a time when they were searching for a secret garden. 'Can this,' he finally conveyed, 'be the key that allowed Nina to enter the gates. If so, I question how Michaelmas entered. Alternatively, is Michaelmas the true prophecy, the one Sage claimed would enter the gates without a key? It does not make sense to have one enter with a key and the other not.'

'So what are you saying?' Michael asked.

'I am proposing this key is the subject of confusion. The key was found in the mouthpiece which was lost one thousand years ago. Or did someone place it between the linings at the time of your birth? Nina, what is your thought on this?'

'I know it was stored gathering dust in the museum since the time it was found. That negates the possibility of someone putting it there when we were born.'

'So shall we assume it may well be a key to unlock the riddle to the lost half?'

'Cedrus claimed the other half was destroyed,' the Thief said.

'Ignore what you heard and tell me where you would look.'

'A key, if not to enter the gates, would open a door but since there are many doors without locks it reduces the search but those with locks have something to hide and there are many that would have something to hide. For my part, I have no locks for what might be taken I can easily take back.'

Quercus looked vaguely impressed. 'What men have something to hide? Not many, since everything is bargained or free.'

'Does anyone know exactly what happened when the Book split in two?' Nina asked. 'I mean, nobody seems to tell the same story. Pussy told me the fight occurred in the palace yet Syringa argued it occurred in the woods. Fraxinus was convinced it was never a fight. That Cedrus poisoned the Keeper in his sleep. But if that was the case, the Keeper must have known for why else split the Book. Even you, Quirky, admit you don't know.'

'The problem is simple. Cedrus wiped the truth from our history books.'

'That's interesting,' Michael said. 'Why would he do that? Was he afraid of what his people would think of him or was he afraid of something else being known?'

'If you are willing to take risk, I can lead you to a man who may shed more light on those events.' The Thief gained their attention. 'He claims to know the truth but he never proffers the truth because no-one has won the game.'

'And what game is that?'

WINTER CHAPTERS

Less obviously, the colours and textures of twigs, branches, bark and berries of deciduous trees and shrubs also have roles to play in providing visual interest during the winter months.

THE GAME

The cabin door was wide open and at a glance he identified Nina hunched over a desk with a pen in her hand. Not far from her feet, the recumbent green leopard gnawing on a fat juicy bone. He never moved until she looked up, scarcely knowing what to say.

'It never worried me,' she said, the humour long gone from voice now. 'To have what years I could spend with you is better than nothing.' She shrugged her shoulders. 'But this is not about the differences in our life spans, is it?'

'Not all is lost, my Nina.' He tried to smile, but the gravity of the situation had finally sunk in. 'I was sorely tempted to stay on Nepenthes and forget others existed except you. But I am, in truth, bound to my destiny and however much I want to share yours it would seem we are only linked in passing.'

She wiped her eyes with the palm of her hand, so much in control of her feelings. 'In England I had my prejudices too but unlike here, you're not able to express your thoughts without someone ready to drown you out, and those people who do most of the shouting have the most to lose. Choice is an illusion created between those with power and those with not. Here was me thinking I was British, routing for my country to stop the madness and close the borders on immigration. They came for a better life, and the government gave them carte blanch to do what they liked, take what they liked and say what they liked regardless of how it affected long established ways. If you allow one society to prosper at the expense of the other then you have created a temple for apocalyptic visionaries. Both of us are in a position to put our needs last and keep established ways but there is nothing to stop us from earning each other's trust.'

'You want to be a politician?'

'To be a politician means cheating and lying. If they are not kissing babies they are stealing their lollipops.' She looked at him with intensity now, trying to read his reaction before going further. 'Michael and I have an opportunity to find our Mother. Perhaps she is still alive, and why not?' She glanced down at her hands, clasping them on the desk. 'We have made arrangements to be dropped off with you.'

'Do you intend to stay?' Quercus asked quietly.

'Where you seek the missing half, we shall seek our place in a land that as yet we know nothing about.'

He took her hand, scribing small circles with his thumb. 'I am proud of you, Nina. Whatever was said in anger these past few days, it was not meant. In part it was shock. I had built castles for us, Nina, a new home on the wooded clad hills, searching for the missing half of the Book and beyond that a life where we could have children and grow old together.' He sighed heavily. 'One cannot change prejudices, Nina. My people have lost so much and their memories dwell on their losses. Cedrus rallied many of his own kind to slaughter my people in the early days and later, well later they grew fat and lazy and did not want to fight once Cedrus was enshrined in the palace at Daylily.'

'There is nothing to say we cannot write to each other.'

'Nina, if I am Keeper I-'

'Shush,' she interjected. 'If you are Keeper, it would make matters worse and you know this to be true. You cannot have one law for you and another law for your people.'

'Remember the words I spoke to Michaelmas when his morale was low. A man is measured for his deeds.'

'But it goes a little beyond deeds, Quirky. It was such a mistake to tell Michael. He just wheedled it out of me. If only I had kept my mouth shut then nobody would have been none the wiser. He would be sailing on lakes and we would be together in Daylily.'

A rap on wood and the Thief poked his head through the door. 'I see the two love birds have finally made up.' He proffered a bottle of hair dye. 'This will last one wash.'

'Give it to me,' Nina said springing from her chair.

'How soon shall we arrive?' Quercus removed his shirt.

'With any luck we shall arrive in five days. I shall leave you to it.'

Quercus knelt in front of her. 'I coloured my hair once before and Father punished me by shaving it off.'

She laughed softly. 'What made you do that?'

'Fagus dyed his red. To be young and stupid must be the time to live. There are no sorrows or concerns, only one day in front of another to chase hares through steeps of wheat and play truant.' He paused as she wiped a runaway drip to the side of his face. 'Nina, can we not meet once a month on the night of a full moon?'

She knelt in front of him. 'You must be strong for me, Quirky. I cannot do this alone. One night will become two, and two will become three and if you don't keep still your face will be full of brown streaks.'

As she worked her fingers deep into his scalp, there was a moment's silence, a hidden understanding of the strain between them. His feelings were such that he wished he could walk away there and then rather than prolong the agony of their parting. But then she laughed, and her eyes screwed up and they were talking the way they used to, finishing sentences for each other, waving their hands for emphasis, choking on funny stories.

Between the once captive women on Nepenthes, the pirates that fought bravely by his side and the flourishing White Tails who underscored their importance in this most ancient world, Quercus slept among men sustained by his craving for the Book of Hortus.

'You are nearly bankrupt,' Quercus told Nina.

'Not yet,' she said moving her token four spaces.

The Thief smiled, moving her token back one. 'Cheats never prosper.'

'Quirky,' she said glancing up. 'Can you lend me some money?'

'And what guarantees will you give?'

Her eyes followed the pile of properties Jubaea had collected. 'You can have Fleet Street to make up your set.'

'That is mine,' said Jubaea. 'You cannot give what I own.'

'Hey,' she argued. 'I thought in this world nobody owns anything.'

'Rules are not meant to be broken. If one keeps borrowing on others' entitlements, the game will never end.'

'Oh, you're so right, Jubaea.' She looked at Quercus. 'I shall offer a kiss for every pound I cannot pay back. Would that suit?'

Indeed a good incentive. 'How much do you require?'

'Wait!' The Thief had other ideas. 'Since she has landed on my property, I am entitled to be her borrower.' The growl quickly changed his mind. 'Perhaps you should lend her the money.'

In their laughter, a White Tail screeched, shrill-calling to Nina spiralling cosily down in the afterglow of dark. It sunk with the turn of the wind and landed on the Monopoly board, dropping its beak-filled message in the folds of her lap. 'Oh, it's from Pussy. She sends her regards. I must tell Michael.' She beckoned the White Tail. 'Come on, sweetie. I have a rat in my cabin.' The bird squawked and waddled behind her.

Quercus shook his head, reclined against cushions. 'Are we continuing the game?'

'Not for me,' Jubaea said rising. 'I am tired.'

'Your new look suits you.' The Thief watched the face, choosing his words. 'Say you find the other half and discover you are the Keeper.'

'Then I would be truly blessed.'

'You think it will give you licence to live with Nina?'

Quercus said nothing to that, tipping the contents of the game into its box. 'We too must sleep.' Keeping in step with the Thief, he was now of a mind to speak. 'If you were in my position, what would you do?'

'A man who loses his love can do one of two things, follow the ways of a swan or collect tokens of affection. Since you cannot kill yourself, the latter is your only option unless you intend to live like a monk. Listen, my good friend, Book or no Book, I gave you a simple plan but you refused. Now word has spread and the firs are stirring. This excursion you take will be risky. If you do find the other half, remember the Keeper rules not an immortal man pining for a life he cannot have.'

Quercus slipped into a hammock. 'A Keeper is entitled to some pleasures.'

The lantern was dowsed. 'We may get a kind Keeper.'

Long moments passed with his eyes closed, thinking she was a few thin walls away. 'Thief, explain your meaning.'

'The meaning is obvious.' Jubaea spoke. 'The Thief would like Nina or Michaelmas to be Keeper then where would we be? No more interruptions. Good night.'

Now Quercus had something else to think about. He sighed heavily, a rumbling gust coming from somewhere far down in the emptiness of his stomach. From his point of view, perhaps there was advantage if Nina was Keeper. There again, perhaps not.

As the nautical miles drifted behind a magnificent frigate, drawing them closer to their dropping off point, so did the blustery winds come upon Sea Winger's sails, her repaired mast creaked and groaned under the strain. The crew and passengers stared into the wilderness of seas, anxious for a scenery change, anxious to meet their loved ones. The conversation ebbed and flowed, they talked about warmer wear for the shivering, duck pate for the connoisseur, and anything else a Juniperus Pirate would steal from the gates.

For Quercus, his nervous system was over-stimulated by chemicals. He looked a different man, fit for purpose. His hair was brown, tied back with a leather thong, two leather scabbards concealed daggers upon his leather tunic and a heavy black cloak made out of sheep's wool hung loose about his shoulders. He was going to set foot on Coniferous land portraying himself as a cross-bred farmer.

Then in the slow grey light of a late afternoon where clouds packaged the sun, land was sighted and the vessel came alive. Men and women leaned against the port-side as Sea Winger dropped anchor, a rowing-gig pulled alongside.

'I shall send word if there is any news.' Quercus told Jubaea.

'Good luck, my friend.'

It was a moment of parting and understanding.

Quercus worked fast, shimmied down the ropes and jumped into the rowing-gig where Nina and Michael were waiting. Then they broke away from Sea Winger, heading towards the shores of Coniferous land where beyond this terrain Quercus would enter Ginkgo territory to find the man who could tell the tale of what happened one thousand years ago. In place of conversation was the acceptance of fate. They might not meet again, might not witness a new Keeper.

Two friends quickly hugged then Quercus stooped and enveloped Nina in his arms, she clutching him tight, burying her head in his shoulder. Neither spoke in their long embrace then he just stood there watching her leave. She never looked back, and suddenly he felt abandoned and bereft, holding the crying into his throat, his chest expanding. Would he ever see Nina again?

As he walked the land of broken dreams, he continued alone, his steady pace carrying him onward. Every night sound was enough to penetrate his thoughts and most were sufficient to rouse him, the hoot of an owl against the roar of a beast. His own limited experience had provided his eyes with nothing inspirational to inhabit, though by the time light broke into the sky, beauty unrolled before him, mile after ambling mile to give him a glimmer of this hungry continent. Post wind-mills appeared to play an important role, their white sails turning on the brow of hills with deeper valleys crazed by rock formations. It was wild and magnificent.

Coming across a settlement, holding sway above a deep ravine, he was more than ready to shake the dust off his boots. Ahead, a boy with brown hair sat on a stone-built wall, drawing a picture with pens sticking out of a jam jar. When he looked up, he quickly gathered his workings and rushed off as though what he saw was frightening.

Quercus went further into the settlement where it was notably different from what he knew in his part of the world. Here, single storey homes were built of stone and eaves sloped to create canopies over yellow painted wooden terraces that captured the views. He looked higher to see some sort of construction crane hanging over a red tile roof top a street away and there was sweetness of a rolling cold wind that was clean from the countryside. But absent were the sounds of human interest, blacksmiths and stonemason mallets, the neighing of horses or the wheels of carts rumbling over cobbles or even the smattering of people that generally wander around. It was evident his presence had caused concern.

Momentum carried him forward to a water fountain, drank his thirst wet then surveyed a wooden hut with its door half off its hinges. There seemed a good place to catch up on sleep. Inside gave him shelter from the winds and he nestled among sacks of flour with his hand clutching the handle of a dagger, his head resting in the crook of his elbow. He was once again bent against the way of war.

'He looks like one.'

Quercus reacted swiftly and drew a blade. Women shot back, some tripping on their footing, fell flat on their rumps. Focusing more clearly, he said, 'I apologize, ladies. You took me by surprise.' He stood and bowed. 'Permit me to introduce myself. I am a farmer wending my way towards Ginkgo territory.'

'For a farmer you act fast in your sleep.' A spokeswoman said.

'A farmer learns to sleep lightly in case wolves should attack.' They nodded. That appeared feasible. 'Where are your men?'

'They are hunting.'

'Is there a spare horse for my travels?'

'The river takes you to Ginkgo land. Are you sure you are a farmer?'

'Madam, I have been cocooned in my own world tending to my animals and studying plants that favour pastures new. I seek to broaden my horizons and find myself a wife.'

'Wife, you say? What woman would want a man that caresses flowers?'

'Then truly I have a hard task.'

'I would be interested in a man who caressed my body like flowers.' A different voice, a different woman wormed her way through. 'Pay no attention to these gaggling geese. They like the rough hands of a warrior whereas I like a man with a delicate tongue such as yours.'

'Perhaps upon my return we may reacquaint ourselves.'

'Perhaps I will come with you.'

He gulped. She was voluptuous, headstrong and like many on this continent. It was strange how this land had nurtured its people to blend with its most beautiful and rugged terrain. There appeared to be an underlying correlation and something he would think further upon when his mind was vacant of other things. 'Although your company would be most welcome,' he said. 'I shall be busy in search of a man called Black Jack in order to hear his tale.'

'No man wins,' the spokeswoman said. 'Your journey will be wasted.'

'I beg to differ. Win or lose, I still gain experience.'

'You see, ladies. This man has a philosophical mind. If he cannot stir the body he can stir the mind.' They laughed again. 'I will join you.'

And that appeared to be that.

He sat in her kitchen breathing uneasy while she gathered her incidentals. Against the fashion she wore her brown hair long and straight. It was so fine and silky it formed a polished sheet over her cotton-clothed shoulders. But there was something vaguely familiar to stir his senses. Was she related to someone he knew?

'So,' he began a little hesitant. 'I heard whispers that Cedrus was killed by the mighty Lord of the Oaks.'

'You were misinformed by your sheep. He was slain by his son, Cedrus Michaelmas.'

A daisy fir. He smiled.

'Where is your farm?'

'Far south where the hills are flatter and the grass is greener.'

'Far south is where the land is hotter and the grass is browner. You are no farmer. You speak with a quick tongue. Hold yourself like a warrior with manners of a tree. Truth would be a good exercise if you care for your life.'

'Bold words spoken by a woman alone.' From behind came a blade to his throat. 'Perhaps not alone?'

'Must I keep saving your miserable hide?' The Thief laughed. 'She is my wily blood sister, and will take you to Ginkgo Country, be your wife so act like her husband.'

'You planned this?'

'If you cannot convince her, you cannot convince the men. I watched your pitiful act.'

'How did you arrive before me?'

'By river of course. But have no fear, your women are safe and will soon arrive at Daylily a little fatter.'

'You lead me on a foot trail when the river is quick, now you wish me to act as husband to your sister. What game are you playing?'

The Thief struck his webbed foot on a stool, let a world map roll its thick length on the table, and pointed with the tip of his blade. 'Look closely, my friend. Before Cedrus, Deciduous land opened wide to the seas. The Juniperus Pirates would sail their vessels into the mouth of Daylily and travel the channels into the heart of your countries. Other mouths were narrowed to halt their traffic.'

'The Keeper did not give the Juniperus Pirates right of access on our lands, only to unload their cargo at Daylily.'

'Ask why your waters stagnate, why your rivers freeze quickly in winters and why your dirt tracks grow thick of mud when the rains come.'

'It is the way of things.'

'Maybe your eyes will widen when you see the way of things here. See how these rivers flow from the sea-salt mouths into the heart of fresh water destinations. I can sail on Coniferous land and reach Ginkgo in less time than you can ride your steed fifty miles. Do you think Hortus would make her seas starve her lands?'

'If, what you say is true, why would Cedrus distrust the Juniperus Pirates?'

'Now you have asked the right question. He wanted control of the gates. By stemming your water highways, we could not attack from behind. He would root us on land. Our only defence position would be at the gates and there his vessels and black robes would pick us off, one by one. When we first heard of the black robes, we made our own plans to seek and destroy their breeding grounds. We found six and sabotaged each one. Next, he sent Lord Acer and his men to Abies Alps. Abies, you met him and his good warriors. We were planning a campaign when low and behold the mighty Lord of the Oaks gathers his army and the prophecy appears through the gates. Abies was marking his territory. He would not have attacked you.'

'I puzzled how the black robes could enter the gates until Fagus pointed out they are not blood and bone but plant matter.' He held the Thief's eyes. 'Why did you not trust me with your thoughts?'

'Why did you not trust me with yours?'

A fair comment. 'Was his intention to bring greater weapons through the gates?'

'Think. Why would he want weapons when he had the world at his fingertips? There is so much we can steal without being caught. He wanted their knowledge, their ability to create machinery, to turn this world into the type of madness they have. In return he would offer some of your women for examination. But he forgot the mighty Lord of the Oaks, and of course the Handsome Thief.'

'The Elders never spoke of our rivers flowing fierce.'

'Cedrus wiped much from the history books. Now, if you are Keeper, you can reinstate the waterways.'

'And you wish to travel them?' Quercus stood, shaking his head. 'Too much has passed between the firs and trees. If we were to widen the mouths it would leave us vulnerable.'

'This is how it once was. The Juniperus Pirates sailed the water highways. In return we heard your tales. It was a good arrangement made possible by the Keeper. Our bellies were full, our thirsts quenched.'

'I have only your word.'

'And my proof is the map which my ancestor stole from Cedrus.' The Thief rolled it up with no intention of handing it over. 'Trust in JP. She will guide you to Ginkgo territory. Guard her back as she would guard yours.' He kissed his sister on the cheek. 'Show him the sights via the enclave. You have four days and no more.'

Leaving the Handsome Thief to find his own way, the two left the stone building and headed for the crane hanging over a roof top a street away. A sturdy basket lowered them two hundred feet down a sheer ravine and into one of the standby canoes. The water was as clear as air and so cold that when Quercus tested the temperature his fingers turned white.

'I shall paddle.' JP piled her hair on top of her head. 'You must call me bitch or woman and try to slump like a farmer.'

Quercus dug into his cloth sack to break bread. 'How far do we go, woman?'

'Two hours at most, husband.'

The conversation was light and trivial and, having established their peculiar accord, they were entering Ginkgo territory. Gone were the aspects of sheer ravines. In their place was gentle benevolent hills, and the river narrowed, winding among a pretty backdrop of colourful sails rotating from post mills and stone built houses awash with red roofs. Upon the last bend, they were entering a city where the river ran through and under wood painted bridges. The populous was heaving and swelling with activity.

'What, my husband? You think the firs are stupid as well as lazy?' JP stopped the canoe close to where musicians were playing their brass instruments. 'Remember to slouch and do not dip your head.'

'Is this enough slouch, woman?'

'You look like an ape.'

'Have you seen an ape?'

'Am I not looking at one now? Close your mouth and listen. Do you see the orange building with the double doors? That is where we go. The doors do not open until sunset.'

Quercus ambled on. 'I have noticed many different things. One in particular is colour and shape. Where we take a simple line, here there is gross ornamentation with bright colours. Even some of your windmills have colourful sheets. It would suggest that because your kind lack colour you seek colour in other ways whereas we are colour and seek only to keep our buildings plain.'

'And winter you have no colour but bare branches and snow.'

'True, winter can be bleak but we use the snow for sledges and games.' He stopped at a shop front, remembered his father making him a box kite. Commerce was indeed rife in this neck of the woods. 'What is the purpose of this shop if not to exchange some form of currency?'

'Gold, diamonds or any precious metals or stones.'

'Where are these metals and stones?'

'Mined in the east. It was Lord Acer who discovered them. That was why he turned traitor. Did you not know this.'

'I did not know this.'

'You are forgetting your slouch, husband.'

'Must I be a farmer? Why not a tool maker or do they slouch?'

'Here, farmers are considered imbeciles. If you play the imbecile with Black Jack it will relax his guard.' She foraged under her skirts and brought out a pouch. 'You will need these, the brighter the colour, the more valuable the stone. As a farmer you only have two diamonds. He will ask for more so act disappointed and walk away. He will call you back. Do you understand?'

He looked into her face, watched as the brows met. 'Do you live among these people?'

'I am my brother's eyes and ears on land. What I do best is gather information and besides, I cannot swim.'

'You cannot swim. That is extraordinary.'

'I sink like a bag of sand. My brother claims I have too much iron in my blood.'

Quercus laughed. 'Your brother needs a chemistry lesson.'

Now the sun was setting, in front of them stood a series of bustling actions, people squeezing to get through a pair of doors that seemed to hold more than the mystery of Black Jack. Inside, it was as expected to be seen based on what he had already established about this area; substantial, ornate, and it conjured up excess as though colour and music were the two most important things in their lives. At every turn there was dazzling opulence, gambling tables, dancers in frilly knickers, fortune tellers and whores who had men lining up for their wares.

Welcome, welcome, are you ready to be distracted.

Cutting through the various smells of heavy perfumes, Quercus ventured towards a large gathering round a black-clothed table. He went on tiptoe to see over the heads and watched a man shuffling three up-ended gold cups. The hands were deft, the fingers laced with gold rings, the hair white, the skin aged and the body rotund. Above, a poster hung of the tales he would tell and priced accordingly.

'The ball is not under any of them.' JP whispered.

Quercus had noticed this too. It was time to turn the tables to his advantage. He drew close, showed interest and waited for the approach.

'You look like an intelligent man,' announced Black Jack. 'Guess the cup that has the red ball and you win a story.'

'How would I know your story is correct?'

'Sir, I am a man of my word. Do you wish to play or run away?'

'I wish to play.'

'What story do you wish to play for?'

'The Keeper's Demise.'

Black Jack rubbed his hands together. 'We have a true gambler in our midst ladies and gentlemen. It will cost you two red stones or five white.'

'I do not have what you ask.'

Black Jack turned to his audience. 'This man wants to run away.'

'If I do, I take the tale of the prophecy.'

He knows the prophecy! Someone shouted and a greater crowd gathered.

'What say you Black Jack, a tale for a tale told in confidence?'

'Can you prove your tale?'

'Can you prove yours?'

The man stroked his stubbled chin, his bead-black eyes fastened on Quercus, no doubt sizing him up. Then he nodded and left the table, motioning to follow behind the curtain.

'This is not a good way.' JP said.

'It is my way.'

They were led through a series of corridors where the smells were less heady and the scenery less extravagant. It was, perhaps, typical of such places where only the façade mattered. Then Black Jack closed the door and pulled Quercus to the table that sat centre stage in a room without a view.

'The woman was not part of the bargain.'

'The woman is deaf. Before I begin my tale, I want proof yours is true.'

'I can give you proof.' Black Jack smelt the wine stopper. 'I am seven hundred and thirty-two years old. My Father was there, every last detail given to me. Now what is your story?'

And so Quercus related his tale and in so doing he reminded himself of the events that played out and considered that perhaps one day he would write his journals. It took nearly an hour with personal details excluded, and with interruptions included. Meanwhile, JP had helped herself to the wine and fell asleep slumped over the table.

'How did you come by this tale?' The question was expected.

'I am Lord of the Oaks, Quercus Coccinea.'

'Lord of the Oaks has red hair.'

Pulling at a chain round his neck, Quercus revealed one of two keys. But still it was not enough.

'That is no proof. Anyone can have a key made.'

'Let us hope your proof is as good as mine.' The dagger unsheathed, Quercus placed a flat hand on the table and rammed the blade hard through flesh, the suffering sufficiently painful to wince before a man who witnessed a healing wound.

Black Jack poured more wine. 'I do not know the Keeper's history or what kind he portrayed. But I do know he was here, on our lands surveying a new bridge constructed by my Father. Attached to his side was a green leopard. Everywhere he went the leopard went too. That day, my Father was honoured by the Keeper's attendance to share food at his table and sleep in his home. Now we come to the point of his death. It was past midnight. My Father woke to a terrible howling and ventured to where the Keeper slept, and there, the green leopard was sprawled on his chest. What happened next is no word of a lie. The leopard rose sharply and flew through a closed window two storey high. Since there was no reported sighting from an injured or dead cat, we must assume the creature returned to your homelands. From that day to this, I have my Father's words memorized in my head, those same words whispered to him by the Keeper upon his dying last breath. Cedrus is my assassin. It was a slow and painful death. There was nothing anyone could do. The poison was administered in the water jug by the bedside table.'

'Did your father fear Cedrus?'

'My Father feared no-one. He was a great man with extreme vision and mental acuity. Cedrus claimed to be the new Keeper and for several years we flourished under his command. Then he paid my Father a visit and made him Commander of a new army to quell dissention on Deciduous land. That was the last time I saw him.'

'And yet Cedrus did not threaten you.'

'He did not threaten me because I made my living from a tale I would never tell. Now the tale is too old to invigorate newcomers and Cedrus is dead. They wish to hear the tale of the prophecy.'

'What proof can you show me?'

Black Jack smiled, his belly wobbling toward a cabinet. 'What I have here will be proof indeed.' He bent down and opened the cabinet door, rummaged inside and brought a tin box to the table. 'I shall now finish my story.'

'You have more?'

'Yes, my good fellow. I have more but it comes at a price.'

'What is your price?'

A belch before he replied, 'I want that key round your neck.'

'It will serve you no purpose.'

'Is that so?' He lifted the lid slightly, offered a quick preview then slammed it shut. 'Are you certain now?'

Quercus swallowed hard. 'What is to stop me from taking it?'

'Do you think me stupid? Beyond that door awaits your fate if you steal from me.' He paused to drink more wine. 'A man,' he said after swallowing 'who claims to be immortal should know he is not immune from capture, to serve his everlasting life behind bars. It would be quite a crowd puller in my business.'

'Council Members serve their kind not their egos.'

'The last Keeper favoured your kind by handing keys. We had nothing.'

'You had nothing because you took without asking.'

'I must be drunk to listen to the piffle coming out of your mouth. It was the old sailors that took. They were the crafty ones.'

'Not true,' JP yawned. 'The firs built boats to claim further lands.'

'Who is this woman?'

'Dead if she interrupts again.'

'Besides, you have misinterpreted my request. I am not seeking your key. I want the other round your neck.'

'Ah, you want the key of Hortus.'

Black Jack snorted. 'The initial is not for Hortus but for Cedrus. It was his seed that dominated their blood, Cedrus blood. That key was delivered to his twins when they were born. How do you think they came through gates?' Colour spots of exasperation had developed on Black Jack's cheeks when Quercus failed to answer. 'Cedrus was just as vacant as you. One entered with the key, leaving the portal open for the other before it closed. Your meddling Sage enticed his woman when she was swollen. The key rightfully belongs to them. Here they will take their place as our Keepers.'

'You argue against your cause, Black Jack. You give a missing artefact in exchange for a key. They cannot be Keepers unless they can read the pages.'

'You forget I have the remaining tale.'

'Open the lid and show me again.'

Black Jack did better than that. He carefully brought out a green leather bound volume with the mid-section missing, laid it on the table and delicately turned the pages over. 'Now do we have an accord?'

As is often the case with men whose thoughts ever dwell in greed, Black Jack was oblivious of time being slowed while Quercus removed the key from his chain, placed it beside the Book, his finger pressed firm on metal. 'Trick me, and it will be your life at risk.'

'I shall keep my bargain and offer the truth.' A pause later and Black Jack returned the volume into the box, unaware of what Quercus had done. 'Why do you think Cedrus altered our history?'

Quercus had this strange feeling he was not going to like this and remembered Michael questioning the same. Was Cedrus afraid of what his people would think of him or was he afraid of something else being known?

BOOK OF HORTUS

'I shall tell you. No-one can read the pages and that is the point. Imagine if you will, a man of great wisdom and power beyond belief. And with such power he could rule the world. Where did he come from? He may have been an outsider or an unfamiliar, who knows. We can debate all night and still come up blank. But he certainly was different and he certainly required validity to his presence. Because of this, he created a book of blank pages and claimed he was chosen by Hortus to be the Keeper of her secrets. Only a Keeper can read the pages thus no-one could challenge his claim. And this is what Cedrus discovered, learnt what he could but not enough before the Keeper realized his student's ambitions. Cedrus did not bargain for the green leopard. My Father watched that creature bite through the spine then fly through the window with the mouthpiece.' He tapped the box. 'This half was found under the bed.' He pushed the tin box towards Quercus. 'Our bargain is complete.'

Quercus slapped his hand over the key. 'Did Cedrus confess this much to your father?'

'By the mere fact Cedrus did not acknowledge my Father is confession enough. If the Book was real, he would be the first to hunt it down. Instead he acknowledges the mouthpiece is lost and the other half destroyed thus legitimizing his position as Keeper.' A hand came forth. 'The key if you please.'

Outside the air was clearing his mind. He looked down at JP with a frown. 'Why did you interrupt? You made me appear an idiot.'

'It will be a tragedy if you are Keeper.' She walked on. 'You are so gullible a chicken could roost in your lap. The man is a liar. It's his business to lie. Now he has the truth of the prophecy and the key.'

Jumping into the canoe, Quercus paddled the distance, away from the blinded centre leaving the lights and the razzmatazz behind before asking, 'Do chicken roosts in laps?'

'You should be asking why you ignore my brother's advice.' She took the paddle. 'You have half of what? A facsimile no, doubt.'

'No, it is not a facsimile.'

'Let us hope it was worth it. The first thing he will do is summon a White Tail and entice your friends to join him along with others more notable. You have placed Nina and Michaelmas in a very awkward position.'

He slipped further into the canoe, his hands behind his head, smiling in the near dark. 'It is perfect. Michaelmas will run circles around him. And Nina, well Nina is inexplicably Nina. She has a heart of gold, a face meant to smile and with such a bank of knowledge she will correct his history. Although I must admit I found his tale fascinating. I rather enjoyed the dramatics of a leopard leaping through the window.'

'I doubt that was truth.'

'Only a leopard can leap such a distance.'

'Leopards do not howl. They hiss, growl and whine like pussy cats. Dogs howl.'

'A cat will howl like a baby for its loss. Within lies are truths because lies are created from truths. Consider the whip of Hortus? If you claim the Book is false then the whip must be false and if the whip is false then the veil of tears are false.' After a long pause he placed his hand to his ear. 'I cannot hear your argument.'

'I am thinking.'

'Then I shall leave you to your thoughts.'

BY MUTUAL CONSENT

From the distant moonlit shores of Coniferous land, dusty, weary and hungry, Quercus shrugged off his cloak and severed a chicken drumstick while Sea Winger weighed anchor.

'I wonder who bit off more than they chewed.' The Thief entered the captain's quarters. 'In one day, Black Jack told his father's tale to a great many others. In two he had the prophecy at his door. In three he elevated his position to Ambassador Ginkgo. The man does not stand still in the wake of progress.'

'And neither do I.' Quercus sat with the closed book on the desk, staring into the wavering shadows, living in full detail the barter with Black Jack. 'Do not consider the exchange unfair. His father's tale will not be substantiated, not when its counterpart is joined.'

'My sister believed your senses were lost.'

'They were lost in her chattering.'

'I take it you have applied for a divorce.'

'Let us see if your senses are lost.'

The blue pirate's eyes missed nothing as he watched Quercus vigorously scribe on a blank page. There was nothing, not even an abrasion which could only mean one thing.

'Did you know at the time?'

'Not before I gave away a story and shed my blood.' Few ever gained the chance to outwit Black Jack. 'I placed the key on the table, his attention drawn to what he desired most allowing me time to be at one with Hortus and test my theory.'

'To slow time,' the Thief amazed, 'is something my kind have forgot. Did he not think in all those years to test it himself?'

'The man lives by a code of greed. He believed if the pages were marked it would invalidate his claim. Paradoxically, he would be unable to mark the pages. I hazard a guess and say he never had intent of parting with what had become a legend in which he had no faith. Yet, when he saw the key, his mind reverted to a greater possibility. As he said, what value is there in an old story when he had the details of the prophecy?'

'By all the destinies, Quercus, if you are not Keeper I will sail into the sunset and never look back.'

They raised their glasses, toasting to the old ways. It was perhaps a little premature when considering the pages had yet to be joined, the secrets yet to be read.

'What is your opinion of Coniferous land?'

'The moods of your rivers change constantly. At places they narrow and race through rock-lined gaps and the long canoe flew like a lance and beyond that the surface was moulded like glass. Some of our rivers act no differently but most emerge on broad shallow stretches in summer, the flow broken by inlets and islands.'

'As I told you, it was because Cedrus narrowed the mouths.'

'When shall we arrive at Daylily?'

'Two days at most, perhaps less if we pick up good wind.'

Quercus began to write. 'I want you to attend our meeting at the Home of Hortus.'

'I do not venture beyond the Harbour Winery.'

'Like leading your men on land to sabotage?'

'You will put your people in a very uncomfortable position. It would put me in an uncomfortable position. I am a Juniperus Pirate, a despised fir, employed as a thief.'

'A Handsome Thief and true to Hortus.' Quercus craned his head round. 'Will you take the same line of defence if the waterways are established?' He held up a note. 'Here is the message of truth, the return of old ways. We have come this far. From chaos to calm, let this time renew our trust and celebration, not one of rage and reckoning.'

The Thief went quiet at the lattice square windows watching the peninsular of Coniferous land make distance. 'The firs will not take kindly to the return of old ways.'

'I do not wish to stir the pond of their history. It must be for them to alter their ways. I wish to reinstate our waterways and give back what was taken by Cedrus.' Quercus stood to share his view. 'This is what you have wanted, my friend. I cannot do it alone.'

'You wish my kind to protect yours?'

'It would give me leverage to convince Council Members.'

'As Keeper you could.'

'Even as Keeper, I would not do it alone. Our society is based on the fundamental principle of true democracy. Yes, Cedrus has influenced some of our Ambassadors but they shall be told there is no room for social inequality or complacency. There must be consensus and free speech. If you ally yourself to us, it would be an example to others.'

'No, my friend, it would show we are taking sides and such men like Ginkgo would take advantage. A Keeper does not turn his back on one society because it suits. You would have your kind enjoy the secrets of Hortus while across the sea others go their separate ways. What of people like Nina and Michaelmas? Would you have them live among your kind?'

Quercus remained silent. This man, he thought, spoke wisdom. Yes, there were those like Captain Twist, and those equally bent on war for war's sake. The inevitable chills of winter had closed his mind. To branch out and touch the weeping hearts longing for change would make a far prettier garden in the world of Hortus. And it could not come soon enough.

Two days of cold weather had brought him to his shores, the winds playing harshly against heavy green cottons, his black boots shiny, ready to walk into his future as Sea Winger drifted into harbour. The faces of men and women, children, the smell of deciduous soil and the distant noises of jubilation where each district and quarter had couples dancing, their arms curled gracefully around one another from blares of soft music, all the noise and the non-stop wonder created an exuberant atmosphere. And it all welled in a rush.

Thrown into the masses of animation and confetti, the crowd thick and cheering, his pace was slow, sometimes suspended, stuck to the ground like glue. He had barely gone beyond the Harbour Winery when another rabble closed in, giggling girls in some freakish attempt to touch any part of his body. To this shambles, he vaulted a dwarf wall and made a dash to the stables a little hard pressed to understand the nature of teenagers. It was the sharp end of fame.

Betula was working the harness on Shadow. 'He has missed you, my lord.'

'He looks well.'

'That is because he has spent his time in the palace grounds watching a transformation.'

'Transformation?'

'You will not be disappointed when you see your new quarters.'

'My friend,' Quercus said as he placed the lost half to the Book of Hortus in his saddlebag. 'I would like you to join the debates at the palace tonight.'

'May I enquire why?'

Quercus swung himself onto Shadow and wheeled the horse. 'It is your destiny.'

With a shake of the mane and flick of the tail, Shadow skirted the rim of the port, which to Quercus seemed life's whole purpose, the buzz of celebration, a spectacular return to those promised days. Tomorrow or the next his people would settle where some will return to their country of origin but for now, further on he felt compelled to visit the charred remains of a home that once stood on the wooded clad hills. It was his land, his scorched piece of earth but it had somehow settled in such a way as to provoke the new beginning of life. Creepers had pushed among the ashes, tiny young leaves pressing home their positions. The black copper kettle lay dormant on the rusty stove as though by any stretch of the imagination he could pour hot water in a teapot and make a cup of tea. To what end and for whose benefit?

He dismounted at a burnt scarlet oak, its branches tarred and laboured like liquorice sticks. There was little to love about this stricken tree except to wonder if this was the tree where a whip once hung among scarlet leaves. He brought out a knife and began to scrape off the scorched bark, working his way round and down the trunk, wistful at the recollection of a bygone childhood. And for a moment he near conceded there was nothing to indicate this was the tree until he had stripped to good wood. Hortus had not forgotten him. The date of his birth came into focus with the words *serve my whip to serve your destiny.*

'What you see is the will of Hortus.'

'Did you guide my Father to his death?'

'You can look at me with those judgemental and incriminating eyes all you want.' Her thin and crooked finger pointed starkly at the oak. 'Your destiny was written on the bark of her tree, linked to another, a good man protecting his son until the time of his ending.'

'It did not occur.'

'Many things do not occur when blinded by love. Do not tempt providence, Quercus. Remember Hortus can be cruel as well as kind. Give me what you have.'

At his saddled bag he asked, 'When will the pages be joined?'

'Not until the snow falls with its deceptive gift so that both time and the winds are stilled. Pending this, your branches lay deserted to serve equally well for establishing new growth.'

'How? How can one establish new growth when you keep the pages parted?'

'Listen and listen well, Quercus Coccinea.' Her strangeness of tone compelled his silence, some peculiar threat in her manner. 'Learn from the past, the fate of a Keeper, his age interminable but not indestructible. Hortus is generous as she is venomous. For one thousand years her anger had profound implications for the fate of two continents where few spent much time wondering why. The Keeper owed it to himself to discover the world in which he lived so what he did he had to do from knowledge not ignorance or prejudice. Cedrus claimed to be chosen by Hortus, to read her pages. He was a false prophet sent by Hortus to wake a sleeping Keeper from his ignorance. Let that be a memory ingrained on your bark. Sleep in a state of ignorance and Hortus will kill your roots. Now go and begin your journey.'

When Sage was gone there was nothing else for him to look at, his land slipped back into silence and not a thing seemed to move. If there had been doubts before, there were certainly none now. He was ready in every way to mould history, to lead his people into a new future and to turn Council Members of his world upon their heads. But he would do it gently and tread softly before the snow fell.

A little later nearing the upland, the dramatics of change built into this scenery came into view. The dominating physical feature of a grotesque wall had gone to reveal a stately building proudly rising from the summit of Daylily. In comparison, there was no question in his mind that this simple piece of architecture had greater impact on the landscape than any overworked piece of construction lost in a maze of colours.

Dismounting at the palace entrance, he removed Shadow's tackle then walked his familiar route, by-passing the chambers and cells that took up the ground floor. If there was something different it certainly went unnoticed as he transcended the marble staircase towards a much calmer environment. Council Members were conferring among their benches. They anticipated his approach but instead he carried on with his tour. For now there were just a few lines, faintly etched and erased and re-etched between a scattering of pillars and angles while he carried on steadily as if he had destination in mind rather than merely setting out for a stroll.

He was told he had his own quarters and widened his search to the ground floor where he finally came across a stone-flagged courtyard. Amid potted palms and bromeliads, he stepped through a door and entered a world that combined both neatness and memories. A grandfather clocked ticked loudly in the hall, a copper kettle hung over a stove, a four poster bed with thick cotton sheets, seating arranged by a fireplace hawking coughs of tinder and everything else which may be considered incidental was in fact significant to him. Here he was able to watch and welcome the wildlife that appeared at different shapes of the moon, or at daylight or midnight hours, according to their different natures.

Beyond all this, there were books, immaculately shelved. More than once he ran his finger along them, tracing one by one the hundreds of spines then looked to his right, recognizing the circular picture of beautiful flowers. Later he would understand their relevance but for now he had found his bearings and established the opposite wall was the wall that once displayed abominations and a hidden panel to a secret garden. It was now a glass partition, which pulled back on runners. He had come full circle into the flagged courtyard.

'Quercus, you make me dizzy.' Syringa smiled. 'A cup of tea is in order.'

'I was anxious to see my quarters.'

She linked her arm with his. 'We rather gathered that.'

'Have you been communicating with Nina and Michaelmas?'

'Oh such sadness, Quercus,' she replied in misfortunate tones. 'How could Cedrus seed good but there again,' she sighed 'their destinies were mapped as surely as yours.'

As he poured hot water into a teapot, he was transported back to the day when Nina offered him a jellybean and later spoke sadly about a mother she really knew nothing about. 'She is searching for her real mother. Has there been any news?'

'Yes, there has been news, a little disturbing, I think. The firs have proclaimed them as Keepers due to the key you exchanged for what? We do not know. You say the Book is real. They say the Book is false.'

'I would not exchange unless I was certain.'

'That as may be, but this notification came from Ambassador Ginkgo, elevated it would seem from a gambling table. What audacity. If the Book is real then what makes this key so important? It is such a worry, Quercus. Are we to assume one of them will be Keeper? If this is so, our lives will be made intolerable again. We shall see an invasion of firs and-'

'Do I have a message from Nina?'

'Has a White Tail delivered one?' She paused to the shake of his head. 'Well then, apparently not.'

'I see they are no longer the flavour of the month?'

'That is not strictly true. But-'

'Ah,' he interjected fiercely. 'We come to the unmerciful but.'

'Do not take that tone, Quercus. I have loved and lost my Fagus. At least Nina is alive albeit on the other continent.' She placed her cup and saucer aside. 'It is true they have accomplished good things. Why, they are hard not to like yet we cannot dismiss their blood line nor can we dismiss the possibility this upstart speaks some truth. Why did they seek Coniferous land, why not return through the gates?'

'Why not return to Daylily?'

'In the murky world of coniferous manipulation, where loyalties shift overnight and a friend can become an enemy by noon, would you be happy to see them here?'

He only just contained the groan that came up his throat. Paradoxically, an owl cried in the yew trees and was answered from another wood, then, far away, still faint and unmistakable a mournful chant sliding towards them, the passage of farewell to brave souls.

'Do you hear?' Syringa asked, her green satin robe rustling as she scrambled to the window, opening it wide. 'Listen, Quercus, it is the song of Hortus sung by our people. Truly this is wonderful. I shall hear my Fagus.'

To this barely audible melody that presently hung over the port, they left his quarters and greeted the waiting Council Members seated on benches. The conversation subsided as they stood to his presence. He had caressed the seams of war, of pain and loss, had felt his own internal fortitude diminishing at times and now he had come to this point, going beyond that little bit necessary to establish his position. The prospect of entering the corridors of power was not one to disturb his equanimity, and the prospect of failure never entered his head. He gestured to sit.

'We have come a long way, my friends,' he agreed indulgently and the Ambassadors gave little cries of confirmation. 'It was no easy task to reach this point. Not all came to aid in the cause, fixed only as far ahead as their balls.' Some guilty gazes seemed to slide by his face without touching it. 'I lay blame at the feet of Council Members who forget how to lead with honour and strength.'

'Honour and strength rolls easily from a tongue serving its own cause.' Lord Alnus, Ambassador for the Alders rose to his feet, his voice resolute. 'It was your father who held grievance, took up the whip, passed it on like an open wound to infect others. We had no quarrel with Cedrus.'

As a collective frown creased the assembled, Quercus stared at the man for a full five seconds, considered the gold round his throbbing neck, the diamond stud earring shining brighter than his yellow fuzzed hair. Solemnity was more fitting than rage. It also warranted drama. He walked silently to the balcony doors and opened them wide. A gust of cold wind tugged at the hem of his green cotton tunic, carried the rolling notes of a haunting melody that drowned the rolling notes of the sea.

'Hear the song of Hortus, Lord Alnus.' He told him. 'It calls to the faithful. I heard tales by the Elders in my youthful years. Their Ambassador, Lord Sambucus sits by your side. There is no fancy trimming round his neck only the scars of war. His kind was the first to fall before mine picked up the whip. If you had cared to unplug the stud from your ear you may have heard his cries when he was rooted not so long ago by Cedrus. Thank destiny for Nina and her tears. For certain you had none.' He processed the floor and pointed his finger, ramming home the truth. 'You allied yourself to Cedrus as surely as Lord Acer turned traitor. Is that honour, a pathway to perfection?' He waited a full five seconds holding his hand to his ear before saying, 'I am deafened by your guilt.'

Quercus remained silent after that, glancing back at the dimming sky, listening to the singing voices drawing near. He could feel their mood, could also feel the cloud of depression lift in the hall as Lord Alnus removed his presence. Now he needed to set the seeds of the future.

'I would like to tell you an interesting story,' Quercus said turning into the room aware the key was causing some consternation. 'Nina queried why White Tails delivered keys to our kind, and keys to the Juniperus Pirates. What of the others, she asked and I had no explanation other than to say it was just the way of things. Yes, there was odd exception. Cedrus had a key. There was also a key found in the mouthpiece. This key really puzzled me. I first believed it was Nina's incentive to come through the gates but that theory was later negated when she told me I was her reason. When I met Black Jack, he gave a very plausible argument by suggesting Nina entered the gates leaving the portal open until Michaelmas came through.' He shook his head processing the floor with his hands behind his back. 'I must admit his story was fascinating. Those firs surely know how to keep the mind invigorated. For my part, I questioned how was it possible that a key was hatched one thousand years prior to Nina and Michaelmas being born? Perhaps the key was placed in the mouthpiece much later or perhaps Hortus had already decided they were destined to be born.' Quercus paused, ready to make his point. 'Know this, from lies come truths. Black Jack was right when he claimed it was their key. Nina did come through the gates leaving the portal open for Michaelmas. It was their destiny to come into this world at the appropriate time, their destiny to put right a wrong. The Book of Hortus is real. Black Jack may have elevated himself to thicken his ego but that key will not serve his wishful thinking.'

Syringa stood. It was expected. 'If the key does not serve his wishful thinking, then it serves the prophecy which can only mean one of them will be chosen as

Keeper. It will spell disaster for our kind. We shall see another invasion of firs sweeping our lands, taking over the Home of Hortus.'

Jubaea was on his feet. 'We must keep our army ready. Recruit and train new warriors. Build ships like Sea Winger and blow them to kingdom come.'

Quercus blinked. 'Are you losing your senses through senseless conceit?'

'Michaelmas demonstrated how to keep men from harm.' Lord Salix stood. 'This is his way so we must fight his way lest our army be totally obliterated. We all know the firs look down on our ways. They will build vessels like Sea Winger and cross to our shores.'

'You forget the Juniperus Pirates control the seas,' Quercus argued. 'They will not allow others to command their highways.'

'You forget they are firs too.'

He held up a hand to their mumblings. 'You jump to heady conclusions. I am reinforcing a point I wish to make. The Book of Hortus is real, the key incidental. Only when the pages are joined will the outcome be served. And the pages shall not be joined until Hortus is ready. Until then we must look to ourselves.'

Jubaea remained standing. 'Fagus believed you to be Keeper.'

'Nothing is certain in an uncertain world, my friend. I am here, have fulfilled your wish where I could have fulfilled my own. Is this not enough?'

'Forgive me, Quercus. It is more than enough. I would hope in this time of uncertainty you will consider taking the platform to our debates and lead us not into temptation.'

The Ambassadors slapped their benches in approval.

Quercus had banked on this. He bowed deeply. 'I am honoured.' But debates could wait for the outer grounds. 'The song draws near. We shall return after we pay our respects to the dead.'

Paradigm, he thought moving on. It was fragile, accidental and difficult to argue. Wishing Michael and Nina were somehow here again, wishing he could hear their thoughts right now he became aware of Zelkova, the Astronomer wringing his hands, standing at the foot of the stairwell.

'I see the rabbit is out of his burrow. Want do you want, Zelkova and make it quick?'

'I beg your forgiveness.' His voice was tremulous and waited for the last of the Ambassadors to pass before falling to his knees. 'I ask you to look upon this simpleton with charity and understanding. There is no excuse for my actions other than to say my senses were stolen, replaced by vanity and nepotism. Any position I would gladly take.'

'You think if I put you to work it would render your position in Daylily acceptable?'

'At least permit me chance to make account for my miserable hide.'

'Since you are a bad forecaster of weather, what else are you good at other than choosing a comfortable bed when it suits?'

Zelkova rose to a hand gesture. 'I can service your requirements and quarters.'

'I do not wish my quarters to be serviced.'

'Perhaps assist others at their command to mop and polish, launder and clean the home of Hortus, be at your disposal for the mundane? My knowledge of wines is vast, so too my experience for stocking larders and tilling land.'

After all, there was need for the mundane. 'I shall personally till your innards if I discover a fault. Do I make myself clear?'

He bowed deeply. 'Abundantly, my lord.'

'Pay your respects to the dead then speak to Lady Syringa.' Quercus walked on. He would watch and study the Astronomer's behaviour, would give him no second chance should he fail in his duties.

Outside, the authentic past was here. Glimpses of candles in lanterns half burnt, glittering balls held by loved ones chanting the melodious song of Hortus, their voices echoing to the light of the stars and the earth of the moon, generations of complex lives and deaths trailing off into limitless space. Grief and madness were not so private now.

Quercus was helplessly bidden to share their tears, his pity welling as he stood on the palace steps watching them pull softly toward him. He could make out the thousands stretching beyond this summit and imagined Fagus was there among them, imagine his father spilling crumbs of carrot cake off his green cotton tunic and the men that fell to their fate. Death rubbing shoulders with life.

As time went on, they grew less sombre; then there was an upsurge of cheers as Quercus swivelled slowly on his heels, emotional austerity reasserting itself. He returned to the hall to meet his newest recruit in quizzical attendance. Shifting from the shadows, Betula exposed his position.

'Keep your presence known and listen, my friend.'

'Will the pages be joined tonight?'

'Not until the snow falls.' Quercus looked back at the approaching green silks, their eyes questioning. 'Betula is here at my invitation,' he told them and watched them take their seats, acceptance now part of their creed. He waited awhile until the hall drew silent then pointed to himself. 'Do not think this man will pander to your whims! Guns and cannon shots indeed.'

Lord Fraxinus stood. 'We have no whims except one. How may we address you?'

'My dear Fraxinus, do I address you any differently than my brother, my friend. Can we at least cast pomp and circumstance aside?'

'Then we shall call you Quirky.'

The hall erupted into laughter. The focus of the debate seemed to be shifting. It was important for Quercus to meet his objective and stood with his hands behind his back, smiling, allowing them their moment. He even took the time to glance up at the ceiling to view someone's handy work. Unnoticed before, a sun dial had been painted round a plastered protrusion. No doubt an effort to create a talking point but then it suddenly occurred why Cedrus kept the pretty flowers on that wall.

When the laughter settled his eyes raked the room. 'The Handsome Thief,' he began. 'We know him well. We thought he roamed the seas accountable only to himself yet he silently waged war against those abominations Cedrus had created. I doubt any of us would be here to tell tales if not for his intervention. He claims he is handsome and I do not disagree but his claim is modest by comparison. While my branches were casting shadows through the gates, the Thief led his men to sabotage a number of breeding grounds on Coniferous continent. Yet he said nothing of this when I vilified his kind in the Harbour

Winery. And still he said nothing when we fought side by side on Nepenthes. My promise I keep. He and his men are to be honoured in our history books.'

Fraxinus was back on his feet again. 'How far should that honour go when I heard he bargained for an island and offered you a retreat from your destiny? I doubt we would be here having this debate.'

'If your desire is to shame him, then your words are lost.'

'Lost?'

'For certain you have to be lost in order to be found.' A collective smiled creased the assembled. 'He is what he is, a Juniperus Pirate who has proven his mettle. But have we proven ours, I wonder? Here is where fourteen Council Members once belonged, and then by sad regret there were thirteen due to the last remaining Elm which cannot tell the time of day let alone tell which side he prefers to stand. Here, right here, Council Members conducted meetings in the home of Hortus not over a flagon of wine in the Harbour Winery. Look at our vacant places to be filled? Where are the men and women born with keys to represent the Maples, the Hollies and the Beeches? Now we have another to fill for the Alders. Why do they fear taking up their rightful positions? No longer must we sit on our laurels expecting problems to resolve themselves. The Birch from the north has yet to see your face, Lord Betula. When last did you visit your country?'

The Ambassador stood up slowly. He was bowed with age, his skin wrinkled and folded, and his hair not so lustrous. 'I am past my prime,' he declared, 'physically slowed but mentally able.'

'With age comes wisdom, old friend. There is one of your kind among you born with a key yet chooses to remain absent from duty. I have asked him to join us, another brave man who waits to serve his destiny. Would you take him under your wing, share your office and let him be titled correctly?'

'A good solution,' the old Birch said looking about. 'I cannot see him.'

'I am here,' said he, his grin almost to breaking point.

'Come sit by me.' The old Birch waved. 'I may later need a lift to my feet.'

Quercus pulled up a chair, straddle the seat and placed his elbows on the back rest to face his audience. 'Before Cedrus,' he began. 'Our continent had wider mouths for the sea to branch into our waterways where the Juniperus Pirates ventured, touching upon our countries to drop off their cargo, to hear tales and fatten their bellies. I motion we undo what Cedrus has done.'

'My people never spoke of such waterways.' Lord Sambucus sat composed. 'Do we take the word of a pirate and to what end and for whose benefit?'

'For both,' Quercus replied. 'He has a map stolen from Cedrus. I have seen it. To let the waters flow their natural course will cleanse stagnated areas and then, only then you will see excellent advantages for transport. I have witnessed the advantages of waterway transport on Coniferous land, how their homes are built close to clean flowing waters. Our roads become dust in summer, flooded in spring, mudded in autumn and iced in winter. Our travels become weary, our horses become weary and our carts creak and groan with the mileage they cover. This is what the Juniperus Pirates crave, to open our waterways and give them right of passage to unload their cargo. This is how we gained knowledge between two continents.'

Lady Tilia stood, projected her voice above their mumblings. 'Have you forgotten what Cedrus did to me? I was paraded in front of a Juniperus Pirate who aided my suffering.'

'Then you would tar all with the same brush. One man, one man who follows the will of Hortus can lead his people into our waterways. Would you deny him that much?'

'And others? When these waterways flow, who is there to cover our backs when unwelcome feet stamp on our shores?'

'Why, the Handsome Thief, of course. He will not lend passage to firs with war in mind or to the likes of Captain Twist.'

'And has he agreed to this?'

Given time, given chance. 'For now you need to approach your people and speak of what has been spoken here. Cedrus has left us with a poor legacy. We have lived on the edge of insanity for so long we have forgotten how to live. Our people's homes are tired and patched, created in tight settlements for fear of invasion. Your men, Lord Sambucus, your men beat blacksmiths hammers and stonemasons' mallets known only for war. Now they must beat for peace.'

Quercus had done enough and accomplished what he could. Tomorrow or the next would bring the coldest of dawns on the coldest of smiles for who was he to go against the will of Hortus.

SNOW FALLS

Alone, Quercus breathed deeply of winter, sat as an inhibitor of doom drinking tea by the fireside listening to the grandfather clock ticking slowly to the tune of his mood. Tick-tock, tick-tock, no snow yet, tick-tock, tick-tock, did Hortus forget.

Jubaea punctured his mood. 'Why do you sit like a bear with a sore head?'

He sighed and watched another presence wending a wearily way towards him. 'Is this a social call or one of complaint?'

'This is like old times, Quercus.' The old Birch lifted the lid to the teapot, bent over as he had bent over the complaining Lord Alnus. 'He has this very day insulted Lord Sambucus in front of our newest recruits. Admittedly he was drunk. Sambucus made Alnus forfeit his key. You must speak to Sambucus. Make him see reason.'

'Alnus had opportunity to defend his deceitful self.'

'No man or woman forfeits their key, only in death. It would set a precedent.'

'The reason why I am here is due to Nina forfeiting a key.'

'But had it returned.' Jubaea reminded.

'Keys are for the gates,' argued the old Birch. 'Yes, we do not wish the now deposed Alnus to return but he is entitled to go through the gates. I am surprised, Quercus. You failed to acknowledge our newest recruits.'

'I shall acknowledge them tomorrow at Council.'

'The meeting was today.' Jubaea reminded again.

'I was busy with my memoirs.' Quercus excused himself. 'Memoirs keep the history books straight.'

'And enlightens the reader why we need keys.'

'Bah,' the old Birch scowled at the Palm. 'Are you deliberately provoking our leader or just reminding? Can you not see his mind is vexed?'

'I am reminding White Tails hatch keys, the very reason why they are chosen to be Ambassadors.'

The old Birch would not leave it at that. 'The key is our doorway to knowledge. Without knowledge we stand ignorant of what Hortus can do. Alnus has strayed in his path therefore he should go through the gates to remind himself on which path he strayed.'

Quercus sat back disinterested as the two expressed their differences on a matter of much conjecture and debate. He had other things on his mind and remembered the question Nina had asked him so long ago. *Are you flirting with my petals again?*

Apart from the politics in managing small and large grievances, he had started his journals intending it to be huge and authoritative on the battles. At a late stage of one chapter, the hero walked diffidently onto the page where Nina was ingrained so heavily and legitimately, it was hard to express her any other way than his Nina of the Atlantic. Sometimes Syringa would drift in, be quiet by the fireside or lay her hand on his shoulder as he hunched over a desk. Finally, when his journals were complete, it seemed the only thing he really achieved was to remind himself how much he missed Nina's deranged sense of fun.

'And this upstart,' the old Birch said, nudging Quercus from his thoughts. 'His voice has become so loud I can hear him from where I sit.'

'What would you have me do?'

'Ignoring our neighbours only promotes his sentiments. I can feel the tempo of preparation for war, of impending siege increasing. The man only knows the ways of Cedrus and manipulates the prophecy to his own ends.'

Quercus seemed to stare momentarily into his own internal distance, his thoughts so easily drawn to Nina. 'Ironic,' he said in dismal tones. 'I can no more exist in the land of sleeping than I can exist without snow.' He looked from the fire into their quizzical faces. 'We should open our borders for immigration.'

The old Birch near choked on his tea.

But what Quercus wished more than anything was Nina by his side. He had found his home too lonely and lived quietly most nights like a prince in deliberate exile, merely dressing his face from time to time with a few astonishing runs on his eyebrows. He sat forward and picked up the poker, ramming it into the coals underscoring his frustration.

'I have received no communication whatsoever. Nothing, I have received nothing since last we parted. Did I place her in such a position she feels aggrieved.'

'I am confused,' Jubaea admitted. 'Are you confused, old Birch?'

'I am too old to be confused. Quercus misses Nina as much as he misses snow. If there is to be snow it comes late. Perhaps Hortus does not wish to snow.'

'We must have snow,' Quercus irritated. 'We have sun to grow, rain to feed, wind to clean and snow to sleep.'

'So you wish to sleep,' Jubaea said. 'Go to bed and sleep, pretend we have snow and dream of flowers for spring.'

'Exactly,' Quercus said rising and pointing. 'What is the point to look upon flowers when they fail to predict snow?'

'I thank destiny I am too old to worry.' The old Birch rose slowly and complained about his aging bones. 'Were I younger,' he said. 'I would not be fixed in this position. Lend me your arm, Jubaea.'

'You have not finished your tea?'

'It is not the tea but our leader's sanity which must be addressed. I am destined towards the flowers if I can get my blessed knee joint to move.' A crack and he smiled. 'We may proceed.' At the wall, he gave a summary account of what he had been told by the Birch from the north. 'My aid was convinced these flowers held significance, that each one offered a magical gift. For my part, I find it a little far-fetched to consider Hortus would be so bold as to show her secrets on a wall.'

'I too was puzzled,' Quercus informed. 'Puzzled as to why Cedrus would look upon such beauty against the opposing repugnance he seemed to attract. Surely his inclination would be to get rid of them. The answer came when I looked up and saw the sun dial painted on the hall ceiling though why someone should do so is a mystery.'

'It was my idea,' the old Birch claimed. 'At school we were taught it was far better to look up with optimism than to look down and grow camel humps on our backs.'

Quercus regarded him. 'That is good, for when the world weighs heavy on my shoulders at best I shall receive a neck ache.' They smiled and Quercus looked back at the wall giving an account to the pictures. 'Quite simply this has to be a mechanism of ancient horology, a most complex arrangement of time and tide, weather and phases of the moon, perhaps the very reason why Cedrus kept that wall untouched. I suspect it was a chance inspiration for there is still an element of chance in life we can do nothing about.'

'Can Zelkova explain how to read it?'

'Jubaea, I have yet to see his shadow though I cannot complain. The man looks like a flower himself. Did it not howl with cold blustery winds last week and yet it showed a torrent of sunshine.'

The old Birch wended his way towards the fire, sat down and brought out a pouch, methodically filling his pipe. 'So the wall has you annoyed because it fails to predict snow. The only conclusion I can reach is that you read it incorrectly.' He applied a flame to his pipe. Billows of blue smoke rolled away to the rafters. 'From my point of view Cedrus would not have kept that arrangement had he been unable to read it. Or perhaps you are misguided in your thoughts.'

Quercus smelt the cork of a port bottle. 'Jubaea, there is bread and cheese in my larder. Perhaps men should think upon a full stomach.'

They lingered over a dense red port and talked for another hour as the night wrapped itself round the palace with its lights springing across frost bitten meadows and trees burdened of ice. And then there was silence of sorts. The old Birch had fallen asleep, curled in an armchair like a child in dreams and Jubaea was near to follow.

Now Quercus took interest in the pipe, drawing weed into his lungs. A shudder of ecstasy closed his eyes and he was borne very far away. Her long sable hair fell in coils of midnight and she drifted in gusts towards him whispering sorry and sorry seemed to be the hardest word. The main door opened and let a breeze back into the tightness of his chambers. For long moments she did not move then sank back into the shadows, like the moon disappearing behind clouds. His journey began from the open flagged courtyard, through corridors and passageways, beyond silent rooms where his end came to a halt. A faint imprint rolled briefly across a door before he stepped inside to be afforded a magnificent panoramic view across Daylily. Roof tops and sails, hills and valleys, seas and land, everything was seen in a fleeting moment, a wild, beautiful place, full of birdsong and light before shadows grew darker and outlines grew weaker. Then music played and he danced in her arms on sand. He had the rest of the moon to sleep off his dream.

For a while he heard faint sounds like birds folding their wings, a far door swinging. He sniffed the room and sensed without needing to look at the state of an early day, the weight of the cloud in the invisible sky and the snow lay in the air waiting to tumble. This was as much as he seemed to need until his eyes fell on a face meant to smile. She wore a simple blue robe of cotton, concern and then relief in her features. Was this Nina?

They held each other in silent embrace, her tears mingling with his kisses. There was so much to rejoice, and too much to say. The Council Members agreed to widen the mouths where the seas would flow to clear waterways, where the Handsome Thief was a talking point and the pages would be joined when Hortus was ready. It had left him scarce able to think beyond the next day.

'Oh, my Nina, am I dreaming, if so, do not wake me.' He looked down into the vivid blue pools of her eyes and the smile flittered through the clouded emotion. 'Nina, a word, a single word was all to set my mind at ease. Why did you not reply to my letters?'

'Quirky,' she whispered, toying with his key. 'Sage requested me not to.'

He buried his face in the crease of her neck, lost in the smell of her skin. It brought memories of the night among the delphiniums, how he kept his thoughts to himself whilst she laid her head on his shoulder.

'Forgive me, Quirky?'

'There is nothing to forgive. I was blinded, wrapped in my own prejudices and sense of worth.' He touched his heart. 'Here is where you have always been.' Then pulled upon a chain hung round her neck. 'How did you get Black Jack to part with the key?'

'Oh, Quirky, he did a terrible thing. He locked Michael up in a cage because he refused to co-operate so I turned him into a tree then Perry chopped him down.'

'How was that possible?'

'I had one bauble left.'

He laughed uproariously. Nothing had changed. She was Nina, her courage burning through poise, her generous heart too large for such a small frame. She climbed mountains without looking up and swam seas without knowing distance.

'I wish to bathe.' Gently he kissed her forehead. 'Speak of your adventures, I shall hear.'

'Well,' she said, making up the fire, 'we never found our Mother, no surprise there since we were squirrelled away to Ginkgo territory. We were taken to the mines, say no more about that. It was appalling. People, children even, were made to work under terrible conditions. Of course that sparked the first row. We met Perry's sister. She told us of your escapades, said you were impossible, would make bad husband material.'

He called back. 'Where is Michaelmas?'

'With Perry on Sea Winger, moored in the harbour and, dare I say two other special people.' Her head popped through the door. 'Quirky, we made them Council Members.'

'Is that so?'

'Yes, that is so. Remember Abies with the diamond studded head band and four hundred warriors? Michael signed him up after flicking his nose. And when Black Jack was chopped, a Ginkgo volunteered to join in the cause.'

'And what cause is that?'

'To become democratic, although democracy really needs a voting system.' She disappeared and carried on talking. 'We heard on the grapevine you were widening your river mouths.'

'A mammoth task, but yes, we have completed our surveys.' He paused, knew he had to find some peace of mind. 'Nina,' he called to her. 'Marry me.' Her face came into view and gave a weary sigh. 'Nina, do you wish to grow old without my arms to protect you, to wither away knowing we could at least share one lifetime, your lifetime?'

'My place is not here and your place is not there.'

'Then what better place than Inbetween?'

'In between we certainly are.'

Quercus hauled himself out of the tub, wrapped a towel round his waist and took hold of her shoulders. 'The snow will fall and the pages will be joined. Things have come to pass, Nina. I have done as she asked, set new seeds to my branches as they lay deserted of love. I will be chosen as Keeper and can serve equally well from an island in between two continents.'

'But the island does not belong to you and a Keeper cannot take to suit his whims. Perry uses that Island, now steps on land without fear of being rooted. You cannot take what has now become his home.'

'Would you deny me chance to barter?'

'Wisdom and silliness go hand in hand.' Her smile increased. 'Go for it.'

She was the way he loved her, a discovery by fate or opportune, it did not matter. What mattered, he reflected, was the fire she ignited in his heart. How happy can a man be? Not as happy as he.

Zelkova emerged with a basket of warm rolls and an apologetic smile. 'Forgive the intrusion, my lord. Lady Syringa begs to inform Sage has called upon Council Members.' He dipped his head at Nina. 'Madam, your party has arrived.'

As the snow began its journey to the ground, the words of Sage came to mind. Not until the snow falls with its deceptive gift so that both time and the winds are stilled. It seemed to fall like starlets, descending gracefully, and yes, there was a remarkable stillness in the air. It was time.

'My lord, do you require dressing?'

'Do you think I am incapable of dressing myself?'

'Forgive, my lord.'

Forgive? Taking a warm roll from the proffered basket, Quercus broke it in half, scattering crumbs on the floor.

'Zelkova,' he said walking into his bed chamber, 'since you are useless forecaster of weather, what purposes did you serve Cedrus?'

'None whatsoever, my lord, except to say I was the next best thing when weighed against his irritation towards Sage.'

'So why counsel him at all, why stay with a heathen among your own kind?'

'You forget, my lord, I am the last of my kind on the edge of survival, where career endings can be so precipitous. I can give no loyalty when I am shunned by many, ignored by all. If the air was not so foul through the gates, that is where I would go for kinder company.'

'You have a key?'

'What good is a key when no more of my kind are left to serve, my country taken, my home ravaged. This was the only shelter in which to hide.'

There was silence save for the Astronomer's fast breathing. Had Quercus been too quick to judge? Slipping across the words of Sage and through the history of man, something much stronger was calling; a greater picture came into view and never before had Quercus felt so close to Hortus. His gaze fell away from Nina and alighted on Zelkova, a man who wore his scars on the inside out.

'To walk alone is not her desire, Zelkova. It is our mistake and one to be remedied.'

'Remedied, my lord?'

'I wish you to attend the joining of pages.'

'My lord, it will-'

'You can sit by me. I make a very good agony aunt.' To know her was merely to know her kind heart. 'See you later, Quirky.'

All the difficulties thus smoothed away, Quercus slipped a white cotton tunic over his green cotton shirt and pantaloons, struck into his boots and moved on, his steady pace carried him forward to the main hall. Here, there was hesitancy in a charged atmosphere while the benches filled to give testimony to the generosity displayed in regard to quantity. Against a backdrop of white, the green silks of the Ambassadors, which now included Zelkova, was deeply satisfying to see; more so the Firs in blue, whether it may be to their advantage or disadvantage. Quercus took a seat beside the Handsome Thief. He had purpose in mind.

'You have been busy, Handsome one.'

'Nina has been busy. I have been on land.'

'So I understand. Is your sister well?'

The pirate glanced to his side, the eyes enquiring. 'You do not sit next to me to ask about my sister.'

'I sit next to you because you have two islands.'

'Ah, you wish to take up my offer.'

'For Inbetween.'

'Out of the question.'

'You can still moor your vessels, build a nice home and be our neighbour.'

'I have neighbours between two lands.'

'But can you hear their stories so far away?'

'To pass what has been in my family for generations is to say to the firs I am allied to the trees. I do not take sides.'

'An argument once used before.'

'Our seas were threatened, the gateway threatened. Unless you are Keeper and threaten, I live on my island in between two lands.'

It was an uneventful discussion. Around, Council Members were talking among themselves, the firs excluded. They had come to see the joining of pages at the behest of Sage, to witness the choice of Keeper, to hope it was Quercus or wonder if it was one of them. Enlightenment was imminent.

In a shape that had slid so eerily into the hall, Sage walked the marbled floor, her black hem weaving a path behind her. She was in no rush, was content to prolong their agony and the moment. In her hands two halves of the Book, held close to her aged and bent form. There was a strong mournfulness, a way of shaking her withered forefinger as she preached.

'I call upon you all to witness the joining of pages. Only the Keeper can read the Book of Hortus, only the Keeper will lead you from nightmares. For one thousand years the rivers of blood have cursed this land, do well to remember why. Hortus punished a Keeper who favoured one more than the other. For this, Cedrus was born to take for his people but he took for himself and left the lands across the sea to lose its direction.' The finger pointed at Michael then ran across to Ginkgo and Abies. 'The Keeper shall recognise them as leaders to their own kind and they will respect the will of Hortus. No more shall their lands be toiled to grow abominations or greed.' Her finger continued to travel.

'One sits as Keeper to her secrets and will know her ways as born to it. If you doubt her choice then look at the pages and see nothing but your own misgivings.'

With that she held aloft the two halves, relished in the theatricals as the pages met, bounded by the workings of Hortus while the snow built up on the land, creating castles. For Quercus, his universe was revolving around her as though she was renewing his entire geography and the earth stood safe beneath his feet.

'Take Hortus into your heart, Quercus Coccinea. Only she can lead you to the summit of understanding.'

For seconds he hung motionless and upright, his hands clutching the green leather bound book, his knuckles rising hard. Then he opened the cover and let out a burst of hysterical laughter. He looked up, watched Sage wending her way to the exit and wondered if she had made a mistake.

So he pushed on leaving the others to ruminate. 'Sage,' he worried-whispered, 'the pages are blank.'

'They are blank like your mind.' She would say no more.

He gnawed at his bottom lip, stood there for a moment realizing he had not taken a breath since he last spoke. He slowly exhaled and began breathing normally, his feeling of extreme doubt quickly supplanted by relief. A plant pot caught his attention. Upon closer inspection he saw lizards gulping down grass.

'What did you see, my friend?'

Quercus sent his eyes to the Thief. 'I see a man, a good man who should take his place among Council Members.'

'I have no need for titles.'

'Let them say, there goes the Handsome Thief, leader of the Juniperus Pirates, has control of the seas, control of the gates and control of the waterways.'

'And for this I am to pass over my island?'

'Not pass, my friend but share. Share with a Keeper who has taken your wisdom to heart. I require a small patch for a cabin no bigger than Sea Winger, a place to sleep with Nina in my arms, a view to ponder before resuming my duties.'

'And those duties will bring trees to my island.'

'How can they come when you have control of the seas? I shall sail to my duties. Here, there, I am in between two worlds in need of guidance. And what better cargo than for Sea Winger, to carry the Keeper under the command of the Handsome Thief.'

It was old Lord Betula who ventured up to them, bowed fractionally towards the Thief and then spoke to Quercus. 'We stand at the beginning of a new era. All we have done up to this moment was to fight, kill and bicker. We are ready for our endeavours.'

Quercus looked back at the Thief. Gone forever were his excuses, the sanctuary of neutral charms. They shook hands. Creation and innovation had a particular rhythm, a wavering beat of their own.

FOOD FOR THOUGHT

Our planet Earth is truly a wonder - a rare, beautiful jewel in space, afloat around the sun, enclosed in its own bubble of atmosphere, manufacturing and breathing its own oxygen, fixing its own nitrogen into its own soil.

And just look at what marvellous, abundant varieties of living things there are - microscopic organisms, insects, plants, fish, bird, animals and humans...yes, us...humans...the only living creatures taking pains to destroy our beautiful planet. For that is what we do every day.

Do you know why
this page is blank?

LEVITY BROWN

ALSO BY LEVITY BROWN
GALLOWS HUMOUR

IT'S A MATTER OF LIFE AMD DEATH

Solomon Monday is ready to jump off the media rungs and accept his bizarre legacy, a converted mid 18th century courthouse tucked in the folds of Norfolk...and so begins an extraordinary mystery which has its roots in the eccentric staff, six poor souls innocently hung at the gallows. It takes the appearance of Izabo Tuesday to force Monday to confront his demons and find their ancestor's book, Week's Work, the element to clar Gallows Humour of its hauntings.

**In a place where love and membership comes at a very high price,
Gallows Humour is simply irrsistible.**

PHANTOM JIGSAW

WAITING FOR REVISION

Strident Cutter, owned by third generation Tony Black, is on the brink of bankruptcy. His twin, Jason, an eminent chemist arrives from America to help with the sale, unwittingly walking into a nightmare. What first appears to be a blank jigsaw puzzle found in the store room, the phantom riddles catapult the twins into the realms of the paranormal.

This mystery is of a soul who needs Jason's expertise to alter the course of history. There is rivalry, revenge and forbidden love; an unforgettable impact of human relationships.

GIDDY MIDNIGHT

THE GRAND EXIT

Warrior Queen Boudicca called upon the Goddess Andate for victory in battle against the Roman army. But what transpired gave rise to a curse inflicted upon two opposing bloodlines.

Lukas Giddy, disadvantaged by the curse, is determined to lift it.

Marcus Metellus, advantaged by the curse, is determined to stop him.

**For one woman caught between the two,
her love for Giddy and his furry companion is an act of courage.**

COMEBACK

THE LADY IN GREY

The Chief Executive

Godfrey Shilling of Fair Life Assurance is limiting the liabilities against his company. Shortly issuing a million pound life policy, the client drops dead of natural causes. Coincidence? With no proof, he calls upon the woman in Grey.

The woman in Grey

Enigmatic, expensive to hire, Miss Grey walks into a Norfolk Town as Godfrey Shilling's Trojan horse. With a 100% success rate as a ruthless private investigator, she is about to turn a carpenter's world upside down.

The Carpenter

Ruben Stone, hiding more than a secret or two, lives above a shop selling beautiful dollhouses and related items. No profit, no loss, no gain, no shame.

**The Black Panther writes again in this stylish mystery
murder is on the menu for those who want to die and live again.**

www.ingramcontent.com/pod-product-compliance
Lightning Source LLC
Chambersburg PA
CBHW071235190726
48292CB00007B/2290